Where I Should've Been

Where I Should've Been

max
New York Times Bestselling Author
monroe

Entangled Publishing, LLC
644 Shrewsbury Commons Ave., STE 181
Shrewsbury, PA 17361
rights@entangledpublishing.com

Amara is an imprint of Entangled Publishing, LLC.

Visit our website at www.entangledpublishing.com.

Edited by Silently Correcting Your Grammar
Cover design by LJ Anderson, Mayhem Cover Creations
Edges Illustrated and designed by LJ Anderson, Mayhem Cover Creations
Cover image by Alena Dzivina/GettyImages, Olga Kurbatova/GettyImages, Sudowoodo/GettyImages, LadadikArt/GettyImages
Interior design by Toni Kerr

Print ISBN 978-1-64937-966-5
Ebook ISBN 978-1-68281-701-8

Printed in China

First Edition July 2026

10 9 8 7 6 5 4 3 2 1

ALSO BY MAX MONROE

Meet Me at Midnight
The Girl in the Painting

Red Bridge series

What I Should've Said
When I Should've Stayed
Where I Should've Been

Dickson University series

Learning Curve
Playing Games

Billionaire Bad Boy series

Tapping the Billionaire
Banking the Billionaire
Scoring the Billionaire

For anyone who's ever tried to outrun grief,
only to trip over love
(and maybe a sheep or two)
on the way.
This is for you.

Author's Note

Dear Reader,

This is a love story for those who don't think they can handle the risk of love, only to find out not loving is the real danger.

Thank you for reading. Breezy and Tad and Red Bridge continue to change us every day. We're so thankful for this series. For your readership. For the chance to tackle real-life topics and share them with you.

All our love,
Max & Monroe

Disclaimer: This book does contain sensitive topics. Areas that may be triggering can include abuse of alcohol, depression, anxiety, child loss, terminal illness in a child, loss of a spouse, fire, loss of a parent.

Prologue

I come over the hill, expecting to see home; instead, the devil bares his teeth in a heated smile, his wicked, dancing jubilation a most unholy welcome to hell.

My memories, my things, my home, picked for its perfect, quaint setting and idyllic white fence—up in flames.

The sight is a punch to the gut in every sense it can be, a glowing mix of orange and thick black and ash curling into the otherwise blue sky.

Before I can even think, my body moves. The truck isn't fully stopped when I'm out, my boots hitting half-melted snow, and my knees jarring on the loose, sloppy ground.

But I don't slow. I *can't.*

The glow of fire through the shattered windows is all I see. All I feel. A living thing devouring everything I know.

I hit the front door with a shoulder, snapping the wood frame with ease and barreling into the house in what feels like a fraction of a moment.

My foyer is dismally dark, the normal laughter of jokes and banter created with love replaced by a smoke so thick I can't even see my hand six inches in front of my face. My lungs feel heavy but not with soot—with the real, raw reality that my limitations as a human are on the precipice of being challenged. I overpower the feeling with urgency.

I can and will do *whatever* I have to do, no matter the cost.

Fear coats my movements, forcing me to rely on my training and muscle memory fully. I can hear my own breath in my ears, feel the thud of my heart in my chest, and see the film reel of a life in this house as it's eaten by the lick of unbearably hot flames.

Palming the wall, I walk along it blindly with nothing to guide me but the experience of walking it a thousand times before and the determination to see if she's okay—to see if *they're* okay. To get them to safety as quickly as possible.

"Where are you?" I yell, my voice muffled unbearably. "Are you in here? Can you hear me?"

Ash and water mix with still-hot embers as they rain down on me, the crew outside fighting to knock down the flames enough to keep the structure standing. Beams above me burn near clean through, and the walls feel hollow to the touch. I use my elbows and fists to knock through barriers, but it gets harder and harder with every step I take forward.

This should be a hall—open and free from debris—to the back of the house, but it's nothing more than an obstacle course now, burned and beaten by a fire that's been unattended for just a little too long.

Words don't seem clear or crisp right now, so I revert to anguish, screaming loudly instead.

I listen intently, and for a heartbeat, there's nothing but my heavy breathing and the crackle and groan of failing wood in response.

Then, a sound. A cry. It's faint, but it's desperate enough to chill me to the fucking bone despite the temperatures being well over a thousand degrees.

The call wasn't wrong. They're *inside*.

Some part of me believed they weren't; some part of me ignored the description of the dispatcher when she said *people may be trapped*. The most naïve part of me believed this couldn't and wouldn't happen to me.

Fuck!

I move more quickly, ignoring the creak and crackle of succumbing wood and pushing myself to my knees to go farther when structural collapse denies me at my full height. I have to get to them. I *have* to.

My brother Randy's muffled yell rings out behind me, but I ignore it, pushing forward anyway.

I can save them, and I will.

Tad Hanson can do anything when he has to. There's no other option.

1

Breezy

Monday, January 11th

If betrayal had a sound, it would be the rip of packing tape—a life redirected, a stage cut short, an eviction notice from best-laid plans.

If it were something new, I'd let myself be surprised.

But in my family, duplicity isn't just common; it's practically an art form. Cheating, arson, divorces, scandals—the Bishops could fill a museum with our disasters and still have leftovers for the archives.

The tape screeches sharply across cardboard and echoes in the newly hollow space of my Chelsea office like a taunt. *Go on, Breezy. Pretend this isn't gutting you. Pretend you're not dismantling your whole damn life, one box at a time.*

I catch my reflection in the big window behind my desk, and a humorless laugh bubbles up. It's giving *The Walking Dead:*

Manhattan Socialite Edition. My makeup is three days old and half sloughed off, my black bob is in wavy disarray, and the same gray dress slacks and white silk shirt I've pulled from the dry cleaner's plastic three too many times tell the tale of a once-successful woman cast aside to the underworld of lost motivation and deep emotional wounds.

I look like shit, I feel like shit, and the lipstick I found rolling around in the bottom of my Birkin bag is the only thing giving the illusion I tried.

Vogue won't be calling me for a feature spread anytime soon, not that they ever have before—but I looked the part, at least. Right now, I don't know what the hell role I'm supposed to be playing.

Outside my glass office wall, the gallery hums with life. Staff members in sleek black outfits flit from one end to the other, adjusting track lighting and arguing over placement for an incoming installation. Phones ring off the hook at the front desk, and somewhere in the lobby, a patron raises their voice over a billing error. The symphony of chaos plays on, even as I pack my exit into cardboard boxes in the room that still has my name on the door.

This office—my office for nearly the past two decades of my life inside the most popular and successful branch of Bishop Galleries—has been a place of comfort and confidence since I was eighteen, working part time as a lowly receptionist fielding calls. I built my career on sweat and fumes until I was the sole person running all the Bishop Gallery locations in the domestic and international markets, and if it weren't for *my* blood and tears tinting every facet of operations, there'd be a different damn color on the walls.

And look what good all that sacrifice did you…

My throat tightens reflexively around thickening moisture, but I snort to clear it, swipe my hand down my face, and grab the next stack of newspapers. Tears are *not* allowed. Sarcasm is my armor, and I'm keeping it on.

My phone lights up on the desk, and I briefly glance at it to see three text message notifications populate.

Logan: *Breezy, please. Just pick up.*

Logan: *We need to talk.*

Logan: *Where are you?*

I have two younger brothers, and for the vast majority of my life, managing them has been my second job.

Logan, the youngest of the three of us, is thirty-two but still plays the baby like it's his full-time job. Though, I suppose, his actual career as a famous Hollywood actor fits his dramatic, self-serving MO perfectly.

Bennett, on the other hand, is thirty-six and hasn't been on speaking terms with Logan since an arson-scandal-turned-cheating-scandal blew everything up. As the art prodigy of the family, Bennett achieved world-renowned success as a barely legal adult, and our father pushed and pushed him until he hit rock bottom and cut off everyone in the family but me. He escaped to a small town in Vermont called Red Bridge with a medically fragile newborn daughter in tow—a long, painful, bitter story involving an ex who wanted nothing to do with a sick child and just enough pent-up rebellion to turn him into a full-blown recluse.

He's doing better now, despite a literal ton of heartbreak and loss that robbed us all of my sweet niece Summer over two years ago.

Our mother, on the other hand, wanted us as babies but traded in any pretense of maternal responsibility for flings half her age after our parents divorced decades ago. Basically, Colleen Bishop is busy sending me tropical selfies with her twenty-eight-year-old surfer boyfriend—whose name I can never remember—while my whole life is going up in flames. *Lovely symmetry, really.*

And our father, Henry Bishop, is dead.

A month ago, he had a massive heart attack on a European vacation with his twenty-seven-year-old wife Serena, died, and as I've come to find out, made one of his most personally vindictive moves to date by leaving all of Bishop Galleries to

Logan in his will.

Logan, who couldn't tell a Basquiat from a Banksy if his life depended on it.

Logan, who's probably Googling "how to run an art gallery," in between firing off texts to me.

I ignore my phone, packing away the evidence of my life wasted until the boxes form a sad little cityscape around me. *One more box,* I tell myself. *One more sharp turn toward a dark road I've never driven before.*

The slam of my office door is violent and jerks me out of my thoughts with no finesse.

Sunglasses shoved into his hair, his leather jacket unzipped, and his usual Hollywood persona of cool at war with unrest, Logan stands in the wake. He looks irritated, but I'd win a contest in that department today.

Seeing as he lives in LA, the last time my baby brother was in New York was at my father's will-reading two weeks ago, and I haven't spoken to him since—not that he hasn't tried.

He's called and texted ad nauseam since I stormed out after my father's lawyer announced that he'd gifted Bishop Galleries to Logan—before the rest of the inheritance bullshit was finished—and since it was just the three of us, my absence put quite the dent in the estate attorney's captive audience. I've got a feeling he still needs me to dot all the i's and cross all the t's, but for some enraged reason, I'm not feeling like making it easy.

"Breezy, what is going on? Are your fingers broken? Why aren't you answering my calls or my texts?" He takes a step inside my bare office, and startled by its appearance, his eyes dart from box to box. "Wait…are you packing?"

"Yes, I am." These are the first words I've spoken to him in over fourteen days, and to be quite honest, I'm surprised they aren't more colorful. "You can consider this my formal notice, *boss*, though you'd have to hit me over the head with something heavy and blunt to convince me to stay for two weeks." I slam the tape gun down onto the desk for dramatic effect, but the only real result is a jarred elbow.

"You quit?" he questions, baffled. "Dad's been gone a month, Breeze. A month. Why in the hell would you quit? Why in the hell—?"

"Get real, Logan. What did you expect me to be doing? Waiting around to babysit *your* inheritance?"

His jaw slackens enough to ruin his bad-boy, devil-may-care persona, and I know the waterworks are coming soon. *Oh Breezy, you can't do this to me. How am I supposed to do this and Hollywood? Wah, wah, wah.*

"Don't." My voice is sharp as cut glass. "Don't act like this is some big shock. And definitely don't act like you're some kind of fucking victim in this. Dad left everything to you, Logan. Even though you haven't done shit for Bishop Galleries, you're the owner now. I guess congratulations are in order, huh?" A harsh laugh contrasts with my burning eyes. "So happy for you, bro. So fucking happy for you."

Look at that. I found the color shaded fuck.

This hurts. I want to cry, but I wouldn't dare.

Not with this audience.

My entire life has been wrapped up in my family's galleries. This location—Chelsea—and Brooklyn were mine. But Chicago, Miami, and Paris were my father's brilliant ideas, which meant they were half disasters that took a hell of a lot of work to build up and keep thriving, but I did it. *Me.* Not Logan, not Bennett, not my father or his much younger girlfriend-turned-wife Serena.

The only other Bishop who ever cared as much was my grandfather Harold, who founded it all. If he'd have been alive to see how cavalier my father was about his brainchild, I'd have found out about the diabolical twist in daddy dearest's will a long time ago.

For nearly twenty years, I've been the pulse that's kept Bishop Galleries alive, and my father's way of repaying me was to give the galleries to the man who's never worked a single exhibition.

"He didn't leave *everything* to me, Breeze," Logan retorts.

"Just the galleries."

Just the galleries. Just *the galleries.*

"I didn't want anything *but* the galleries, Logan," I toss out. "Dad can take the twenty million dollars he pity-lobbed at Bennett and me and shove it straight up his dead, cold ass."

I still don't know why my father didn't leave the galleries to me after the astounding number of conversations we had assuring me he would, but I shouldn't be surprised. Henry Bishop was prideful and egotistical, and he used people like pawns in his everlasting game of greed and money.

I witnessed the way he treated his own father when he was on his deathbed—not as a fountain of knowledge or a visionary to be thanked, but as a cash cow headed for slaughter. And when it came time to divide the Bishop fortune with his brother, he flat-out refused. He always took full credit for Bishop Galleries' success instead of acknowledging his daughter's hard work, but I guess I thought the ego of a man died with him.

I never expected him to slice me open from the grave.

"I get you're angry. I do, Breeze. But how about we take a breath here before we do anything impulsive," he says cajolingly. "Because this all feels a little crazy to have you just up and fucking quitting on me on a random Monday."

"Oh, I'm so sorry for throwing this on you so suddenly, Logan. What a surprising inconvenience." I shove the last box toward the rest of the pile, and it skids across the marble floor. "Dad leaving *everything* to you after what it's cost me to keep these fuckers alive and thriving?" I shake my head. "If anything, you should be shocked I'm not already gone by now."

"Breezy, trust me, I was shocked too when he told me about the will."

I pause menacingly, turning to face him with my hands on my hips. "What do you mean, when he told you about the will? You *talked* to Dad about his will?"

Logan sighs and runs a hand through his silky hair. "It's not a big deal, Breeze. It was, like, six months ago."

"You and Dad talked about his will *six months ago*?" My heart pounds wildly in my chest, and I think I might throw up. This keeps getting worse. "What was said? What was decided, Logan? Did you know he was giving you the galleries?"

His long, dagger-shaped silence is all the admission I need.

"Are you fucking kidding me, Lo?" My bottom lip quivers traitorously until I dig my top teeth into it so hard I taste blood. "You knew about me getting cut out of the galleries before Dad died, and you didn't tell me?"

My brother Bennett might not have a relationship with Logan, but I always have. I've defended him, gone to bat for him, loved him despite all the trouble he causes. But this? It's duplicitous. It's deceitful. It's fucking treason of the highest order.

"It's not how you're imagining it."

"Then how about you tell me how it went," I demand. "Because I can tell you, from where I'm standing, you're looking more and more like the biggest asshole on the planet than you ever have."

"You know how Dad was, Breezy."

"No, actually, I don't. Clearly. Not like you. Because if I did, this wouldn't be nearly the shock that it is. So, why don't you tell me how Dad was? Why don't *you* tell me why he cut me out of my life's work without so much as a warning?"

Logan sighs again. "He was a macho prick. You know this. He wanted the galleries to go to one of his sons."

"And so, what? You stepped up and decided to fill those shoes for him to win the merit badge of macho-prickdom for yourself?"

"I did it to protect you."

"You stole the most important thing in my whole fucking life to protect me?" I yell. "Well, ding-ding-ding, that's some of the most patriarchal bullshit I've ever heard, so congratulations, you're a badge winner!"

"It's complicated," he hedges. "Dad was determined. Bennett is incommunicado these days. And honestly, I didn't think he'd fucking die so suddenly. I figured we'd find a way to make him see the light. I figured we had another twenty fucking years before he'd kick the goddamn bucket."

"If you wanted to protect me, you could have stood up for me. You could have fought him on the half-baked idea that Bishop Galleries should go to anyone but me," I bite out. "You could have done anything besides sit there, complacent, while I got screwed over."

He takes a step closer. "I can't run this place. You know it and I know it." His voice is low and raspy around the edges. He seems sad, upset, even earnest—but he's an actor, and I refuse to forget that one very important fact. "I'm not cut out for it. But you're the galleries, Breezy. You always have been. I thought…you'd keep going. That we'd figure it out together."

I stare at him, hurt and fury rolling together in a wall cloud of impending change. "Since I was eighteen years old, I've done nothing but figure it out, and the only acknowledgment I get is being erased from Dad's will because I don't have a fucking dick. I'll be forty next year, Logan. Forty years of dedication to the Bishop legacy, and what do I have to show for it? *Nothing.* Not even my name on the door."

I've quite literally sacrificed everything to run these galleries. Other career possibilities, relationships, marriage, babies—all of it was put on the back burner for years and years so I could catapult my family's wealth and reputation.

No more. I'm *done.*

Panic flickers in his eyes. "Don't walk away. Please. Don't let him take this from you."

"No." I hold up both hands and shake my head, already increasing the distance between us again with a giant step in the opposite direction. "It's done. The only thing left to do is finish packing up my shit and get the hell out of here."

"I don't know the first thing about this place," he argues, following me as I backtrack to gather the final remnants of my desk. "You do. You always have. You *are* the galleries, Breezy. If you go—" His voice cracks. "I can't do this without you. Let's do it together."

"Together?" I laugh, but it's hollow. "Where was *together* when you were talking about Dad's will with him? Where was *together* when I sacrificed everything to keep our family's galleries running while you Holly-whored it up under the bright lights of stardom? You can tell yourself we're a team, but I've been the only one on the field for a while. I'm tired. I'm done."

"So, that's it? You're just leaving?" His face falls. For once, it feels like Logan Bishop isn't acting. He looks lost. "Where are you even gonna go? You live in New York. Your life is here."

"Not anymore."

I reach for my stack of newspapers to wrap up my paperweight, the latest issue of the *Red Bridge Chronicle* right on top. The weekly subscription I secured almost a decade ago to keep tabs on Bennett when he moved to Vermont is usually nothing more than a habit, but today, it feels a lot more like fate.

Tad Hanson: Keeping Red Bridge Warm, One Fleece at a Time, the headline reads, a photo of a sheep farmer I've met more than a few times holding a lamb like it's a Gucci bag right below.

Handsome-as-hell Farmer Tad looks like he belongs on the cover of a Ralph Lauren ad rather than on the front page of the newspaper in one of Vermont's smallest towns, but that's probably why Eileen Martin, the editor of the *Red Bridge Chronicle*, is always finding something to interview him about. If I gathered all the issues I had with his smiling face on the front page, I could fill my now-empty office two times over.

But right now, it beckons of a new, quieter life. Somewhere where the snow falls heavy and people notice when you walk into a room. Somewhere without the teeth of wealth-chasing, where you end up chewed up and spit out on the sidewalk with the gum. *And somewhere where sheep farmers look like* that.

"Please stay," Logan begs once more.

"No." The answer rolls off my tongue with ease. "I'm done here, Logan. I'm going to Red Bridge."

"Are you serious?" His disbelief sharpens into anger, his sad act ending in a flourish. "You're going to fucking Red Bridge?

Running off to Bennett, the golden brother."

"Yeah. I am." My voice is calm now, steady even, a sharp contrast to the sounds of his envy and regret.

"Fucking figures. He was always the untouchable one. Dad wrapped him in bubble wrap and threw me to the wolves so Bennett could keep painting. Ten million dollars to keep his little prodigy clean. I took the fall, did what Dad asked, and Bennett's still the only ass anyone ever tries to kiss."

"You and I both know that if there's anyone who understands walking away from the Bishop bullshit, it's Bennett," I say. "He saved himself. And right now, he's the only family I can stand to be around."

Logan stares at me, chest rising and falling, but he doesn't speak. I sling my bag over my shoulder, heels clicking against the floor like punctuation marks as I pass him on my way to the door. "You've got the galleries, Logan. Good luck."

He spins in place to follow me with his gaze, his arms coming up to his sides. "What about all of your shit, Breezy?"

"I already have a courier coming in a few hours to handle it."

It's my last official stead as head of the galleries. From here on out, Logan can figure out what to do with the empire I don't want anymore.

For all I care, he can burn the whole damn legacy to the ground.

2

Breezy

The wipers can't keep up as snowflakes smear across my windshield in thick and frantic strokes.

"Visibility is near zero," a man's voice warns on the radio. "If you don't have to be on the roads tonight, don't. Conditions are expected to worsen and won't let up until three a.m."

Welp. That's not ideal. I immediately flick off the dial because I don't want to hear it. I didn't want to hear it when I called Bennett earlier today to let him know I was coming and he advised me to wait out the weather until morning, and I don't want to hear it now, when I've already made it this far.

I couldn't stay in the city a single minute longer, dangerous blizzard conditions or not.

My hands grip the steering wheel so tightly that my knuckles are as white as the snow. I ease my foot off the gas of my Range Rover as it slips and slides gently from side to side, and then I put power back into it when I see a freshly plowed patch of highway ahead.

The snow keeps coming down, but I swallow hard against the anxiety and tell myself if I managed to keep my grandfather Harold Bishop's art legacy alive amid arson scandals and piss-poor financial management from just about everyone but me, I can certainly handle a little snow.

Except this isn't a little snow, Breeze. It's a blizzard.

The sky is ink-black, the road ahead barely visible, and my back is so stiff I think my body might've replaced my spine with a metal rod. The drive from New York to Vermont has been nerve-racking to say the least, but I'm so close I can almost taste the cider donuts, and if I did stop now, I don't even know where I would go.

RED BRIDGE 5 MILES, the roadway sign harkens as I blow by it at a mind-bending one mile per hour.

See? Only a little while longer, I tell myself, instead of daring to do the actual math. *You're almost there.* I speed up when the equation solves itself against my will, knowing I don't have another five hours in me. *Fifteen miles per hour, it is. Life on the edge.*

I just have to keep my eyes focused on the road, and I'll be inside my brother's warm house in Red Bridge in no time at all.

In fact...

I should give him a heads-up that I didn't take his advice to wait for morning, so he knows to expect me.

I take one hand off the wheel and unearth my phone from my purse, dialing Bennett's number and waiting for it to ring. I pull it away from my ear at the sharp bleat of a failed call and try three more times before I realize I'm not getting any damn service.

"Of course," I mutter, dropping my phone in the passenger seat and returning my hand to its previous position to grip the steering wheel tighter.

I drive along at a snail's pace as a big tractor-trailer truck zooms past me like they haven't a care in the world, and the New Yorker in me wants to flip them off and honk my horn, but I'm too busy trying to keep myself from sliding off the road to give in to the urge. Mile by mile, I fight to keep my jaw unlocked until the exit off the highway comes into view.

The snow is relentless, but the back road I just turned onto is mostly empty, and I even see Red Bridge's infamous yellow bridge in the distance.

"Yes! I did it! I'm he—oh shit!"

In an instant, I go from straight and steady to the back end of my Range Rover fishtailing violently. My tires skid as I try to correct it, but the SUV ends up spinning across the empty road before I can even figure out what's happening.

"Oh no!" I mutter to myself as a big snowbank on the side of the road comes into view, my car bouncing toward it like the Plinko disk on *The Price is Right.*

I slam my foot on my brakes and scream, but it's useless—the Rover noses straight into it with a sickening lurch that I half expect to trigger the ghost of Bob Barker.

"Son of a bitch!" I cry out into the quiet of the cab, my heart trilling at a gallop. *I'm so close! I can make it!* I put the engine in reverse and hit the gas, but spitting snow and the perilous crunch of my hood as it strains against the bank in front of me are the only results.

Shifting from reverse to neutral and back again, I try it again, making the car rock. And again. And again, to no avail. My situation doesn't change; I'm officially stuck.

"Damn it!" I slam both hands onto the steering wheel.

Now what do I do?

A deep, strangled sigh escapes my lungs, and I throw the engine into park. I yank my gloves out of my Birkin bag on the passenger seat, shove them over my hands, and climb out, squeezing through the sliver of space the snowbank leaves me to open my door. The snow is still coming down hard, and the cold air is a bitter slap to my face, but the real kicker is the feeling of wet feet as my favorite black suede YSL heels sink instantly into the drift.

Ugh. That's just perfect.

I step back and survey the tilt of my SUV half buried in a snow mountain and pull my coat tighter. Well, *shit.* Unless I can miraculously gain the strength of ten men, I am well and truly fucked.

Behind me, a beam of light blooms through the thick white bluster. I move to the side of my SUV again, anxiety over the level of visibility I know the driver of whatever's coming doesn't have ratcheting up to an eleven. My legs shake and my lip quivers, as the silhouette of a truck finally appears. The engine is loud, and the combination of snow and headlights makes it impossible to see who's behind the wheel, which makes the relief over not being physically run over as it pulls to a stop behind my Rover incredibly short-lived.

I've hardly had time to watch television or follow true crime podcasts on the internet for the last two decades of my life, but I've seen and heard enough to know this is how the worst stories start.

Eleven at night. Lone female. Stranded on a snowy back road. No witnesses. *I sure hope Bennett and Norah use a nice photo on my missing person's poster.*

The passenger door squeaks on old hinges as it busts open with a bang, the shadow of a man climbing up and into the V between the door and the cab about all I can make out in the heavy snow. The sky is absolutely shitting it at this point. "Breezy Bishop, is that you?" a male voice calls out, way too jovially for the circumstances.

My panic eases slightly—*happenstance, snowbank murderers don't normally know your name*—and I answer hesitantly, my voice quavering with the cold. "Um, yeah. Unfortunately, that's me."

When the driver's door opens in kind and another tall figure steps out, I finally recognize the shadows as the sheep-farming Hanson brothers. Everyone in Red Bridge knows them, *especially* the ones who are of the single female variety.

Tad Hanson jumps down from the passenger side and stumbles a little as his boots skid across the slippery road, nearly eating it before catching himself on my bumper. His face is lit up in a sloppy grin, and his cheeks are as red as Rudolph's nose. Behind him, his brother Randy moves steadier, and his mouth is set in a neutral line as he assesses my current stuck-in-the-snow situation.

Unsurprisingly, tonight, Tad is Chatty Cathy and Randy is

Broody Betty. It's not a change from their usual dynamic, but it is an interesting twist to my evening as a damsel in distress.

"Nice car," Tad announces proudly, patting my Range Rover like it's a prized cow. "But that's a god-awful parking spot."

"Oh, this snowbank isn't an ideal place to park?" I toss back. "You know us city girls. We don't drive much."

Tad's grin grows.

"You'll learn. Red Bridge has plenty better spo-ots," he says, the words moving loosely over his tongue in a way that suggests Tad Hanson is more than a little boozed up. He rubs a hand over his light brown beard as he weaves just slightly on his feet. His cheerful eyes look me up and down, but when his gaze catches sight of my shoes, that grin of his dials up again. "You're wearing heels. In a blizzard."

"They're weatherproof," I deadpan.

"Woman, those shoes are ten seconds away from calling 9-1-1 themselves," Tad answers with a chuckle. "Please, Mr. Emergency Man, our suede is mel-ting."

"Tad." Randy's voice cuts through the cold and Tad's laugh. He throws me an apologetic glance. "Ignore him. He's a little indisposed."

"Definitely had enough drinks to feel good and numb. Been a real great night," Tad chimes in. He slaps the hood of my SUV again and nearly tips over as his feet tangle on the stacked snow, catching himself on the wheel. "Whoops."

Randy exhales through his nose. "God help me."

Tad keeps on chattering away as he looks between me and my SUV. "Breezy, you're bee-you-ti-ful, but your driving could use a little work."

I should be annoyed, but Tad Hanson's handsome grin and teasing charm have me laughing instead. "Can't argue that tonight," I agree on a snort.

"Would you like a hand?" Tad offers, bowing gallantly and making Randy groan.

Before he can finish his descent, and before I can answer, his boot slips on the ice and he windmills both arms, fighting to keep his face from smacking the ground. I lunge forward out of instinct, only to end up slipping too, and Randy curses behind us like he's seen this show before.

"Oh, for fuck's sake."

Somehow, despite his drunken state, Tad manages to stabilize us both by wrapping me up in a bear hug. He grins down at me and winks. "I got ya, Breezy."

"You do realize you're the reason we almost fell, right?"

"The ice is a little icy." He's still holding on to me tightly. "By the way, you smell real good. Like flowers and fucking sunshine and soft breeze on a summer day. Pretty Breezy smells like a breeze." He snorts. "It's kinda perfect."

"Thanks." I gently remove myself from his embrace. "But if one of us dies out here, I want it in my obituary that I was dragged down by Tad Hanson."

Tad beams. "I'd be honored."

Randy shakes his head, his eyebrows drawing together as my whole body jolts with a giant shiver. "Why don't the two of you go get in the truck while I finish assessing this situation?"

"You think you might be able to get me out?" I ask, hopeful. After being emotionally sucked dry by my baby brother, a seven-hour, white-knuckle drive, and fifteen minutes standing in the middle of a blizzard, I'd give anything for a warm bed and dry feet right now.

Still grinning, Tad fumbles toward the truck bed. "Fear not, Breezy! The sheep farmers are here to save the day!"

"Tad, why don't you get in the truck and let me handle this?" Randy suggests again. His brother ignores him.

"We'll get you out!" Tad calls over his shoulder. "Gonna take us five minutes, tops!"

"Good grief," Randy mutters. "Again, I apologize for his drunk ass."

I shrug and smile at that. "At least someone is enjoying themselves."

"Oh, he's enjoying himself, all right," Randy retorts. "Too fucking much, if you ask me."

"Shut your trap, Rando!" Tad yells as he fumbles around with God knows what in the bed of their pickup truck. "We gotta focus or else pretty Breezy here is gonna end up sleeping in her fancy SUV!"

Randy heads in Tad's direction, setting him to the side while he pulls a chain from the bed. Tad does a jig that almost plants him on his ass again, and Randy catches him by the elbow before coming back to me.

"If you think you can, hop back in your car and roll down the window. I'll tell you when we're ready."

"Ready? Ready for what?"

Randy smiles just enough to flatten his usual frown. "I'll give you instructions."

Shrugging, I climb carefully through the snow to my driver's door and squeeze back inside. With the engine back on and my window down, I listen intently to everything they throw my way.

"Give it a little gas!"

"Turn your wheel to the left!"

"Let off the gas!"

Tad tries to insert himself into a conversation with me more than a few times as they work actively and strenuously, grunting and cursing and swapping out chains for cables and ropes and the like, but when he stops in the middle of the whole debacle to peek into my window and ask me, *"Why are you so pretty, Breezy Bishop?"* Randy finally meets his limit.

"I hate to say this, but you're stuck, Breezy. We'll get you out tomorrow when it's light." The gloves on his hands are covered in snow, and he breathes heavily into the cold night air. I don't like it, but I can't ask him to try anymore.

"So what now? I just walk to my brother's house?" I ask, my jaw clenched as I climb back out the door.

"Hell no!" Tad exclaims, nudging Randy out of the way and wrapping an arm around my shoulders. He's still drunk and annoyingly smiley, but he worked just as hard as Randy at getting me out, so I can't be mad at him. "You're coming with us."

"I gotta drop Tad off at home anyway before I head back to my place," Randy agrees. "It's no trouble." The last update I got from my good friend and Red Bridge lifer, Josie, Randy Hanson bought her grandmother Rose's old house that sits just on the outskirts of her and her husband Clay Harris's property, which is a drive in the opposite direction, but his explanation makes sense—Tad's farm is right beside Bennett's property, and he's way too drunk to get anywhere on his own.

"See?" Tad says, still grinning and gently squeezing my shoulders at the same time. "Everything is coming up like roses in the Breeze."

I laugh at that. "I don't know about roses, but a ride to Bennett's will certainly help my situation."

"We got you, girl," Tad says, flashing a wink in my direction.

I grab my purse and the Louis Vuitton travel bag that has my laptop and most important shit in it from my SUV and turn off the engine. Once I'm sure the doors are locked and Randy puts my bags in the bed, I climb into the truck and a Hanson Brother Sandwich.

Randy drives and Tad sings along with the radio, the air in the cab thick with the scent of hay, snow, and the whiskey on Tad's breath.

Yeah, he definitely had some drinks tonight.

But damn, when he flashes that lopsided smile at me, I can't do anything but return it with a laugh. It's downright comical that the man whose picture I saw plastered across the *Red Bridge Chronicle* this morning while I was packing up my office is the first person to greet me when I arrived in town.

"It sure is good to see you, Breezy," he says, his head drifting down to my shoulder and back to the window on every bump we take.

"You too, Farmer Tad."

"Farmer Tad? Fuck me." He lets out a half groan and half

chuckle. "You talk to Josie Harris too much."

"You don't like being called Farmer Tad?" I question and he sighs.

"How about you just call me Tad?"

"Okay, Tad. Who just so happens to be a farmer."

Randy laughs, but Tad laughs even harder. "Breezy Bishop, the linguistic gymnast."

I grin. "At your service."

"You know, you should come to Red Bridge more often," he says. "Hell, you should move here!"

It's my turn to crack up. "I don't think I'm small-town material."

"I think you're the kind of pretty that can fit in anywhere."

Is it just me, or is Farmer Tad flirting with me?

"Leave her alone, Tad," Randy mutters. "Pretty sure she's had to deal with enough bullshit tonight."

"Relax, Rando." Tad holds up both hands like he's being arrested. "I'm just being hospitable."

"Pretty sure you're being a pain in her ass," Randy retorts.

"Don't mind him," Tad attempts to whisper to me, but there's no doubt that Randy can hear him. "He's mad at me 'cause he had to pick me up from the bar. I like to have fun. Randy likes to be a buzzkill."

"I'm mad because you told Maybelline Ross I'd give her a ride home, and she lives five goddamn miles outside of town."

"Now it's making sense why you guys were on the road tonight," I say, and Randy nods.

"Guess it all worked out, though. I wouldn't have wanted you stuck out there like that."

"The Maybelline Ross thing wasn't my fault," Tad interjects on a sigh. "She was asking to stay at my place, and you know I'm not down for that bullshit."

Randy snorts and rolls his eyes. "Whatever you say, brother."

I've heard enough of Farmer Tad's lore to know all the single ladies in Red Bridge want a piece of him. Hell, Josie says there are women from Molene—a town that's about thirty minutes away—who come to her husband Clay's bar just to see Tad Hanson. He's apparently quite the hot commodity out here in small-town Vermont.

Though, on all my visits to Red Bridge, I've never actually seen him with anyone. Maybe he's just a one-night-stand kind of guy? I don't know.

It's a slippery journey, and by the time we pull into the long gravel drive of Tad's farmhouse, the time on the clock glows red with 1:30 a.m.

Shit.

That's about four hours too late to be barging into Bennett's house where his not-even-two-year-old toddler, Autumn, is asleep, and up until now, I was too busy worrying over the snow to realize. But I can't go in there. I'd rather die of hypothermia than risk waking a sleeping baby, to be honest.

"Home sweet home!" Tad exclaims as he hops out of the truck and holds out a hand for me to follow. I do, but my mind whirls as I try to figure out a plan for where I'm going to go until the sun comes up. "What an honor spending the evening with you." He literally bows in front of me like I'm royalty. "Anytime you get stuck somewhere, give me a call, yeah? Day or night or afternoon."

"Uh…thanks," I say.

"You good?" Tad asks, weaving on his feet a little as he leans back into the truck. Evidently, even in his buzzed-up glory, he can see the hesitancy on my face.

"Yeah. Yes," I say, but a sigh escapes my throat. "I just…I didn't realize it was so late."

"Does Bennett know you're coming?" Randy asks, leaning across the bench seat to meet my eyes, and I cringe a little.

"He knows I'm coming, but he *might* have been under the impression that I was coming tomorrow. Something about a snowstorm I should wait out before making the drive."

"Oh! I know what you should do!" Tad exclaims with a giant grin on his face. "You should stay at your buddy Farmer Tad's house!" He winks. "That's me, by the way. I'm Farmer Tad."

"I'm aware," I answer, shaking my head as I do. "But I don't know if that's a good idea."

"C'mon, Breezy. It's a great idea. No use in you waking up Bennett and Norah and little Autumn. I've got plenty of beds here."

"Uh..." I pause, completely unsure of what to do. I mean, I definitely don't want to risk waking up my little niece at two in the morning, but spending the night at Tad Hanson's? That's quite the turn of events.

"If you'd rather, you can stay with me," Randy offers kindly. The idea of getting back in a vehicle right now, however, is akin to the most brutal of psychological torture.

Tad takes charge, grabbing my hand and pulling the two of us a couple steps away from the truck. I grip him tightly back, but it's only because the ground is so freaking slippery. "Let's go, sweetheart. You can stay here. No problem! And I'll be very gentlemanly, okay? Make sure you got your own bed and everything."

I hesitate for a long moment, but when I look past the tree line to where Bennett's house sits, a wide expanse of snow-covered darkness the only thing between here and there, I exhale.

"Okay, yeah."

"Fan-fucking-tastic!" Tad cheers.

Randy makes sure I'm good with the plan before heading on his way, even taking my keys with him and kindly offering to get my car out of the snow in the morning, and I follow Tad's jovial lead up the porch steps and into the warm farmhouse.

It's a sweet, old place—the kind where the wood floors bounce a little with each step—and reeks of bachelorhood in every way. The walls are bare, the couch is old, and the cords from the giant TV run unhidden down the wall.

He unearths a blanket from a cabinet in the corner of the living room, accidentally hands me his coat before realizing his blunder with a laugh, and then gives me the lay of the land.

"This here's the living room. And the kitchen's over there. This woodstove'll keep you hotter than any electric heat ever could, but if you need the extra blanket, you've got it." He shrugs. "I'll be in my bedroom down the hall, but you can sleep in the guest bedroom or here on the couch because I'm not in the mood for any of your funny ideas. Nothing handsy from you, okay?"

I roll my eyes. "Sounds good." I clutch the blanket to my chest and shift from one foot to the other. "Anything else I should know?"

"There's a bathroom in the hall, and oh! Don't get too close to the stove here, 'cause she'll roast your ass."

I laugh. "Noted. Goodnight, then. And…thanks. For the help in the snow and the hospitality now."

"Anytime, Breezy Bishop. Anytime."

As Tad stumbles down the hall, I sink onto the couch and pull off my wet shoes, leaving them by the woodstove to dry.

It's late and I'm tired and I desperately want to sleep. But I can't help marveling at how far the mighty have fallen.

A month ago, I was single-handedly running one of the biggest art gallery empires in the country. Now, I'm without a job, temporarily without a car, and completely adrift in all aspects of my life.

And I'm about to have a sleepover at a small-town sheep farmer's house.

Goodness, things have certainly taken a drastic turn.

3

Tad

Tuesday, January 12th

My head pounds and my stomach turns, but the thing about sheep is...they don't give a damn about your plans or your hangover.

I've just finished up with the morning feed routine, and some of my flock is already trying to find a way to get into trouble—which isn't new, but it *is* inconvenient.

"Back in!" I yell, clapping my hands like an idiot as three woolly little bastards try to shove through a sagging section of fence. *Again.*

They scatter into the snow, bleating like they're in on some private joke at my expense. *Good one, Tad. How about we shove a giant rod in the middle of your already vibrating brain?* Sheep have that smug, blank look that says *we win, you lose,* and they're usually right.

Or at least, *my* sheep have that look. I don't know about other farmers because I've never researched it.

Randy keeps telling me we need dogs. Border collies, heelers—apparently, it's a *must* for people who take this shit seriously. *Every shepherd worth his salt has dogs, Tad,* he lectures almost daily, all the while missing the whole fucking point.

I'm not in this business to *succeed*. I'm in it to forget.

Plus, my general inclination when it comes to my older brother is to do the opposite of what he wants me to do because it's his fault we're in Red Bridge in the first place. The whole state of our lives today, as it were, is his own damn fault, even if he doesn't see it that way.

Don't get me wrong; I love my brother. Randy is a good man and an even better older brother, but he should've stayed in Chicago and focused on himself instead of worrying so goddamn much about saving me from myself.

But that's Randy for you. He's only two years older than me—forty-three to my forty-one, but he refuses to drop the protective older brother act, and as a result, he's farming sheep—which he fucking hates—while I'm *pretending* to farm sheep in the name of passing time.

I have nothing to lose and nowhere to be because almost a decade ago, I already lost everything. I basically closed my eyes and randomly pointed to a spot on a map, drained my savings to purchase the one and only farmhouse that was for sale in Red Bridge, Vermont, at the time, and moved here.

It's not my issue that Randy's dumb ass followed.

"Ah, ah, Mabel. Get your pregnant ass over here." My girl Mabel darts around me, beelining straight for Bennett Bishop's property, of course, my flock's homing beacon for pissing off my neighbor alive and fucking well.

I skid on my feet and nearly fall on my ass, but I manage to stop her while two other sheep halt dead in the drift and stare at me like they wish they had some popcorn to eat while they enjoy the show.

"Mind your business, Crosby and Nash!" I shout over at them. "Go make yourselves useful by sticking with the group!"

They bleat at me, but thankfully, they actually listen.

I'm at least grateful Randy bought Rose Ellis's old house from Josie and Clay and is no longer all up in my shit twenty-four seven—and blissfully missing now—because the constant stream of shit he'd be giving me would only serve to make Mabel's escape ruse ten times more annoying.

With Mabel on her way back toward the barn, I grab the useless fence wire she broke on her way out in my hands. I sigh. *Another repair I'll try to fit in before Randy sees it and has a conniption.*

Trust me, a little space from each other is a good thing, for me and for him. I'm no fucking picnic to deal with, I know, but he has a habit of riding my ass that I'm not too fond of either.

I head back toward the barn to grab some tools, but as I pass the farmhouse, a female mess of long legs, fancy clothes, and wide eyes poised at the top step of my porch grabs my attention.

"Hey."

Soft, feminine notes of a night I should but can't remember grip me by the balls and stop me in my tracks. It takes a couple seconds for recognition to kick in, but when it does, the news gets even worse.

It's not just any woman. It's Breezy, my neighbor Bennett's sister, standing on my snowy front porch in heels and tailored pants I'd bet cost more than my entire truck and making it so hard to breathe, I feel sickish. She's *beautiful.*

But if I fucked with her while I was too drunk to remember, I'm about to be in a whole world of trouble.

Breezy is a city girl through and through. She lives in New York. She runs prestigious art galleries. She probably spends her days drinking expensive coffee and having dinner dates with men who have seven-figure bank accounts.

And her brother hates me. *Oh boy.*

It's not out of the ordinary to see her in Red Bridge on occasion—she makes frequent weekend stops to visit her brother and sister-in-law Norah and her niece Autumn, and she's close friends with Norah's sister Josie and her husband Clay, but the way she's standing on my porch like she just came *out* of my house is a new one, to say the least.

"Uh…hey," I eventually manage in reply.

"So…thanks for last night," she says.

"Uh…you're welcome."

My memory might as well be Swiss cheese with all the holes it has, a barely there scrap of last night clinging to the edges. *Drinking at The Country Club. Randy dragging me out before I ordered another round. Something with that woman Maybelline Ross needing a ride home. Snow. Maybe headlights.*

And then…nothing. A blackout curtain.

My stomach drops. I look at her—polished, confident, heels not even wobbling in the snow—and then at myself, boots, old jeans, flannel, and looking like a dumbass covered in snow and mud from wrestling sheep.

The two of us mixing is a recipe for disaster.

She doesn't give me any more details on what last night entailed, instead moving down my front porch and crouching gracefully near one of my escape-artist sheep to stroke his head.

"Oh, I remember you, Crosby," she says through a soft laugh. "You're a little troublemaker, aren't you?"

Breezy and Clay had a run-in with Crosby over a year ago, on the day of Clay and Josie's wedding, on their way into town from the airport. They had to drive the obstinate bastard all the way home in Clay's back seat because of his Oscar-worthy performance as an injured damsel, but her remembering him by name still comes as a surprise.

Crosby bleats and looks up at Breezy like she's the fucking sun, clearly in love with her, and she gently pats him between the ears.

With one final pet, she waves to the rest of the herd that's managed to surround her. "Bye, cuties," she tells them lovingly, their role switching quickly to beloved pets from what I know them to be—woolly terrorists.

"Bye, Tad." She leaves me with a wink and a smile, and the pit in my stomach collapses even deeper.

I don't know what happened last night. Hell, when I woke up this morning, I didn't even know she was in my house.

Probably because you drank your weight in whiskey—and Randy's weight too.

She's on the move, heading across my yard and straight for Bennett's house, walking through snow and ice and obstacles she wouldn't have to if I had the wherewithal to do the gentlemanly thing and offer her a ride, but I'm fucking frozen, mind swirling with foggy memories. *Drinking. Snow. Breezy Bishop. At my house. All night long.*

Surely she slept on the couch. Or in the guest room. Or…

The more I think, the less I know.

I'm not an expert in much these days—and I don't pretend to be.

But I'll be damned if two plus two on this one isn't adding up to a four-by-four to the head when Bennett Bishop finds out I slept with his sister and have zero memory of it.

4

Breezy

It's been years since I've taken a nap—or even slowed down enough to consider it—but at a little after five in the evening, I'm already yawning so much I'm seriously considering it.

Last night wasn't exactly restful with Tad Hanson, in all his drunk, gentlemanly glory, popping in on me every five minutes for the first hour after we arrived to make sure I had enough blankets and pillows and knew my way to the bathroom. Even after he was done and passed out in his own bed, I lay awake, staring at the ceiling for another full hour, my body heavy with travel, grief, and too many thoughts.

By the time I unlocked the back door of Bennett and Norah's house this morning with a key I've had since before the two of them got together, I'd only slept a whopping two hours, and exhaustion was a second skin. But Norah was already in the kitchen with Autumn, and the sweetest smell in the universe—coffee brewing, toast in the toaster, the faint pureness of baby shampoo and sugar clinging to my niece's curls—was enough to soften all my rough edges and give me a second wind.

Now, the late-afternoon sunlight slants through the windows of Bennett and Norah's house, and I press my cheek into Autumn's hair and breathe her in. She smells like innocence. She smells like hope. She smells like the breath of fresh air I need right now, and I cling to the feeling by tightening my hug.

She giggles and wiggles like a worm in my arms. "No squishes, Bee!"

God, those curls. Glossy brown spirals that frame her round cheeks and startling blue eyes that grab ahold of your chest and suck you inside, heart first. I swear, if her hair were blond, she'd be Summer's twin. The thought makes my whole body ache. I miss her so much.

I kiss the crown of her head one last time. "You sure make cute kids, Ben. Goodness, Summer would've adored her."

Norah's eyes are warm, her hand resting on Bennett's, and my brother's mouth tugs into a ghost of a smile, though his eyes hold a little moisture.

"She would've," he agrees. His voice is quiet but certain.

I set Autumn down, and she toddles off toward the basket of dolls in the corner. The silence she leaves behind is thick but tender, full of love and loss braided together.

Forever seven, that's our sweet Summer. We lost her two years ago, and sometimes it still feels like yesterday.

"Here," Norah says, handing me a cup of coffee as I sit down across from Bennett.

Immediately, I wrap my hands around the mug. The warmth helps steady me. We don't have to have the toughest conversation about my dad's final fuck-you—I already called Bennett after the will-reading and had it, so that wound isn't fresh anymore, but it's certainly bruised and pulsing in the background.

Still, I find myself filling him and Norah in on the rest. "Logan showed up at the gallery yesterday," I say, my voice weary. "I was already packing up my shit and ended up telling him I quit. He looked panicked and begged me to stay and run things for him.

Apparently, he knew about Dad's will before he died. He knew the galleries were going to him." I shake my head. "God. After everything Dad did, after all I sacrificed...and he just...cut me out of it all. And Logan knew and agreed to it. It's all so awful. I don't even have words."

"I hate to say it, Breeze..." Bennett pauses, his jaw flexes, but his eyes hold no surprise. Which, frankly, shows how fucked up our family is. "But that sounds about right for Logan. Thinking you'd just run the galleries for him. You're seeing the side of him I've been privy to for years."

Bennett and Logan's relationship has been *strained* for more than a decade. I don't know if there's anything that would have brought them back together after all that's happened between them, but I'm sure Logan's role in Dad's will planning and the galleries being taken away from me are only serving to nail the coffin shut.

"And the money," I add carefully. "I didn't tell you before, but...it wasn't just the galleries. He left us twenty million each."

Bennett's expression hardens instantly. "I don't want a dime of it. Not from him. Not after everything."

"I figured." I nod, affirming that his message is the one I conveyed on his behalf. "I told Logan that. And I said the same thing for myself."

"Dad never saw me as a son," Bennett says. His tone is flat, but the words land heavily. "I was an asset. A machine to produce work he could sell. Work that brought attention to his precious galleries that had you as a workhorse behind them the whole fucking time. That's all I ever was to him. And sadly, that's probably all you were to him too. I hate this is how you had to find out, though."

Norah squeezes his hand, her thumb brushing over his knuckles.

"Mom's not much better," I murmur.

"No, but at least she's not worse," Bennett says with a shrug. "Flighty, selfish, off chasing cabana boys on some beach. She never cared about my paintings. That made her easier. She might not be mother of the year, but she sees me as her son, not a paycheck. And she never would've faulted you for telling Dad to fuck off and run the galleries himself either. I don't need her around, but there's a little less dancing on the grave to it, if you know what I mean."

"That's true." I lean back in my chair, watching him. "Though, as her daughter, I could never trust her around any men I dated." My mother loves to flirt and seduce, especially when the men are younger. Even her daughter's boyfriends weren't off-limits. "Our family is so screwed up."

"Yeah." Bennett laughs, and he squeezes Norah's knee. "However, Norah's family might take the cake for the most fucked up."

"You won't hear me refuting that one. I mean, my mother is currently sitting in an orange jumpsuit to prove it." She snorts at that, but then her eyes turn kind toward me. "Breeze, I know what it's like to have your world turned on its head. I know what it's like to need to escape to somewhere you feel safe. I don't know what your plans are, but just know you're welcome to stay here as long as you need without pressure or judgment."

"Thanks, Norah." I'm grateful, but I'm also exhausted and sad and confused and so many other emotions I could scream. I sigh. "I wish I had plans. I wish I had even an inkling of a direction to go right now."

No career. No job prospects. No boyfriend or husband or happy family. I'm basically aimless at the moment. The reality pinches sharply.

"You'll get there," Norah reassures, and Bennett nods.

"You will, Breeze. Dad and Logan's bullshit won't drag you down the rest of your life. Just give yourself a little time to work through it all," he says.

We all go quiet for a long moment, but there's a part of me that can't leave this conversation without saying something on our brother Logan's behalf. Sure, I'm pissed at him, and yes, he's probably one of the most selfish people you'll ever meet, but he's still my baby brother and I will always try to see the good in him, despite all the chaos his rebellion and bad decisions have created for our family over the years.

He said he went along with Dad's will to protect me, and deep down, I believe his intentions weren't malicious. It doesn't make it all better, but it's something—a something I'm trying to hold on to.

I know better than to say anything aloud, but Ben can read the look on my face anyway.

"Don't do yourself the disservice of underestimating him, Breeze. I know exactly what that motherfucker is capable of." Bennett barks out another laugh, but it's not amused. "And now, clearly, you should too."

Maybe someday my brothers won't be estranged. Maybe someday I'll convince Bennett—and hell, myself too—to give Logan another chance. But I know today isn't that day, so I don't argue.

Thankfully, the front door creaks open before the conversation can dig deeper.

"Hello?" Josie's voice floats in, followed by Clay's deeper timbre.

"Is our little Autumn in here?"

"JoJo! CayCay!" Autumn squeals, barreling toward her aunt Josie and uncle Clay. Josie drops her bag and sweeps Autumn up, kissing her face until our niece is nothing but a curly ball of giggles and squeals.

Clay follows suit, taking Autumn out of Josie's hands and raining kisses all over her chubby little cheeks. Instantly, everything dark and dismal about our conversation disappears, and the room feels brighter.

"All right, Clay." Bennett rescues Autumn from her uncle's affection on a laugh. "Any more kisses and she might puke."

Bennett and Clay have been friends for years and years. Clay was actually the first one to move to Red Bridge and start a bar in spite of his own father, and Bennett ended up following in his footsteps when Summer was born.

The two of them have seen each other through the worst and

the best and everything in between, and they handle it all with love—and incessant razzing.

Clay flashes his best friend a shit-eating grin. "Aw, Ben. You want some sugar from Uncle Clay too?"

See what I mean?

"You can f-u-c-k right off with that," Ben mutters as he sets Autumn on her feet. She runs across the living room on quick feet and doesn't stop until she reaches the little dollhouse I bought her from a boutique in New York for her first birthday.

"Weeee!" she exclaims as she takes one of the dolls out of the house and pretends she's flying in the air. "Fast gurl! Go fast gurl!"

Finally released from the cute toddler spell by Autumn's exit, Josie notices me sitting here for the first time, and I laugh as she starfishes her limbs in shock. "Hold the freaking phone! What are you doing here, Breezy? When did you get here? Why didn't you call?"

She crosses the room in three strides and drags me from the couch to pull me into a hug.

"I literally just got in," I laugh, hugging her back.

"Well, it's good to see you," she says with a smile.

"Hey, Breeze. Happy to see you in our neck of the woods." Clay grins and slings an arm around my shoulders to give me a friendly side hug before Autumn demands his attention over at the dollhouse once again.

Norah joins Josie and me on the couch in a kind of girl-gab-pow-wow while the guys field the toddler. When there's a lull in our conversation, Josie pulls a folded copy of a New York newspaper from her purse and hands it to her sister.

"I have something you need to see, Nore."

"What is it?" Norah asks, but Josie just taps the front-page article with her index finger.

"Read it."

I lean in slightly as Norah does just that, taking it in for myself and gritting my teeth at the headline. ***Ellis & Conrad Appeal Denied: Thirty-Year Sentences Stand.***

Mug shots of Norah and Josie's mother Eleanor Ellis and Norah's ex-fiancé Thomas Michael Conrad waste ink and paper right below it.

It's good news, but anytime these sweet women have to confront their past, my loins practically gird. The article is clinical, but the reality isn't. Eleanor's and Thomas's crimes were ugly and tangled in the most disgusting things you can think of. Honestly, whenever I think about what the two of them did, it *still* makes my stomach twist, and I don't have the confusing pleasure of sharing DNA with one of them. I can't imagine how hard it is for Norah and Josie.

Norah's face stays composed, but her voice is clipped. "I already heard. Carlton keeps me updated."

Josie's eyebrows jump upward, toward her own curly hairline. "I'm always shocked you keep in touch with our stepfather, even knowing you do."

"Hey, he was always good to me." Norah shrugs. "I keep in touch with Alexis too, and she hand-delivered the note that nuked my life in the first place."

Oh, Alexis. The sweet, young girl who exposed Thomas and Eleanor's whole sordid façade, even when the risk was so high she could've lost everything. She may have delivered the bomb, but she didn't build it. They did. She was a victim, just like all the rest.

"How is she doing?" Josie asks.

"Good, actually," Norah updates.

"I'm sure it's easier for her to breathe with those two assholes behind bars."

Norah snorts. "From your lips to God's ears."

Josie opens her mouth to say something else, but Autumn toddles back with her doll and plops it in my lap. "Dolly say hi, Bee!"

Bennett and Clay are no longer on toddler duty, having disappeared down the hall to tinker with something unknown.

I paste on a smile, grateful for the distraction, and kiss Autumn's forehead. "Hi, Dolly. Nice to meet you."

Her curls bounce as she nods and giggles. “Meets you! Dolly meets Bee!”

“Dolly is so pretty,” I say, but before Autumn can answer, Clay and Ben’s return formally announces itself with a remark from Clay.

“Not as pretty as me!” He picks up the princess crown and a little purse from the top of the dollhouse and dons them while we all look on.

“CayCay so pwetty!” Autumn exclaims as she runs back over toward Clay. “Smiles, CayCay!”

Clay flashes a full-toothed grin, and Autumn claps her hands.

“So pwetty!”

The princess crown ends up on Autumn’s little head but not before it makes the rounds on Bennett, Norah, and Josie first. Norah and Bennett take Princess Autumn into the kitchen to get her a snack, and Josie sits down beside me and places her hand gently on my knee.

“All in all, are you doing okay?” she whispers.

“As good as I can be.” I shrug. “I mean, being here with you guys is a nice distraction.”

Josie’s smile is soft. She knows about Dad’s death. She knows about the will and the gallery betrayal. She knows all there is to know up until about twenty-four hours ago. In a weird way, Josie Harris is one of my closest friends, even though we don’t live in the same city. When all of the drama and heartbreak was going down between her and Clay, I was her shoulder to cry on.

And now, even though it’s been mostly via phone, she’s been mine.

“Breeze, did you miss all the shit snow on your way into town this morning?” Clay asks, and I shake my head.

“Unfortunately, no. I was stuck driving in it last night.”

“You were driving last night in that blizzard?” Bennett asks, overhearing the conversation from the kitchen. He peeks around the oak doorjamb with a furrowed brow.

I sigh. “Yes, brother, I was. And yes, I know that was dumb

and that, in the future, I should listen when you tell me not to do something."

He smiles, waggling his eyebrows. "So long as we're on the same page. Where did you end up staying?" he asks, undoubtedly assuming I ended up staying in a hotel off the highway when the conditions got too bad to continue.

Clearly, I'm a grown woman, fully capable of making my own decisions, but telling my brother I spent the night under the-sheep-farmer-next-door's roof feels like signing up for an inquisition I do *not* have the energy for.

He'll either laugh his head off and tease me relentlessly, or he'll try to give me a lecture about safety. Neither one is on my short list of experiences I'd like to have.

"Just somewhere easy," I say with a shrug, my words as light-hearted as my name. "No big deal."

I don't know if Bennett would have pushed the issue—his hands are a little busy scooping peanut butter and apple slices off the floor—but a knock at the front door saves me either way.

Bennett wipes his hands on a paper towel while Norah wrangles the toddler with another precarious plate. "I'll get it, baby," he offers, confirming all the things I know about my brother in his role as a spouse. With Norah, his hard turns soft, and his heart lives on his sleeve.

He heads from the kitchen to the foyer and opens the door, and from my vantage point on the couch, I get a perfectly clear view of the person on the other side as soon as he does.

It's none other than Randy Hanson, the keys to my stranded car hanging on his finger. *Whoops.*

"Hey, Bennett," Randy greets as he dusts snow off his boots on the front mat and holds up my car keys in the air. "Just bringing Breezy's Rover over. She's out front."

Instantly, Bennett's gaze whips from Randy to me, his brow arched, his mouth quirking in that way that says, *Well, isn't this something...*

I'm a little upset with the universe for choosing *right now*, with a literal audience, of all times to bring Randy to Bennett's door, but I am thankful for the fact that my car is here and, evidenced by Randy's arrival with it, roadworthy.

"So..." Ben pauses, looking between me and Randy. "You didn't drive here this morning?"

"She ended up—" Randy starts to chime in, but I'm very quick to cut him off, jumping up from the couch in a flash and snatching my keys from his outstretched hand.

"It's no big deal, Ben. I had a little car trouble last night, but all's well that ends well." I turn directly to Randy, poising my palms together in prayer hands, my keys smashed in the middle. "Thank you, Randy. Again. Can't say how much I appreciate it."

"It wasn't a problem at all, Breezy," Randy says, and I'm grateful when he just tips his ball cap toward me and boot-scoots back down the steps and across the driveaway, headed in the direction of Tad's on foot. Thankfully, Randy is the broody, quiet Hanson brother and not talkative Tad, who I have a feeling would have spilled each and every single bean.

As I step inside and shut the front door, I don't miss the way Bennett's eyes narrow at me, and I don't give the questions that will inevitably follow time to sprout either.

"I'm going to go lie down for a bit," I say as I head toward the guest bedroom I always stay in when I'm at my brother's house, exhaustion and the need for excuses commingling perfectly. "Got a headache."

"A headache, huh?" Bennett says, and I can hear his footsteps following behind me. "You think it's from partying with Randy Hanson last night?"

"Shut up, Bennett." I flip him the middle finger over my shoulder.

"What? It's an honest question. I mean, he just dropped off your car, Breezy."

"Because he's a nice man. Unlike you!" I snap, still walking.

"I'm nice!" Bennett refutes on a laugh. "I'm very nice. Doesn't mean I show up to random women's houses with their car keys in tow."

"It'd better not mean that," I hear Norah chastise as I close the door behind me, their voices only muffling slightly. "Leave her alone, Ben. Or else."

"Or else what, Norah?"

"Or else I'm going to kick your a-s-s," Norah retorts smartly, which is quickly followed by shrieky laughter and an *"Oh my God, stop it, Ben!"*

Maybe I should be embarrassed. Maybe I should be defensive or feel like I owe an explanation. But my life is already in splinters. I'm jobless. Directionless. And there are two suitcases in the back of my Range Rover with enough clothes to last me a good month because the thought of being in New York right now, near all my usual spots—*near the galleries*—makes me feel like crawling out of my own skin.

At this point, what's it matter what my brother or anyone else thinks?

Bennett could think I got rip-roaring drunk with Randy Hanson and did a naked snow dance with his flock of sheep, and I don't think I have it in me to care.

With my life at a standstill, I've got bigger things to worry about.

5

Tad

Wednesday, January 13th

I like my coffee the same way I like my relationships. Hot. A little sugar. No fuss, no muss.

Red Bridge offers more in both departments, though, even if I'm not interested in consuming them. At Josie Harris's coffee shop, CAFFEINE, you can go wild with twenty kinds of syrups and foam-art shaped like hearts, and if you're looking for a long-term relationship, there are at least fifteen different women with the tenacity and desire to take you up on it to choose from waiting on every corner of Main Street on any given day.

Fiona Blue, the children's librarian at the Red Bridge Library, is one of them.

"Tad Hanson," a voice sings, sweet as syrup. For me, it's the kind that sticks to your fingers after sticking to the bottle, but I'm sure it'd taste good if the feeling didn't annoy me so much.

Fiona makes her way up the sidewalk, having spotted me the moment I stepped out of my truck in front of CAFFEINE, wearing a fuzzy pink coat, a wool hat with antennae that look suspiciously like butterfly feelers, and a smile that could power the town's Christmas lights.

"Well, if it isn't our town's most eligible sheep farmer," she teases, adjusting the strap of her oversized tote bag.

"Morning, Fiona," I greet, smiling over at her. "What's the costume this week? I'm guessing *caterpillar* season's over?"

She's a local celebrity for the performances she puts on in the library every Wednesday afternoon, the town's unofficial morale booster, and her pretty face is the number one reason all the single dads show up to toddler story time.

She laughs. "Yep. This week is all about the butterfly. And next week is ladybug bonanza, so prepare yourself for lots of polka dots."

"I'll alert my sheep," I reply. "They're real fashion-forward these days."

"You know, Tad, you should come read to the kids sometime," she says, and her eyes are bright as she briefly puts a gentle hand on my shoulder. "They'd love it. You could bring a lamb. You'd be the hit of the century."

"Oh, I don't know," I say, rubbing the back of my neck. "Not sure if you've noticed, but my sheep aren't much for behaving."

"I think that's just because your sheep like to be around people." Fiona winks. "But Sheep Farmer Tad at story time? You'd steal the show. But then again, you always do."

Her voice drips with flirtation, and I smile politely out of habit. Fiona's sweet—hell, everyone in town loves her—but my brain is doing its usual autopilot thing. The kind of natural gear that knows when to smile and when to charm but isn't looking to get anywhere.

"Just think about it, okay?" Fiona says and reaches out to squeeze my bicep. "And also, maybe, if you ever want to grab a bite to eat or something, let me know."

I smile and nod, letting her down easy. It's not her fault I'm unattainable for anything other than a quick shag. "That's very kind of you. Pretty sure ol' Randy's got a complex about me eating dinner without him, though. Thanks for the offer."

"Pity you're always so busy, honey. You'd be surprised just how kind I can be for the right man." She winks. "I'll see ya around." Marking her exit with a floppy wave, she flutters off toward the library, her butterfly hat bobbing in the cool winter air.

I shake my head, smiling despite myself, and head for the door of CAFFEINE.

It's warm inside, smells like espresso and cinnamon rolls, and the bell above the door chimes as I walk in. Most mornings, it's crowded, but that's probably because half of Red Bridge stops here before work. It's also where the newspaper bulldog Eileen Martin usually tracks me down, notebook in hand, claiming she needs "just a few quotes" for the *Red Bridge Chronicle.* I don't know how one woman can come up with that many questions about sheep, but I suppose the motivation of a chance to check out my ass is a creative catalyst.

I don't really mind—I've taken to embellishing my answers for fun just to see if she'll print them—but I'm thankful not to see her in here today.

After stomping snow off my boots on the rug, I get in line behind Sheriff Peeler, who's so busy complaining to Marty Higgins, one of the bartenders from Clay Harris's bar, The Country Club, about the Red Bridge youth, he's forgotten the art of volume control.

"I'm tellin' ya, Marty," Sheriff Peeler says through a shake of his head. "The damn kids wrote obscene words in the snow outside town hall. Took Deputy Felix two hours of plowing to remove it all, and Betty Bagley just about broke her hip when she saw the word d-i-c-k on her way to Melba's bakery to get some pastries."

"Pete, I'm pretty sure the youth haven't changed." Marty chuckles. "I recall hearing some stories about your wild teenage days."

Sheriff Pete huffs. "Things were different back then. We didn't have any fancy-schmancy cell phones. Stirring up a little trouble was the only damn thing to do."

"Yeah, yeah." Marty grins. "Speaking of which, you gonna be in to stir up some trouble at the bar later?"

Besides The Diner and CAFFEINE, The Country Club is a top Red Bridge hangout spot for locals, so I'm not surprised when the sheriff says *yes*. It's a home away from home for many of us—probably more than it should be. But far be it for me to judge anyone else for the overconsumption of Clay's alcohol. I'm a lot of things, but I try like hell not to be a hypocrite.

As the line shifts, so do Marty and the sheriff, and I get a clear view of the woman standing directly in front of them.

Beautiful Breezy Bishop, in the flesh. I suck in my stomach and lick my lips as my balls jump inside my body.

It's not that she's not a fair damn sight to look at; it's that I still don't know what happened between us Monday night.

She's at the counter talking to Josie, her dark hair shining under the lights, jeans tucked into sleek boots, and a soft gray sweater on top that looks straight out of a fancy magazine spread. Her outfit is perfectly practical for the snow, but she still looks like Red Bridge accidentally ordered her from the city. I don't imagine she'll be blending in anytime soon either. She's too fucking beautiful for people not to notice her.

Josie hands her a cup, shaking her head with a smile. "Bishops and their coffee. Strongest stuff in the house, every time."

Breezy laughs, low and easy, and my stomach does a slow, guilty somersault as I'm reminded that less than forty-eight hours ago, this woman walked out of my house like it was the most casual thing in the world, looking like she looks, and I can't even remember a damn nipple. It's criminal, really.

Maybe I *should* judge the overconsumption of Clay's alcohol. I'd remember whether we had sex.

I'd remember the sight of a damn fancy nipple like hers.

I wouldn't have had to let Randy be the knight in the shining armor and drop her keys and car off at Bennett's place to assure

I wouldn't end up with a black eye or two. Randy *and* I drove out to the main road with Tommy Lockland's tow truck; I could have taken a little credit.

Breezy stays glued to the counter, chatting up Josie and Todd and Camille—two of CAFFEINE's full-time baristas—regardless of the line behind her, and this small town has everyone acting so nice, nobody even says anything. Back in Chicago, even in the suburb of Elgin where I lived, curses would have been lobbed by now about being late.

I don't have anywhere to be per se—the sheep don't own a clock—but I'm sweating like I'm about to sit for confession.

I'm not used to playing the fucking fool. I've kept a hard rule of never bringing any women home when I've been drinking, up until now, and clearly, that rule was for a damn good reason.

Marty and Sheriff Peeler place their orders, yammering about their piss-poor deer seasons—everybody always sees a monster they don't kill—while they wait, and I play Russian roulette with eye contact with Breezy every time she turns a little bit toward me.

I want to see her eyes, but I'm terrified to let her see mine.

Get it the fuck together, man.

I'm a forty-one-year-old adult man, not some Red Bridge high schooler who just finished drawing dicks all over the town hall lawn. If we fucked, we fucked.

Right?

Right.

The pep talk works until it's my turn, and Breezy looks directly at me. Her smile is devastating, and my tongue gets tied in a fucking knot.

I clear my throat and try to find my easy talk—the rhythm I'm known around Red Bridge for falling into—but it's a struggle. "Hey, Breezy. How have you been?" I manage, which isn't too bad, but when the next words out of my mouth are "It's good to see you here in Red Bridge," I feel like punching myself in the dick.

One of her perfectly shaped brows arches, and a smile tugs at her mouth. "Tad, I'm pretty sure we just saw each other the other morning...unless you forgot."

It's half tease, half dismissal, and it knocks the wind out of me. I'm used to women caring a fair share more than I do. Meanwhile, this time, it's the opposite. Ironic, I suppose, that sex I can't even remember is all I can think about.

"Definitely didn't forget," I say quickly. "Just...making conversation."

"Mm-hmm." She crosses her arms. She's amused. She's relaxed. She's the exact opposite of me, and it's a humbling moment, to say the least. "Well, conversation accepted. I've been fine. You?"

"Good. Great." I clear my throat *again*. I lean in a fraction, lowering my voice to something that sounds far too much like a guilty whisper. "You, uh, sleep okay the other night?"

Her brow furrows for half a second, then smooths. "I slept fine. You were very *hospitable*."

Hospitable? Is that code for something? It sounds like it was. Especially in the oogly googly way she said it.

"Did I...uh...meet all your needs?" I ask, rubbing the back of my neck. Beating around a bush you're not even sure exists gives new meaning to awkward. "You know, despite my being so drunk that night."

"Meet my needs?" She scrunches up her nose. "Tad, everything was fine. Seriously."

"Fine?" As in, *I was completely respectful, and we didn't sleep together?* Or fine, as in, *we were tangled up in my sheets together, and my performance was mediocre at best?*

"Yes. Everything was fine. Entertaining, even. Never had an experience like it, and I'm in a little bit of a new experience phase." She grins, reaching out to squeeze my shoulder. It's firm, it's friendly, it's *torturous*. "I think you worry too much, Tad Hanson."

An *entertaining experience*?

Are we talking *put a clown nose on my face while I do a jig* entertaining or *very pleasurable, gave her a million orgasms with my tongue* entertaining?

Before I can process it—before I can say another dumb

fucking thing—she glances at her phone, clicks her tongue, and immediately slings her purse over her shoulder. “Shoot. I’d better get out of here. I promised Norah I’d watch Autumn while she’s on a conference call. It was good to see you, Tad.” She gives my shoulder another little squeeze before offering a wave to Josie. “Bye, Josie!”

“Bye, Breezy!” Josie exclaims with a smile.

And just like that, she’s gone, her fancy boots finishing their floor-clacking with a final punctuation mark just as the door closes.

Josie slides two steaming cups toward me and props her chin on her hand as she assesses me closely. “You always this twitchy before noon?”

“Coffee jitters,” I mumble, grabbing Randy’s and my coffee from the counter.

“You drink coffee before coming to my coffee shop?”

“Sometimes,” I lie with a shrug.

I like my coffee and my relationships simple.

This morning, I only managed that for one, and truth be told, it’s not the good one. I’d rather have foam fucking hearts in my damn coffee.

• • •

My sheep are out again, and that’s par for the course on the Hanson sheep farm. My brother hates it; I think it gives us something to do.

As we have many times before, we agree to disagree.

Crosby and a few other woolly assholes toddle toward the road, another three head for Bennett Bishop’s fence line, and my big girl Mabel stands there, chewing on hay and staring at me like she can’t believe her sheep friends are acting a fool while Randy and I wave our arms like idiots trying to get them to respond, knee-deep in crusty, refrozen snow.

She’d be rebelling right along with them if she weren’t

pregnant, but she's tired and fucking over it entirely right now. Frankly, since this is my fifth trip through the field, my breathing ragged with overexertion and laser beams shooting out of Randy's eyes, I'm feeling a little pregnant myself.

I juke and weave as Randy sends the flock in my direction, forcing them back through the gate and into the smaller, still-secure fenced area near the barn. I follow the group in with a loud yell and wave of my arms to assure we don't have any runners turn back, but Nash makes a break for it anyway.

"Dammit!" I scream as he scoots past me, belly-flopping in the snow in a failed attempt at a grab, but thankfully, Randy's behind me as a second line of defense.

"Back in," Randy snaps, grabbing Nash by the neck and wrestling him inside until he can get the gate closed enough to create a pinch point. His knee drags in the snow as Nash takes off to rejoin his buddies, and I laugh at our matching outfits.

Randy doesn't find the mud and melted snow quite as entertaining. "I swear, one of these days I'm gonna sell this whole fucking flock behind your back."

"And then what?" I grunt, shooing an onery Crosby away before he can start chewing on the one area of fence that's in good shape.

"I'll find some fucking peace. Maybe retire somewhere tropical. Never touch a fence ever again." He shrugs. "Anything but fucking this, Tad. Anything but this."

Normally, I'd be laughing and tossing out smartass remarks, but there's a small part of me that feels bad every once in a while for trapping Randy in purgatory with me. I guess, because of Breezy Bishop getting me all discombobulated this morning, this is one of those times.

"You can leave, you know. I don't need a babysitter."

He snorts, and I, of course, take offense.

"What? What's that sound mean?"

"It means you absolutely need a babysitter. How the fuck would you have gotten home the other night if it weren't for me?"

I sigh. I want to go to war—lash out and shit. But his bringing up the other night so organically is too good an opportunity to pass up.

"I guess I wouldn't have. I don't fucking know." I pull my gloves off and tuck them into my back pocket, wiping sweat and melted snow from my forehead. "Did everything...go okay?"

"Did everything go okay?" he repeats, confused. I can't blame him. I don't really even know what I'm asking myself. "I mean, you were drunk. So, that wasn't ideal. But Breezy's Range Rover got stuck in the snow, and we did our best to help her out."

"Right," I say, kicking at the snow. "So...when you dropped us at my place...what was the vibe?"

Randy squints at me like I just started speaking French. "The what?"

"The vibe," I repeat, trying to sound casual.

"What the hell does that mean?"

"You know—" I wave my hand vaguely "—the...*energy*."

"The energy?" His brows knit tighter. "Should I know what the fuck you're talking about right now?"

No, Randy. No, you shouldn't. Because I don't fucking know either.

"I just mean, how was Breezy acting that night? How was I acting?"

"Tad, it was snowing, you were shit-faced, and she was tired from driving and didn't want to wake up Bennett and Norah's little girl in the middle of the night. Pretty sure she just wanted to go to bed, you know? And you...you needed to sleep off the booze."

My heart skips. "Go to bed like...?"

"Go to bed like sleep. As in, the human thing we all do when the sun goes down. Jesus."

"Why didn't you stay with us?"

His face scrunches. "Why would I stay at your house when I have a house of my own?"

"Forget it," I mutter quickly.

"No, brother. You want a damn itinerary? You want me to tell you the exact times I picked you up from The Country Club and dropped Maybelline Ross off at her place because you apparently think I'm some kind of Uber driver when you're shit-faced?"

His voice is thick with years of pent-up aggression, and it takes everything in me not to give it right back. He hates me deep down, I know it. But I damn well have reason to hate him too.

"No, Rand. I'm good," I grind out.

He growls and storms off toward the barn, and I move toward the house to put on some dry damn clothes.

I don't have any answers, but I have a routine. And Clay's damn bar is the next fucking part of it.

6

Breezy

Thursday, January 14th

It's been three days since I landed in Red Bridge, and I've spent all seventy-two hours feeling like a glossy Manhattan fish plopped into the drained fountain of a very snowy small town.

Out of breath, out of resources, and out of freaking water.

Three days of playing third wheel in Bennett and Norah's idyllic farmhouse life and unpacking my stupid suitcases and putting my clothes and toiletries away in the guest room like I'm planning on staying awhile.

Three days of my brain spinning like a broken record over a million different things.

Dad's last voice mail to me before he died.

Past conversations with my father about the galleries and his will.

Logan's face when I told him I quit.

Logan telling me he'd known about Dad's plan with the galleries for a whole six months and how I was painfully oblivious the entire time.

All that thinking, and still, I've done absolutely nothing to figure out what the hell I'm supposed to do next.

For someone who's made a career out of crisis management and high-stakes openings, this particular limbo feels like the earth's gravity has disappeared and I'm floating around aimlessly while the world below keeps spinning.

Ugh. I really need to get my shit together.

I glance at my phone out of habit—the fast-paced life I left behind creeping into my subconscious even if I am in a small-town respite—and the three texts I haven't read or cleared from my littlest brother taunt me once again.

Logan: *Breezy, call me.*

Logan: *Please.*

Logan: *Just talk to me so I can explain. Groveling via text is so disingenuous.*

It doesn't matter how many times he texts or calls or pleads; I have no desire to respond.

Dimming the screen again, I walk toward the gurgling, faintly misting coffeepot as it finishes its brew, waiting not so patiently for the beep of finality before stealing the pot and filling a cup for myself. I sit down at the big farmhouse kitchen table across from my sister-in-law and niece and soak in the smell of dark roast and vanilla creamer.

They're trivial in the grand scheme, but in the little moments like these, they help—as does the sight of Norah feeding Autumn breakfast while my niece giggles and smiles in her high chair.

"Bee! I eat! I eat!" Autumn exclaims as a big plop of yogurt drops from her spoon and onto the floor.

"Good job, Autumn," I say as I flash a secret smile at Norah. "You're such a big girl."

"Big gurl! Me! Eat!"

This kitchen is all wide-planked wood and barely filtered sun, a mocking, far cry from my sleek Chelsea office, and there are no ringing phones, no Richters or Rothkos or Warhols, and no interns with clipboards—just my sister-in-law in one of Bennett's favorite flannels and my giggly niece trying to feed herself yogurt with a spoon.

It's not the gallery, but it *is* art. And I work hard to center myself enough to take it in.

The warmth. The comfort. The homey feel of a family and its love.

As Norah patiently helps a very determined Autumn, I mull over the most shocking part of my life imploding—that I don't hate this moment as much as I should or thought I would. That it's a joy to be getting so much unfettered time with Autumn. That strangely, the tension I normally carry deep within the walls of my chest has eased.

When Summer was this age, I was too busy jetting between galleries, juggling exhibits, and trying to impress a father who never saw me. I missed so many breakfasts like this one. So many "I eat!" moments.

I'm glad I'm not missing these.

Heavy boots on hardwood signal the arrival of another, and I recross my legs in my cashmere pajamas and billow my shirt to make sure I'm decent.

"Morning, ladies," Bennett says, his voice still rough with sleep as he ambles into the kitchen, stopping at his girls. He's wearing one of his usual paint-stained Henleys—smudges of blue or pink or sunflower yellow that never quite come off littering the fabric in ways reminiscent of Bennett past. The Bennett who was a part of the canvas both literally and emotionally.

"Dada!" Autumn squeals as Bennett leans down to touch his lips to Norah's. When he returns to full height, I lift my coffee in the air in salutation.

"Morning."

"Morning, sis." I smile at the moniker, reveling in the feel of being something so simple.

For years, I managed Bennett's career *and* his emotional well-being in ways that went well beyond the normal call of duty. I was the agent, the assistant, and the go-between during his most difficult years as he turned down seven-figure checks for his paintings and declined MoMA exhibitions without blinking. I was the call of desperation while he poured everything he had into Summer and her complex medical needs. I was the last stop before the inevitable outcomes of jail, bankruptcy, or worse.

Now, Norah manages his career and his mood swings, and I get to just be...Bee.

And he and Norah and Autumn get the life he's always deserved.

I'm so happy for him. And for the first time ever, I find myself a little jealous too. Of the creative outlet he has to take chaos and make something beautiful out of it. Of the sanctuary and security of a family that loves him. Of knowing exactly what he wants and sitting in it wholeheartedly.

I thought I had some of that with the galleries, but I was wrong.

I know Bennett deserves this beautiful life. But I can't help but wonder what kind of life I deserve.

I sip my coffee as he scoops Autumn into his arms, her little hands smearing yogurt on his sleeve, and something tender and bittersweet catches in my chest.

Something foreign—something that feels an awful lot like possibility and hope.

Once he sets Autumn back in her high chair, Bennett grabs a cup of coffee and stands at the kitchen island, flipping through the latest copy of the *Red Bridge Chronicle* and sipping on the plain brew.

Norah and I chat and laugh as Autumn finishes off her meal and mess, but when they get up to clean Autumn's hands and face, I'm left with the vision of a smirking Bennett, his hips against the counter with the folded paper in his hand.

"What?" I ask, unsettled by the way he's staring at me.

"Really making a splash in Red Bridge, huh, sis?"

I frown. "What are you talking about?"

He sets the paper on the table and taps his finger on the headline. "Front-page material."

I follow his finger to the text, half expecting some kind of ridiculous small-town nonsense about a sheep sale for the library roof, but what I find instead is altogether more outrageous.

Bishop in the Barn: Breezy Bedding Both Hanson Brothers!

"Ahh!" I gasp. Snatching the paper off the table, I stand, my eyes flying across the page.

Move over, Mary's little lamb! There's a new shepherdess in town, and she's keeping both Hanson brothers warm this season.

You've *got* to be kidding me! Eileen Martin, the little snake, wrote an entire exposé saying that I'm sleeping with Tad *and* Randy Hanson!

I keep reading, desperate to pull the words from the page and swallow them whole so no one else can see them as I go.

Our favorite Red Bridge realtor Hillary Howard has been saying property values are up in Red Bridge, but apparently, the Hanson brothers' values are skyrocketing too. Rumor has it Breezy Bishop's subletting space in both brothers' beds.

What the fucking fuck?

Someone needs to tell Ms. Fiona Blue that this isn't the kind of sharing we want her to teach our sweet children during story time at the library.

I finish scanning her ludicrous words quickly before taking in the stalker-esque grainy photos at the bottom of the page. One is a shot of me and Tad at CAFFEINE, caught mid-conversation. Another of Randy behind the wheel of my Range Rover, the New York plate zoomed in like it's a smoking gun.

Heat floods my face.

"What the hell?" I look up at Bennett, who's barely holding in laughter, the bastard.

Norah leans over to look at the paper with a furrowed brow. "What's going on?"

I stab the headline with my finger, tapping furiously as I shove it at her face. "According to Eileen Martin, I'm bedding both Hanson brothers!"

Norah's eyes widen. *"What?"*

"You know, I thought the article Eileen wrote about me years ago—the one where she said I fought off a gang trying to kidnap Norah—was peak crazy. But this is truly the cherry on top of the Eileen Martin bullshit cake." Bennett pauses, but his eyes glint in the most annoying way as he studies me closely. "Or...is it...*not* bullshit?"

"Oh my God, Ben." I huff, folding the paper in half like that'll make it disappear. "Of course I'm not sleeping with the Hanson brothers!"

But I *am* about to ream some asses. And I'm about to do it right now.

7

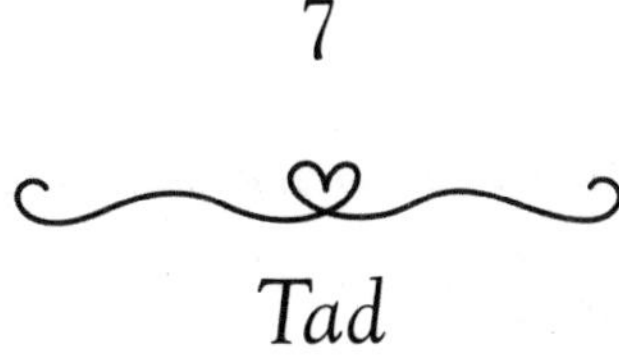

Tad

Earl's Grocery is the only place in Red Bridge where you can buy milk, sushi, and fishing bait all in the same aisle and still wait fifteen minutes to check out.

Lance—Earl's most lethargic and unenthusiastic employee—rings up my groceries one item at a time like he's being paid per sigh. He scans my bread, then he sends a few texts on his phone. He scans my peanut butter, then he zones out for ten seconds. He scans my bananas, then he just stands there looking at the next item on the conveyor belt.

It's a *slow*, unpredictable process.

He's got an AirPod in one ear, head bobbing to what sounds like heavy metal, and the kind of posture that screams *I hate this place and everyone in it*. Not to mention, when I got to his checkout line, he greeted me with an eye roll.

I try not to groan aloud, for I know Lance loves to pay impatience back with spite.

I tap my fingers on the counter, settling for fake pleasantries instead. "Real busy today, huh?"

He side-eyes me without stopping his slow-motion scan. *Beep.* "Yeah. Wild."

I'm pretty sure I'm the only one in the entire store, which makes us both liars.

While Lance hunts for the barcode on an apple like it's a hidden treasure map, my gaze drifts to the rack of newspapers beside the counter. I peruse headlines with little to no investment other than the passage of time, but three shelves down, a subconscious hiccup sends me racing back to the one I just passed.

Bishop in the Barn: Breezy Bedding Both Hanson Brothers!

I blink once. Then twice. Then promptly inhale my own saliva and start choking on it.

What the fuck?

Sound blurs to white noise as I lean over the conveyor, snatching the paper from its rack and reading frantically.

There's a lot of fancy language about a three-way fuck fest between me and Breezy and my brother Randy, and yet, a whole lot of nothing that gives any indication how Eileen got the information.

Information *I* don't even have, for shit's sake.

The more I read, the more obvious it becomes that it's bullshit—or at least half of it is. I know my brother didn't sleep with her because, for as many offers as he gets from women, he never takes them up on any of them. He's a creature of habit, with a mother-goose complex for taking care of me, so he doesn't drink and keeps to himself so he's available to get my frequently-drinking-ass out of trouble.

As for the stuff about me, I'm not really sure, but that's not anything new. I haven't known what's going on—truly—in a really long time. I live life like I have to—by going through the motions.

"You gonna pay?" Lance asks, put out by *me* now.

"What?"

"Are you gonna pay? Sometime this century would be nice."

Frustrated by the switch-up from Lance, the article from Eileen, and the huge fucking gap in my recollection, I growl.

He barks. Like an actual dog. Clearly, I'm not equipped to win a battle of the weird with this guy.

I sigh, digging my wallet out of my back pocket and swiping my card in the machine.

He nods. "You want a bag for all your shit?"

"Yeah. That'd be helpful."

"Cool." He pops his gum. "You want me to double-bag it?"

"What?"

"You want me to give you two bags?"

"Honestly, Lance, I just want to pay and get out of here."

"Dang, bro," Lance answers with a roll of his eyes. "Just trying to be friendly. You in a bad mood or something?"

I have no words. Honestly. No words. But I try like hell to be nice. "Just one bag will be great, Lance. Thank you."

I'm grateful when the charade finally ends and Lance hands me my bag and receipt, but the article burns a bright hole in any feelings of relief.

Time to go to the source.

• • •

The *Red Bridge Chronicle* sits right next to Fran's flower shop because nothing says "Get well soon" like a side of gossip. And, because this is Red Bridge, the *Chronicle* shares its office with Tracey-Jayne Lintott, the town's self-proclaimed pet psychic. People bring in their cats and dogs to read their horoscopes or figure out why their pets are mad at them, and I'm pretty sure, if Randy had his way, we'd be using her to hone our craft for sheep farming by now.

I, however, have no desire to get good at the sheep or the farming.

When I push the door open, the smell of flowers mixes with the smell of wet dog. Three golden retrievers are barking in a waiting area, a tabby cat hisses from inside its carrier, and a woman in a red sweater is wiping tears from her eyes while Tracey murmurs about her pug's "emotional blockage."

It's all par for the course until Breezy's voice cuts through the chaos like a whip.

"You can't just *make up* lies about me, Eileen! It's illegal!"

I round the corner to the reception area of the paper, and when she comes into view, she leaves an impression. Spine straight, her fancy boots making a comeback with a new and complicated sweater, and eyes blazing, she jabs her finger at Eileen across the desk. She's polished and beautiful and furious, and I feel an involuntary tingle in my dick.

Eileen, though, is calm and coy, tapping her pen against her notepad.

"But *is* it a lie, Beatrice?" Eileen challenges. "You've only been in town a few days, and I've seen you with *both* Hanson brothers."

"Seen with, sure. Bedded, I think not!"

As Eileen's eyes cut past Breezy and latch on to me, she smiles. "Oh, well. Hello, Tad Hanson. Perfect timing. Would you like to offer your side of things?"

I gulp. "My...side of things?"

"Yes. Your side of things." She nods toward the crumpled paper in my hands. "I take it you read today's cutting-edge news story."

"Cutting-edge news story?" Breezy scoffs. "Give me a break, Eileen. This isn't news. It's trash slander! Outright lies."

Eileen purses her lips. "Tad?"

"Well...I... Well...uh...I mean... I was pretty drunk that night... I don't *think* anything happened. I mean—"

"Tad!" Breezy snaps. "We *didn't* sleep together."

I blink. "We didn't?"

"Oh my God, no! We didn't. You were hammered drunk. I was *sober*. We slept—separately."

Eileen poises her pen at her notepad, eager to take down all the new details, and Breezy smacks it out of her hand. "Don't even go there, Martin. If you print one more lie about me in your little paper, you'll be eating your notepad for breakfast."

Eileen gasps. "Are you threatening a journalist, Beatrice Bishop? A pillar of the free press?"

Breezy rolls her eyes. "Oh, please. The whole damn town knows you make up your sources. Normally, it's cute. I mean, no one's life is ruined by a scathing article about where the grocery store gets oranges. But *this*? No way. This ends now. I'm watching you."

Eileen huffs. "I should call Sheriff Peeler."

Breezy smirks. "Oh, I *dare* you. But maybe remind him about that little exposé you ran on how he naps at the Red Bridge Inn during shifts?"

"I've had enough of this. You can see yourselves out." Eileen storms away from her desk and toward a back room down the hall.

Two of the golden retrievers bark like they're applauding Breezy, and the little pug previously sitting on Tracey-Jayne's lap—now peeking around the corner in Tracey-Jayne's arms—snorts.

"Good grief." Breezy exhales hard, muttering, "I need a drink."

I rub the back of my neck. "I'm pretty sure I need to cut back on my drinking. Because if I can't remember whether I slept with a pretty woman, that's a problem."

Her blue eyes cut to me.

"I'm sorry I was so blitzed that night."

"Well, far be it for me to encourage liver-bending drinking, but you did nothing wrong, Tad. You were a gentleman. Friendly. Accommodating."

"Yeah?" I question, running a hand through my hair.

"Yeah. Eileen is the problem here."

Something about Breezy's confidence is infectious, and I find myself shooting a shot of my own. "Would you let me buy you lunch?"

8

Breezy

Metcalf's Diner smells like bacon grease, burned coffee, and small-town curiosity. Every booth is packed. The hum of voices rises and falls around us, silverware clinking against porcelain, the coffee machine hissing like it's part of the conversation.

"I still can't believe you thought we slept together," I say, leaning across the booth table and lowering my voice to make sure no busybody ears can hear me. "Now that awkward conversation at CAFFEINE makes a whole lot more sense."

Tad doesn't flinch. He doesn't apologize. Instead, he grins.

"*Did I meet all your needs?*" I tease, mocking his exact words in a deep tone that sounds more like a cartoon cowboy than him.

"Damn, Breezy. Run my ass over the coals, why don't you?" His laugh is a low rumble that makes heads turn from the counter. Several eyes stop and stay once they're there, too. I imagine that's a perk of the trumped-up article.

"Hey," I say, smiling at him. "I'm not the one who was walking around Red Bridge for *three days* wondering if we slept together that night or asking you if I *met all your needs*."

His grin expands. "Can't risk a bad Yelp review. I've got a reputation to uphold."

God help me, it's hard not to laugh. "Pretty sure no one in Red Bridge even knows what Yelp is, and the things you thought we did don't have a review section." I stab my fork at my salad and take a bite before allowing myself to ask the really *hard* question. "What is…your *reputation* exactly?"

He guffaws, a dangerous smirk melting his chocolate eyes. "It's *big*. The highest standard in both physicality and performance. By far the best in the business."

On any given normal basis, I'd find the remark smug—disgustingly egotistical, really. But under these circumstances, it's funny, and I react accordingly.

"Oh boy, that *is* a big deal."

He leans back in the booth, arm stretched casually along the top, and I use the opportunity to take him in. Everyone seems to know him, and yet, with the way they're watching his every move during this lunch, it's like they don't understand him at all.

His eyes are so entrancing, I swear they could melt reason right out of my skull, and his striking smile could talk a reverend into sinning. He's tall, but there's something relaxed in the way he carries it, slender but muscular and strong at the same time.

Honestly, Tad Hanson is unfairly good-looking, and I think he knows it.

His shoulders are broad in a sexy way that reminds me of Olympic swimmers, and his body language is a cool, confident kind of chill. There's something under it all, though—something rigid under the layers and layers of happy paint.

"So, how long are you sticking around in Red Bridge?" he asks, watching me over his cup of coffee.

"You know, that's a great question." I huff out a laugh, and his features pull toward center.

"Sounds like there's more behind that."

"Oh, trust me. There is." I drop my fork, sit back, and spread my hands wide. "A truckload of baggage, with three more trailers and a cargo ship behind it."

His grin deepens. "Baggage is the number one contributor for moves to Red Bridge, you know."

"Oh my God. Me? Move to Red Bridge?" That earns him a sharp and genuine laugh. "I mean, come on, Farmer Tad, do I look like a Red Bridge gal?"

"Not exactly," he admits, eyes twinkling. "But there's more than one way to shear a sheep, you know?"

"Do you even know what the fuck you're saying right now?"

"All I'm saying," he drawls, leaning closer, "is you look like the kind of person who can fit in anywhere. If you're looking for refuge, Red Bridge isn't a bad place to blend, you know?" He snorts. "Though, you're a little too pretty to blend anywhere, I suppose."

The compliment lands harder than it should. Warmth creeps up my neck, and for the first time in weeks, I don't feel like a woman who's lost everything. I feel seen. Wanted, even.

I can't remember the last time I actually felt desired by a man. *Has it been months? Years?* I don't freaking know. My head's been up the gallery's ass for so long that I hardly know who I am without it.

"I'm not staying in Red Bridge. This is just temporary until… I figure some stuff out," I contend.

"Suit yourself." He smiles, but this one isn't as easy as the others. "I'll never judge someone for handling anything they're going through in the exact way they need to." He takes another drink of coffee, rubbing his beard dry with a napkin when some escapes the rim of the mug. "But, hey, while you're here, feel free to call on me anytime. You've got a friend in me…"

Visions of Tad Hanson and me spending time together are suddenly way too vivid. His easy laugh. His broad shoulders filling this booth. The way he doesn't take himself too seriously and how he has this way of making everything feel fun. It wouldn't take much to turn friends into something a hell of a lot more intimate.

But is that really so bad?

I mean, goodness knows, I deserve a little fun in my life these days. I deserve to flirt and date and laugh. *And find out what Tad Hanson's* big reputation *really entails.*

Prying eyes pull me out of the spell when a glass tips over and Sheriff Peeler curses. Eileen Martin shushes him, her notepad balanced on her knee and at the ready, while Mayor Wallace hurriedly wipes at spilled ice and soda.

I give our main stalker the stink eye before returning my attention to Tad. "I just now cleared up the rumor that I slept with you and your brother. The last thing I need is to feed that shark Eileen more material."

"I don't know, Breezy," he says through a smile. "With the way you went all New York mob boss on her at the *Chronicle*, I feel like she's going to keep her distance from you."

"She's literally in this diner, right now, taking notes for her next supposed exposé."

His brow furrows as he follows my gaze over his shoulder to the table of busybodies. A shocked laugh leaves his lungs. "Gotta admire that level of tenacity just a little."

I roll my eyes, and he chuckles.

"I can be tenacious too, you know?" He says it with that easy trademark grin of his, the one I know for a fact works on half the women in town. But his eyes don't calculate or assess or take. I'm no pawn or playmaker for him—I'm a shot at a good time.

He gets up from his side of the booth and tosses a wad of money down on the table. His smile is a goodbye—tinged with a hopeful plea of *see you later.* "Whatever you need, Breeze. My door's open any time."

Maybe I still have a little spark left under all the burnout and heartbreak and betrayal after all.

Still, logic butts in. Sure, my bank account is fine, but I'm unemployed, emotionally scrambled, and living like some homeless vagabond in Bennett and Norah's house. If I should be doing anything right now, it's focusing on piecing my life back together.

Spending more time with a sheep farmer has *bad idea* written all over it in bold Sharpie.

But then again…bad ideas are the only kind I haven't tried.

9

Tad

Friday, January 15th

Friday nights in Red Bridge aren't glamorous. Not for me anyway.

Most weeks, I'd be sitting on a stool at The Country Club right about now, nursing a whiskey or three, letting the live band or local karaoke singers drown out the noise in my head. Half the town is usually there, ringing in the weekend with some fun. And I willingly play along, being the charming, happy, talkative Tad they all know and love, while I use alcohol to momentarily forget all the shit that eats away at me.

But tonight, I didn't feel like numbing it all.

I didn't feel like drinking until the edges blurred and faces became meaningless or getting cut off just in time for Randy to show up to play chauffeur.

Maybe it's the snow. Maybe it's that stupid newspaper article.

Maybe it's the fact that I was working on the farm until well past ten this evening. *Or maybe it's Breezy Bishop, coming into town like a beautiful, complicated reminder that you're still alive.*

Instead of whiskey, I drank water. Instead of the live music, I listened to the hum of the old heater as I made a late sandwich.

Now I'm standing in my living room in nothing but boxer briefs, towel slung around my shoulders, hair still damp from a shower hot enough to scald the day off me. I've got three weak spots in the fence to patch tomorrow—weak spots my damn sheep made from constant head-butting. If I don't fix them, I'll wake up to find the whole flock parading down Main Street again and Randy being taken away in an ambulance on account of a stress-induced heart attack.

I'm about to call it a night when there's a knock at the door.

Instantly, I groan. *Probably Midnight Randy here to bitch some more about my lack of planning, my half-assed gate repairs, and my nonexistent strategy.* I swear, we argued enough earlier today to last a lifetime, but that's my brother for you—never met a dead horse he wouldn't beat.

I swing the door open, already gearing up for round two, but freeze solid instead. Because it's not Randy.

It's Breezy Bishop.

Her black bob is sleek and shiny even under the weak porch light. Her boots are dusted with snow, and her striking blue eyes are steady on mine.

"Everything okay?" I ask, thrown completely off my easygoing script. I tucked it in for the night, thinking I was alone.

Her mouth curves like she knows exactly how much she's knocked me sideways. "You tell me." And then she steps past me, straight into the house like she belongs here.

The scent of her perfume cuts through the faint smell of soap that's still clinging to my skin. And I stand there dumbly for a second, hand still on the door like my brain needs a reboot.

"You said your door's always open," she tosses over her shoulder, a casual, cautious flirt. "Or was that more of a...neighborly thing.

Like, in case I needed a bag of sugar or a wrench."

"I don't have any sugar. And you don't look like you'd come looking for a wrench."

She grins. "I'm not here for a wrench." Her eyes sweep over me, taking in my bare feet, damp hair, boxer briefs, and towel slung over my shoulders. "Or a bag of sugar either." She closes the distance between us. "I'm curious, what do *you* think I came here for, Tad?"

Her voice is playful but direct. Her smile is charming but deadly. If she's a black widow, I'll gladly tangle up in her entrancing web.

I arch a brow. "You sure you want to risk Eileen finding out about you coming over here this late?"

"Please." Breezy laughs. "I waited until everyone at Bennett's was in bed before I came over. I even checked your bushes before I knocked and didn't see any camera lenses or hear heavy breathing."

"Smart woman," I murmur.

Her smile softens as she tilts her head. "What do you think I came here for, Tad?"

I glance at her boots, her perfect jeans, the way her sweater fits her like it was tailored. She's so beautiful she doesn't seem real. For a guy like me, that's all the better. "I think you came here so you can be fully educated before leaving your Yelp review."

"Finally." Her responding laugh is warm and amused like she's enjoying this game. "He's catching up."

"Hey, I'm not slow," I protest. "I thought we slept together three days ago, remember? Maybe it was more fantasy than amnesia."

She laughs, low and genuine, and damn if it doesn't go straight to my chest. "You're something else."

"Something good?" I ask, playing dumb.

"Don't push it."

For a second, we stand there, the air buzzing between us. She doesn't look away. Doesn't fidget. She's confident as hell, and it makes me feel like I'm the one being measured here.

Finally, she steps into my space, close enough I can smell the faint citrus of her perfume. "Relax, Tad. I'm here because I want to be."

"Good. Because I want you here too."

Her eyes flick down to my mouth, and it's the green light I didn't know I was waiting for.

I lift a hand, slowly, giving her the chance to back off. She doesn't. My fingers skim her jaw, cool skin warming under my touch, and she leans in like she's been waiting for this too.

"You sure?" I whisper, because I have to ask.

She smiles, small but certain. "Positive."

And then, we're kissing.

Her lips aren't tentative or testing. They're direct and confident and hold zero hesitation. They move against mine like she's claiming me, and all I can do is match her, meet her, let her set the pace until I can't help but take over.

Her hands grip my bare shoulders, pulling me closer, and I slide my arm around her waist, anchoring her to me. The kiss deepens, heat sparking, and suddenly the whole day—the sheep, the fences, Randy's nagging—falls away.

It's just her and me and this insanely arousing fucking kiss.

Her mouth is firm and insistent, and I meet her with everything I've got—every ounce of want I didn't know was still in me.

Her hands tug at my bare shoulders and pull me closer, like she wants every inch of space gone. I don't argue. I slide my palm down her back, over the curve of her waist, fitting her to me until there's no more breathing room between us.

She breaks the kiss just long enough to catch her breath. Her forehead rests against mine, and her voice is low and teasing as she says, "Is this what your fantasy had in mind?"

"Oh, Breeze. I've just barely started," I whisper back, earning a small laugh that goes straight through me.

I kiss her again, and this one is slower. Deeper. The kind of kiss that makes the rest of the world vanish.

Her laugh is muffled against my mouth when I back her toward the hall. She keeps at me like she's dared herself not to stop.

Her confidence is intoxicating.

By the time we reach the bedroom, I'm half undone. Her sweater's in my hands, her hair's loose, and her pulse thrums beneath my fingertips. She looks up at me—eyes bright, lips swollen, cheeks flushed—and something in my chest goes quiet.

She smiles like she knows exactly what she's doing to me. "You gonna kiss me again—or just stand there thinking about it?"

I answer with a kiss that's rougher this time, a low sound escaping her throat as I press her back against the sheets.

The world narrows to skin and breath and the heat between us. It's not frantic. It's deliberate. A slow, hungry rhythm that feels like remembering how to live.

And for the first time in a long damn time, everything I'm fighting in the background gets lost because I can't find my way out of her.

I remove her boots and clothes with methodical but quick precision before she does the same with my boxer briefs, and I have to catch my damn breath when I see her sprawled out naked on my bed. Her breasts move up and down with each panting breath, and her pussy shines with arousal between her thighs.

My cock is hard and jutting out from my body as I stare down at her, every cell inside me craving to bury myself deep.

She hands me a condom, and I laugh. "I love a woman with the *prepared is best* mentality." She smirks, and I put it on and crawl over her body until the tip of my cock is pressed at her entrance.

I kiss her again, and the world dissolves away to heat and breath and desire. Her bare skin against mine and the way her hips move from side to side, desperate for me to push inside, feels unreal. I can't remember the last time I let myself want something this freely, defenses down with no time spent calculating the risk.

Tonight, I'm not punishing myself. I want her too much to stop. Plain and simple.

I roll onto my back, taking her body with mine, until she's

lying on top of me. "Put my cock inside you," I demand. Her dark hair spills over her eyes and pulls my mind deeper into ecstasy. It's another layer to peel, another sensation to feel.

Breezy's confidence takes my fucking breath away and makes me want to match it.

She kneels around my hips and guides my cock inside her. The pace is mind-bendingly slow but so incredibly addictive at the same time. And she's warm and tight and her pussy squeezes my cock with a grip that makes my head feel like it's going to explode.

She's also wet—so fucking wet, I can practically feel her through the condom.

Fuck me.

"Now, ride me," I tell her, gripping her hips tightly and guiding her up and down my length. The sight of my hands on her skin amplifies every sensation.

Her tits bounce with each thrust, and her lips part every time my cock fills her up.

"Goddamn," I whisper. "You're perfect."

She moans. But she keeps going. Up and down. Up and down. She rides my cock like she needs this release as much as I do.

Fuck, she feels so good. *Too good.*

I flip her onto her back and spread her thighs wide. I push myself to the hilt, but I stay there. "You're going to come on my cock," I say and move my hands down her body. I grab her perfect breasts, feeling their softness in contrast to my work-roughened hands. I lean forward and suck her nipples into my mouth, flicking my tongue against the sensitive buds until her hips start to squirm against me.

And when the urge to keep fucking her grows too strong, I get on my knees and move my hand to her clit, drawing lazy circles with my index finger. Her arousal coats my skin, and her moans mix with mine, echoing off the walls of my bedroom.

She arches her back, and her eyes damn near roll to the back of her head as the first waves of her orgasm consume her body.

As she rides the waves of her pleasure, I drive my cock inside her at a deep and frantic pace. Her pussy clenches around me, gripping me like a fucking vise, and I can't hold back any longer.

I come hard with my cock pushed deep inside Breezy Bishop, and *this time*, I know for sure it really happened.

10

Breezy

Saturday, January 16th

The snow crunches under my boots as I cross the yard, and my breath puffs white in the predawn dark. *Talk about a walk of shame, Breeze.*

One-night-stand-style sex with the sheep farmer in my brother's small town, initiated and pursued by me, was not on my post-gallery-apocalypse bingo card. In fact, it's so outside the realm of possibility I considered while fleeing New York to come here, it's practically paranormal.

Add in that it's five a.m., there's a fifty percent chance of a deranged woman with a camera and a notepad sleuthing somewhere in the vicinity, and the tenuous return to a house my loudmouth brother lives in, and you've got a trifecta of brain-eating circumstances nipping at my heels.

Still…it was *good*. Mind-bending, limb-melting, Yelp-review-worthy in all the ways suggested.

But the buck has to stop there. I left Tad asleep, sprawled across his mattress with one leg out of the comforter and hair in disarray, donned last night's clothes, and hit the icy tundra without saying goodbye to establish a baseline—I don't want a commitment. I don't want a boyfriend. I don't want expectations and responsibility.

I've spent my life meeting the needs of others, but this felt like meeting my own.

Tad Hanson, while incredibly handsome, charming, and all the fun things, will be nothing more than a fun distraction while I try to find all my damn marbles.

By the time I use my key to slip through Bennett's back door, my fingers are numb and my lungs sting from the cold. I rub at the pins and needles in my legs with closed fists and tiptoe down the hall, but the kitchen smells like coffee, and the low murmur of cartoons hums in a way that terrifies me.

Five was supposed to be before the sunrise *and* before the inhabitants of this house were up, but I guess with a toddler involved, nothing is guaranteed.

Unfortunately, I don't have any options for a route to my room without passing the living room, and by the sound of things, that's where the people are.

Okay, Breeze. Confidence is key here. Act like nothing is weird.

Straightening my spine and shaking off the nerves, I follow the noise through the kitchen and down the hall to Bennett on the couch. *The worst of two options—I'd have rather dodged Norah—but it's fine.* His hair is mussed from sleep, he has a mug in one hand, and Autumn is in his lap. My niece is wearing fuzzy pajamas with kittens on them, clutches a fistful of Cheerios like they're diamonds, and her still-sleepy eyes are set to the TV.

My footsteps across the hardwood floors draw Bennett's eyes toward me, and a slow smirk robbing him of his previous lethargy sounds all my warning alarms. "Huh. What an interesting surprise." Murmuring to Autumn even though she pays zero attention, he taunts me. "Aunt Breezy's either been out super late or got up super early, and seeing as we ended last night with her headed to bed, I can't wait to hear which it is."

"Well, good morning to you too," I deadpan, unwinding my scarf and hanging my coat on a chair.

"Aha, the avoidance technique," he says lightly, taking a sip of his coffee. "I've used it myself, many times before."

I shoot him a flat look. "I'll have you know, I'm a grown woman, Ben. I don't need you keeping tabs on me."

"Didn't say otherwise," he answers, and his mouth twitches in a small but very annoying smile. "But your silence is deafening."

I roll my eyes and flop onto the opposite end of the couch, crossing my legs and arms because the cold still tingles.

"I mean, I'm not saying Eileen Martin's bullshit newspaper articles are ever right," he continues, "but—"

"Shut. Up."

"Just saying," he adds, and his smile turns into a full-blown grin. I want to smack it right off his face. He picks up his phone with exaggerated slowness, pretending to dial. "Autumn, sweetie, say hi to Eileen."

"Hi ya, baby!" Autumn chirps without looking away from the TV, then pops another Cheerio into her mouth.

I narrow my eyes at my *very* annoying brother. "I will murder you."

Bennett lifts the phone to his ear. "Yeah, Eileen, you won't believe this..."

"Slow. Painful. Death," I warn.

He laughs, the bastard, before setting his phone back down. "Ah, small-town life. Gotta love it."

"I'm starting to miss those eight million people back home who didn't give a single shit what I was doing."

"Shit!" Autumn crows, still staring at the little cats that are dancing across the television screen.

"Nice one, Breeze," Bennett says, coughing to cover a laugh.

I groan. "Oh, don't act like you're innocent. I've heard you drop plenty of f-bombs."

"Maybe," he says. "But when Norah wakes up, I'm definitely telling her Aunt Bee expanded Autumn's vocabulary."

"You're such a *s-h-i-t* stirrer, you know that?"

"And you love me." He grins. "Which is why you should tell me where you were last night..." He waggles his brows like an idiot. "Did you finally find someone to rev the old engine before it never turns over again?"

"A Hanson brother," I retort with pure sarcasm—which is a fun twist on the truth.

His laugh is so loud, I can only hope it doesn't wake up his wife.

"Okay, okay. But for real, Breeze," Bennett pushes after comedy hour subsides. "Where were you?"

"I took a drive."

He quirks a brow. "Your car was here."

"I walked, rented a car, and took a drive."

"There aren't any rental companies for, like, a hundred miles."

"I took an Uber."

Bennett chuckles. "This story has more holes than a sponge, sis."

"And you have more questions than flipping *Jeopardy*."

When I see Autumn yawn, her little body softening against Bennett's chest, I stand up and scoop her up into my arms. "Want to come cuddle with Aunt Bee?"

"I's seepy." She nods, and I cuddle her closer.

"I see how it is," Bennett calls over my shoulder. "Using my adorable daughter to avoid my questions."

"Avoid your *interrogation*," I correct.

Bennett's soft chuckles follow us all the way down the hall to the guest room. "Bee's woom," Autumn mumbles before she slides her thumb into her mouth.

Her words are innocent, but they hit a mark.

My niece thinks the guest room at her parents' house is my room—as in, I'm living with them permanently. I know it's been less than a week, but I really need to start figuring some shit out. I can't spend the rest of my life living with Norah and Bennett and facing the Red Bridge Inquisition every time I do something like slink home in yesterday's clothes before the sun comes up.

I have a whole apartment in New York that's now probably filled wall-to-wall with all the boxes the courier dropped off from the gallery, but that doesn't call to me even a little bit.

Parts of this...like this moment with my sweet niece, feel *right.*

We curl up in the guest bed, her curls tickling my chin as she burrows into me. She cups my cheeks in her tiny hands, presses a sloppy kiss to my nose, and whispers something that sounds like "love ya" before sleep steals her away.

I let myself just...be. In this small, quiet moment I never would've had if life hadn't detonated under me.

I should be panicking. Should be figuring out how to rebuild everything I lost. But instead, I hold my niece, breathe her in, and admit the other truth pounding in my chest.

Maybe I could use a little more distraction in my life...

And Tad Hanson sure did a good job of distracting me last night.

11

Tad

Monday, January 18th

"You realize we're terrible at this, right?" Randy's voice cuts through the cold Monday morning air, sharp as the bleating sheep.

"We're not terrible per se," I mutter, chasing after a woolly escapee by the name of Bob Dylan who looks way too pleased with himself.

"Tad." His tone is flat and completely unforgiving. "This morning alone, we're missing four sheep. We're shit at it."

I straighten and let out a deep exhale. My breath fogs in the cold. "We're not *missing* them exactly. Betty Bagley called and said they're in her front yard."

Randy stares at me like I've grown a second head.

"What? They can't be missing if you know where they are."

He sighs, and I resist the urge to bury him in blame. It's his fault we're doing this in the first place, and he knows it. If I'd had my way, he'd be doing whatever the fuck he wanted without me to worry about.

"Just…keep the rest corralled," I instruct instead. "I'll grab the four at Betty's and be back."

"Yeah, go play shepherd," Randy calls after me. "I'll just stay here and wait for the other half of the flock to chew their way into traffic!"

I leave him to his bitching, hopping in my truck and heading down the road with a bucket of feed and my sanity hanging by a thread. I've got a lot of pent-up anger with my brother—and I know it's not a one-way street—but you can't meld two minds when they're on opposite sides of the same damn coin. His greatest frustration with the sheep is that we don't excel—but we're never going to. The point, for me, is to exist.

Main Street is awake and active as I make it into town. Storefront lights are already on, the smell of coffee and donuts and fried food wafts in the air, and snow is pushed along the curbs in tired gray piles.

Sheriff Peeler's cruiser pulls up beside me at the one and only stoplight in town, and I rev the engine playfully like I'm reckless enough to race the sheriff. Some days, I am. Today, though, I'm feeling pretty good, still high off the unexpected, incredible sex of two nights ago.

Frankly, I'm thinking getting Randy laid might help a tremendous amount with his disposition.

Pete rolls his window down, grinning at me like he's been waiting all morning for this. "Morning, Tad. Lost sheep again?" I follow his eyes toward Fran's flower shop, where all four of my missing sheep are currently munching from the flowerpots outside like it's an all-you-can-eat buffet.

Shit. Apparently, they had their fill of Betty Bagley's yard.

"Morning, Sheriff," I say, tipping my ball cap toward him. "They're not lost. They're just…uh…sight-seeing."

He chuckles. "Let's hope they don't make it down to

Melba's again."

He's referring to the Melba Danser Bakery Disaster about a year ago. That was before my sheep Mabel got pregnant and managed to sneak into Melba's shop and raid her bread display.

Frankly, it's a day I'd prefer everyone in Red Bridge forget.

"Oh, no worries. I'll have them wrangled up before they get that far."

The light turns green, and Sheriff Peeler chuckles as he drives away.

When I pull my truck to a stop outside Fran's, Mayor Norman Wallace is the next person to call my attention from across the street. "You ever thought about pigs instead, Tad? I hear they're much easier to keep in a pen."

I pretend to laugh to keep the peace. Mayor Wallace's ego knows no bounds when wounded—the yellow bridge in a town named for a red one is evidence enough of that.

He moves on with a wave, his head bobbing with pride over his joke, and I head toward my woolly hooligans who have now destroyed all the flowers Fran has sitting outside her shop.

Shit. Landscaping bill is going to be big this month, given the destruction to Sheila and Marty's Japanese maple, Betty's hedges, and now this.

As I wrangle the flock toward the back of my truck, where a big pen waits for them to climb their asses inside, Cindy Jo Barringer offers a flirtatious finger-waggle in my direction. She's Red Bridge's one and only wedding planner and moved here from Texas about two years ago. She's also single, in her late twenties, and always ready to mingle.

"Oh hey, Tad," she says, stopping to watch me muscle fluffy ass after fluffy ass up the ramp and into the trailer.

"Hey, Cindy Jo."

"Missed you at karaoke on Friday. You still owe me that duet."

"How about a rain check?" I say, managing a friendly smile through the sweat dripping into my eyebrows. "I should have these troublemakers contained by the end of the week."

I wink, and she laughs. "Those sheep of yours need leashes," she teases.

"I'll be sure to tell Randy. Maybe we can tie them all to his legs."

She cracks up and then scuttles away toward her boutique next to The Diner, but before I can finish up, I field two more single bloodhounds as they sniff out their chances of turning my eye.

After Cindy Jo, there's Peggy, and after Peggy, there's Nicole. Nicole is fully single, but technically, Peggy is in the middle of a divorce—she's just handling her social life like the papers have already been signed.

I'm kind and friendly and everything a man should be when a nice woman greets him, but I don't dare invite attention that goes further than that. They seem like vipers, but I know for a fact that they're the type to cling and clang about relationships and marriage as soon as their backs hit your bed.

Unlike Breezy Bishop, who snuck out early Sunday morning without a word or a trace. I don't even have her fucking phone number, and it seems she actually wants it that way.

Though, it's hard to really ghost someone in a town this small. It's almost a certainty I'll see her at some point.

Unless she already went back to New York, that is…

I ignore the uncomfortable ping in my chest and refocus on my sheep.

By the time I get them squared away in the trailer and pay Fran for all the flowers they've destroyed, I'm parched.

CAFFEINE is the perfect solution. I figure Randy deserves a peace offering anyway, and if Breezy Bishop just happens to be there to see her best friend Josie, all the better.

Two birds, one stone, you know?

I push open the door of CAFFEINE, the bell chimes above my head, and Josie is waiting behind the counter. "The usual, Tad?" she asks, her morning rush clearly already over.

"Yeah, but make it two and toss in a few cinnamon rolls as well."

"Randy pissed at you again?" she asks, grinning at me as she rings me up. "Saw a few of your sheep make their way from Betty's house to enjoy a buffet of flowers across the street."

"When isn't Randy pissed at me," I retort on a snort. "And trust me, I know. I just paid Fran for seven bouquets worth."

Josie makes my coffees and packs up the cinnamon rolls in a cute box, and I scan the tables around the café for the second bird.

Breezy sits at a table near the window, laptop open and fingers typing furiously. She's dressed to the nines, even in a small-town coffee shop on a Monday morning, and makes the rest of us look like we just fell out of bed.

Jackpot.

I turn my baseball cap around, grab my coffees and cinnamon rolls, and head in her direction.

"Hey there," I greet, drawing her blue eyes up to mine on a startled jerk.

"Oh, hello," she says casually. "Can I help you, sir?"

Did she just call me sir?

"What?"

"Did you need something?" she asks, and my head fucking spins. I know how to play it cool, but this is more like fucking ice. I mean, I did lick this woman's pussy not even two nights ago.

"Well. I guess not. I just...thought I'd say hello."

"I love chatting with all of Bennett's friends and neighbors," she says sweetly, nodding toward me. "But I'm in the middle of something right now."

My jaw runs tight. "Bennett's friends and neighbors?" I ask with a whisper. *So that's how it's going to be.*

A wicked, teasing smile softens her face, and instantly, I eat crow. She had me fucking going good—too good for shit that's so in line with my own damn terms of use sex policy.

"You're messing with me, aren't you?"

She scrunches her nose and grins. "Maybe a little."

I groan, scrubbing a hand down my face. "You're cruel."

"Or...funny," she tosses back. "Depends on how you look at it."

And damn it, she is funny. Infuriatingly so. Beautiful and quick and confident enough to make me feel like I'm twenty again and out of my depth.

"You left early," I say quietly, leaning closer.

"Pretty sure I left right on time."

Before I can find the words to agree, with the caveat that we should arrange a time for her to hop in my bed, ride my cock, and leave expeditiously again, Clay Harris's voice fills my ears.

"Tad Hanson," he says, clapping a hand on my back. "Haven't seen you in a while, bud. You planning on stopping by The Country Club tonight? I'll be bartending."

I flick a glance at Breezy, whose eyes are fixated back on her laptop, but it's clear to me she's listening. I look back at Clay. "Nah. Planning on staying in tonight. All night. *By myself.*"

It's a hint and an invitation that would go over a dumb head like mine without notice. But Breezy Bishop is smart. Sophisticated. Educated.

She'll pick up the nuance. I'm sure of it. She doesn't look up from her screen, but the corner of her mouth curves just enough to let me know she heard while Clay and I say our goodbyes.

My dick tingles, and my heart picks up speed.

The rest of sheep-battling with Randy today just got a lot more interesting—I can't wait to spend the day planning some moves for round two.

12

Breezy

The house is quiet when I slip out.

Bennett and Norah are asleep, and Autumn is tucked cozily in her bed with her curls spread over her princess pillow. The whole place hums with domestic peace, and I step into the night like I'm a teenage girl breaking my parents' rules.

It's close to midnight, and it's snowing again. Small flakes drift lazily down from the sky, catching silver in the light of the high, bright moon. My boots crunch on the old ice underneath as I cross the yard on quick feet, and my heart beats faster with every step toward Tad Hanson's house.

I should feel ridiculous. Or guilty. Or at least hesitant. But instead, I am *excited*. Thrill and passion and impulsivity commingle in newness, challenging me to explore a different side of the woman I've always been.

For the first time in years, I'm not the girl with the 4.0 GPA, the gallery director who gave up her twenties and almost all of her thirties to keep her family's empire afloat, and I'm not the Bishop who got erased in the end anyway.

I'm not thinking about responsibilities or legacy or how my life looks on paper. I'm taking action, reveling in instant gratification, and toying with the idea that I could be someone entirely different if I wanted to be.

Knuckles poised at Tad's wooden door, I startle when it swings open before I make contact.

Tad's barefoot, wearing jeans and a t-shirt, and his slightly damp hair curls a little at the edges.

He grins at me like I'm *both* expected and surprising, which only makes my pulse race faster.

"Well," he says, leaning a shoulder against the doorframe and crossing his legs at the ankles. "And here I thought I'd be spending the night alone."

I smirk, brushing past him into the warmth of the house, turning my neck to taunt him over my shoulder. "That's funny because I came over to fix that problem for you."

"Generous," he drawls, shutting the door behind me.

"Don't get cocky." I shrug off my coat, tossing it over the back of a chair. "You just so happen to be conveniently located."

"Conveniently located?" His laugh is low and amused. "Careful, baby, it's counterproductive to shoot a man's horse before you expect him to gallop."

I glance at him, at the way his shirt clings to his shoulders and the way he's watching me like I'm the only thing in the room worth noticing. "Fine. You've also met certain performance qualifications. But don't read too much into it."

He steps closer, slow and steady, until the air hums with quickly dwindling space. His eyes lock on mine, and his easy smile tilts sharper. "See, that's where you've got it backward, Breezy. I plan on reading every damn inch of you."

My pulse trips, betraying the cool girl I'm trying to project.

When his hand brushes up my neck, his grip on my chin firm and sexy in a way that shows he wants to be in control, my whole body tenses. "And I know you want it. Because you came here," he murmurs. "Not the other way around."

"And?" I don't break eye contact. "You'd rather be spending the night alone?"

"Not even a little bit." He dances his fingers along my jaw, and his grin softens into something hungrier.

And then, his mouth is on mine.

His lips take and claim, and for once, I don't want to be the one in charge; I want him to make me *feel* something.

The kiss steals my breath, not because it's rough but because it's certain. He's leading, and I'm following, and it's a relief to have someone else running the show.

My entire life has been about control. Everything planned, perfected, and polished. But Tad takes the reins without asking, and instead of resisting, I fucking melt.

His mouth is sure on mine, steady and unhurried, and it has me unraveling faster than I want to admit. By the time he threads his fingers through mine and leads me down the hall, my heart is all the way up in my throat.

His bedroom is dark except for the wash of moonlight spilling across the floor and the small lamp on the nightstand creating golden shadows on the wall.

He doesn't rush. He stops in front of me, hands sliding down my arms until his palms rest at my hips.

His bedroom smells faintly of cedar and soap, the kind of simple, masculine scent that makes me dizzy before he even touches me. The low lamplight paints him in warm yellow, catching the edge of his jaw and the curve of his mouth.

Tad steps closer, but his movements are deliberate, like he has all the time in the world to undo me. His knuckles skim my jaw, tracing down my throat, and the sensation sends a shiver through me I don't even try to hide.

"What do you want, Breezy?" he asks me, and for the first time in my outspoken life, I can't form words. But it doesn't matter because he answers for me. "Right now," he says, eyes burning into mine, "I want to fucking lose myself in you."

The words land heavy and hot, knocking the air out of me. Not a promise. Not a lie. Just raw truth.

His mouth claims mine before I can respond, a kiss that's both greedy and unhurried. His hand cups the back of my neck, keeping me right where he wants me, while the other slides to my waist, pulling me flush against him. He makes me feel small and delicate—two things I've purposely avoided as labels because they don't lend themselves to being a boss bitch who takes charge.

I sink into it, into him, into the way his body presses me backward until my legs hit the edge of the bed. He doesn't break the kiss as he lowers me down, bracing his weight carefully to keep from crushing me, but making sure I feel the strength behind every movement.

I tangle my fingers in his hair, desperate, hungry, while he trails his lips down my jaw, my throat, and they leave fire in their wake. He murmurs something against my skin, a rough sound that could be my name, could be a curse, could be both.

I've never felt more wanted.

He removes my clothes slowly, starting with my sweater and my bra and finishing with my socks and jeans and panties. Contextually, I expect him to remove his clothes too, but he doesn't.

His focus is kissing me. *Everywhere.*

My breasts. My stomach. My inner thighs. His lips and mouth and tongue touch every square inch of my body before pausing to hover over the apex of my thighs. I'm wet. Drenched. Insanely aroused. And he doesn't take the invitation lightly.

I arch my back, and my soft moans echo against the walls of his bedroom as his lips feast on my pussy.

In this moment, time is a construct I can't understand. Awareness is a myth, and the only thing happening on this big spinning rock is what Tad is doing—how good it's making me feel and the way my body is strung tight like a bow as the intense pressure of my impending climax builds.

I weave my hands into his hair, gripping the silky strands tightly. "Tad," I urge, desperate for something. For what, I don't know, but I need *something.* I need to come, or I need him to put his cock inside me, or I need both to happen at the same time. I need *more.*

"Tad," I pant again.

"Ah, ah," he says, and I actually *feel* his smile against my pussy. "I'm not stopping until you come on my tongue."

I moan.

"Be a good girl, Breezy. Be a good girl and come on my tongue."

His words are my undoing. My eyes roll back in my head and my spine curves off the bed, and Tad keeps on licking and sucking and eating at me during each intense wave as my climax barrels through me like a freight train.

I'm still coming down from my high, but I feel him move away from my body, and an ache takes hold.

"N-no," I mutter, but when I find the strength to open my eyes to tell him I need more, I find Tad standing before me, completely naked now. *Fuck, he's a beautiful specimen of a man.* He's strong and lean and muscular. And his cock is swollen and hard in a way that has it jutting out from his body.

He wants me. That much is clear. But I want him too. Right now, I want all of him.

I move myself toward him and wrap my mouth around his cock.

He lets out half a moan and half a groan. "Fuck."

He's hard as stone but soft as silk against my tongue. He's big and swollen, and I can't fit all of him in my mouth, but goodness, sucking him deep is only awakening more arousal inside my body.

"You're such a good girl, Breezy," he tells me, and I don't know why that's such a freaking turn-on, but it is. Maybe I have daddy issues. Maybe I've spent too much time avoiding men. Or maybe the feminine side of me finally has the freedom to exist.

I want him to finish inside my mouth, but he has other plans.

Gently but firmly, he moves me back to the bed, grabs my thighs, and spreads them wide. His cock is poised at my entrance, and I don't know when he managed to get a condom on, but I don't care. I'm fucking mesmerized by the sight of him.

I'm entranced by the way his muscles flex and curl as he rubs the tip of his cock across my clit.

"What do you want, Breezy?" he asks, and his voice is raspy and deep and guttural. He doesn't hide the fact that he's using every ounce of willpower he has to hold himself back.

I'm high off all of it.

"I want your cock inside me."

He complies with a deep and hard thrust, and I feel so full it makes my eyes water in the best way.

"Fuck," he mutters as he continues to drive himself inside me. His hands still grip my thighs, spreading them wide, and his eyes flit between my face and where his cock is sliding in and out of my pussy. "You're perfect, Breezy."

I want to tell him he's perfect too, but the deep, aching pleasure that's building inside me renders speech impossible.

So, I do the only thing I can do and hold on for the ride.

Sure, it's temporary and fleeting, but so is every roller coaster I've ever been on, and I've never looked back on experiencing one and considered it a waste of time.

13

Tad

Tuesday, January 19th

I wake up to an empty bed.

The sheets are still warm on the side Breezy slept on, and a faint trace of her perfume lingers in the air, but she's nowhere to be found.

And damn if it doesn't make me grin.

Some men might be insulted, waking up to nothing but a dent in the pillow, but I'm downright entertained. Hell, I'm relieved. Serious is bad. Serious is heavy. *Serious ends in a fucking sheep-farm-driven pointless existence and never-ending sibling resentment.*

But a temporary little fling with the visitor next door? That's safe. That's easy. That doesn't end in destruction.

I stretch, rub the sleep from my eyes, and I'm still grinning when my bedroom door bangs open.

"Tad!" Randy's voice is sharp enough to cut steel. "We're missing half the damn flock."

I groan and sit up. "Morning to you too, sunshine."

Randy stomps into the room like he's auditioning for a cattle drive. "I mean it. Gate's wide open. I counted, and we're down by at least twenty. I think that bastard Crosby figured out the goddamn latch."

I scrub a hand over my face. "See? We're not bad with sheep, Randy. We're bad with fences. The flock's healthy. So healthy, in fact, that I think we should get Crosby's IQ tested. That bastard is abnormally smart."

His glare could curdle milk. He lets out a deep exhale and runs a hand through his hair. "I'm going to choose to ignore every stupid thing you just said in the name of keeping myself out of prison." He sighs. "I swear, I'm throwing a fucking party when spring hits and we can take these fuckers to market. And I'm hoping that's that on the sheep shit."

Oh, here he goes again. The "we need to be done with sheep farming" conversation that comes up every two weeks or so like clockwork.

I swing my legs out of bed and tug on my jeans. "Sheep soothe me, you know that."

"Fuck right off, Tad."

I laugh, which only makes him glower harder. "Okay, okay. I'll go find the flock this morning, princess. You can relax and have some breakfast."

Randy crosses his arms, still fuming. "I've been going along with this for so long that I'm starting to wonder if *I'm* the crazy one, Tad. When are you going to give up the sheep farce and use the damn insurance money to invest in something that might lead somewhere other than Betty Bagley's front yard every other day?"

The words hit like a sledgehammer to the ribs, and my grin dies swiftly. The air in the room thickens into a cold and heavy mist of lines crossed and unearthed demons. We may volley, but he's crossed a line this time, and he knows it.

"Don't." My voice is cutting. Randy opens his mouth, but I interrupt him before he can say another word. I don't want to hear it. Not even if it's an apology. "Don't even fucking go there."

For once, he listens. His jaw works, muscles ticking, but he knows the cost of honesty on this subject.

I stand, yanking on my shirt. My movements are clipped and mechanical, and I grind my jaw so hard I feel it in my molars. When I slip on my boots, my ears buzz with all the unsaid things between us, burning me alive from the inside out. But I can't give this tailspin legs, and I know the risks of breaking open the dam of guilt and shame, and the worst kind of grief could pull me under in ways I'm never sure I'll come back from.

Randy didn't mean to hit the nerve, I know that. But intent doesn't matter when the nerve is always this raw.

"I'm going to get the fucking sheep," I announce.

Randy mutters something under his breath as he stomps down the hall and toward my kitchen, but I barely hear it over the rush in my head. I grab my coat and head for the door, anger still boiling under my skin.

Ten minutes ago, I was in a decent mood, still riding the afterglow of hot sex with Breezy Bishop and a rare night that didn't feel heavy. But it doesn't take much to kill a spark.

Or light one, for that matter. One wrong word and I'm right back where I always end up—standing in the ruins, trying to pretend they aren't still burning.

The cold hits my face as I step outside, but it brings none of the invigoration it usually does. The sky is gray and viscous, and the world smells like hay and frost and the faint ghosts of smoke that never really leave me.

I know the sheep don't fix anything. I know the farm doesn't *fix* anything. But they give me something to hold—something to do with my hands when my mind gets too loud. Something to playact for the world around me.

And most days, pretending is the only thing that keeps me standing.

• • •

By the time night rolls around, I'm fried.

My body aches from chasing down half a flock, my pride aches from handing Betty Bagley another wad of cash for her chewed-up flowerbeds, and the silence between Randy and me feels heavier than any argument we've ever had.

He didn't bitch after this morning. Not once.

He worked beside me all day—quiet, efficient, and steady—but I could see the unspoken regret in his shoulders. The whole damn reason my older brother came to Red Bridge in the first place was to keep me from falling apart, and the thought of being the reason I might cuts deeper than any amount of broken barbwire and electric fence for him.

By the time I roll into The Country Club, I'm bone-tired. The place is boisterous with music from a bluegrass band playing live on stage. The sounds of fiddles sawing and banjos clicking spill across the whole bar and even outside into the parking lot, and the bar is packed like a tin of sardines. Couples line dance in the center, regulars loiter over by the pool tables engaging in their competitive games, and the sounds of the usual small-town gossip bounce off the walls.

I slip into the rhythm effortlessly, because that's what I do.

I put on the easy grin, that mask I've gotten too good at. Laugh at the right moments, buy rounds, slap a few backs, and make Clay Harris and the rest of Red Bridge believe I'm fine.

Clay has insight—more than a few occasions of me blitzed to oblivion while I weave my sad tale and confront my demons head-on directly across from him—that no one else does, but he doesn't press. He never does.

I'm on my second rocks glass of whiskey when the door opens, and in walks Bennett Bishop with Norah on his arm, and the one woman I gladly let linger in my head these days trailing behind them.

The arch of her back, the sound of her moans, the perfect pink of her pert nipples—yeah, they hang around rent-free.

At the sight of her, my pulse does something stupid. Even in this little bar, under too-dim lights, Breezy shines.

Clay slides me a fresh pour. "Another?"

I stare at the glass, the amber catching the light like temptation itself.

For a second, habit almost wins. That familiar itch to blur the edges, to let the world fade into background noise, has my fingers tapping toward the glass.

But then Breezy laughs, carrying over the noise of the bar and the music and straight into my ears, and another agent for changing the way I feel tips the scales. I won't be numb, certainly. But I won't feel any pain either.

Enough brooding. Enough drinking. I don't want to forget tonight.

I shove the glass back toward Clay and shake my head. "Nah, I'm good. Thanks."

And before I can second-guess it, I'm on my feet, crossing the room.

The crowd fades and the music buzzes as the Molene bluegrass band picks something fast and twangy. But all I can see is her, standing there in the middle of it all, magnetic as hell.

"Well, hello, Breezy Bishop," I greet when I reach where she stands at a high-top table with Bennett and Norah. "Happy to see you're still in Red Bridge."

"Hi, Tad," she replies, a secret smile on her lips like us pretending to be mere acquaintances in front of everyone else is her new favorite game. My new favorite is seeing her in my bed and making her come.

"Bennett. Norah." I tip my head toward them, but my eyes never leave Breezy's face. "Good seeing you all here tonight."

I don't know what Bennett says, but that's probably because I'm one hundred percent focused on his sister.

"Band's pretty lively, huh?" I say, nodding toward the stage where the bluegrass players are tearing through a fiddle run that could wake the dead.

Breezy shrugs. "They sound pretty good."

"How about a dance?"

She blinks quickly, first at me and then at her brother and sister-in-law. "A dance?"

"Yeah," I answer, a smile curling my lips up. "A dance."

Her eyes narrow playfully. "Are you good at dancing?"

"I don't know, but I'm hoping we're about to find out." I smirk and hold out my hand toward her. "C'mon, Breezy. I won't bite, I promise."

"It's not the biting I'm worried about. It's the stepping on my feet."

I wink. "I won't do that either."

She hesitates just long enough to make me sweat, but when she slips her hand into mine, I celebrate the victory.

Her palm is warm, her fingers small but sure, and instantly, something in my chest unclenches. I lead us onto the dance floor, where boots shuffle and skirts sway, and the air smells like beer, wood, and dust.

I'm sure there are a dozen busybodies watching us, including Fiona Blue with an expression like she's swallowed a bug, but I don't give a damn. Because right now, with Breezy's hand in mine and her laughter brushing my throat, I feel good.

That's a dangerous thing for a man like me. Good isn't something I trust. Good never lasts.

But with her body close and her perfume cutting through the smell of booze and sweat, I decide to stop thinking.

Just for a song.

Just for a dance.

Just long enough to let the noise in my head fade away and remember what it feels like to be alive.

14

Breezy

The music is loud, the floorboards are shaking, and I'm laughing so hard my stomach hurts.

Tad's hand is warm in mine as he spins me into the crush of people line dancing in The Country Club. Clay is on the other side of the floor hollering like a rodeo announcer, and Bennett and Norah are tucked into a corner table, enjoying a date night while Marty Higgins's wife Sheila babysits Autumn, and watching me with identical amused smiles. Even Bennett—my perpetually broody brother—looks halfway entertained by my flailing attempt at a grapevine step.

"Left foot, Breezy!" Tad calls over the music, his grin wide and his eyes wicked.

"I *am* left-footing!" I yell back, but I'm laughing too hard to actually figure out which foot is which. He doesn't care. He catches me by the waist, hauls me closer, and twirls me until I'm breathless.

It's ridiculous. And fun. And nothing like my life in New York.

Back home, nights were quiet dinners, charity galas, perfectly composed smiles under dim gallery lighting. Here, I'm sweaty in my designer boots, my hair falling out of its sleek blowout, and the whole damn town seems to be watching me laugh like an idiot.

And I don't even care.

I catch sight of Norah nudging Bennett, both of them laughing, and Clay saluting with his beer. But it doesn't feel like they're laughing *at* me; it feels like they're laughing with me.

And I honestly can't remember the last time I let myself go like this. Maybe I never have.

The thought catches in my chest. Over the past week, I've *entertained* the idea of figuring out my next move—scrolling through job postings at museums and galleries, clicking in and out of listings that all blur together. I even thought about reaching out to a headhunter once or twice, but something about it feels...I don't know...too soon. Or maybe it feels wrong, like I'm admitting the career and life I built in New York is really over.

Instead, I hired someone to deal with the chaos in my apartment and paid movers to take all the gallery boxes to a storage facility down the street because the housekeeper couldn't find the floors under the mess.

Everything's technically "handled," but nothing feels settled, and I've basically resigned myself to the fact that I don't know what comes next.

For once, I'm just...here.

The song shifts and the beat slows down dramatically. Tad slides in behind me, one arm circling my waist. I lean back into him, chest still rising and falling with laughter and my cheeks aching from smiling so damn much.

To anyone watching, it all probably looks sweet. Innocent, even.

Sure, we're probably engaging the rumor mill a little after Eileen Martin's ridiculous article, but everyone in Red Bridge knows that woman makes shit up.

Plus, I can't really find it in me to care what anyone else thinks right now because I'm enjoying myself too much.

Tad's lips dip close to my ear, his breath hot against my skin, and the rumble of his voice changes everything. "Meet me at my place in thirty minutes," he whispers, low and rough. "I want to make you come on my cock."

Heat spikes through me so fast I stumble a little and have to catch myself against him.

The people around us keep laughing, clapping, and moving with the music. They're completely unaware of the dirty command Tad left in my ear or the growing arousal in my belly, born of eagerness to take him up on it.

I manage a smile, shaking my head like it's nothing, but my pulse is thrumming everywhere.

When the music ends, Tad gives me a friendly hug and says, "Thanks for the dance, Breezy Bishop," before he starts his goodbye tour around the bar.

I head back over to where Bennett and Norah are, pretending I have no plans to leave anytime soon, but as soon as I come up with an excuse, I'm gone.

My libido is already grabbing her purse and making a beeline for Tad Hanson's bed.

15

Tad

I don't look at Breezy when I leave the dance floor. Frankly, if I did, I'd be tempted to drag her out of here in front of half the damn town.

Instead, I plaster on my grin, clap Clay on the shoulder, and head out the door.

Act normal.

Be normal.

That's my role. That's what everyone in Red Bridge expects from me.

But by the time I make it back home and I'm climbing up my porch steps, headlights sweep across the snow. It takes me less than a second to realize it's Breezy's Range Rover.

She kills the engine and gets out, boots crunching against the ice. She looks like a fucking goddess under the moonlight. It bounces off her sleek hair and pretty eyes and only makes her look more mysterious.

More alluring.

More tempting.

More encompassing of the beautiful distraction I so desperately need right now.

Losing myself in Breezy is better than drowning myself in booze. She's entrancing in ways that make me feel high for hours and days after being with her.

I unlock the door, shove it open, and wait at the threshold as she climbs up the stairs. But when she closes the distance between us, I don't even give her the chance to speak. I wrap my arms around her and crash my mouth into hers.

I kick the door shut behind us, and I pin her gorgeous body against it, kissing her like I need her to stay alive.

"Breezy," I whisper her name against her lips like a fucking prayer, and she moans into my mouth. It's a low and hungry sound, and it wrecks me.

"Fuck," I mutter. "I want you."

"I want you too."

All my senses home in on the press of her body against mine and the way her hands thread through my hair. She's soft and lush in all the right places, and I relish the way she bites my bottom lip.

Fuck, I need this. *I need her.*

There's no room for talking, and there's certainly no space for thinking. Because if I think—if I really let myself think—Randy's words from earlier today will crawl back in. And then I'll have to think about the ghosts that are always clawing for air and the things I can't change, no matter how many fences I fix or sheep I wrangle.

So, I don't think. I take.

I scoop Breezy up, her legs wrapping around me in a smooth sweep and her heels digging into my back as I carry her down the hall. She's light, but the weight of her feels grounding, anchoring me in the present.

"You'd better make good on your promise," she whispers. Her voice is teasing, and her smile is sly.

I growl in answer, lips crashing back onto hers. My grip on her tightens, and she gasps into my mouth. I don't bother with clever comebacks because my actions will speak louder than words.

The bedroom door slams open, and I lay her down hard, hovering over her, caging her in. Her sweater rides up, and I skim my hand along the soft line of her stomach. She arches into my touch like she's daring me to keep going.

"You feel like fucking heaven," I murmur, and my voice is rough and raspy like sandpaper.

Her lips curve. "And you feel...hungry."

"That's probably because I'm starving."

Clothes fall away fast. Too fast. It's clumsy and frantic and not at all polished, but I don't care. She's bare beneath me, and that's all that matters.

The instant I sink into her, we both groan, and the desperate sounds tangle together and bounce off the walls of my bedroom.

She grips my shoulders, pulling me closer. "Tad."

I press my forehead to hers, thrusting harder, deeper, chasing something I can't even name. And she takes me with a gasping moan, her nails biting into the skin of my back.

It's not making love. It's not soft or slow. It's straight-up fucking. It's heated and intense and all-consuming.

Her sexy little smiles, the way she bites her lip, and the sharp press of her heels against the backs of my thighs only fuel me further. And when she comes undone beneath me, her body clenching, her voice breaking on my name, I fall with her. *Hard.*

The room is silent after, except for our breathing.

I collapse beside her, sweat cooling on my skin and my chest still heaving. She curls onto her side, hair mussed, lips swollen, and eyes half lidded but sharp as she looks over at me.

"Damn," I manage on a raspy chuckle, my words dragging in the air.

Her smile turns lazy. "You say that like you didn't expect it to be good."

"Oh, I expected good," I say, grinning. "Just wasn't prepared for *holy fuck* good."

She laughs, low and pleased, and the room goes quiet for a second, until I realize that my dick is feeling a little too free at the moment.

"Shit." My brain finally catches up, and my stomach dips. "Shit. Shit. Shit."

"What?"

"I...I didn't use a condom," I admit. "I...fuck. Yeah, I completely forgot to put one on. I'm so sorry, Breezy. I didn't—"

"Relax, Farmer Tad," she cuts me off, but her voice is incredibly calm. Hell, she's not freaking at all. She props her head on her hand. "I'm on birth control. Have been for quite a few years now."

Instantly, relief rolls through me.

"And," she adds, smiling over at me, "I haven't exactly been on the rodeo circuit lately, so I'm, you know, clean."

"Well, that makes two of us." I huff out a short laugh. "It's been a while since I've been with anyone." After the truth leaves my lips, something in my chest stirs and memories threaten to flood my brain, but I force them back to the deep recesses before they can bubble to the surface.

"Yeah?" she asks, outright surprised. "Could've fooled me. I've seen the way half the women in town look at you."

I eye her with a teasing quirk of my brow. "Looking and doing are two very different things."

"Well, then." She grins, trailing a finger down my chest. "Guess I'm just lucky, huh?"

"Woman, pretty sure I'm the lucky one here," I say, catching her hand and kissing her knuckles.

The truth is, I am the lucky one out of the two of us. Lucky she even walked through my door. Lucky she's in my bed. Lucky a woman like Breezy would waste a single night on a broken man like me.

This might just be a fling, a distraction, a hell of a night, but I'll catalogue it as a fleeting period of time when I let myself feel good.

I know it'll have to end soon, but right now, I let myself savor it—the ease, the laughter, the way it feels so damn uncomplicated.

Just another amazing night with a beautiful woman who's way out of my league.

It's nothing more than that. Because with a guy like me, it can't be.

16

Breezy

Wednesday, January 20th

I can't remember the last time I slept through the night.

Not since the funeral. Not since the will-reading. Not since my whole life tilted sideways and everything I thought I'd built turned out to belong to someone else.

But last night…last night, I did.

No tossing. No turning. No recounting all my life's choices. No staring at the ceiling until my eyes burned. Just…sleep. And I just so happened to do it in Tad Hanson's bed.

When I finally blink awake, sunlight is cutting through the curtains, and Tad is standing at the side of the bed, holding out what looks to be a to-go cup.

"Mornin'," he says, his voice is raspy in a way that has memories of last night rushing into my mind. "This is for you."

"Uh...thanks." I sit up, taking it from him and brushing my hair out of my eyes. Once the to-go cup is in my hands, the smell of fresh coffee hits my nostrils.

"Hopefully, it's good." He shifts awkwardly on his feet, eyes darting from me to the floor and back again. "Wasn't sure how you like your coffee, but I remembered you ordering it with some sugar and cream at CAFFEINE."

I take a sip. It's hot, smooth, and about three spoonfuls too sweet. A smile tugs at my lips. "You went a little heavy on the sugar, Farmer Tad."

He grins and rubs the back of his neck. "Guess I was trying to sweeten my odds."

The line earns him a tiny laugh, but the moment still feels... off. The coffee might be sweet, but the *to-go* cup tastes a lot like goodbye.

His broad shoulders tense, as if he's waiting for me to get dressed and head out, and I guess normally, I'd already be gone. I think he's surprised I'm not.

Pretty sure the to-go cup is a hint, Breeze.

"I'm glad you were here last night." His words are soft and unexpectedly sweet, but his back is tense. He clears his throat. "And...this morning, too." The last part comes out so discreet that I almost don't hear it, and he's angled to the door so hard, I'm surprised he didn't take the opportunity while I was sleeping to strap on my shoes.

Mixed signals, thy name is Tad Hanson.

Regardless, the time to get going is now, and Norah and Bennett will undoubtedly be wondering where I am. I don't owe anyone explanations, but if the roles were reversed, I would be worried. By the time I've tugged on my sweater and slipped into my boots, the air between us feels even more baffling. It's like he's two different men at the same time. One wants me gone, and the other seems to be searching for a reason to ask me to stay.

I sling my bag over my shoulder and head into the living room. Tad follows closely behind me, and we both stop and turn toward each other in an awkward dance of goodbye. This part, it seems, is definitely easier when I leave before he wakes up. I pat his arm and turn for the door, but Randy swings it open with so much force I jump back in surprise and bump right into Tad's chest.

"Tad! Get your ass out here!" the other Hanson yells, having unleashed the command before his vision could catch up.

"What the hell, Randy?" Tad barks, but his brother's already spinning back toward the porch, eyes wide and body panicked at the sight of me, seemingly, in Tad's arms.

He gives a half-startled, "Uh...morning?" before bolting back outside. Tad follows after him quickly, and I follow behind the two of them in confusion and curiosity.

The cold hits instantly, sharp and biting, and then I see...

Well, I'm not entirely sure *what* I'm seeing.

A cluster of woolly shapes crammed half in, half out of a squat little building. Some of them are bleating, some are shoving each other, and one has what looks like a giant sack over its head.

The snow is trampled into a muddy mess, and the air smells... ripe.

"What in the actual hell?" I whisper.

Tad grabs my hand, already dragging me forward. "They broke into the feed shed."

"The what?"

"Where we keep the grain." He points with his free hand. "That idiot Nash—" he jerks his chin toward the sheep staggering blindly in circles "—managed to get a whole bag stuck on his head."

I blink. "Oh my God! Is he suffocating?"

Tad snorts. "No. Just stupid."

We're running now, snow spraying up around us, my coffee splashing dangerously close to my wrist. "Why are they all shoving each other?" I call out, trying desperately to keep up.

"Because sheep are greedy little bastards. One gets a mouthful, the rest want in. It's like a Walmart Black Friday circa 1995 in there."

Randy throws his arms up when he sees us coming. "Wow,

Tad! Isn't this fantastic? A true vision of our *sheep-farming excellence!*"

Tad ignores him, letting go of my hand and wading into the wool storm.

The sheep with the bag stumbles into another one, knocking them both into the snow. Grain scatters everywhere, and suddenly, there's a mad dash of bleating, wool, and tiny hooves scrambling over one another to get a bite.

Tad curses as he lunges forward to use some muscle against the flock. "Come on, Breezy. Help me block them in!"

I freeze. "Block them in? With *what*?"

"Your body!"

"My *what*?"

"I promise, Breezy. I would never put you in harm's way," he says as he nods toward where he wants me to stand. "I just need your beautiful presence right over there to distract them. They won't do anything besides move in the opposite direction of you!"

Tad is in the thick of it, muscling sheep back into the shed while Randy wrestles the bag off the one's head.

And somehow, against all odds, I find myself edging sideways in the snow, arms flung wide, trying to shoo woolly bodies back where they belong. My boots are not made for this. My pants are not made for this. *I* am not made for this.

But Tad glances back at me—sweaty and laughing—and suddenly, I don't care.

Instead of being horrified, I'm laughing right along with him. Something about snow, sheep, and the smell of farm feces unleashes ducts I thought were clogged a long time ago.

I feel alive.

• • •

The sun is higher now in the sky, and somehow, the yard looks ridiculous and right all at once.

After this morning's debacle with the feed shed, my clothes and boots were destroyed. Now, I'm in Tad's clothes. His jeans hang off my hips like a tent, his flannel is huge, and his boots are about five sizes too big.

I look like some badly styled country music video, and I'm grinning anyway.

There's mud on my cuffs and grain dust in my hair, and for the first time in a long time, I'm not thinking about how I have no idea what I'm going to do with the rest of my life or the fact that I'm currently squatting at my brother's house with absolutely zero plan.

Instead, I've spent the whole morning pulling sheep out of places sheep should never be, slipping through mud, and laughing more than I probably have in months.

After we got the feed shed under control, Randy didn't ask any questions about what I was doing at Tad's place. He just gave me a quiet nod, the kind that said he'd seen more than he'd comment on, and went about his morning. He's been out in the back fields ever since, working the snowplow near the creek that's started backing up. But Randy Hanson is steady like that. Quiet when Tad is not. He's brooding in a way that somehow feels protective instead of cold.

Tad is fixing the last bit of fence near the feed shed. His jaw is set in a firm line, and his strong hands work the wire with competence. He glances over, and for a second, his face softens before he goes back to focusing on the task at hand.

And I'm currently sitting on a bale of hay, taking a short break while watching him work.

When my eyes catch sight of the discarded and hardly drunk to-go cup of coffee he made me this morning, I can't stop myself from pointing out the giant elephant in the room.

"You didn't want me there this morning," I say. My words are blunt and direct. I don't sugarcoat it or wrap it up in a nice, tidy bow of pleasantries. I just state the truth.

He drops the wire for a beat, and a deep, heavy sigh escapes his lungs. "It's not about not wanting you." He rubs the back of his neck, but his eyes don't quite meet mine. "I've just got some shit, Breezy. My life doesn't allow me to be anything more than casual." His gaze finally meets mine. "I'm not the guy you settle down with."

"Good thing I'm not looking to settle down," I say and keep my eyes locked with his. "I have my own shit, Tad. I'm only temporarily here in Red Bridge. But I don't need to be worried about falling asleep in your bed and you having a breakdown over it. I'm too old for that. I deserve more than that."

He stands there for a moment, like he's choosing whether to step toward me or away. Then he steps closer, and his voice is raw, not performative. "Breeze, you deserve the fucking world." The line is smooth, but the way he says it makes it feel unpolished in a raw and genuine way.

Honestly, it threatens to knock the breath out of my lungs, but I lift one shoulder and grin instead. "Well...how about a very casual, playful kind of world where you occasionally fuck me senseless while I'm in Red Bridge?"

For a heartbeat, he looks stunned, but then his reply is a crooked, dangerous smile. "In this world..." he says, lowering his voice, "do I get to lick your pussy too?"

Instantly, heat blazes up my spine. There's a beat—ten, maybe twenty seconds—where the farm noise, the flock, everything, falls away, and it's just him and me.

"You know," I say, offering a flirty wink in his direction, "I think that can be arranged."

He laughs, low and quick, and closes the small space between us. His hand finds my face, and his thumb brushes my bottom lip. The world tilts, not because of anything he says, but because of how he makes me feel—seen and wanted and dangerously easy to unravel.

When he kisses me, it's soft and deliberate at first, a promise without anything heavy attached. But then, it quickly slides into something hungrier. More desperate. More passionate.

I let myself fall into it, into the warm press of his body, forgetting about the fact that I'm wearing boots five sizes too big and have hair full of grain.

Eventually, we break apart with laughter on both our lips, and it's messy and sweet and exactly where I want to be.

Because I don't want serious or commitment.

I want casual. I want easygoing. I want freedom.

Frankly, this right here is the only kind of complicated I can handle right now.

I rest my forehead against his and let out a small breath. "Also," I whisper quietly. "How about we keep this between us?"

"Ah." A slow smile starts on his lips. "You sure do love the thrill of playing that 'we're just acquaintances' game, huh?"

"Maybe a little." I giggle. "But also, I fear Eileen Martin would run out of ink if Red Bridge knew that I was hooking up with the most eligible bachelor in town. I mean, there'd be daily front-page spreads, Tad."

That earns an amused chuckle from him. "You're right," he says. "Wouldn't want to bankrupt the *Red Bridge Chronicle*."

And when he kisses me again, it feels as if we've made a pact.

But it's not love or promises or commitment.

It's just a secret.

A distraction.

A very spontaneous kind of freedom.

And I tuck my chin against his shoulder, smelling dirt and cedar and the faint ghost of his shampoo, and I let myself believe that a very casual, playful world with Tad Hanson is exactly what I need.

17

Tad

Friday, January 22nd

It's been two days since Breezy Bishop and I made our little pact—casual, discreet, and absolutely nobody's business but ours.

Two days of pretending to be acquaintances in public and trading the filthiest text messages imaginable in private. Two days in which my phone lights up with something from her, and I'm instantly fifteen kinds of distracted.

It's been blissfully quiet on the farm, which is a miracle in itself. No missing sheep. No broken fences. No feed shed fiascos.

Mabel had her vet appointment this morning, and Dr. Michael said her pregnancy's right on track. She's due to deliver her lambs toward the end of February.

And Randy didn't say a word about finding Breezy at my house the other morning, which tells me one of two things: either he didn't really notice, or he doesn't really care. Frankly, both options work great for me.

My brother is in Molene today, sorting through tax paperwork with our accountant, and I managed to get most of the farm chores finished this morning before taking Mabel to see Dr. Michael. She's currently sound asleep in the trailer, and I decided to make a pit stop at CAFFEINE to grab some coffees for Randy and me before heading back home.

It's also highly possible that I've noticed a certain beautiful woman has made CAFFEINE part of her morning routine and I'm hoping to see her.

I push through the coffee shop door, stomp the snow off my boots, and smile over the fact that it's not even ten in the morning and Josie has outlaw country blaring from the speakers. The smell of cinnamon and espresso hits my nostrils, and it feels like half the town is here trying to look busy while they drink their coffee.

"Morning, Tad," Josie calls from behind the counter. "You want the usual, or you want to cheat on yourself with a fancy foam-topped latte?"

"Let's not make me a liar," I say. "Two drip coffees. And extra cream to one and make sure you write *Joyless* on it."

She laughs. "I take it *Joyless* is Randy."

I grin and nod. "Consider it a very loving nickname."

While she grinds, I scan the coffee shop out of habit. Though, at first, I'm mostly just looking for Eileen Martin. A few days ago, she ambushed me by the cream station to ask if sheep experience seasonal affective disorder. I said *yes*, which was then published in the *Red Bridge Chronicle* like it's fact and not utter bullshit I just spouted to get her off my ass.

And that's when I see her.

Breezy.

She's sitting at a corner table, tucked away from the crowd. Her laptop is open, and her phone is next to her like it's expecting VIP calls. She looks polished, perfect, and nothing like the woman from two nights ago who had my sheets twisted around her legs while my mouth was on her pussy.

"Order for Tad and Joyless!" Josie slides my drinks across the counter.

"Thanks," I say, grabbing both cups before my grin can give me away.

I take a slow sip, glance Breezy's way one more time, and wander straight over toward the woman I can't keep my eyes and thoughts off.

When she finally notices me standing there, I let a grin pull slowly across my face. "Well, Breezy Bishop," I say lightly, "fancy running into you."

She stays cool as a fucking cucumber with only a small but friendly smile lifting the corners of her lips. "Mr. Hanson. You want to sit?"

"I wouldn't want to interrupt..."

"You're not. I was just answering emails." Her smile is polite but sharp-edged. "Always a pleasure to chat with an...acquaintance."

Fuck me. I don't know why this game is so fun, but it is.

I slide into the seat across from her, trying like hell to look casual while my mind flashes straight back to the way her body arched under mine two nights ago. The taste of her still feels branded onto my tongue.

But maybe that's *exactly* what makes this game so fucking fun.

Because I know exactly what Breezy Bishop's pussy tastes like on my tongue. Because I'm actually imagining it right now. And because I know every inch of what she's pretending not to think about.

"Acquaintance," I echo, leaning back in my chair with a grin I can't quite fight off. "That's a good word for us."

She tilts her head. "I thought so. Very casual, you know? Like us."

Her tone is light, but her eyes are pure challenge. There's a heat there that doesn't belong in a public coffee shop.

The air between us tightens. I can smell her perfume from across the table, and her leg shifts under it, the fabric of her jeans brushing just slightly against mine. It's enough to make every rational thought in my head scatter like startled birds.

"Casual," I murmur. "Sure."

Before I can push it, before I can lean in and remind her just how *casual* the other night wasn't, a familiar voice cuts clean through the tension.

"Morning, Beatrice. Morning, Hanson."

I look up to find Sheriff Peeler standing at the edge of our table. His hat is in his hand, and he's beaming like a man with zero awareness that he just stepped between two people on the verge of combusting.

"Sheriff," Breezy greets in a crisp, polite voice.

"Sheep staying where they belong, Hanson?" he asks, grinning down at me with crossed arms.

"Always," I lie and smile.

Peeler launches into a story about misplaced traffic cones out on Route 7. Breezy listens with picture-perfect grace, chin resting on her hand, lashes low, but I can see the pulse fluttering at her throat. She knows exactly what I'm thinking.

And I know she's waiting for me to prove it.

While Peeler rambles, I slide my phone from my pocket beneath the table and type fast.

Me: *All I can think about right now is how wet you got last time I had my mouth on you.*

Her phone lights up. She doesn't miss a beat with the sheriff, but the faintest pink creeps into her cheeks.

Breezy: *Big words for a man pretending to care about traffic cones. Are you all talk, Hanson?*

It takes everything in me not to laugh *and* not to drag her out of here right now. I text her back while Sheriff Peeler continues to ramble on.

Me: *Woman, I'm all action. You already know that.*

Her hand dips below the table, and I hear the faint tip-tap of her fingers on the screen.

Breezy: *Maybe you should prove it to me. Tonight.*

Heat licks low in my gut.

Me: *You show up, and I'll ruin that perfect composure of yours all over again.*

She doesn't so much as glance my way. Instead, she just blows gently across the rim of her mug, lips parted, eyes half lidded, as she responds to Peeler. "That's fascinating, Sheriff. Truly. Red Bridge is lucky you got it all squared away."

Peeler beams, satisfied with the proverbial pat on the back, and, eventually, tips his hat and ambles toward the door when Deputy Felix Rice waves at him through the big glass window of the coffee shop.

"Well, Ms. Bishop," I say, standing to my feet, and my voice is rougher than I intend. "It's always nice to see you. Hopefully I'll see you around again soon?"

She looks up, perfectly composed but with that secret smile playing on her lips. "Maybe."

Maybe, my ass.

I take my coffee, head for the door, and the second I step into the cold, my phone buzzes in my pocket.

Breezy: *Don't lock your door too early. I'll be late.*

I grin into the rim of my cup, heat crawling up the back of my neck as I already start to picture her in my bed with wild hair and bare skin.

Oh yeah. We're just acquaintances, all right.

18

Breezy

Sunday, January 24th

Sunday morning in Red Bridge feels like I'm living someone else's life.

Instead of being hunched over my laptop in Chelsea, answering twenty emails before nine a.m., I'm sitting at my brother's kitchen table in leggings, hair in a half-bun, sipping coffee while my adorable niece creates what can only be described as culinary carnage.

It's just past nine, and breakfast is a full-body event. There's yogurt on the high chair tray, a spoon clattering rhythmically against the bowl, and Autumn babbling through a mouthful of banana.

"Mo' nana!" she insists, pointing to the counter behind her with her chubby hand.

"You've already had a whole banana, sweet pea," I tell her and point to the bowl that still has some strawberry yogurt in it. "How about you finish your yogurt now?"

"Yo-yo, Bee!" She giggles, then smears yogurt across her cheek like war paint.

It's just me and this little cutie for the next few hours. Bennett is in Paris for the next two days for a gallery showing, and since Norah is his manager now, she had to start the day on a few conference calls for his ever-expanding art empire and just left about twenty minutes ago to run some errands in Molene in the name of restocking Bennett's studio with his favorite paints.

Truthfully, old Breezy would've bristled at that. I would've felt edged out of the inner circle I helped build. I mean, I spent years handling Bennett's shows, his deals, his entire damn trajectory. I was the PR machine behind his art, even though I was running Bishop Galleries and that was more than a full-time job in itself.

But sitting here now, watching Autumn dunk her entire hand into a bowl of yogurt like she's mining for treasure, I don't feel left out for the first time in my life. I feel...relieved.

And that scares me.

"Uh-oh," Autumn says solemnly after she manages to flick a handful of yogurt onto the kitchen floor. It lands on the hardwood with a wet splat.

"Uh-oh," I say, wiping up the mess with a paper towel while simultaneously biting my lip to fight my laughter. Goodness knows, once a toddler figures out they can make you laugh by doing something, they'll keep doing it over and over again. "Bye-bye, yogurt."

"Bye-bye!" She delightfully kicks her little sock-covered feet. "Bye-bye, Yo-yo!"

It's been two weeks since I landed here in Red Bridge, and somehow, I've slowly become a part of their household rhythm, helping out with grocery shopping or watching Autumn whenever I can. Norah even did some of my laundry earlier this week, and when I found my sweaters folded on the dryer like some kind of domestic peace offering, I teared up.

To be cared for is...new. Quietly frightening. I can't decide if my growing comfort here is a good sign or a bad one, but for now, I've resigned to sitting in the unfamiliarity until I figure it out.

Norah's also been forwarding me emails she's received from gallery owners and museum curators, even a couple of headhunters from the art world, asking what I'm doing now that I'm no longer with Bishop Galleries.

Apparently, word travels fast when you fall off the pedestal.

And every morning last week, I took my laptop to CAFFEINE with full intentions of responding to them. I'd sit there with my coffee, staring at the blinking cursor in an empty draft, and then... nothing. I couldn't bring myself to type a single word.

Because the truth is, I don't know what to say.

Because I don't know yet if I even want to say it.

Autumn hums to herself now, a tuneless little song, yogurt dripping from her spoon, and I smile at her cute little face.

"Bee sing!" she demands. "Sing, Bee!"

I don't hesitate to dive right into her demand. "Old MacDonald had a farm..." I start, pausing long enough for her to join in.

"E-I-E-I-O!" she shouts, clapping her hands excitedly.

Her joy is infectious, and before I know it, we're both going through all the farm animals together, Autumn giggling and smiling and clapping the entire time.

We manage three rounds of "Old MacDonald" and five rounds of "Itsy Bitsy Spider," and considering how I spent my weekend, it's a miracle I'm capable of keeping up with her pace without yawning.

Friday night, I stayed at Tad's. And last night, I went to his house but came back to Bennett's at three in the morning because I promised Norah I'd watch Autumn today.

Neither she nor Bennett has asked me any questions about where I've been disappearing to at night, but I'm not naïve. They *have* to know. I mean, I've been caught by both of them in the walk of shame act a few times at this point. But they haven't said anything. Besides the one morning I came home and Bennett was up with Autumn, my brother hasn't asked me any more questions about my late-night whereabouts.

Maybe it's out of respect. Maybe it's out of quiet amusement. Or maybe Norah read him the riot act and told him to stay out of my business.

I don't know, but I'm not sure either of them would guess I'm spending my late-night free time in the hot sheep-farmer-next-door's bed. Frankly, it's not something the old me would've ever done. But I'm starting to wonder if she died the instant my father's betrayal slapped me in the face from his grave.

I don't know if this new version of Breezy is improved, but I know her body still hums from the memory of Tad last night—his laugh, his hands, the warm, reckless tangle of us that made the rest of the world blur out.

Whatever this casual fling thing is that we're doing, it's safe to say it's working. Maybe a little *too* well.

And still, as much as I love the way Tad makes me forget, mornings like this remind me how uncertain everything else still feels.

Honestly, I don't know if this is real or if I'm just compartmentalizing.

Am I going to wake up one day hysterical, undone, unable to move without the galleries anchoring me?

Or is this strange, floaty reality of having no plan and no title actually what peace feels like?

I don't know if I've ever had peace. But right now, watching Autumn grin with yogurt smeared across her nose, I think maybe I do.

"All dones, Bee!" Autumn cheers from her high chair, and I make quick work of wiping off her face, earning a few belly giggles as I do.

Once she's back on her feet, she runs toward her favorite dollhouse in the corner of the living room and starts playing.

But only two minutes into playing, she pauses and yells, "Juice-y, Bee! Juice-y, Bee!"

"Do you want apple juice or grape juice, sweetie?"

"Aaa-pull!"

"You got it, girl," I answer and grab the new cups Norah has been letting Autumn try to drink from because the pediatrician encouraged her to go lid-less.

A minute or two later, Autumn is all set up at the living room coffee table with her apple juice, a little bowl of Cheerios—an additional request while I was getting the juice—and her favorite kids' show playing on the television.

And I head back into the kitchen to clean up our breakfast mess.

But I'm only a few dishes in when her little voice pulls my attention again.

"Uh-oh, Bee!" She's looking down at her overturned cup of juice spilling across the table. Her big blue eyes are wide, and guilt blooms inside them. "I sowwy."

Aw. My heart squeezes.

"It's okay, sweetie," I say softly and head into the living room with a towel to clean up the mess. "Accidents happen sometimes, okay?" Once it's all cleaned up, I tell her it's okay again and give her forehead a little kiss.

Her relief is instant. She beams up at me, cheeks dimpling, and then holds out a Cheerio toward me like a peace offering. "For yous."

"Thank you." I take it with a smile and pop it into my mouth with exaggerated delight. "Yum. Best breakfast I've ever had."

She giggles, and that sound might as well be music to my ears.

She grins wider. And that grin… I swear, it's Summer's grin, and it never fails to hit me like a sucker punch. Autumn never met her sister, but she's a carbon copy of ringlet curls, blue eyes, and pure sunshine. I can *see* the bond they would have had—Summer putting her little sister in an all-pink princess outfit while playing dress-up, Summer bossing Autumn around with big-sister pride, and Autumn following her around in sparkly shoes.

The ache catches me low in my chest. It's sharp but sweet and tethers me to both what's gone and what's still here.

"I love you, Autumn," I tell her as I press another kiss to her forehead.

"Luv ya, Bee!"

Autumn runs back over to her dollhouse, and my phone buzzes on the kitchen counter.

Logan: *Everything is going to shit without you.*

Logan: *I don't know what the fuck I'm doing. You know that. I know that. Help me. Please. I've already fucked two artists into sharing an exhibition slot because I don't understand how this scheduling program works.*

My throat tightens, but I won't give him that power. Instead, I slide the phone to dark, but not even ten seconds later, it buzzes again, and the screen comes to life.

Serena: *We should do a girls' trip. Ibiza, maybe? Henry would have wanted us to support each other through such a difficult time.*

Serena: *Also, do you have the number for the private banker in St. Barts? I'm here and need to move some funds. I tried to get ahold of Logan, but he didn't answer.*

Good grief. My father's widowed wife is apparently having such a difficult time with his death that she's currently on vacation in St. Barts. Not to mention, she wants to grieve together in *Ibiza* and find a way to get access to more of my dead father's money.

But seriously, why is my family so screwed up?

I laugh out loud. A bitter, genuine, but ridiculous laugh. Autumn notices.

"Funny?" she asks.

"Nothing, sweetheart," I murmur.

She goes back to playing with her dollhouse and I'm about to sit down on the couch, but my phone vibrates again in my hand, and a deep sigh escapes my lungs. *Good God. Who is it now? My dead father texting me from the freaking grave?*

Tad: *I'm knee-deep in riled-up sheep. And it's so cold outside, I'm questioning my life choices. How's your Sunday going?*

Now *this* is a text I can entertain. Want to, even.

Me: *I'm babysitting Autumn. We're still in our pajamas.*

Tad: *Wanna trade?*

Me: *You know what? I really appreciate that offer, but I think I'll pass.*

Tad: *What? Why? You have so much potential as a sheep farmer, Breeze. I'll even offer my mentoring services.*

Me: *From what I hear from the Red Bridge busybodies, those sheep mostly farm you…*

Tad: *Lies. Slander. Unfounded rumors.*

I snort, shaking my head.

Me: *Uh-huh. And what excuse do you have for me literally seeing five of your sheep in the town square two days ago?*

Tad: *Sabotage. Clearly, someone planted them to ruin my reputation.*

Me: *HAHAHAHAHAHAHA*

I laugh so loudly Autumn joins in, though she has no idea why.

Tad: *Glad I got you laughing. I like picturing that.*

Heat prickles at the base of my neck. *Damn him. Why is he always so much fun?*

Me: *Careful, Farmer. You're supposed to be tending your flock, not distracting me from being a good babysitter.*

Tad: *Who says I can't do both, City Girl? It's called multitasking, and I'm a pro. Wanna come over tonight, and I'll prove it to you?*

Me: *And how exactly are you going to multitask?*

Tad: *You'd be surprised what my mouth and my fingers can do at the same time.*

Me: *Challenge accepted.*

I school my face into perfect neutrality, but inside, I'm melting.

Autumn claps her hands along with the song that's now coming from the television. "Dance, Bee! Dance, Bee!" she demands as she wiggles her hips in this adorable little side-to-side motion.

I set my phone down and do exactly that, shaking my hips and clapping my hands right along with Autumn.

She's giggling and beaming at me with a full-toothed, toddler grin, and I'm laughing like a woman who doesn't have the weight of a fallen empire on her shoulders.

When the music fades, I collapse onto the couch, breathless and smiling. Autumn curls up beside me, her eyes fixated on her television show and her little hand clutching mine.

While I enjoy my niece's sweet little cuddles, my gaze drifts to my half-finished knitting project—*fingers crossed it actually turns into a scarf*—sitting on the armchair. Peggy Samuel had been working on one at CAFFEINE last week, and since I wasn't doing much besides staring at a blank screen, she gave me a free lesson over coffee.

Now, I've got a tangle of uneven stitches and a ball of yarn the color of sunshine. And even though it's probably not going to turn into a scarf someone will actually want to wear, I still kind of love it.

And deep down, I love that I'm giving something like knitting a chance.

But maybe that's the real reason I can't seem to settle on any plans that have me heading back to New York. Currently, my days aren't dictated by deadlines, exhibitions, high-priced art negotiations, or anyone else's expectations.

Instead, they're filled with my niece's giggles and smiles, and Norah's and Bennett's warmth and support, and Josie's friendship, and the simple rhythm of a town that actually notices when you walk through the door.

And my nights? Well, they're filled with Tad Hanson.

Maybe staying in Red Bridge a little while longer is one of those bad ideas I should entertain...

19

Tad

Monday, January 25th

It's pushing two in the morning, and my kitchen smells like bacon and batter.

Breezy showed up at my door around midnight, all New York confidence in a snow-dusted coat, and I barely got the lock turned before she was pressed against me. There was no time for food then; we barely made it to my bed.

But two hours later, her head was still on my chest when her stomach let out a growl loud enough to make both of us laugh.

"I didn't really eat today. My little Autumn kept me busy," she admitted, sheepish.

So here I am, standing over a skillet in nothing but boxer briefs, flipping bacon like it's the most natural thing in the world.

The last time you felt so domesticated—

I clear my throat and cut off that thought before it can grow legs and run me into the ground.

"Tell me, Hot Farmer Tad, do you always cook in your underwear?" Breezy asks, and the playful humor in her voice has me glancing over my shoulder to find her sitting on my kitchen island, legs swinging and looking too damn good. Her hair is messy, and one of my flannels is the only thing that covers her body. She's holding a chipped coffee mug like it's fine china, and an adorable little smile tugs at her lips as she watches me cook.

"Hot Farmer Tad?"

"Hey," she says with a little shrug of her shoulders. "It's what all the single ladies of Red Bridge call you."

"Bullshit."

"Oh, come on, Tad," she retorts on a snort. "You and I both know it's the truth. You're a hot commodity around these parts. Hell, you've been referred to as *Studly McSheepman* in the newspaper."

"Fuck me," I mutter and run my free hand through my hair. "That's worse than Hot Farmer Tad."

Breezy laughs.

"And to answer your question, I only cook in my underwear when I've got company to impress." I flip the bacon and wince a little when the grease pops onto my bare stomach. "By the way, welcome to late-night breakfast at *Casa de Studly Sheepman*. There are no Michelin stars, but I've got maple syrup and orange juice in the fridge," I add with a wink. "It's vintage, last Tuesday."

She laughs again, and God, I'd put the sizzling bacon straight on my chest to hear that sound again.

I pour batter into the pan, focusing on keeping it round, though my eyes keep flicking back to her. *Because fuck, Breezy is beautiful.* Sleek black hair falling loose, bare thighs peeking out from under my flannel, and toes curling against the counter like she's been here a hundred times. *Like she belongs here.*

"You sure you know what you're doing?" she asks with a cute grin kissing her lips. "I've never really painted you as a cooking kind of a guy."

"Are you questioning my pancake skills?"

"Judging by the state of your stove..." Her gaze drops pointedly to the grease splatters. "I think it's a fair question."

I waggle the spatula. "Careful, woman. You mock the chef, you don't get pancakes."

"Oh no," she says and dramatically moves her hand to her chest. "How will I survive without your slightly burned delicacies?"

"Breezy, baby, I'm a pro at pancakes. Trust the process." I flip the pancake. Of course, it arcs too high, lands half off the pan, and Breezy covers her mouth to stifle a giggle.

"Pro status, huh?"

"I'm just getting warmed up." I grin, toss the pancake in the trash, and pour another onto the skillet.

She watches me, smile softening, and after a beat, she says quietly, "I like this."

"Like what?" I glance at her over my shoulder. "Burned pancakes?"

Her eyes flick to mine. "No. This." She gestures at me, the stove, the ridiculous scene. "You making me food in your boxers at two in the morning."

Something sharp pulls in my chest, but I play it off by shaking my ass at her. "Careful, Breeze. If you keep complimenting my ass, it might start sounding like you want to keep me and my sexy boxer briefs around for more than breakfast."

And I punctuate that statement by slapping the spatula on my own ass.

Her laugh is quick and deflecting. "Don't push it, Farm Daddy."

"Farm Daddy?" I question through a groan. "If you tell me Eileen has been calling me that in the fucking newspaper, I swear I'll croak right here."

"Nah." She grins mischievously. "That's a Breezy trademark. I use it in my secret diary." Her smile is equal parts teasing and sarcastic. "And of course, when I doodle *Mrs. Farm Daddy* all over my notebooks in study hall."

"You're such a smartass," I tell her, and she just keeps on smiling.

"I might be a smartass, but I'm a very lovable smartass, you know?" she retorts with a wink. "Pretty sure that's why you're currently twerking and cooking for me in your boxers."

"I did not twerk."

"Whatever you say, Farm Daddy."

She's still smiling, but her eyes flicker with something she's not saying. A thought neither of us wants to name.

Suddenly, my heart starts pounding so hard it's like it wants to dive-bomb straight out of my chest. It's a strange feeling. A confusing fucking feeling. It's the kind of feeling that digs under your ribs and threatens to mean something.

I immediately shove it down.

And I slide a few pancakes and bacon onto a plate and walk over to the kitchen island to hand it to her. But before I can stop myself, the question just slides off my fucking tongue. "You made any decisions about Red Bridge?"

She tilts her head to the side. "Decisions?"

"Yeah." I grab my coffee and take a sip, pretending the question doesn't matter. "You've been here, what…two weeks now? Just wondering how long I get to feed you midnight pancakes before you run off back to the city."

She looks at me for a long beat until she exhales a quiet laugh. "Honestly? I don't know. My life's kind of…a mess right now. Nothing feels steady enough to plan past tomorrow. I'm still figuring out a new and exciting direction to go in." She shrugs and spears a bite of pancake. "So, I guess I'll stay until I figure out where I should go or where I'm supposed to be. Or until you run out of bacon."

It's a simple answer, but it lands harder than it should.

I tell myself it's nothing. Just curiosity. Just conversation.

She's free to leave whenever she wants. Hell, that's the whole point of this. No strings. No expectations.

Still, there's this weird heaviness in my chest that I can't quite shake.

I ignore it and pour more batter into the skillet. "Guess I'd better stock up on bacon, then," I say and flash a teasing smirk I don't quite feel.

"That sounds like a good plan," she says through a giggle and mouthful of pancakes. "By the way, *Farm Daddy*, midnight pancakes taste pretty dang good."

"Farm Daddy." I groan. "Don't tell me that Breezy trademark is sticking."

"I don't know," she singsongs. "It truly has a nice ring to it. Really rolls off the tongue, you know?"

A laugh jumps from my throat, and the heaviness that sits on my shoulders dissipates. And when I turn to look at her and find her still sitting on my counter with her legs swinging adorably and her bare thighs peeking out from my oversized flannel shirt, I set the spatula down, flip off the stove, and cross the room to her.

I grip her thighs in my big hands and spread them wide so I can step between them.

"What about the pancakes?" she asks, searching my eyes curiously.

"I'm not hungry for pancakes," I murmur and kiss her deeply. Her mouth tastes like maple syrup and bacon and something I shouldn't want as much as I do.

Something I should be running far away from.

Something that feels a lot like the one thing I swore to myself I'd never do again.

But I'm powerless when she starts kissing me back and threads her fingers into my hair.

I'm completely entranced when she wraps her thighs around my waist and lets me guide her back into my bedroom.

And even though this is starting to feel less like distraction and more like pure, unfiltered trouble, I let myself drown in her anyway.

20

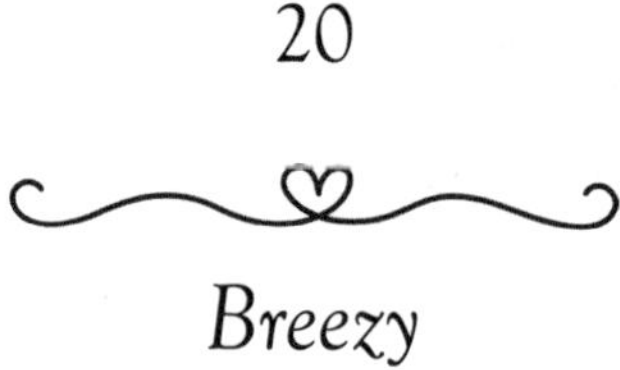

Breezy

Sunday, January 31st

Another week slips by before I even realize it.

Seven more days in Red Bridge, and most of them end the same way—me tiptoeing across Bennett's snow-covered yard long after everyone else is asleep and ending up in Tad Hanson's bed. Sure, sneaking out feels pretty dang juvenile for a thirty-nine-year-old woman, but the heat of Tad's hands and how fucking good he makes me feel makes it possible for me to ignore that fact.

Of course, I could tell Bennett about it. I could definitely tell Norah. I mean, I'm a grown fucking woman. Hell, I'm older than both of them. But this is something I want to keep to myself.

The Red Bridge cemetery is about a two-mile drive from Norah and Bennett's house, and it's a quiet, serene stretch of rolling hills and leafless maples bowed under the weight of frost.

When we step out of the car, the morning chill surrounds us, and our breath clouds the air as we follow the gravel path that winds between the headstones. The quiet winter morning is so silent it presses into my ears and makes every crunch of gravel under our shoes feel loud.

Bennett carries Autumn on his hip, Norah is beside him, and I'm beside Norah. The four of us move slowly across the stone path until we stop at the gravestone I've seen a hundred times but will never get used to seeing.

SUMMER BEATRICE BISHOP

Her name is carved deep, the letters filled with shadows and ice. I kneel, brushing away a drift of snow, and the chill bites through my glove. For a moment, I swear it's like she's still here, like I can feel her small hand lacing with my fingers again.

Her sweet, melodic voice floats through my memory. *"Aunt Breezy, I want to be a painter like my daddy!"*

God, I miss that girl so much.

Norah crouches nearby, helping Autumn arrange a tiny bouquet in the vase at the base of the stone. Autumn chatters the whole time, serious and loud in her toddler way. "Pinks! Smells good! Me picks dem!"

"That's right, Autumn. You picked out pink flowers for Summer," Norah hums encouragement, smoothing her daughter's curls away from her face. "And she would've loved them."

Autumn grins and leans her little body against Norah's side. And I can't get over how natural they look together, like two puzzle pieces that always belonged.

Behind us, Bennett stands a few steps back, hands shoved deep in his coat pockets and his face carved tight. While my brother is happy in his life, it's a fact that losing his daughter Summer has made grief live in him permanently now. It's quieter than it used to be, but it's stitched into the fabric of who he is.

I rise slowly, standing beside him, not sure if I should speak. Honestly, words feel clumsy here. Even two years after losing Summer, I never feel like I can fully convey how I feel or how much I miss Summer or how much I loved her. But when my sleeve brushes his, his hand shifts from his pocket and finds mine, squeezing once in a silent and steady gesture.

It undoes me more than words ever could.

After a while, Bennett steps closer to Norah and Autumn. He wraps his arm around his wife's shoulders, and Autumn finds her spot beside his legs, hugging her daddy tightly. The three of them—grief and love and life all knotted together—make a perfect, imperfect whole.

I hover in the back. The spare piece. The ghost on the edge of their little family.

And my chest aches with something sharp and new.

I've never let myself wonder about motherhood. Never really wanted to. My life has always been noise and deadlines and gallery openings and a very curated version of purpose that left no room for anything else. I've measured years in profit margins and successful exhibitions, not birthdays and bedtime stories. But watching Norah guide Autumn's tiny hands toward the flowers again, I feel something deep inside me tug.

It's quiet but powerful. It's a desire I don't know if I even want to name.

I'm thirty-nine years old. I've never missed what I never thought I wanted, but it's as if I feel the sharp edge of something I've always ignored. The absence of a life I never gave myself the time or permission to want.

A buzz rattles in my coat pocket, jarring me out of my own head.

I glance at the screen and see *Incoming Call Logan*.

Without hesitation, I press the side button and silence the call without looking at the screen. He doesn't get this moment. Not here. Not today.

We stay a little longer, silence consuming us all.

Autumn places her palm against the stone and whispers, "Summy-bee."

It's as close as her little toddler mouth can get to saying

Summblebee—the nickname my brother always used for Summer.

Bennett turns away, blinking too fast, and Norah squeezes his hand, and I have to swallow the lump in my throat and force the liquid emotion out of my eyes.

Summer would've loved her little sister Autumn. And Autumn would've loved her too. That's a fact. That's the bittersweet and tragic truth. Summer was taken from us too soon, and I'm certain there will never be a time when any of us feels okay with that.

We can live through it. We can cope with it. But we'll *never* be okay with it.

Eventually, we drift back toward the car. Autumn skips between Bennett and Norah, clutching both her parents' hands while her curls bounce like springs in the pale sunlight. They look whole. Complete.

And I trail a few steps behind, my boots crunching in the frost, the sharp ache inside me still very present.

For most of my life, I told myself I didn't need family or the love of a good man or the kind of steady devotion that roots you somewhere.

But watching them now, I find myself silently wondering if I somehow managed to miss out on my own life.

• • •

After Norah, Bennett, Autumn, and I left the cemetery, we stopped at the Diner to eat a late brunch.

Now, the three of them are outside, bundled in coats, helping Autumn build what she insists is a *castle*, though it looks suspiciously like a snow mound with twigs sticking out of it.

I'm back in the guest room, sitting cross-legged on the bed, the faint smell of syrup still clinging to my sweater and a half-finished yellow scarf pooling in my lap. My knitting needles click quietly in the silence in a soft rhythm that's almost meditative. My stitches are uneven, my yarn keeps tangling, but somehow, it feels grounding.

My phone buzzes on the quilt beside me.

Logan's name lights up the screen again, but this time, it's a text.

Logan: *Breeze. For fuck's sake, stop ignoring me. Call me back. Clearly, I'm struggling without you, but I also really miss my sister.*

I stare at his name for a long beat, the familiar frustration and feelings of betrayal coiling in my belly, but I still can't bring myself to respond to him. I swipe the notification away and open my ongoing text thread with Tad instead.

My thumb hovers over the message bubble, and before I can stop myself, the truth spills out in typed words that feel like a confession.

We went to the cemetery to visit Summer's grave today. I miss her so much. I don't know how my brother survives it. And I keep wondering if I spent my life chasing the wrong things. If I let time run out on something I didn't even realize I wanted until it was too late.

The sight of it on the screen makes my chest ache. Because it's true. All of it. But it's too much for what I have with Tad. Too open.

I stare at my own words for a long time, biting my lip hard enough to taste copper.

Eventually, I delete every word, backspace by backspace, until the screen is empty again.

And I start over, sending something safe and teasing and casual. Just like it's supposed to be.

Me: *Hope your sheep behaved today. Or should I be watching for your mug shot in the Chronicle tomorrow?*

Three dots appear immediately, and a smile already tugs at my lips.

Tad: *They've been plotting all day. Crosby's their ringleader. I swear he's one union meeting away from demanding benefits.*

A laugh slips out, and I set the knitting needles aside to text back.

Me: *You should probably give them dental. Or at least better snacks.*

Tad: *You volunteering to bring treats, City Girl? You seem to have a thing for lost causes.*

Me: *Oh, c'mon, Tad. You're not a lost cause. I can name at least fifty single ladies in Red Bridge who would sign that petition.*

Tad: *Would you be one of those fifty ladies?*

Me: *Hell no. I've seen how badly you burn pancakes.*

Tad: *You LOVED my pancakes.*

Me: *I couldn't even finish them, Farm Daddy.*

Tad: *That's only because I distracted you with orgasms.*

Me: *Oh, that's right. I forgot about that.*

Tad: *Woman, you best not ever forget the power of my tongue.*

Me: *Is that a threat?*

Tad: *It's a promise. One I'd like to make good on tonight. My door will be unlocked.*

Me: *Door unlocked? That sounds like a safety hazard…*

Tad: *Only if you're planning on breaking in.*

Me: *What if I am? Hypothetically.*

Tad: *Then hypothetically, I'd have to frisk you for weapons.*

Me: *Oh boy. That sounds dirty.*

Tad: *Farm Daddy better see your ass tonight.*

The fact that I've now got him referring to himself as Farm Daddy has me cracking up. Out loud.

Me: *LOL. I'll be there.*

Eventually, I pick my knitting back up, yarn sliding through my fingers as my heart thuds lighter than it has all day.

Outside, Autumn's laughter carries through the cold air. And inside, my scarf grows by another few uneven rows.

And for the first time all day, I don't feel so alone.

21

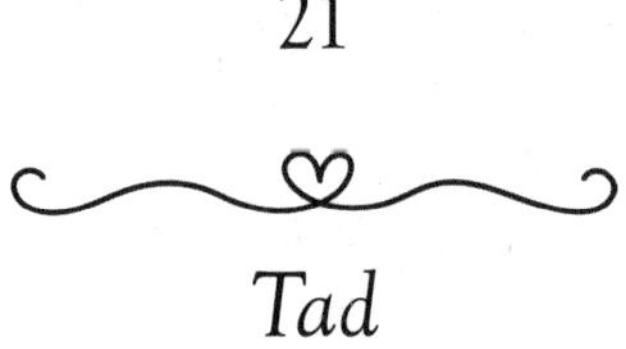

Tad

Monday, February 8th

"You realize this makes three times in the last two months? We're idiots, Tad. Certified dumbasses," he gripes, kicking at an empty sack of feed like maybe it'll magically fill up with grain.

The farm's feed delivery is late, and Randy's pacing the barn like he's rehearsing for a one-man show called *We're Doomed*. It's not even ten in the morning, and the day's feeling like spoiled milk before the sun can burn off the frost.

"We're not idiots, Randy. Just a little unlucky."

He snorts and shoulders open the barn door. "Unlucky's stepping in dog shit on your way into a restaurant. This is incompetence."

"We're not incompetent," I mutter, checking the latch on a stall. "Life is just handing us some lemons, and we're being resourceful."

"Resourceful?" He barks out a laugh. "Tad, we're down to one bag of feed because our sheep keep getting into the feed shed, and the delivery's still in Montpelier. We've got to buy local. *Again.* Which costs us twice as much. Which makes us idiots. And makes this farm not profitable."

He's not wrong, but I've learned not to fuel the fire. The thing he can't face is that this farm isn't about profit; it's about existing. I bought it so I'd have a reason to get out of bed every day.

I bought it to save me from myself. *Because Lord knows, I'll never be able to forget.*

Fifteen minutes later, we're loading into my truck and heading into town. By the time we arrive, Main Street's wide awake. Josie's chalkboard sign is propped outside CAFFEINE, the scent of fresh bread sneaks out from Melba's bakery, and a couple of locals scrape ice off their windshields.

Red Bridge Feed & Grain sits behind the hardware store, a small, squat brick building with a tin roof that rattles in the wind, and I pull into the gravel parking lot.

"Fuck me, what a waste of money this is going to be," Randy mutters as I shut off the engine. "How about you let me handle this one? Last time, I know we could've gotten him to come down on his price at least twenty or thirty bucks if you hadn't been so nice."

"By all means, have at it, brother."

On a huff, he hops out of the truck and marches inside to haggle with poor Mr. Donnelly like it's a sport. And I climb out of the driver's side to get some fresh air and lean against the hood of my truck.

My phone buzzes in my pocket, and I pull it out to see Incoming Call Dad on the screen.

I swipe. "Hey, old man."

"Hey, stranger," Dad rumbles, and I can hear what sounds like poker chips clattering in the background. I guess my dad's and Uncle Cal's Caribbean cruise has got them spending far too much time in the casino on the boat. "You busy?"

"Depends on what you'd call busy. Randy's in the feed store, and I'm outside waiting on him."

"Uh-oh." He chuckles. "You run out of feed again and have to buy local?"

I sigh. "Randy needs to stop bitching to you so much."

"In his defense, Tad, it wasn't his idea to move to small-town Vermont and run a sheep farm. Bitching is his coping mechanism."

"I didn't force him to follow me here ten years ago, and I'm not making him stay now. I'm in my forties. Pretty sure I can handle my own shit."

"He's your big brother," my dad tosses back. "He's protective. And in your own damn words, it's been ten years. His life is in Red Bridge now, whether the two of you like it or not."

He's not wrong. Randy's life *is* in Red Bridge now, and if I'm being frank with myself, things wouldn't feel right if he weren't here. Though, I'd more than support his choice to leave and finally choose himself over being worried about my bullshit.

"Dammit," he snaps, a teasing laugh preceding something unintelligible from my uncle Cal. "You're not the only one with a pain in the ass sibling, son. Count your blessings for good old boy Rando. You could have a poker cheat for a brother like me."

"I'm not a cheat. Your father is just inferior," Uncle Cal says, leaning into the phone enough for me to hear him clearly.

I laugh and sigh at the same time. "There a reason you called while you're cruising the Caribbean seas? I don't wanna cut you short, but I've got shit to do."

"Relax, son." His responding chuckle sounds weathered but warm. "I'm just checking in while we have a day at sea. I won't keep you long."

Dad and Uncle Cal are retired firefighters, brothers like Randy and me, and Chicago born and bred like us too. They were the backbone of my entire childhood. Shifts at the fire station together, softball games on their off days, and Sunday cookouts in the backyard, they've been inseparable since birth.

Now they're balls deep into retirement and spend their days on golf trips, poker nights, and vacations with other retirees from their station.

I love them both dearly, but I'm not naïve enough to think they're calling me from a fucking cruise for any reason other than to take the temperature of my mental state.

"So...everything all right out there?" he asks subtly, diving predictably into probing. He and Randy are two peas in a pod when it comes to checking in on me.

And is *everything all right?* I mean, the sheep are fine. The fences mostly hold. Randy's still Randy. But lately, my nights don't end alone.

Instantly, my mind pictures Breezy, her bare feet padding across my kitchen floor, my shirt sliding off one shoulder, and her laugh wrapping around me like something I shouldn't need as much as I do. She's still here in Red Bridge. And somehow, that feels like the best and worst kind of relief.

I still don't know the whys or hows of what brought her here—has kept her here for the past month—or when she's going to leave. But that probably stems from the casualness we agreed to.

Though, Breezy did say she's just taking things day by day and doesn't plan to become a permanent fixture here.

And I tell myself that's a good thing. *But do you actually believe it?*

"You still there, bud?" Dad asks.

"Yeah," I answer quickly, voice flat enough to hide what's under it. "And everything's all right."

He hums like he doesn't buy it. "You sure things are good in that small town of yours?"

In the background, Cal yells, "Don't let him fool you, Freddy! That boy was always a bit of a ladies' man. Probably busy dating half the women in that Podunk paradise by now."

"Everything's good, Dad," I reassure. "Sheep are healthy. Randy's cranky. Business as usual."

"Hold on, Tad. Cal wants to talk to ya."

"Tadpole!" My uncle Cal's voice is now in my ear. "How's the sheep biz?"

"You'd be surprised how exciting and glorious it is."

"That's funny. Exciting and glorious weren't the adjectives your brother used when I last talked to him."

"Yeah, well, Randy has a flair for dramatics," I retort. "How about you old geezers tell me how the cruise is going?" I ask, trying like hell to change the topic of conversation.

"Well, I'm certain it's a lot better than mucking around in sheep shit," Uncle Cal retorts on a chuckle. "I just cleaned out half the poker tables on this boat. You and Randy want me to send a care package when we land in Jamaica? Maybe some whiskey and cigars to take the edge off all the farming mundanity?"

Before I can answer, Dad cuts in. "Ignore him. He's only had one good gambling day on this boat, and he won't shut up about it."

My dad and I continue chatting, but we both dance around the deep shit.

We don't mention Mom or the fact that the anniversary of her death was just a few weeks ago. We don't talk about how Dad still hasn't sold the house and has been splitting his time between it and Cal's condo, the two of them basically bachelors again in their seventies. I tell him the sheep are fattening up for spring, thanks to them basically overfeeding themselves and making us run out of grain earlier than we should. And he tells me to call more often.

All in all, it's exactly how I'd expect a call with my dad to go. But then again, he's always been a good man, a good dad, and everything in between.

Eventually, we hang up, and the quiet that follows feels heavier than it should. I tuck the phone into my pocket and just stare down Main Street without any real focus.

But my attention is pulled when Sheriff Peeler turns the corner and heads through the gravel parking lot on foot with a

Styrofoam cup of coffee that has CAFFEINE written on the side of it.

"Mornin', Tad," he greets.

"Sheriff," I nod. "How's it going?"

"Been better," he says through a deep sigh when he comes to a stop in front of me. "Did you hear about the vandals?"

"Vandals?"

"The graffiti artists who keep painting wieners all over the side of the high school." He lets out another deep sigh. "I swear, this is the fourth year of this shit, and I'm growing tired of trying to track these little hooligans down."

I bite my lip to hide my laughter. Truth be told, the dick-and-ball masterpieces that appear on Red Bridge High every year are part of an ongoing senior prank. Everyone in town knows it to be true. Everyone besides Sheriff Peeler, the man responsible for tracking them down, that is.

You'd think he would've figured it out by now, but Red Bridge protects its own. Also, their law enforcement is too busy flirting with the ladies at the bingo hall on Friday nights to thoroughly investigate the matter.

"That's horrible," I eventually say, my face as neutral as I can force it.

The sheriff shakes his head and purses his lips. "Tell me about it."

Before he can start in on the weather or some other random Red Bridge gossip, a fire truck

blasts past the feed store, lights strobing and horn rattling the windows.

My whole body locks up.

My lungs forget how to work, my throat seizes, and it's like the air thickens in an instant with smoke where there is none to be found.

Sheriff Peeler stands right beside me, squinting toward the lights and sirens on Main Street like it's no more alarming than a garbage truck. "Metcalf's Diner, I bet," he says, casual as anything. "That oven's older than Moses. Bastard needs to replace it before someone actually gets hurt."

I can't tear my eyes from the red truck as it slows, sirens still screaming, men in turnout gear leaping down. My nails bite into my palms, and my spine grows rigid as the blood in my veins pumps through my body at a jolting pace.

"Did you hear about Old Man Gellar's house?" Peeler keeps talking, oblivious to the turmoil that's rumbling inside me. "The damn roof caved in from all the snow we've been getting. He's staying over at the Red Bridge Inn while some of Harry Kyman's boys are fixing it up."

I can barely hear him. But that's on account of my heartbeat hammering inside my skull.

The firefighters vanish inside the diner just as my phone buzzes in my pocket and startles my spine straight.

Breezy: *You should make me dinner tonight.*

The words ground me like a rope thrown across a cliff's edge. I stare at the glowing screen, her words a cute reminder of her blunt confidence and bossy charm, and I inhale air that doesn't taste like smoke.

Though, I can't respond. Not yet. Not right now.

"I think they've got it under control," Peeler says, nodding toward the fire truck. There's currently no smoke pushing through the roof or flames licking the sky, but the firefighters who jogged into the diner have yet to come back out. "Probably nothing more than a whole lot of song and dance for an ancient oven that should've been condemned twenty years ago."

After a quick pat to my back, Sheriff Peeler ambles over toward The Diner, his posture relaxed and his strides slow and easy. It's the opposite of my tense body and legs that still feel like they want to bolt.

A few pounding heartbeats later, the sirens cut off, the sudden silence ringing louder than the noise ever did, and the firefighters who went into The Diner are walking back to their truck.

Instant relief is a whip to my nerves.

Thank fuck.

Eventually, I force my hands to unclench, refocus on the screen of my phone, and thumb out a reply to Breezy.

Me: *And what time are you wanting this dinner, Bossy?*

Breezy: *I'd prefer 7 p.m. Unless you think Randy will still be hanging around?*

Me: *And what about Bennett and Norah? Won't they notice you leaving the house so early?*

Breezy: *They took Autumn to Miami with them for the night. Bennett had a gallery showing.*

Me: *7 p.m., it is then. Guess it's a good thing I cook better than I farm.*

Breezy: *Are you sure about that, Farm Daddy?*

Farm Daddy. *Fuck me.* It's the nickname she refuses to give up on.

Me: *I think I'm going to start tallying every time you call me that. You know, for future punishment's sake.*

Breezy: *Uh-oh. You gonna spank me?*

Me: *I guess that depends on how much you keep using that fucking nickname.*

She texts back with the same two words—*Farm Daddy*—repeated at least twenty times.

And just like that, I'm laughing. No longer tense. No longer internally battling the ghosts of my past.

• • •

The rest of the day felt stressful as fuck; Randy bitched for most of it because of our feed shortage and the subsequent price-gouging Mr. Donnelly did with the grain. Though, I hardly think an extra $3.75 should be considered predatory.

Thankfully, Randy called it a day by three, and after I made sure my pregnant sheep Mabel was comfortable in the barn and the rest of our flock was keeping a low profile, I spent the rest of the late afternoon and evening preparing a home-cooked meal for Breezy.

A meal we devoured.

A meal Breezy might've wanted seconds of, but I was too determined to eat my dessert—*aka her pussy*—in my bed to accommodate that request.

It's now a little after eleven. Breezy and I are curled up on my bed, under the fleece comforter, and the house feels cozy and calm as soft silence wraps around us like another quilt.

She is stretched out naked beside me, and her skin is warm against mine. The sheets are a mess from what we just did, and the air still hums with the electricity of it.

Her sigh is a cute, dreamy little thing as she traces lazy circles on my bare stomach with her fingertip. "That pasta…" Her voice holds a hint of drowsiness, but it's playful too. "Where the hell did you learn to cook like that?"

I tilt my head toward her, and a smirk tugs at my mouth. "My mom."

Her finger stills. "Really?"

"Yeah." I stare up at the ceiling for a beat. "She was Italian. The kind who thought boxed noodles were a crime. Every Sunday, she'd start her homemade sauce before sunrise, and the house would smell like garlic and basil all day. She kept a wooden spoon in her hand like it was a weapon. And if Randy or I would even dare to get in her way when she was cooking, she'd threaten to hit us upside the heads with it." I laugh at the memories. "Needless to say, she was a tough-as-nails woman who made sure we knew our way around a kitchen before we could drive."

Once my mind catches up with my mouth, with what I've just revealed, I'm shocked at how easily the words even came out. I honestly can't remember the last time I said anything about my mom out loud.

"Your mom sounds incredible." Breezy props her chin on my chest. "I bet she'd be proud of that pasta."

"Maybe." I breathe out. "She actually passed away twelve

years ago. Pancreatic cancer."

Her expression shifts, tender in a way that makes something inside me ache. "I'm sorry, Tad."

"Yeah," I murmur. "Me too."

I'm surprised how easy it feels to talk about my mom with Breezy. I honestly can't remember the last time I talked about Mom to even my dad or Randy. Frankly, it's been years since we've reminisced on memories of her at all.

But then again, she died two years before…I ended up in Red Bridge. *Before everything happened.*

The quiet settles around us, but it's not uncomfortable. It's just there, pulsing between us, and neither of us feels compelled to fill it up with chatter.

But the bubble of silence is popped when Breezy's phone buzzes against the nightstand.

She reaches for it and groans the instant her eyes check the screen.

"Something wrong?"

She turns her phone for me to read it.

Serena: *What was the name of Henry's favorite cologne? I'm thinking of getting a tattoo of it.*

I blink. "I'm sorry, but is that a real text? From an actual human?"

"Unfortunately." She tosses the phone back down, disgust rolling off her. "It's my dad's widow who, yeah, is technically my stepmother but is only twenty-seven."

"And she wants a cologne tattoo?" I furrow my brow. "Like of the bottle?"

"You're asking the wrong person that question," Breezy says through a laugh. "I won't pretend to have any idea what's inside that woman's head." Her laughter fades, and her hand drifts back to my chest. Suddenly, her face is shadowed by sadness. "My dad died two months ago. Unexpected heart attack. He was in Europe with Serena."

"I'm sorry to hear that." I don't say anything else. Instead, I just slide my hand over hers and hold it against my chest. I give her space to say or not say anything she wants.

"Did you know I used to run my family's art galleries? They were basically my whole life," she says, but her voice has dropped to a near whisper. Like whatever she's about to tell me is too difficult to use her full voice. "They're a Bishop legacy that my grandfather Harold started. World-renowned, truthfully. When Grandpa died a long time ago, my father was supposed to run the show, but for the last two decades, I've been the workhorse behind them. Pretty much running them all by myself."

She pauses, and I just keep giving her whatever space she needs while I hold her hand against my chest the entire time.

"I sacrificed everything to keep Bishop Galleries going," she admits quietly, and I don't miss the way her voice shakes a little around her words. "To keep them successful. To keep my family's legacy intact. And then, my father up and died, and he left them to my littlest brother Logan, who hasn't done jack shit for the galleries. He doesn't have a clue about art."

She exhales a shaky breath.

"And if that's not bad enough, I found out that Logan knew, Tad. He knew for six months before my father died that the galleries were going to him, and he never told me. I was blindsided. Everything I built—everything I gave up—just handed over like I wasn't good enough. Like what I built and created and sacrificed for didn't mean anything." She blows out a shaky breath and moves her head from side to side. "Now, even though I still have a place in New York, I'm living in Bennett's guest room like I'm twenty again because going back to the city is...too much for me right now. Too big of a reminder of everything I sacrificed and everything I lost."

She scrubs a hand down her face, lifts her eyes to mine, and lets out a self-deprecating laugh. "So there it is. The story of why I'm hanging out in Red Bridge. Why I currently have no plan. No direction. Why I'm basically just lost...lost *and* pathetic."

"You're not pathetic, Breezy," I refute, reaching up to gently run my knuckles along her cheek. "You're the exact opposite of pathetic, actually."

She searches my gaze closely, like she's trying to measure if I mean it. And I don't hesitate to keep going.

"That's fucking terrible, what happened to you. I'm sorry it did. I'm sorry you were betrayed by the people who should've protected you," I say and brush my thumb across the firm line of her lips. "And again, you're *not* pathetic. Not at all. Whatever you're feeling, whatever you're doing or not doing right now, it all makes sense, Breeze. Everything you built got tragically ripped away from you. That'll rattle anyone. It would make anyone feel untethered and completely fucking lost. And that doesn't mean you're weak. It just means you're human."

Her mouth quirks at the corners, though it doesn't quite turn into a smile. "Sounds like you know a thing or two about being rattled."

"I guess maybe I do." I shrug and look away, toward the window and the way the shadows of the trees are pressed into the glass.

I don't say or do or reveal any more. I don't fill her head with the kind of dark, heavy shit that sits inside my soul on a daily basis. Don't tell her that most nights I dream about smoke and ash and everything I couldn't save.

Instead, I press a kiss into her hair, pulling her closer until her leg hooks over mine and her breath evens against my skin.

And I try not to think too hard about the fact that having Breezy here keeps my ghosts at bay better than anything else ever has. *Or the fact that when she does eventually leave Red Bridge, I'm not sure how that'll feel.*

"Yeah. Okay. I think that's enough sad shit for the night," Breezy says, and she leans up to press a gentle kiss to my lips. "Sorry for being a Debbie Downer for a moment there."

"I'm glad you told me," I say, meaning every word, even though I *know* it's dangerous for me to feel anything when it comes to her.

"And I'm glad you told me about your mom."

All I can do is nod.

"By the way," she says and surprises me by reaching up and literally booping me on the nose like you would a cute dog. "We do have something important we need to discuss. Something very serious, actually."

I laugh, but it's a little nervous. "Okay..."

"We need code names."

I blink. "Code names?"

She grins up at me, and her face is all teasing sparkle again. "You know, for risky situations like when you have to call me on the phone and I'm in public. That way, I can be, like, 'Oh hey, *Tom*, so glad you called,' and all the Red Bridge busybodies will be none the wiser."

"Tom?" I laugh. "*That's* my code name?"

"I figured you'd like it better than Farm Daddy." She waggles her eyebrows. "Plus, you pull off being a Tom. Reliable. Steady. Probably owns too many flannels."

"I'm not so sure I'd peg me as reliable, but if I'm Tom, who are you?"

"Hmmm." She tilts her head to the side and taps her chin. "Has to be something close to Breezy. Belinda?"

"Feels too church choir."

"Bianca?"

"Too fancy. I don't think Bianca would want anything to do with reliable Tom."

"Oh, I know." Her grin widens. "*Betsy.* Short and sweet and kind of perfect, if you ask me."

"Betsy," I repeat, liking the way it slides off the tongue. "Okay, *Betsy*. How do you feel about a round two with Tom?"

"A round two?" She giggles, and I catch the sound with my mouth as I kiss the corner of her smile.

"Oh, come on, Betsy. You know Tom's dependable," I murmur against her lips. "You can *always* count on him."

That makes her laugh, full and unguarded, before she pulls

me in and kisses me deep.

And I let myself get lost in it. In her. In the way she looks at me like I'm not broken Tad, but steady, dependable Tom.

Which, yeah, is a dangerous fucking thing for a man like me to do.

22

Breezy

Friday, February 19th

The past month and a half that I've been flitting aimlessly about this small town, I seem to end more nights in Tad Hanson's bed than anywhere else. But tonight, I'm spending the evening at The Country Club.

And when I say *seem to,* that's clearly me lying to myself because let's be real, my primary hobby has been being a freak in his sheets.

Sex with Tad Hanson is out-of-this-world addictive.

Apparently, so are midnight pancakes with Tad. And dinner with Tad. And TV with Tad…

What can I say? The man's stupidly charming, dangerously easy to be around, and I'm a woman who's overdue for some fun.

Tonight, the bar's still packed, but instead of karaoke and beer-soaked dancing, it's poker night.

The lights aren't as dim as they usually are, and green felt-top tables are filling every nook and cranny of the bar. The hum of conversation blends with the clink of glasses and the shuffle of cards.

Poker night in Red Bridge is as close as you get to high society around here, and it's all for a good cause. Betty Bagley, self-appointed queen of small-town fundraising, announced earlier that tonight's buy-ins and side pots are going to "Operation Playground." Red Bridge Elementary's swings are evidently so rusted they look like tetanus on chains, and the town decided poker might be the fastest way to get the kids something safe to climb on.

One might've thought a bake sale would be more appropriate, but the people in this small town apparently prefer gambling to cupcakes.

My table is a mix of family and familiar faces. My brother Bennett sits to my left, looking like he'd rather be anywhere else, and Norah leans comfortably against him, playing with her chips like she's been doing this her whole life. Josie Harris is across from me, bright-eyed and competitive, and her husband Clay is dealing. Sheriff Peeler, Betty Bagley, Eileen Martin, and a few other townsfolk are at the next table over, already bickering about rules, and Marty Higgins is behind the bar, his wife Sheila perched on a stool beside him.

"Breezy, you play a lot of Texas Hold'em in New York?" Tad asks as he folds his hand to Clay. He's two seats down from me, and his broad shoulders are framed in flannel, while his forearms showcase strength from beneath rolled-up sleeves. His favorite faded ball cap is turned backward—which, damn, I'm starting to understand the appeal. Basically, he looks like sin in denim, and it's no wonder half the women in this small town want a piece.

Randy's wedged between us, grumbling over his cards, and I put on my most neutrally friendly face to look over him to meet Tad's eyes as I answer his question.

"Occasionally," I answer smoothly, glancing back at my cards like I'm easy peasy, cool and breezy, and haven't spent the last week sneaking into his bed every night. "But this is certainly my first time playing where my Hold'em skills can affect children."

He chuckles at that. "Small-town stakes are high."

"Who taught you how to play poker, Breezy?" Bennett asks, one brow raised.

I don't even hesitate. "Just some guy named Tom."

Across the table, Tad coughs into his ice water to cover a laugh, and I have to look away before my face gives me away. To be honest, ever since Norah told me I had to come to this little charity event a week ago, Tad has been teaching me how to play Texas Hold'em.

Mind you, most of the time we've been naked and in his bed, but lessons were definitely being had.

"Tom?" Bennett repeats slowly, his tone suspiciously casual. "Would that be the same *Tom* I've heard you on the phone with at night?"

Uh-oh. Maybe I've gotten a little too comfortable with those secret code names I made us choose two weeks ago. I freeze for half a second before I jump into offensive mode. "You're eavesdropping on my phone calls, Ben?"

"It's kinda hard not to hear your calls when you're cackling like a lunatic." Bennett smirks. "And when were you going to tell me you're seeing some dude named Tom?"

"I'm not *seeing* him," I say quickly. "He's just…uh, a business contact. Likes to call late because of the time difference."

"The time difference?" Bennett echoes. "Where's he based, Mars?"

"London," I blurt. "He's British."

Josie laughs into her drink. "A *British* Tom. How fancy. Maybe he should teach *me* poker."

"Slow your roll, woman," Clay interjects, and Josie just sticks her tongue out at him. "Shall I remind you I'm a very jealous man when it comes to you?"

"Oh, trust me, I know," Josie retorts. "You were the one who kept me married to you for five years against my will."

Clay just smiles. "And I still don't regret a single second of it."

"Me either." Josie leans over to press a playful kiss to his lips. "Macho man."

Clay waggles his brows. "Oh, I'll show you macho, baby."

"Get a room!" Norah shouts, a giggle on her lips. "We're trying to gamble for the kids here!"

Clay just chuckles and dives straight back into his dealer role.

The whole table breaks into easy laughter, chips clinking and cards shuffling again. It's loud and warm and full of small-town energy, but under it, there's something quieter. A pulse I can feel from two seats away, where Tad's shoulder shakes with silent laughter.

The bastard is loving that Bennett's overheard some of my phone calls with "Tom."

I send him a discreet glare, but he just meets my gaze, a slow, infuriating grin tugging at the corner of his mouth.

The smug bastard. I shake my head and smile despite myself.

To anyone else, Tad and I are just acquaintances. Just neighbors-of-neighbors, nodding and smiling politely, and occasionally teasing each other the way small-towners do.

But under the table, my phone buzzes against my thigh.

Tad: *Honestly, Betsy, I would've thought a New Yorker would've been better at bluffing…*

I school my face into neutrality, sliding two chips into the pot.

Me: *Well, Tom, I think it's safe to say you're shit at teaching. Also, I just saw your ass fold pocket queens three hands ago.*

Tad: *Maybe I just wanted to keep my hands free so I can text you about how fucking delicious your ass looks in those jeans.*

Tad: *PS: I've been imagining your thighs wrapped around my face all night.*

Heat rises in my cheeks, but I keep my gaze steady on the table.

Clay flips the river card and reveals a nine of hearts. The table hums with tension as it's quite clear that anyone holding two hearts in their hands is probably going to win this one. Norah pushes a small stack forward, Josie raises, and Bennett sighs like the tortured artist he is.

Randy mulls over his decision, alternating between cursing under his breath and staring at Josie across the table like he can see into her skull. My hand is utter garbage, and I definitely should fold, but I wait on Randy to decide his move.

Tad: *If I were you, I'd cut my losses. You and I both know your hand is shit.*

My head snaps up, but his face is unreadable. *How the hell?*

Me: *And how would you know that?*

Tad: *Because you've got "bad hand" written all over that pretty face.*

The urge to kick him under the table nearly wins, but once Randy folds on a curse, I follow his lead and fold my cards too, flashing a discreet scowl toward Tad.

Tad: *Don't be mad. I just saved you money.*

Me: *What if Josie's hand is shit too?*

Tad: *It's not.*

Me: *And how would you know that?*

Tad: *Because her knee is bouncing under the table. She's too fucking excited.*

Josie flips over her cards, revealing not just a flush, but a *straight* flush, and Norah groans when her sister whoops in excitement over her lesser-than flush.

"Jeez, Josie," Norah says on a groan. "You do remember this is for the kids, right? You're not pocketing the money."

"Yeah, but I can be excited for the kids and getting to kick my sister's ass at poker at the same time."

Norah sticks out her tongue at Josie, and Bennett chuckles as he wraps his arm around his wife.

"Nice hand, sweetheart," Clay says, and Josie turns her competitiveness up several notches.

"Oh, honey, you're next."

Clay just laughs and starts shuffling the cards, and my phone buzzes in my lap.

Tad: *Told you.*

I roll my eyes.

Me: *It's a shame your stack of chips over there doesn't showcase how good you think you are at poker.*

Tad: *I'm slow-rolling, woman. It's only a matter of time.*

"I'm going to sit out this hand," I tell Clay as I rise to my feet. "Need a quick bathroom break."

Clay nods and starts dealing to the rest of the table, and I don't miss the little smirk Tad flashes me as I head for the bathroom.

The hallway is quiet, a stark contrast to the buzz of the bar. I make quick work of using the restroom, and as I'm finishing washing and drying my hands, my phone buzzes in my jeans pocket.

I check the screen, expecting it to be a dirty text from Tad, but I'm stunned into silence when I find I have a voice mail from Logan.

Against my better judgment, I press play as I step back into the dim hallway.

"Breeze, it's me. Look, I know you hate me, and you feel betrayed and everything else. I know I'm the last person on the fucking planet you want to talk to, but I don't know what the fuck I'm doing here. I'm drowning. Everything is going tits up with the galleries. You're the only one who knows them inside and out. Just...call me back. Please. I'm begging you."

His voice cracks on the last word, and the ache that follows is sharp enough to steal my breath. I lean back against the wall, phone pressed tight to my chest.

There's a small part of me that wants to step in and save him. But the part of me that's tired of sacrificing myself for everyone else's needs prevents me from doing anything at all.

"You okay?"

My head jerks up, and there's Tad, half shadowed at the end of the hall. His gaze is steady, too steady, like he can see the crack in my armor even in the dim light.

I waver between telling him the truth or just keeping it surface-level. Deep down, I want to tell Tad everything. And boy oh boy, that's fucking scary.

Sure, one night I confessed to him about Logan and the galleries and how I ended up on hiatus in Red Bridge and he revealed fond memories about his mom, but that's not something we need to be doing all the time.

Frankly, we shouldn't be doing it all.

Because we're supposed to be casual.

We *are* casual.

"I'm fine," I eventually say and tuck my phone away.

He doesn't look convinced. He takes a step closer, then another, until his presence is a wall in front of me. "You sure? You don't look fine."

"It's nothing." I force a smile that doesn't quite fit.

For a second, I think he's going to press, dig deeper, and urge me to be vulnerable with him in ways I shouldn't be with a man I'm not in a serious relationship with.

But he doesn't do that at all.

He kisses me instead.

His mouth crashes against mine, and it's not gentle or teasing. It's hungry. It's raw. It's deep and powerful in a way that I can feel all the way to my bones.

His hand cups the side of my face, the other anchoring at my hip, and every part of me screams *yes*, even as logic whispers, *"we're just casual"* into my ear.

But the only thing I can do is kiss him back.

A little moan escapes my throat as I clutch at his shirt and pull him even closer to me. The world narrows to the taste of him, the feel of his tongue stroking mine, and the deep, throbbing ache between my thighs that's screaming for more.

"Ladies and gentlemen," Clay's voice booms over the speaker system, jolting us to abruptly end the kiss. "We're going to take a fifteen-minute break. Grab a drink, use the bathroom, and remember, if you're not back at your table in time, you're disqualified."

Instantly, footsteps start echoing down the hall as people spill from the poker room, and we break apart as quick as we can. We're both breathless, and our eyes are still locked like we've just been caught doing something forbidden.

Which is ridiculous, I know. We're both adults. We could walk right out there hand in hand, and no one could say a damn thing.

But there's a rush in the secrecy. An electric, dangerous thrill that makes my pulse skip and my knees a little weak and makes me want more.

More of his kiss. More of being in his bed. More of his hands on my body. More of *him* and the way he makes me feel.

Tad leans in, and his mouth just barely brushes my ear. "Betsy," he murmurs, low enough that only I can hear, "you better be in Tom's bed tonight."

A shiver dances down my spine.

By the time I walk back into the crowded poker room, my lips are still tingling and my pulse is doing its own wild shuffle.

As I slide back into my seat and catch Tad's grin from across the table, I remind myself what this is supposed to be.

Light. Casual. A distraction.

No strings. No stakes. No promises. That's the deal.

But the longer this game goes on, the harder it is to pretend I'm not tempted to go all in.

23

Tad

Monday, February 22nd

Snow comes down like it has a grudge against the entire state of Vermont. This winter has been a real bitch. I'm honestly starting to wonder if the universe has decided she wants to bury us until spring.

It's nearing four in the morning, and instead of being curled up in my bed with Breezy, I'm outside while she's still sleeping, handling the responsibility that comes with being a sheep farmer.

I could've called Randy, but I decided to let him stay in bed.

The snow switches from big, fat flakes to the tiny, relentless kind that stings your cheeks and finds the gap between your collar and your neck, no matter how tight you pull the zipper of your coat.

And with the way it's coming down now, by dawn, the world will be erased and redrawn in white. Which means every daily farm chore will be twice as fucking hard if I don't lay some groundwork now.

The only reason I'm up in the first place is because my girl Mabel is due to go into labor any day now, and the camera in the barn had my phone pinging with notifications of her restlessness.

Once I saw it was snowing cats and dogs, I decided to get up and get some work done while I kept an eye on her.

I'm breaking ice on the troughs with the back of a shovel when the wind shifts and carries a thin, high bleat across the pasture.

"Shit."

Instantly, I drop the shovel and start for the barn in the lower field. My boots crunch through drifts that've swallowed the fence posts up to their bellies, and the rest of my herd is huddled like a gray cloud near the line of spruce trees. They're clearly too annoyed with the snow to try to escape, and their bodies are pressed so tight that steam comes off them in a faint cloud.

Another cry cuts the air as I'm rounding the last gate and heading into the barn.

And there she is, my poor girl Mabel, lying in the hay. Her sides are rippling, and her breath is fogging the air hard. Immediately, I see the problem—one slick lamb leg is already out and appears to be stuck.

"Easy there. I'm here." I crouch near her and place my palm to her neck. She's warm and trembling. "You had to pick a blizzard, huh?"

Mabel bleats in discomfort.

"Don't worry, girl. I got you, okay?"

As I start to assess the situation, the sounds of quick footsteps crunching in the snow fill my ears. I glance over my shoulder to spot Breezy sliding across the front of the barn doors and literally slip on the ice, falling to her ass on an *"Oof!"*

She gets to her feet with ease, and I quickly realize she's dressed in my biggest coat, my flannel underneath, my sweatpants covering her legs, and my wool hat slouched over her head. The outfit and my boots damn near swallow her, and it shouldn't work at all. But somehow, I don't think I've ever seen her look so fucking beautiful.

"What are you doing up?" I ask as she steps into the barn.

"I saw the barn notifications on your phone and figured it was Mabel." She holds up a roll of paper towels and a few bathroom towels like an offering to the gods. "I tried to bring supplies, but I don't really know what supplies you need. Also, I almost died on your front steps, so we probably need to salt them."

"Noted." I try not to smile. "You okay in that?" I nod at the coat that's practically a sleeping bag.

"Um...pretty sure I look adorable," she says, dead serious. "Extremely capable and adorable to help with bringing a new baby sheep into the world."

Another contraction hits Mabel. She moans, long and low.

"Is she okay?" Breezy's face changes on a dime. "What do you need?"

"Your small hands," I say, and her brows jump. "Clean ones. You're gonna help me."

"I...okay." There's the briefest flicker of *really?* in her eyes, and then she's kneeling beside me as I quickly shove the paper towels at her.

I slide my palm along Mabel's belly, checking the angle of the leg. "We've got a shoulder hung up," I tell Breezy. "If she pushes and it's turned wrong, she could tear something. So we gotta stop that from happening."

"And by *we,* you mean...?"

"Well, you, because your hands are smaller than mine." I tug off a glove and guide Breezy's smaller fingers where mine can't go. "Just follow my hand. When she pushes, don't fight. Just ride it. Assist her. Give some counterpressure so the lamb's leg goes in the direction we need it."

"O-okay."

"And don't forget to breathe."

"Don't forget to breathe, Mabel," she encourages, and a short laugh escapes my lungs.

"You," I say. "I meant you shouldn't forget to breathe."

"Oh." She swallows, eyes fixed on Mabel, and nods. "Me. Breathe. Right."

The wind hisses through the barn, and Mabel moans again. Her body bows with the contraction, and Breezy does exactly what I need her to do. She rides the push, giving counterpressure where Mabel needs it. The stuck shoulder turns a hair, then another hair, and I feel the moment it gives in the ewe's body—a tiny click the world might miss if you weren't touching it.

"There," I say, and I don't realize I'm actually holding my breath until I'm light-headed.

The lamb slides free into my hands, slick and steaming in the cold air, a beautiful little miracle covered in blood and fluid. I clear its nose, rub hard with Breezy's paper towels until a tremor runs through its body, and then the little thing gasps like it's offended by the whole concept of oxygen.

"It's breathing!" Breezy exclaims through a choked sob.

"Welcome to earth, kid," I tell the lamb, which replies by sneezing on my chin. "Now, we need to get her under Mabel's nose."

Breezy and I work fast to position the little girl lamb near its mother. And once she's under Mabel's chin, she's already lifting her head to her mama and licking with single-minded determination.

But when another contraction rolls through Mabel, I know we need to focus again.

"It's time for the next one," I say, and Breezy looks at me with teary-eyed confusion.

"The next one?"

"Twins."

Breezy blinks but quickly jumps back into action with me as I give her clear instructions on how to assist Mabel.

We're faster the second time. Breezy's hands don't shake. She doesn't flinch at the steam or the blood or the way Mabel releases guttural sounds with each contraction. She just does the work, and she does so with the kind of bravery that makes me feel proud of her.

Ten minutes later, there are two little lambs blinking at the blizzard like it personally inconvenienced them, wobbling to their feet under a mother who looks outright exhausted.

Breezy helps me get them all tucked in straw to keep them insulated, and by the time we're done, my body aches in a good way.

"You did amazing," I tell Breezy, wrapping my arm around her shoulders and tucking her into my side as we watch Mabel with her lambs.

Her grin hits me square in the chest. "*We* did amazing. But also, I did amazing."

"Yeah." I grin. "You did."

"But you were incredible too, Tad," she says, her voice quiet. "If you hadn't known what to do, I don't like to think about what could have happened."

I shrug. "I guess there are some aspects of sheep farming I'm good at."

We trudge back toward the house, boots squeaking, and a red scarf Breezy grabbed at the last second flapping out of my coat that covers her body. For a second, the flash of red steals my breath. *Red. Sirens. Heat. The—*

No.

I blink hard, and it's just a scarf again, just snow, just Breezy bumping her hip against mine and saying, "Admit it, Farmer Tad. You need me on staff."

"And how much do I gotta pay ya?" I ask.

"I accept payment in pancakes, orgasms, and your mother's marinara," she says through a giggle.

Inside, the house fogs up with the sudden invasion of two people and a storm. I shuck my coat, take hers, and hang them both near the door. She toes out of boots that are five sizes too big and shivers dramatically, then beelines for the kettle like she owns the place.

Once we've got two mugs of hot water, I doctor hot chocolate with a finger of whiskey. She takes one sip, and a combination of a cough and laugh leaves her lungs. "You trying to get me drunk?"

"I'm trying to take the edge off," I explain. "There's not even a shot in each of our mugs, but I promise it'll help take the shakes away."

The last time I drank whiskey, drank any alcohol at all, was shortly after Breezy came strolling into town in a blizzard and I was so shit-faced I didn't know if we slept together. I guess I haven't had the need to reach for it to numb the pain.

Truthfully, I only put it in our hot chocolates because of the way Breezy's hands have been shaking since we helped Mabel bring her lambs into the world.

"Oh, so the fact that I feel like my body is vibrating from the inside out is normal?"

"It's the adrenaline." I smile knowingly at her. "Happens whenever you find yourself in an emergent situation."

"You find yourself in a lot of sheep emergencies?"

The mere thought of an emergency has the always-in-pain, masochistic side of my brain wanting to fold like a deck of cards. But I take a sip of my hot chocolate and refuse to give in. "Well, you know how Crosby can be."

"I sure do." Breezy laughs.

In this moment with her, it's easy to forget the farm exists. To forget fences and sheep and the ghosts of my past and all the ways a life can go sideways. It's easy to just be. *With her.*

We make our way into the living room, curling up together on the couch.

Her phone buzzes on my coffee table, which has both of us looking puzzled at someone texting her at such a late hour. But when she grabs it to check the screen, she lets out an exasperated groan. "You've got to be freaking kidding me."

"Who is it?"

Her mouth twists into a smile, but it's more annoyed than amused. "Heyyy, so I was thinking of hosting a memorial party in Ibiza. Henry would've loved that. Do you want to help plan?" she reads the message aloud before turning the screen for me to see.

There's a little champagne glass emoji. A sun. A palm tree. Three question marks. The kind of punctuation you'd expect from a teenage girl.

"That from Stepmother Dearest?"

"Yep," she says, voice flat. "Twenty-seven going on fourteen."

She laughs in a sharp burst, but it shatters on the second breath. Her eyes go wet, and she tips her head back like she can stop emotional gravity. "What an incredible idea, right? A memorial party…in Ibiza. I mean, we already had a funeral, and a will-reading where my father completely fucked me over, but sure, who needs grief or closure when you can have bottle service?" she says, but it's to the ceiling.

"Breezy." I set my mug down. "Hey." I gently press my hand to her thigh, but she flinches a little.

"I'm fine, I swear." She drags a sleeve over her eyes. "It's just, some days, it's like… How am I almost forty, and I don't know what I want? I used to have a plan for everything. Now I'm—" she gestures around "—wearing your clothes and delivering lambs and making zero plans for my future because I don't know what I'm doing anymore, and instead of telling anyone how I really feel, I ignore their stupid voice mails and calls and texts like a coward."

"Or like a person who has been betrayed. A person who has been hurt deeply," I say. "A person who doesn't deserve any of that bullshit, and despite all of it, somehow still manages to remain strong."

"Strong?" She snorts. "That's debatable."

"No, it's not, Breeze." I reach out and tuck a piece of hair behind her ear before grazing my knuckles gently down her cheek. "You're incredible, Breezy. You're strong and intelligent and brave. You're quite literally the opposite of a coward. I mean, you didn't have to come out there in that storm," I remind her. "You didn't have to help me deliver those lambs, but you did. Because you're amazing. Because you're an incredible person. Because you're the kind of fucking person we all strive to be."

Her eyes find mine, and something in them softens. "You

always say the right thing."

"I don't think it's so much that I say the right things, Breezy. I think it's more that you're simply one of the most amazing people I've ever known."

"That's really...sweet."

"Well, it's the truth," I tell her and mean every fucking word. "Now, how about you ignore that text message, for tonight at least, and focus on the very important task you still need to do?"

She quirks a brow. "And what exactly would that task be?"

"You helped bring two baby lambs into the world. And that means you get naming rights."

Her face brightens. "I get to name them?"

I nod.

"Holy moly...okay...no pressure, huh?" She thinks it over carefully before finally saying, "Tom."

"Tom?"

"Uh-huh." A big smile stretches across her face. "Tom."

"And the other lamb?"

"Also Tom."

I chuckle. "Breezy, the other one is a girl."

"I'm just messing with you," she says, and her voice is light and airy and happy in the way that makes me grin. "Obviously, her name is Betsy."

"Tom and Betsy?"

"Yep." She nods. "Tom and Betsy."

Breezy sets down her mug and slides closer to me until her knee is propped up on my thigh and the hem of my flannel rides up her leg. Her hand rests on my sternum, just above where my heart is already starting to increase in rhythm inside my chest.

She doesn't say anything at first. Just looks at me. Really looks. The kind of look that feels like she might have the power to see past everything I've built to keep people out.

Her voice is soft when it finally comes. "You make it easy to forget what I came here to figure out."

"Maybe that's not such a bad thing." *Because she does the*

exact same thing for me.

Her mouth curves up, but it's not a smile; it's something smaller and more fragile.

She responds by leaning in and kissing me.

It's not the grab-and-burn of the hallway or the kitchen or every other place we've tried to outrun ourselves. It's slower. Steadier. More intense in a way I can't put my finger on.

Heat follows, because it always does. She tastes like chocolate and whiskey and the kind of trouble you choose on purpose, but underneath it all runs an undeniable current. One that I won't let myself name.

The snowstorm continues to drum on the roof. Somewhere far off, a plow passes.

But inside the house, it's just us.

Breezy smiles against my mouth, and I kiss her deeper as I rise to my feet and carry her into my bedroom.

I want and need to be with her tonight. *And tomorrow night. And the next night after that.*

Every time I'm with her, every time I touch her, every time I kiss her, the world feels lighter.

For a man who swore he'd never get too close to the sun again, I know I'm doing a piss-poor job of keeping that promise.

But it's like I can't fucking stop.

24

Breezy

Tuesday, March 9th

Norah has been nudging me about this headhunter call.

She hasn't exactly been pushy, but she's definitely offered quiet reminders and soft encouragements, all while juggling Bennett's stuff and Autumn's adorable chaos with the kind of grace that makes me wonder if she ever actually sleeps.

"Just take the call, Breeze," she'd said more than once. *"It doesn't hurt to listen."*

And I brushed her off each time, because why would I want to listen? I walked away from that world. Technically, I buried it with my father when he buried me in his betrayal.

But the art world isn't letting me off the hook so easily. Everyone knows my name. Everyone knows what I built.

And according to Norah, who still very much has her toes

dipped in the art world water because of Bennett, there are a lot of people out there who want a piece of me now that Bishop Galleries stopped calling dibs.

"I don't know how that headhunter got my number or email, but with the way he's been hounding me over getting a chance to speak with you, I feel like you need to give in to his desperation. Maybe use it to your advantage, you know? He probably has some opportunities worth hearing. Maybe even ones that spur a little excitement in ya."

That was the one statement that came out of Norah's mouth that ended in me scheduling a Zoom appointment with the headhunter who wouldn't leave my sister-in-law alone.

Though, I did let two more weeks of time fly by in Red Bridge before I hit send on the email to him. And fourteen more days in this small town have been a blur of snow and Tad Hanson. Nights in his bed and mornings sneaking back across the yard and afternoons lost to laughter in his barn.

Besides when I'm spending time with Autumn, most of my time goes to him.

Sleeves rolled up, boots borrowed, and pretending I know what the hell I'm doing, I've even started hanging around the Hanson Farm during the day *without* trying to hide it.

Randy eyed me suspiciously the first time I showed up, leaning against a fence post like I might faint if a sheep sneezed too hard. But Tad shrugged and said, "Breezy has been kind enough to offer us some temporary help while she's in town."

I'm not so sure Randy bought that story, but he didn't question it. He went about his usual farming business. Though, he's yet to assign me any chores or tasks. If anything, he keeps his distance.

And my fake gig as a temporary helper on the Hanson Farm has become the official story.

When I started disappearing for full days and coming home smelling faintly like hay and sin, I had to tell Bennett and Norah *something.*

So now they think I'm helping the Hanson brothers with farm

chores like some kind of city-girl-does-manual-labor redemption arc. It honestly sounds like a plot from a Hallmark movie more than real life, but whatever.

Nothing about life feels real or predictable these days.

Of course, Bennett's reaction was a mix of annoyance and hilarity. He's never been a fan of Tad Hanson. Pretty sure being neighbors with a sheep farmer whose sheep never stay behind the fence is at the foundation of that ire. But after he'd bitched a while about how incompetent Farmer Tad is, he couldn't stop himself from laughing at my expense. "Breezy Bishop, cleaning up sheep shit?" he'd choked out. "I fear Red Bridge might be going to your brain, sis. If you hang around here any longer, you might end up selling scarves at the farmer's market."

He's not even wrong in his teasing. I mean, *maybe Red Bridge is going to my brain?*

However, what my brother doesn't know would probably kill him. I mean, if there are any fresh callouses on my hands, they have nothing to do with mucking stalls and everything to do with clutching Farmer Tad's bedsheets.

And trust me, my brother does *not* want to know that information.

Tad even tried to pay me money once, really make the cover story seem real, and I laughed in his face. "The only currency I'll take comes in orgasms and late-night cuddles," I told him.

He wasn't exactly upset about that. Managed to give me three orgasms that very night, in fact.

Basically, I'm living a double life—fake farmhand by day and shameless sheep farmer groupie by night. But when it comes to real jobs, today, I'm officially giving the relentless headhunter my listening ears.

The house is quiet since Norah and Bennett took Autumn over to Josie and Clay's house to have brunch. And I'm as ready as I'll ever be for this call, sitting cross-legged on my bed with my laptop propped on a stack of art books.

On a deep breath, I tap the trackpad, and Zoom flickers to life.

A man in expensive glasses and a perfectly knotted tie appears, smiling as we make eye contact through the screen.

"Beatrice Bishop," he says warmly. "My name is David Smith. It's very nice to finally meet you."

"Nice to meet you too, David. And please, you can just call me Breezy," I correct, plastering on my most friendly smile.

"Of course. Breezy." He consults his notes, the glow of his screen reflecting off his frames. "Let's get down to business and talk opportunities. I'm honestly not sure if I've ever had someone get so many offers at one time. Needless to say, the interest for you has been significant. MoMA is seeking a Senior Curator of Contemporary Works. Art Basel has an opening for Global Acquisitions. And a foundation in London is *very* interested. Excellent salary, extensive travel, and as you know, quite the prestige."

He continues rattling off more job opportunities, and I nod in the right places, hands laced tight in my lap.

Frankly, each job should thrill me. At twenty-five, I would've killed for them. At thirty, I did the work of all those titles combined. But at thirty-nine, listening to him list them kind of feels like hearing the door of a prison cell slide shut.

"So...what do you think, Breezy?" David asks, steepling his hands on his desk.

"They all sound...good," I manage, but my voice sounds flat to my own ears. I clear my throat and try to add a little pep in my step. "Great, even."

"I thought they were all pretty great too," he says, already typing. "How about I push your name forward, and we can arrange some conversations as soon as next week? I think that's what will really help you figure out where you want to land."

All I can do is nod, even though, deep down, I don't want to bother with any of it.

When the call ends, I close the laptop harder than necessary and sit in the hush of the room. My chest feels hollow, my throat is dry, and my stomach is aching with nausea. Not to mention, my head is spinning like a top.

I'm not so sure diving back into the art world is where I want to be.

Not so sure? Feels like the nausea is a pretty telltale sign of your true feelings.

I grab my phone to take it off silent and see if Tad sent me any texts, but I find three missed calls from Logan. They're stacked on the screen like bricks, and a new voice mail banner is highlighted at the top.

I stare at it for a long moment before I press play.

"Breeze, it's me. Logan. You know, the brother you hate and refuse to talk to." His voice is raw and stressed in a way I'm not used to hearing. *"Look, I... This is bad. I'm drowning here. The board's on me, the attorneys won't stop calling, I don't even know half the fucking curators' names. All I know is they're not happy at all. They don't want to work for me. They want to work for you. I'm supposed to be on location in Santa Fe in three months, and there is no fucking way I can keep up with this. I've already had to cancel photo shoots and press junkets and a million other fucking things. Please. Help me."*

The message ends abruptly, as if Logan were in the middle of cursing at someone before he had the sense to hang up.

After all the years I needed someone and did it alone, and *now* someone needs me?

After I've been kicked out of my own life, out of the empire that I was holding up for the past twenty years, *now* someone acknowledges what I achieved?

Not to mention, I had to hear about all the shit *he's* had to sacrifice for galleries that should be *mine.*

Anger bubbles up from my belly and makes my throat burn.

Because, fuck you, Logan. Fucking fuck you.

But something heavier edges in behind the rage. It's not exactly sympathy, but a tired ache where love and family used to sit. As pathetic as it is for me to feel this, I don't get satisfaction in hearing Logan suffer. I don't get any sort of vindication in hearing that everything I built up with my bare fucking hands is slowly crumbling into chaos.

I set my phone facedown on the comforter of my bed like I can smother the sound of his now-nonexistent voice with cotton.

Outside my bedroom window, a drift slumps off the porch rail in a soft, collapsing sigh. And I let the hush swallow me for a full minute before swiping Logan's voice mail into the trash.

Not today. Not now. *And maybe not ever.*

I pull on a hoodie I stole from Tad the other day—warm from the radiator and faintly smelling like him—and head for the kitchen. I need coffee. I need air. I need something that isn't a title or a plea.

Later, maybe, I'll figure out what I want. For now, I want the world to stop asking.

For now, I want to distract myself, and I know two little lambs by the names of Tom and Betsy that always bring a smile to my face.

It's not long before I'm pulling on my boots and heading out the front door, across Bennett's yard and straight to the farmhouse I'm starting to know like the back of my hand.

Straight to the sheep farmer, huh, Breeze?

This is really starting to seem like a pattern…

25

Tad

Breezy and I were working out on the farm all day. Well, *I* was working my ass off cleaning up the stalls in the barn, and she stayed busy playing with Tom and Betsy. The little lambs follow her around like she's their second mother. Hell, even Mabel gets excited whenever she sees Breezy arrive on the farm. But that's probably because she's just happy for a little break from her constantly bleating babies wanting to nurse from her every five seconds.

Randy, Bennett and Norah, Clay and Josie, and whatever other nosy busybody who's inside this small town have been made to believe Breezy has taken a job as a Hanson farmhand.

It was Breezy's big idea, said it was a means to an end to keep her brother and Norah off her trail. And since it gives me unfettered access to her, I went right along with it.

But I know how word spreads around these parts, so I wouldn't be surprised if Eileen Martin shows up tomorrow morning demanding the inside scoop for an article.

Now, we're in my bed, and Breezy lies beside me, propped on one elbow with her phone in hand and her thumb flicking as emails slide past her screen. The sheets are tangled around her waist, her hair still damp from the shower she took before dinner, and she's glowing in that effortless way that makes me want to stop time.

But her face is tight with focus and thoughts.

"You all right?"

She sighs, tossing the phone onto the mattress like it weighs too much. "You want to hear something crazy?"

I tilt my head toward her. "Always."

She lets out a short, humorless laugh. "Since the call with the headhunter today, I've had offers pouring in. London wants me for a foundation position. The MET's sniffing around about curation. MoMA's circling. Even Art Basel and galleries in Chicago, LA, San Francisco all want meetings." She pinches the bridge of her nose. "I haven't answered any of them yet."

I don't know about any of the shit she's talking about, but I know enough to know that when her words come out of her lips, they should sound like triumph. But all I hear is defeat.

I keep my mouth shut for a second, because when I hear her mention places like London and San Francisco, a sharp, uncomfortable ache spreads like a vine inside my chest. And my mind whispers, *Don't go, Breezy. Stay here in Red Bridge.*

It's fucking selfish, I know. It's selfish that I want her to stay in this bed where her hair smells like my shampoo and her laugh fills my otherwise-quiet house. It's selfish that I want her to stay in Red Bridge where I can see her nearly every morning, hear her tease Randy while he chases sheep around the farm, and watch her make my world bigger without even trying.

It's selfish because I know I'm a broken fucking man and I can't give her anything worth getting in return.

I swallow it all down and force myself to focus on things that make sense.

"Sounds like the art world's rolling out the red carpet," I finally say, keeping my voice light. "Clearly, they know talent when they see it."

"Yeah, I guess so." She sinks back against the pillow. "And you'd think after twenty years of killing myself to keep Bishop Galleries thriving, I'd want this. That I'd want to prove what I'm capable of to myself and anyone who doubted me. But..." Her shoulders lift in a helpless shrug. "I don't know. The thought of packing up, starting over, diving headfirst into a new career that will demand all my time and energy..." She trails off, shaking her head. "I feel...tired."

I shift onto my side, close enough to see the three tiny freckles scattered across her cheekbones.

"Sometimes I don't even know who I am without the galleries," she murmurs.

Damn if it doesn't gut me to see a woman as perfect and beautiful and smart and funny as Breezy Bishop look like she doesn't know where she belongs. She deserves more than that. She *is* more than that.

"You're more than a job title, Breezy," I say quietly. "More than a gallery or a city. More than the art world. Don't forget that."

"I don't know if you're right about that." Her throat works as she swallows, and for a second, I think she might cry. Instead, she presses her forehead against my chest. I wrap my arms around her without thinking and pull her tight against me.

"Breezy, you're the woman who helped me deliver twin lambs in a snowstorm," I whisper into her hair. "The woman who can make Randy stop bitching, which is a damn miracle, by the way. You're an amazing aunt to Autumn. You're an amazing sister and sister-in-law to Bennett and Norah. My sheep listen to you more than they listen to me, and Crosby refuses to take off that fucking yellow scarf you knitted because I honestly think he believes the two of you are dating in his pea-sized little brain."

A soft laugh bubbles up from her throat.

"Breezy, you're the incredible woman who everyone in town is happy to see. Including me. You're intelligent and beautiful and bossy as hell, but fuck, I think you're pretty goddamn great." *Just your smile alone has the ability to make me forget how fucking broken I am.*

"Thanks. Really. That means a lot." That earns me a small smile, and it's all I need to tip her chin up, brush my thumb along her jaw, and kiss her.

The kiss is soft and lingering and something that feels like a promise even though I can't give her one. She slides her hand up my chest, fingers curling into me like she's holding on for more than just tonight.

I roll her beneath me, easing the phone out of reach, and when she looks up at me with those big blue eyes of hers, I silently fear that I'll never be ready for her to choose London or Miami or anywhere that isn't *here*.

Which makes me the world's biggest asshole because I can't give her more than these fleeting moments of time.

I kiss her again, deeper this time, because it's the only way I know how to keep her close without asking her to stay.

26

Breezy

Friday, March 12th

If there's one thing I've learned about Red Bridge, it's that these people can turn absolutely anything into a holiday.

And tonight is evidence of that fact.

It's the town's tenth annual *Winter Line Dancing Festival,* which isn't even an actual holiday and lands a mere eight days away from spring on the calendar.

No one outside Red Bridge has ever heard of it, but tonight, Clay's bar is packed shoulder to shoulder like it's Mardi Gras. Apparently, it's a Red Bridge tradition for everyone to get together to celebrate winter's last gasp by stomping boots in unison to whatever fiddle music the band cranks out.

I can't decide if it's ridiculous or charming. Maybe both.

The air is thick with beer and fried food. Josie's behind the bar with Clay, and a big smile is on her face as she teases her husband in between pours. Bennett and Norah have already claimed a table, Autumn sitting between them in her pink cowgirl boots with a Shirley Temple and a pile of maraschino cherries. Sheriff Peeler is making the rounds, clapping everyone on the back like he's grand marshal of the parade.

And I'm standing off to the side of the dance floor, half amused and half wondering if I should get the hell out of here before I end up line dancing with Mayor Wallace.

"Fancy seeing you here." I know the voice before I see his face and turn to find Tad standing beside me, a grin of pure confidence on his face. "Dance with me, Miss Bishop?" His hand is already outstretched like he knows damn well I'll take it.

I arch a brow, playing along. "Isn't that against boss-employee relations?"

Tad leans in, close enough that his breath stirs the hair at my ear. "Don't worry. I won't tell the sheep."

Before I can answer, a voice cuts through the crowd.

"*Beatrice Bishop!*"

I turn to find Eileen striding over to us, a notebook in her hand and her eyes alight with bulldog focus.

Oh, here we go.

Once she closes the distance, I don't hesitate to tease her. "Eileen, I don't think now is the time to be harassing people for an article you will undoubtedly embellish and dramatize."

Eileen ignores the dig and gets straight to the point. "Oh, honey, it's always time for that. Rain or shine or festival. And since you're here tonight, I'd be remiss in my duties as Red Bridge's most trusted reporter if I didn't ask you how life on the Hanson Farm is? Word on the street is that you're working there nowadays?"

I smile sweetly, already knowing exactly what I'm doing. "Oh, you know, Eileen. It's been *very* hands on."

Her brows shoot up. "Hands on?"

"Mm-hmm. Early mornings. Long nights. A lot of...manual labor." I pause long enough to let the innuendo hang between us. "But I'm adjusting. My boss is an excellent teacher."

"And Breezy is an excellent student. Very hands-on kind of woman. Always up for a challenge," Tad chimes in, and Eileen's eyes go so wide I fear her eyeballs might pop out of her skull.

"Good with her hands?" Eileen chokes out. "Please expand."

"There's not much to expand," he says. "She's a real natural… with the flock. A real go-getter."

I have to bite my lip to fight my laughter. But I also can't stop myself from adding to the mental fucking Eileen is currently getting. "Well, I couldn't do it without my boss's very thorough training or the way he insists on such *close* supervision."

"This is all very...fascinating." Eileen's pen flies across the page. "Local art dealer trades city life for sheep and…uh…hands-on…*mentorship.* Does this mean you'll be staying in Red Bridge longer…maybe *permanently?"*

Well, *shit.* Apparently, she's turning the tables on me.

I clear my throat, my heart and mind completely at war with the answer to that question. "Oh, I don't—"

"I think what Breezy is trying to say here is that she wants to enjoy the rest of the night now," Tad interjects with a smile. "Been real nice chatting with ya, though, Eileen. Be sure to make the headline a good one." He winks. "Something like *Bishop Gets Down and Dirty on the Hanson Farm* feels apt. But hell, what do I know? You're the brilliant reporter, right?"

Eileen, scandalized and thrilled all at once, clutches her notebook to her chest like it's holy scripture. "I'll definitely take that into consideration."

The moment she's moved on from us and to some other poor soul in the bar, Tad bursts out laughing. "Hands-on training? Way to bury the lede. I thought we were trying to keep our dirty deeds on the down-low."

"Oh, like you should talk." I'm glaring and smiling at him at the same time. "That headline suggestion is going to have everyone in town thinking I'm sleeping with you *and* Randy again."

Tad cracks up. "Hey, I was just rolling with *your* punches, Betsy. And man, oh man, you sure rocked Eileen Martin hard with the *close supervision* line."

"I didn't know you were going to take it up fifty notches by suggesting a *Breezy gets down and dirty* headline!" I whisper-yell, but I'm also laughing. "You're insufferable."

He waggles his brows. "And yet you keep showing up for *work*."

"Must be the benefits package," I answer with a knowing, devious smile. "Though, I do regret that I forgot to tell her that my boss makes me call him Farm Daddy."

"Woman, you're trouble." He chuckles, the sound rolling deep and warm in my chest, and before I can blink, he takes my hand and pulls me into the crush of dancers.

The fiddle kicks into something fast and wild. Boots pound. The floor trembles. Tad's hands find my waist, guiding me through steps I clearly don't know, and I'm laughing so hard I can't even care.

"Left foot, Bishop!" he shouts.

I accidentally step right and crash into Sheriff Peeler, who gives me a friendly pat before spinning off again. Tad keeps me on my feet with a steady and sure hand at my hip.

"Easy," he teases. "Or else my new farmhand is about to embarrass the whole Hanson Farm. What would Crosby think if he found out his girlfriend can't do a two-step?"

"Oh, shut up. I'm trying over here!" I shoot back through a cackle. "It's not my fault you have ginormous feet!"

Tad waggles his brows, a devious grin striking his lips, and I roll my eyes. However, what I don't do is refute whatever gutter his mind has crawled into. I've seen and experienced his cock, and I'd be a liar if I didn't say he lives up to the *big feet equals big dick* saying.

A month ago, I would've been paranoid that everyone was going to see through our "we're just friendly game," but after my teasing conversation with Eileen and the fact that I'm dancing with Tad Hanson in the middle of a town festival that isn't even real, that must prove I currently do not give a single shit what people think.

Maybe it's the two glasses of wine I consumed when I got here.

Maybe it's the ambiance of this silly festival.

Or maybe it's the man who looks like sin in a pair of jeans and is currently smiling down at me as he twirls me around the floor.

Tad's hand brushes my hip as he spins me around again, his boots pounding the beat, and I try like hell to keep up. We fall into the rhythm badly, but we're laughing so hard it doesn't matter.

And I'm not thinking about New York. Or the galleries. Or the headhunter who emailed me again this morning with job offers in Milan and Chicago and Rome. I'm just…here.

Living. Laughing. *Feeling.*

My phone buzzes in my pocket. I ignore it at first, until Tad dips me low on the last note and the crowd erupts in claps and whistles. When I sneak a glance, the screen glows with a name I don't want to see.

Logan: *What do I have to do to get you to talk to me, Breeze?*

I slide the phone back into my pocket, shoving Logan back into the dark corners of my brain. Because tonight, under these string lights with fiddle music roaring and Tad's grin daring me to keep up, I don't owe anyone anything.

This night belongs to me.

The song changes, the beat faster, and Tad leans down so close his lips brush my temple. "Need you in my bed tonight."

It's more of a demand than anything else. *But you fucking love it.*

I've never been anywhere that actually felt like home. When I was a teenage girl and my parents were going through a divorce, I chose to go to boarding school to escape the madness. And as an adult, my life in New York wasn't exactly cozy. Busy? Definitely. But cozy in a way that it makes you want to curl up on the couch and stay a while? Not even close.

But this small town is starting to crawl under my skin. It's starting to pull me under the comfy quilt of its quirky charm and funny gossip and easy chatter and sexy sheep farmers whose laughs and smiles and dirty talk breathe some life into my veins.

And *oh man*, I can't decide if that's something I should feel happy about or straight-up terrified.

27

Tad

Saturday, March 13th

The house feels wrong without her.

But it's not because Breezy's loud in a way that demands attention. Hell, she's graceful as fuck. Half the time, she moves like a cat, barefoot and soft, humming nonsense under her breath while she raids my fridge or steals my clothes.

I don't know what it is about her presence in my house, but the place breathes differently whenever she's around.

Tonight, the air feels too thin. Like half the oxygen has been sucked out.

Norah and Bennett had to make an overnight run for some art thing for Bennett, so Breezy's at their house in the room Autumn calls "Bee's woom," probably with a toddler foot dug into her ribs and a cartoon murmuring low on the television.

And I've gotten so accustomed to her being in my bed that I kind of feel like one of my limbs is missing, but I tell myself it's good she's spending time with her niece.

Still, the quiet sits on my chest like a brick house.

I try to make myself useful. I try to find remnants of my old evening routine before Breezy started staying here most nights. I make a lap through the kitchen and open the fridge, but when nothing inside it urges an appetite, I close it.

Though I keep standing in the kitchen anyway, I have zero desire for food. I even grab my phone off the counter and see if I have any missed messages from Breezy. There's nothing to be found besides my lock screen with the time and date staring me back in the face.

Saturday, March 13th

11:58 p.m.

My tongue goes dry.

I look away from my phone. And then I look back. 11:59 p.m.

The house hums with noise—the fridge, the baseboards, and the wind sweeping across the roof. Under it, though, something starts up in me I don't invite. A faint ringing. Heat where there isn't any. The sharpest whiff of smoke that is absolutely not in my kitchen, not in this life.

I wish Breezy would text me something silly to yank me out of it. A simple *Hey, Farm Daddy* would do. But when I thumb my phone awake again and pull up our ongoing text thread, the photo of Autumn in tiny cowgirl boots she sent me a few hours ago stares back at me. Still, my fingers hover over the keyboard long enough to feel stupid about it until I set the phone back on my counter.

The last thing I'm going to do is text her and risk waking up her and Autumn. That'd be cruel. That'd be fucking selfish.

I'm not even trying to look at my phone, but the date and time on the screen manage to pull my attention.

Sunday, March 14th

12:00 a.m.

Every muscle in my body goes tight like they got the memo

first. My breath pulls short, my ribs constrict, and the refrigerator hum becomes a siren a mile away. The kitchen light is suddenly too bright, and I have to squint to cope with it.

Sweat starts to bead at my forehead, and I brace both hands on the counter. *Officially ten years. You'd think that number would blunt it.* It doesn't. The body remembers what the mind can't stand to.

Out. I need out.

Boots. Keys. Coat. Door. The cold night air hits my face sharp and clean, but all I can taste is ash on my tongue. The farm is a hunched shadow, fences and bare trees and the squat dark of the feed shed. For a split second, I swear I see a lick of orange behind my eyes, and then I blink and it's gone.

But I'm already moving, in my truck and out of my driveway, ten miles per hour faster than I should.

I don't know where I'm driving until I get there.

And I park in the familiar lot I've left my truck in overnight hundreds of times.

When I step inside, The Country Club is jam-packed with laughter and live music and people drinking and dancing and having a good time.

The door shuts behind me, and the noise thumps my bones. It's too much and exactly what I came for all at the same time.

Clay looks up from behind the bar and does a double take. "Well, I'll be damned. Didn't expect you tonight, Hanson."

"Figured I'd grace you with my presence," I say, and my voice sounds like it's been dragged over gravel. I grab a stool and plant my ass on it. "Whiskey."

He studies me a half second longer than I like. "You sure about that?"

"Just one," I lie. *It's never just one.*

The first glass slides down easy, and I finish it off in two small gulps. The second bites a little meaner, like the booze is trying to remind me I'm still here.

By the third, I stop tasting and start forgetting. *Thank fuck.*

The band drops into a fiddle run that makes the room clap along, but the music kind of turns to static white noise in my head. Somebody laughs too loud. Somebody hollers, "Hell yeah!" But it all feels far away. Like I'm hearing everything from underwater.

Clay sets the fourth down and doesn't let go of the glass for a moment. "You're really making up for lost time, huh?"

"Yep. Clock's ticking," I mutter and toss back a long gulp.

After I finish the last drop of I don't fuckin' know or care what number, my forehead finds the cool of the bar top. The wood smells like lemon oil and old beer, and somewhere way back in the room, a woman cackles at a joke I don't care to hear. The floor vibrates with the bass drum, and my chest vibrates with it too, whether I want it to or not.

"'Nother, Clay-man," I mumble without lifting my head.

He leans closer to me, and his voice drops low. "You sure, Tad? Thought you were done with this shit."

"Done?" I give him a laugh with no humor in it. "Cants be done with a life sentence."

He tries to pry the empty glass from my hand, but my fingers decide they don't want to let go.

"Happy anniversary to me. March fourteenth," I whisper to the top of the bar. The words crawl out on their own. "The day I shoulda died."

Clay eventually gets the glass out of my hand, but there's a beat when everything goes still. All I can hear is the soft rush of air in the taps and the faraway clatter of pool balls. I can't see for shit because my eyes don't feel like stayin' open, but what good are my eyes that couldn't see the risks that had the power to take everything away from me.

"Fill 'er up, Clay-man!" I shout, but when I find the strength to open my stupid eyes, there's no whiskey beacon to be found.

"Think you've had enough, Tad," Clay says like he's my fucking dad or something.

"Nope. Just gettin' started."

"I'm calling Randy."

“Call the whole damn county!” I tell the wood grain of the bar. “Tell ’em to bring a shovel!”

He moves away. Or the room does. I don’t know; it’s hard to tell.

The music floats up and away like balloons pulling against their strings, and the faces of people I should probably know blur into smears of color.

The thing about anniversaries is you don’t need cake to know what you’re marking.

Your bones tell you. Your skin tells you.

The fucking clock tells you when it clicks over and you’re forced back on the ride to hell.

28

Breezy

Sunday, March 14th

By the time the sun drags itself over Red Bridge, the world feels wrong.

Not *bad*, exactly. Just…off.

Maybe it's because I didn't sleep much. My sweet little Autumn decided last night was the perfect moment to test how many times she could roll across a queen-size bed.

For the record? It was a lot.

I'm pretty sure her cute little butt didn't fall asleep until nearly midnight.

Thankfully, she didn't wake up until eight thirty.

Once we get out of bed and make our way into the kitchen, I cook her breakfast, put some of her curls up in a half-pony, and pretend not to check my phone every five minutes. No text from Tad. No "Morning, Betsy." No smartass sheep memes or dirty innuendos. Nothing.

It's weird. We've talked every single morning for nearly two months straight now.

By ten a.m., I'm telling myself he's probably busy. Feeding the sheep, fixing a fence, doing whatever rugged farm stuff he does that somehow always ends with me naked in his bed.

By noon, the logic stops working.

I call him. It rings four times and kicks to voice mail.

I text. Nothing.

I text again. Still nothing.

Me: *You alive, Farm Daddy?*

Me: *Or did the sheep finally revolt?*

Me: *Answer your phone, Tom. Betsy is trying to call you.*

When Autumn goes down for her nap, and Bennett and Norah are back home, and I've texted Tad more messages than I can count, I finally give up pretending I'm chill and grab my keys.

But Tad's truck isn't in the drive when I pull up to his place. The house looks dark.

I knock. No answer.

I knock again. *Nothing.*

I circle around back, boots crunching in the snow. His barn's quiet except for a few soft bleats from the sheep. I half expect him to pop out, grin tugging at his mouth, and a funny explanation about whatever chaos his sheep brought for the day, but the only thing I find is Randy tossing feed, his breath a cloud in the cold.

"Hey," I call. "You seen Tad?"

Randy glances up, his expression flickering—surprise, then something else I can't name. He wipes his hands on his jeans. "No. But he's probably gonna be unreachable for the rest of the day."

"Unreachable?" I echo. "Did he go somewhere?"

Randy hesitates, eyes darting toward the house and back. "Yeah. I guess that's one way to put it."

My stomach twists. "What does that mean?"

"It means..." He shakes his head on a pause, like he can't find the right words. "Just...give him a little space, okay, Breezy?"

That's it. No explanation. No reassurance. Just the word *space* echoing in my chest like a slammed door.

By the time I drive back up Bennett and Norah's driveway, I've run out of theories, and my hands won't stop gripping the wheel like I can keep something from falling apart if I hold tight enough.

Inside, Autumn's giggling in the living room with Norah. The sound should make me smile. Instead, I mumble something about being tired and escape to my room.

The minute the door closes, the silence hits hard.

And when I pull my phone out of my purse, every text and call to Tad is still unanswered.

I tell myself it's fine. He's fine. He's probably off…I don't know…doing something.

But when the first tear slides down my cheek, I realize I'm lying.

Because the truth is, I'm hurt. And scared. And I don't really understand why the mere idea of space between Tad and me feels devastating.

Tears clog my throat, and the emotion catches me off guard.

I'm not a crier. If anything, I'm what you'd call a show-no-emotion type of gal.

But when I can't contain the tears and I start to outright cry, I bury my face in the pillow, breathing in detergent and salt and something that feels a hell of a lot like heartbreak.

Which doesn't make any sense, given this was just supposed to be a casual fling to pass the time.

But I keep crying for reasons I don't understand—reasons, deep down, I probably understand way too much.

I'm shaken, and my normally strongly constructed walls are cracked. Clearly, all this turmoil and uncertainty in my life is starting to get to me—maybe even changing me as a person.

You might be too far gone to turn back…

29

Tad

Monday, March 15th

By the time the sun cracks over the ridge, I'm already knee-deep in the barn, trying to outwork my shame.

Every year, I know when the day is coming, and still, it always pulls the fucking rug out from under me.

The barn smells like hay and thawing earth and my own mistakes. My head pounds, my mouth tastes like regret, and my hands ache from gripping a shovel I don't need to hold this tight.

Randy's somewhere out back plowing the lower fields. He didn't say much when I rolled in this morning—just a short nod and a muttered, "Snow's still heavy in the south pasture. Gonna clear it before the lambs break a leg."

He knows what yesterday was. And he deals with it by pretending it's just another day and gives me space. He never asks questions, even though he got a phone call from Clay to pick my drunk ass up from The Country Club at two in the morning. And yesterday, he didn't try to track me down when I wasn't at home all day and night and he was left dealing with the farm on his own.

Years ago, that's not how he would've reacted. But now, he doesn't try to move me out of my own way. He lets me circle the drain quietly.

When I woke up yesterday morning, hungover as fuck and March 14 staring back at me from the screen of my phone, I felt like I was going to crawl out of my fucking skin.

I left the house before seven and started driving. As if the more distance I put between myself and Red Bridge, the more oxygen I'd be able to successfully breathe into my lungs.

I ended up two hundred miles outside of town and made myself pull over and stay in a rickety highway hotel because it felt pretty fucking apt for my current state. Run-down, dusty, seen better days, it wasn't the kind of place you'd want to take your family.

But it felt like what I deserved.

I slept like shit, tossed and turned the whole fucking night, and when the sun started to rise high in the sky, I got back in my truck and drove home.

Now I'm back, trying to bury myself in mundane farming routines.

Shovel. Feed. Water. Wrestle a few sheep from the fence. Repeat.

But my phone keeps burning in my pocket because of all the unanswered texts and calls Breezy sent me yesterday.

Eventually, I pull it out and make myself reread the messages she sent.

Breezy: *You alive, Farm Daddy?*

Breezy: *Or did the sheep finally revolt?*

Breezy: *Answer your phone, Tom. Betsy is trying to call you.*

Breezy: *I mean, me Betsy, not sweet little lamb Betsy, by the way. Boy, that's confusing now that I think about it. Maybe I should've given the twins different names.*

Breezy: *Probably too late now, huh? I mean, I'm certain they* *know their names by now, and that feels cruel to confuse them. Plus, they look like a Tom and Betsy.*

Breezy: *Hello? Earth to Tad? Where are you? Are you okay? I'm starting to get worried…*

An hour of time passes between the last and next text.

Breezy: *I talked to Randy. He said to give you space. I guess that's what I'm doing, even though I don't know what the hell that even means.*

Guilt hits hard enough to knock the wind out of me. I stare at the blinking cursor, fingers suspended over the screen. And then I type the only thing that feels honest.

Me: *I'm sorry about yesterday.*

The message sits there. It's delivered, but there's no response.

I wait, but there are no bubbles indicating she's responding. There's no Breezy at all.

I shove the phone back into my pocket, jaw tight, and get back to work. I don't know how much time passes, but I'm startled to a stop when I hear Breezy's voice behind me.

"What are you sorry about exactly?"

It's soft, but it cuts straight through me.

I turn. She's standing in the doorway of the barn, framed by the cold light bouncing off the snow outside, and her phone is in her hand. Her hair's pulled up in that messy knot she often wears whenever she's pretending to be my farmhand.

She looks beautiful as fuck, and I feel like the world's biggest dick for being so selfishly MIA yesterday. I could've at least answered her. Could've given her a reason not to worry about me.

But I didn't because I was too wrapped up in my own bullshit and misery.

"Breezy," I manage, but my voice sounds rougher than gravel.

"You didn't answer your phone yesterday." She steps closer, and her boots make the straw on the ground crunch with each step. "You didn't answer my texts. You weren't home all five times I checked. I drove around half the town, thinking maybe your truck broke down or you got eaten by your sheep. So forgive me if I need to hear your apology in person."

"I know. I'm sorry." I drag a hand down my face.

"What happened?" she asks. "And why did Randy tell me I needed to give you space? I know you don't technically owe me anything. I know we don't have a label on whatever it is we're doing, but I do care about you. A lot, actually. And I thought you cared about me, too. I thought you cared enough not to leave me hanging in the wind like that to worry."

"Breezy, I do care about you. And you're right. You're completely right. I should've called or texted back. I shouldn't have left you wondering like that," I answer as honestly as I can. "But yesterday wasn't about you. Truly. It's…it's me."

Her brow furrows. "That feels vague as hell."

"I know, but it's not something I can really explain."

"Well, how about you try?" She crosses her arms over her chest. "Because I honestly think that if I disappeared for a full twenty-four hours, it would make it very fucking hard for you not to take it personally too."

She's right. With how attached-at-the-hip we've been the past two months, I would probably lose my mind if, all of a sudden, she went MIA for a full day. I'd think the worst. I'd scavenge the whole fucking town to make sure she was okay.

"Okay, you're right. I *can* explain, but I refuse to fill your head with the dark shit that's in mine," I admit, quieter now.

She tilts her head. "So, what, you pull a Luke Danes and have some kind of 'dark day'?"

"A what? A who?"

"Luke Danes. *Gilmore Girls*."

"Are they from Red Bridge?"

That gets me the first smile I've seen on her face all morning. "No, smartass. He's a TV character because it's a TV show. Broody, emotionally unavailable, and wears flannel. Honestly, you're doing a pretty good job of playing the part right now."

"I don't watch TV," I say, a small smile on my lips to try to detour this conversation away from my fucking demons. "Too busy wrestling sheep."

It doesn't work, however.

Her brief smile fades and is replaced by something more fragile and vulnerable. "I know you don't owe me an explanation, but…I've shared things with you. And I just thought maybe you felt comfortable enough to do the same with me…?"

"I do feel like I can, Breezy." I swallow hard. "But this isn't something I want to fill your head with."

"I can handle dark shit, Tad."

"I know you can, but…" I pause, completely unsure of what to say or do in this moment.

"But you still don't want to tell me?"

"No. This isn't shit I talk about with anyone." *Even myself.* "I'm sorry." I shake my head, avert my eyes to the ground before lifting them to meet hers again.

For a long moment, she doesn't speak. The air between us is cold enough to see our breath, but warm enough to burn anyway. Then she takes a step closer.

"Okay," she says quietly. "You don't have to tell me. Just… Can you promise me something?" she requests. "Don't up and disappear on me like that again. At least…tell me it's not a good day. Then I'll at least understand, you know? Then I'll at least know you're safe." Her voice cracks on the last word, and it hits like a steel-toed boot to the gut.

I reach out, grip her hips, and pull her close until her chest brushes mine. "Spending time with you has made a lot of things better, Breeze. You have to know that. You're…special to me." I already feel like I'm telling her too much, revealing too much, but she deserves to hear it.

She looks up at me, and her eyes are a little glossy as they meet mine. "You're special to me too."

A tiny smile tugs at my mouth. "So special that you'll forgive me for being an MIA asshat yesterday?"

"Yeah," she whispers.

"You mean it?"

She nods, and that's all I need. I lean in, pressing a kiss to her mouth—slow, grateful, still trembling with things I don't know how to say. Things I wish I didn't feel for her but still feel anyway.

When I pull back, she rests her forehead against mine.

"I probably should go check on Tom and Betsy."

"I think that's a good plan." I smile. "Pretty sure Mabel was confused when she saw me out here but there was no Breezy to be found."

"So, I'll go play with them for a bit, and then you'll make me some dinner as your final apology to me for being such an idiot?" she questions, and a soft chuckle escapes my lungs.

"I'll even include dessert."

"Okay. Yeah. That'll definitely get you back in my good graces." Breezy winks and heads for the pasture, where Mabel and her lambs are enjoying a little fresh air.

And I find myself watching her as she walks away.

A small, fragile kind of silence wraps around me, and my mind whispers, *When are you going to realize that woman feels more like home than the farm, the house, or anything you've known in years?*

But I don't accept it. I *can't* accept it.

Because Breezy Bishop doesn't deserve to be attached to a fuckup like me, and I don't deserve the chance to let someone down again.

30

Breezy

Saturday, March 20th

My phone buzzes against the blanket I'm pretending to knit.

Tad: *How's the headache, Betsy?*

I smile as I start to type out a response.

Me: *A little better. Though, I might try to take a nap soon. The twins doing okay without me?*

Technically, I was supposed to "help" on the farm this morning. But I woke up with a borderline migraine and decided cold wind slapping me in the face wasn't going to improve my condition.

Tad: *How about you just worry about feeling better. Take a nap. Rest up. Tom and Betsy will be good, but you let me know if you need anything.*

I stare at the message for a second too long, warmth spreading through me despite the dull throb behind my eyes. That man. The same man who not so long ago vanished for a full twenty-four hours and made my stomach twist with worry is checking on me to make sure I'm feeling okay.

Whatever that dark day was for Tad, I guess it's behind us. *For now, anyway.* We've spent the past five days falling back into the companionship that always seems to come so easy.

I know we started out as hot sex and a casual fling, but now I don't really know what to call it. I don't know what to call us. But then again, I don't even know what in the hell I'm doing with my life, so uncertainty is pretty much at the foundation of everything.

I still have questions—a million of them, actually—about Tad's past, about what made him disappear for twenty-four hours, about whatever he feels is so dark he doesn't want it in my head.

Maybe a lot of women would be demanding answers. Maybe I *should be* demanding answers. But I know what it feels like to be pushed before you're ready, and I refuse to do that to him. He'll talk when he wants to. Until then, I'm content with the way he shows up for me. I'm content with whatever this is between us.

And really, who doesn't carry some darkness these days? At least Tad's comes wrapped in kindness and quiet strength. He's never been anything but a gentleman to me.

Well, except when we're in bed.

But clearly, that's an exception. A very hot, very manly, very much makes me melt faster than butter in a cast-iron pan exception.

I set my phone down beside me on the bed, glancing at the half-knit blanket in my lap. My latest attempt at domesticity. It's soft and crooked and, like everything else in my life right now, unfinished.

Crosby still wears the yellow scarf I made, and Tad laughs every time he sees it.

But this new project is for Tom and Betsy. The twins are growing like weeds but still sleep curled together in the barn beside Mabel. Tad told me they don't need the blanket, that sheep are supposed to be able to tolerate the cold, but I'm a you-can-never-have-enough-blankets kind of gal.

My phone buzzes again, and I see another email notification

from headhunter David Smith pop up on the locked screen. I still haven't responded to any of his messages. Haven't even attempted to set up times to chat with all the museums and galleries he says want me. I've tried—trust me, I've tried—but every time I've started an email draft to him, I...close right back out of it.

It just...doesn't feel right. And I can't decide if it's because that world simply doesn't feel like me anymore or if I'm pushing it all away because I'm scared.

Or maybe it's because Red Bridge isn't feeling like a detour anymore, but a place you're putting down roots you didn't even know you had.

I don't know what I want yet. I just know that I'm not running toward anything—or away from it.

I'm just here. *In Red Bridge.*

I let out a long exhale and focus back on my knitting. I'm halfway through another crooked row when raised voices break the quiet.

"What the fuck!"

Sharp, escalating, very male voices break the sound barrier of my bedroom wall, jarring my attention away from the blanket and drawing a knot in my brows instead.

My heart thuds, a sudden sense of panic building as I try to make sense of the argument between Bennett and some unknown foe. My ears are perked, my attention set, but because the honest people of the early 1900s cared about quality construction, I can't understand a damn thing.

It's all just...muffled. Like the parents on *Charlie Brown.*

I don't like not knowing who Bennett's opponent is—not a surprise since the ambiguity of the unknown has always been one of my biggest fears—and with the way Red Bridge does small-town vibes, it truly could be anyone.

Norah isn't home yet from getting her nails done—at least, I don't think—and Autumn went down for a nap a little over an hour ago. As the only hen left in the house and fighting a migraine at that, I chose seclusion in a dark room.

But I would've never guessed a street fight would break out in the living room.

When I toss my needles to the side quickly, my knot comes undone and unfurls all the yarn I've been weaving for the last half hour, the tiny piece of blanket I'd conquered promptly no more.

"Shit." Moisture stings my eyes with raging disappointment I don't understand. I already know Tad is right and Tom and Betsy don't really need a blanket to keep them warm at night, but I am emotionally distraught.

My gosh, Breeze. It'll be fine. You can literally buy them a blanket if you're so inclined.

"Crying over a blanket for baby lambs. A blanket that wasn't even looking good, at that," I mutter to myself, annoyed. "Who am I, and what have I done with the tough-as-nails bitch from New York?"

I move toward the door and pull it open in one smooth motion, quickening my pace to a jog as the voices get louder.

I can't make out what they're saying yet, but the tone is *not friendly*. And to think, I left all my pepper spray in my place when I left New York over two months ago because I was certain the crime statistics in Red Bridge were rock-bottom low.

By the time I reach the hallway, my chest is tight and my morning headache flares into something heavier. But I squint against it and move on quick feet into the kitchen just as Bennett reaches out and pushes Logan, sending him back into the counter and bending his back over it like Gumby.

Logan is here? What the *hell*?

Logan's face stutters, slipping into his old mask of trouble, and I know if I don't get this situation in hand soon, poor Norah is going to come home to a bloody kitchen. I can't believe my two freaking brothers are at each other's throats. It's been years since I've witnessed this, but then again, it's been years since they've been in the same room.

"Hey!" I yell, pulling Logan up short from retaliation. His eyes flit to mine with the benefit of my surprise appearance, but Bennett uses the opportunity to land a sucker shove to his chest, banging him into the counter once again.

I jump forward, putting myself between them like I've done a million times in our youth and far too many times in my twenties and early thirties. *Being the only sister to two rowdy brothers is a freaking job and a half, let me tell you.*

"Hey! Stop it right now!" But even as the words leave my mouth, a dizzy wave rolls through me. I press a hand to my forehead, fighting the sudden spin of the room.

"Yell at him! *I* didn't do anything!" Logan rebuts, a typical sibling declaration.

"You showed up!" Bennett spits back. "That's enough, considering I told you I don't want you at my fucking house."

"I came to see Breezy, not you, asshole!" Logan shouts back, and his eyes move to me. "Breeze, come on. We need to talk."

"No offense, Lo, but I don't want you here either." I shake my head on a sigh. "I don't have anything to say to you."

"See!" Bennett booms. "You are not fucking welcome here!"

Instantly, I regret my honesty as another rage-fueled screaming match starts up around me again.

"This isn't your fucking business, Ben!" Logan shouts back.

"Not my business?" Bennett retorts on a sharp laugh. "You're in my fucking home, so it is my business. And you're not—"

"Ben, please. Stop it," I implore when I see the bulging vein in the center of Bennett's forehead appear. The damn thing is already pulsating. He's beyond angry, and my patience is waning significantly as another wave of dizziness washes over me.

"*Ben, please?* Are you serious, Breeze?" Bennett retorts. "I'm not the one who showed up here to start shit! I'm not the one who destroyed your life!"

"I'm not here to start shit!" Logan roars. "I'm here to try to talk things out!"

"But she doesn't want to talk to you. When are you going to get that through your thick fucking skull? What you did was unthinkable. It was pure betrayal."

"It wasn't my choice!" Logan argues. "I—"

"Shut up. Just shut up! Both of you!" A sheen of sweat coats my forehead and neck, and I use my T-shirt to swipe it off my skin as I try to talk both of my brothers off the ledge. "Seriously. I need the two of you to find some way to calm down. If not for me, for the sake of your daughter, Ben. She's in there taking a nap, and if you wake her up—"

My stomach bubbles, and my anxiety ratchets up.

Ugh. I think...I think I might get *sick.*

Is it the migraine?

Is it the stress of seeing Logan again after months have passed and having to be reminded of everything I've lost while still basically being a squatter in Bennett's house who doesn't seem to have the motivation or gumption or desire to leave?

Or is it the fact that our father died unexpectedly a few months ago and completely betrayed me from the grave, and my brothers can't seem to act their fucking age whenever they're placed in the same goddamn room together?

Or maybe, and this might be a terrifying thought, it's all those things combined, plus a million other things that include the reality you won't face—you're secretly falling for the sheep farmer you swore was just a distraction—and it's all hitting you in one big wave?

Holy fuck. My stomach gurgles and nausea climbs my throat, and I am most definitely going to puke.

Putting a hand over my mouth, I make a dash for the trash can, flipping up the lid and throwing up the coffee and eggs Norah made a few hours ago. The taste is putrid, and my whole body shakes with the unexpected upheaval.

"You okay?" Logan asks as Bennett moves to put a hand to my back. I wave them both off, trying to get my bearings and decide whether I'm done. I feel awful all of a sudden, and I swear if I don't use all my strength to fight it, I might pass out right here on the floor.

"Dammit, Logan. You've got Breezy so fucking stressed with all this, she's getting sick. When is your selfishness going to be done? When is it going to be enough?"

"Me?" Logan tosses back, his voice rising once again. "I'm trying to make things right. I'm here, hanging out in fucking Mary Poppins Land, fighting a damn flock of sheep to get to your house, trying to rebuild a bridge. You're the one who fucking yells and takes out his fists every time you see me. Maybe you're the one stressing Breezy out? Ever think of that?"

"Oh, screw you! I didn't steal her fucking galleries. The ones she's been working at since she graduated high school!"

"I didn't steal them. Dad left them to me. And I'm trying—"

"You're trying to ruin everything! You're always trying to ruin everything!" Bennett yells. His voice is loud and raw with thirty-plus years of aggression. This isn't a normal sibling rivalry—this is trauma bonding and perfidy and a powder keg load of testosterone.

Autumn's cry is soft, but aside from Bennett's heavy breathing and Logan's wide eyes, it's the only thing left in the accusation's wake.

"Great," Bennett growls. "You woke the baby."

"Me?" Logan protests. "I'm not the one huffing and puffing the whole damn house down."

"I'll get Autumn," I offer, willing my stomach to settle and then stepping back to the trash can when it turns again. I lose the rest of the contents of my stomach in a violent swoop that burns my throat and makes my eyes tear. Embarrassment rests on my lips atop the aftermath of throwing up. I reach for a paper towel from the roll next to the sink, falling into the counter when my legs unexpectedly go out from under me.

"Okay, fuck. Sit down, Breeze," Bennett orders, and Logan pulls out a chair from the kitchen table and puts it behind me.

I barely manage to sit before the front door slams open with a crack that rattles the hinges. Cold air knifes through the kitchen, and Tad fills the doorway in three long strides.

His jaw is clenched, and his eyes scan the room wildly until they lock on me.

"Breezy?" His voice hits like a thunderclap—rough, panicked, *protective*. "Are you okay?"

Both Bennett and Logan whirl toward him, startled, but Tad's already crossing the room. His chest heaves like he sprinted the whole way here.

"What the hell's going on in here?" Tad demands, voice booming enough to cut through the lingering echo of the slammed door.

But before I can say something, before I can intervene, nausea grips my throat, and I have to shut my eyes as the world spins on its axis.

Which is a fucking shame because I'm basically in the middle of an old Western film and a street-style shootout appears imminent now that a third gun-wielder has arrived. And without sight, all I can do is listen.

"What the fuck?" Bennett shouts at Tad. "What are you doing in my house?"

"Who the fuck are you?" Logan bellows at the same time.

My eyes are still closed firmly shut as another wave of nausea clutches me, and the edges of everything blur. The sound of them—three men, all muscle and ego and tension—feels far too loud for the pounding inside my skull and the nausea wreaking havoc on my insides. My stomach rolls again, and I grip the table in hopes it will anchor me.

"I expect a fucking answer," Tad spits, ignoring their questions entirely. "What the hell is going on? What's wrong with Breezy?"

"Excuse me?" Bennett's voice booms, and I try to calm him before he can fly off the handle. "*You* demand an answer in *my fucking house*? Are you—?"

"Bennett," I plead, my voice dull, even to my own ears. It has nothing of the take-charge woman I'm used to, and her absence is worrisome, given the circumstances. I have a feeling things are about to get a heck of a lot more volatile, and, perhaps more horrifying, the sting in my eyes foretells a soon-arriving wave of more tears.

"Yeah, I do demand answers!" Tad shouts, not catching my

let's-calm-shit-down vibe. "What the hell is going on?"

"What's it to you, Farmer *fucking* Ted?" Bennett's voice cracks like a whip, and more tears flood behind my lids.

I don't know why I'm so emotional. It's never really been in my DNA—something about being a Bishop and dealing with all the family-induced trauma hardens your soul or something.

But I don't open my eyes because I can't. I don't say anything else because the world is spinning, my pulse is hammering somewhere between my ears and my ribs, and the tears start up again before I can swallow them back.

What on earth is going on with me?

31

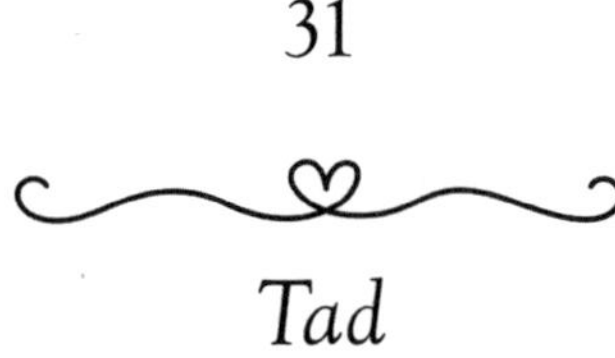

Tad

I didn't exactly plan on getting in the crosshairs of a shitstorm in Bennett Bishop's house.

But my sheep had other plans.

Crosby figured out a way to unlatch the new gate Randy and I installed on the side of the fence that butts up toward the Bishops' house a week ago. We thought it was bulletproof. Evidently, it wasn't Crosby-proof.

Half my flock was in Bennett's yard before I knew it, some in his driveway, some in the pasture near his studio, and I headed over that way to get their asses back over to the farm.

But then I heard screaming and hollering.

The yelling wasn't of the toddler variety or a happy family house boisterous with noise. It was sharp. It was angry. It was strong enough to shake the fucking walls and urge a gallon of adrenaline to pour into my veins.

And I swore I could hear Breezy's soft voice somewhere in the violent mix.

I didn't think. I acted, and I ran as fast as I could across the yard and straight to the house.

My boots hit the porch hard enough to rattle the boards, and I didn't even bother knocking. I turned the knob and yanked the door open as my pulse climbed straight into fight mode. And I busted into the house, eyes searching frantically for Breezy.

Any manner of burglary or attempted kidnapping or Breezy being held at gunpoint was running through my head, but what I found was entirely confusing *and* infuriating, considering she looked more upset than I've ever seen her.

And that's how I ended up here with a livid Bennett and a dude I've never met staring me down while a now-sobbing Breezy hops up from the kitchen table and runs over to the trash can to puke her guts out.

"Earth to Farmer Ted, what are you doing here, in my fucking house?" Bennett asks for the second time, but I'm too focused on Breezy to listen or care or respond. I'm also feeling really pissed that she's in this state, and I have to assume someone in this room is the cause.

"Breezy?" I question, walking over toward her and gently putting my hand on her back. "Are you okay?"

When she doesn't answer, probably because she's too busy hurling and dry heaving between sobs, I turn toward Bennett and the other dude I don't know. Both still look angry as fuck, but guess what? I'm fucking angry too. "What happened?"

"Why the fuck should we tell you?" the man next to Bennett asks. "I don't even know who the hell you are."

"He's the fucking sheep farmer from next door," Bennett interjects, just as I crack back.

"Yeah, well, I can say the same about you. Who the fuck are you, and why've you got her crying?"

"Why don't you leave our sister to us, Farmer Ted?" Bennett intervenes, but his words are all the clue I need to put the rest of it together. *Our* sister. Our.

"Wait...Logan?" With angry eyes, I turn back to the other

brother. "*You're* Logan?"

He lets out an exasperated sigh. "Listen, I know it's rare for celebrities to land in this town, but I'm not here to entertain small-town folk with autographs and fucking selfies."

Breezy is crying, and he thinks I came in here to get his fucking autograph? I'm two seconds away from throttling this guy.

"How about you go back to whatever farm you came from and give us some privacy," Logan adds, his voice an egotistical snarl, and the cries of Bennett and Norah's little girl start to ring out again from somewhere down the hallway.

But I hardly hear anything besides the piercing buzzing in my ears. Can hardly see anything besides red.

Everything I know about Breezy and Logan and how fucked up he's handled everything since their dad's passing overwhelms my already adrenaline-stocked veins with a surge of rage.

And before I know it, I step forward, cock my fist, and let it fly, landing a ringer of a punch directly to his right eye.

"Fuck!" He stumbles back through a shout, and the whole room erupts into chaos.

"What the *fuck* are you doing, Farmer Ted?" Bennett yells just as Norah comes through the front door behind me, her voice rising to a screech as she surveys what's going on.

"I don't know what's happening right now, but someone better tell me why I can hear my daughter screaming from her room while a bunch of adults are in here having a shouting match, and they'd better do it quick!"

"I'll get her, babe," Bennett offers, subduing immediately, and I don't blame him. I've never seen Norah's head so ready to pop off, and she's been in Red Bridge—and through all manner of trauma—for a while now. A crying, unattended daughter is very much the straw that broke the camel's back for almost any mother, and Bennett is smart enough to recognize it.

I look down at Breezy, intent to check on her as she leans over the trash can and throws up again, but Logan steps forward and shoves me back with a hand in my chest. "Stay the fuck back."

I don't think, and I don't hesitate. In one smooth motion, I hit him again, a harsh jab to his left eye.

"What in the actual hell, Tad?" Norah yells.

"Are you kidding me?" Logan groans, holding his other eye now. "Why do you keep fucking punching me!"

"Bam! Bam!" Autumn screeches from Bennett's arms, unfortunately having entered the room while I was zoned out in the red mist of anger.

"Oh my God," Breezy cries as she moves back over to the kitchen table and collapses in a chair again, pulling the collar of her shirt up over her mouth.

"I'm gonna fucking kill you," Logan yells, lunging toward me with an outstretched arm I easily deflect.

"Fucking try!" I challenge back, waggling my eyebrows and my fingers all at once. The aggression is long repressed but cathartic and reminds me a little bit of my old life—the one I lived the few months before I made the decision to move to Red Bridge and swore I'd never go back to.

There were plenty of dark nights in Chicago when I would go to bars just looking to get in a fight with someone. Back then, it was the only thing that stopped the pain. But now, it's like it's the only thing that's making me feel in control of whatever is going on with Breezy. *Like my sole purpose of being here is to protect her.*

"Hey!" Norah yells as Autumn repeats something that sounds an awful lot like "fucking."

Bennett hands Autumn off to Norah and steps into the fray, which only escalates things more. He puts a hand on my chest, which I answer with a shove. Logan lunges, seemingly in Bennett's defense, but Bennett stops him with a fist to the chin.

"What the *hell*?" Logan yells, yet another part of his face succumbing to the role of punching bag. "Why am I the one who keeps getting punched?" And when he starts to move forward, his eyes and fists very much intent on returning the violence, Norah's voice booms him to a stop.

"Enough!" she screams, her voice guttural and loud in a way

that shakes the windowpanes. Shoving through us, she grabs two bags of frozen peas from the fridge and shoves them at Logan. He opens his mouth to yell, and she cuts him off with a hand. "No! No, I don't want to hear it! I'm done! Get out of this house! Right now! All three of you!"

"Me?" Bennett questions.

"Yes, you! In fact, especially you! So help me, if the three of you aren't out of this space in five seconds, I'm getting the shotgun!"

Logan moves first, the back screen door slamming behind him as he jumps down all the deck stairs and falls to his ass in the grass. Bennett opens his mouth to argue, but when Norah snaps her fingers, he follows with the same hurried movements.

I linger, trying to check on Breezy and actually get a look at her face before I leave, but Norah isn't having it. "Tad Hanson, I swear to everything holy, you better get out of this house right now!"

"Bye-bye!" Autumn shouts. "Bye-bye-bye!"

I reach out to squeeze Breezy's elbow, but exiting as directed and depositing myself in the backyard where Bennett and Logan reside.

Logan is sitting down in one of the Adirondack chairs that look out toward the rolling hills, and Bennett is pacing behind him.

But when Logan pulls a cigarette out from the carton in his pocket, before he can light it, Bennett snags it, breaking it in half.

"Hey!" Logan jumps to his feet and drops the bags of peas behind him.

Bennett's finger is a sword, pointing aggressively in Logan's face. "Smoke somewhere else if you want, but you're not doing it here, anywhere near my house or my daughter."

"Fuck me," Logan remarks, smacking Ben's hand away. "It's not like I planned to blow the smoke in her face. I only smoke when I'm stressed—which I am now because the two of you freak shows felt like making me bleed."

"Please," Bennett groans. "Don't be such a pussy, Logan. Before Hollywood, I could have broken your arm, and you wouldn't be complaining this much. Fucking actor pricks made you soft."

"Well, excuse me for not expecting the stupid fucking sheep farmer to have such a strong arm!"

I chuckle, and the two of them turn on me in unison.

"You shut the fuck up."

"Go home, Ted."

No way in hell I'm leaving without talking to Breezy, angry brothers or not.

"My name is *Tad*. Not fucking Ted," I answer on a sigh, rolling my eyes. "And I'm not leaving."

"I'm not either," Logan declares.

"Well, that's just fucking great. I guess we're at a stalemate." Bennett turns angrily and walks toward the backyard, Logan calling after him, when all I have to offer is a shrug.

"Where are you going?"

"To get a burn barrel," Bennett calls back, annoyed. "It's cold as fuck, and if we're gonna stand around with our dicks in our hands, we might as well burn some shit."

Great. Burning shit. Just the thing I need.

32

Breezy

"All right, what's going on? Two hours ago, I left a quiet house to get my nails done, and now I come home to some Fyre Festival-level disaster with black eyes, bloody knuckles, a screaming baby, and you throwing up into my trash can."

Norah's voice is pitched somewhere between disbelief and mom-level authority. She bounces and rocks Autumn on her hip with my niece's sweet head tucked under her chin, and tears spring to my eyes against my will.

"I don't even know where to begin. Logan just showed up here. You know how complicated shit is with Logan and me. And you know how much Bennett hates him…" I pause, not even sure where to start, because honestly, I don't really know what the hell is happening with me or the Three Violent Stooges out back.

"So, Logan showed up, and Bennett lost his shit," Norah repeats, trying to understand it all herself. "And where exactly does Tad Hanson throwing punches come into that equation?"

"He busted through the door out of nowhere," I say, trying to swallow back the onslaught of tears that want to escape. But when my throat clenches with emotion, I hold my breath to calm myself, even swiping at my eyes with my shirt.

It doesn't help. They spill over before I can catch them, hot and humiliating, and a sob bubbles up from my throat.

"Breezy?" Norah asks, horrified, her eyes wide and confused over my sudden emotional outburst.

"Bee sad!" Autumn says. "Okay, Bee?"

I nod, even though I *am* sad. But I don't fucking know why I'm sad. Or this insanely emotional. Or dizzy. Or puking like some woman who…

The wheels of my brain cells start spinning a tune that's straight-up horrifying in its chorus.

Oh God. I'm not pre—

Another sob bubbles up from my throat before I can even think the word.

"Bee is sad, but she'll be okay," Norah reassures, but when her eyes land on me again, her expression is still one of shock and dismay before realization starts to set in. "Breezy?" My name is tight with question, and I know without even having to investigate further, she knows what I'm beginning to fear the most.

"Are you…? How could you be—?"

I cut her off quickly with a shush, nodding to the toddler in her arms whose favorite pastime these days is repeating everything she hears.

Norah squeezes Autumn in a quick hug and then hustles toward the porch door, opening it just enough to place her daughter down gently and yell at Bennett across the yard. "Ben! Come get your daughter. And please, if you would, watch her responsibly this time."

It's a burn as cold as ice, and I'm unavoidably filled with pride at the sound of it. My sweet little Norah, who was a people-pleasing sweetheart when she found my brother tearing his own life apart, has developed a spine of steel. I love to see it.

The handoff goes smoothly, and Bennett is smart enough to

tell her he's sorry for being such an asshole. Norah *sort of* accepts the apology but mostly shoos him back out the door and on his way with Autumn on his hip now.

"Okay," she says as the door slams closed behind her, rushing toward the table and sliding into the chair across from mine without delay. "The little ears are gone, so you'd better get talking. I don't want to assume anything crazy, but I walked in to you puking in my trash can. And now, you're hanging on by a thread of tears..."

I shake my head, as if I can will away the possibility.

"Breezy," Norah says and puts both hands on my shoulders. "I'm not a doctor, but you're acting a lot like a woman who is..." she drops her voice to a whisper "...pregnant."

And there it is. The word my mind is shouting inside my brain, but I'm trying not to acknowledge.

The word that makes the most sense for my current state of absurdity but would be the biggest mindfuck of all.

The word that has me mentally calculating, *When's the last time I had my period?* And *When's the last time I had unprotected sex?*

Sadly, I can't even remember the answer to the first, and the second? Well, let's just say Tad and I haven't been the best about using condoms. Frankly, I don't know if we've used one since the first time we forgot about one. And that was weeks and a lot of sex ago.

I'm on birth control, but anyone with a brain knows it's not an ironclad prevention. It's why they tell you to use condoms too.

"Breezy, are you *pregnant*?" Norah whispers *the word* again.

And sadly, I can't tell her no in this scenario and actually believe it. Instead, I sigh. Hard. "It's sure looking like a possibility," I say, and a laugh that's dangerously close to a wail escapes my lungs. "Though I imagine I can't know for sure without a test."

"Okay, but how? With *who*?"

I gesture toward the group of hoodlums outside, my eyes widening and my hands tossing up with dramatic effect. "Well, it's not one of my brothers, so I'm pretty sure it's the third freaking troublemaker, Rocky Balboa himself out there."

"Farmer Tad?" she shrieks loudly enough that I wave both of my hands aggressively, suggesting she lower her volume by about thirty decibels.

"Norah! Only the screen is closed!"

"Okay, okay, I'm sorry. I just can't believe you might be *pregnant.* With *child.* With *Tad Hanson's child.*" She's whispering again. "I knew you two were spending a lot of time together, and I certainly had my suspicions about you *helping out* on his farm. I thought maybe you were messing around with him, but I didn't think you were over there getting pregnant!"

"Yeah, well..." I burst into tears. "You're not the only one!"

"Oh, Breeze..." Norah's hand shoots forward, covering mine and squeezing. "It's going to be okay. I promise."

"It doesn't feel like it's going to be okay, Norah. I'm lost. Wandering. Completely freaking untethered from everything I've ever used to guide me. And now...this. I mean, what if I'm really freaking pregnant with Farmer Tad's baby?"

Norah snorts. "I just have to know... Do you call him that in bed?"

"Norah!" I chastise, even though the teasing nickname *Farm Daddy* comes to mind a little too quickly for the grave nature of the situation.

"Okay, okay. You're right. No sex jokes allowed right now. Instead, we're going to drive over to Molene, get a pregnancy test, and take it in the supermarket bathroom. After that, we'll make a plan based on the results."

"Do we really have to take it in the supermarket bathroom? That seems a little...uncouth."

"Your city is showing," Norah says through a laugh, standing from the table and grabbing her purse and keys from the countertop by the fridge. I guess she ditched them there when she walked in on Celebrity Death Match in action. "But we can drive to Josie's and take it there if you prefer. Clay will be at the bar to open up with Marty, so we'll have privacy."

I don't move, clinging desperately to the table instead. "What if we don't and say we did?"

"Come on, Breeze, don't go soft on me now. Time to woman up."

"I'm scared, Norah." The words are as quiet as air.

"Oh honey, I know. But I promise...scary as it is—and it is *terrifying*—being a mother is the best thing that could ever happen to you."

I nod. "Let me go brush my teeth really quickly."

Norah nods. "Take your time. We'll go whenever you're ready."

"Funny thing about being ready when it comes to this—I don't know if I'll ever be."

Norah's wink is comforting in the strangest way. I can't explain it, but it's unlike anything I've ever felt. "Then, honey...you're right on schedule."

33

Tad

Snow still blankets most of Red Bridge, but Bennett Bishop apparently took that as an invitation to start an outdoor bonfire like it's the Fourth of July.

"We've got a problem," I say, circling the old, rusted barrel he's using as a burn pit and watching as the flames lick dangerously high. He's already tossed in a pile of cardboard, a busted chair leg, and—God help us—a splash of gasoline from a red can that may be on the back deck but is still way too close for comfort.

The snow around the barrel is melting fast, revealing patches of muddy grass and steam rising in ghostly curls. I dig my heel into the slush, dragging a line of dirt between the blaze and the nearest pine tree like it might somehow stop Bennett Bishop from burning down half of Red Bridge.

"Yeah," Logan agrees. "We do, Ted. And it's your attitude."

"You don't call him Ted," Bennett sings, bouncing Autumn from hip to hip while she laughs. "I call him Ted."

"You don't own the name," Logan asserts, his smile as brittle as Bennett's high notes.

"How about the two of you call me Tad since that's my name," I suggest. "And I'm not the problem. The three of us being dismissed to the outdoors without any answers or resolution to why the heck you were shouting down the whole world while Breezy cried in the first place is the problem." I sigh. "Not to mention, this burn barrel is getting a little wild."

"Zip it, Ted," they say in unison, making me sigh.

Autumn is still on Bennett's hip, and he hands her a piece of cardboard, which she tosses into the fire hazard burn barrel with glee. "Burns! Poof!" she exclaims in glee, making her little pigtails bounce up and down.

Bennett looks over at me, and whatever he sees on my face makes him chuckle like a real asshole. "Don't get your panties in a twist over the barrel, Ted," he says. "There's too much snow to start a forest fire. And trust me, if I wanted to blow up your farm, I would've done it a long fu—effin' time ago."

It's on the tip of my tongue to tell Bennett—and that dickhead Logan too, frankly—to fuck off, but being responsible for one toddler-repeated f-bomb is enough on my conscience for the day.

"You know, Ted, I am curious, though. Why are you still here? In fact, why are you here at all?" Bennett asks, his eyes moving back to me as his gaze searches my face closely. "Even though Logan isn't welcome here, I know why he showed up like an uninvited di—dummy. But you? I don't—"

Before he can finish that thought, Norah and Breezy bust out of the house.

"We'll be back!" Norah calls out, making pointed eye contact with Bennett as she leads the way by holding open the door and ushering Breezy through.

"Where are you going? When will you be back?" Bennett asks, and Norah doesn't hesitate to answer with straight-up sass.

"None of your business. And we'll be back when we get home." No doubt, she's still ticked off about the scuffle that just occurred in her house.

"Love you, Nore," Bennett says, the man clearly trying to gauge just how pissed his wife is.

"Love you too, you big dummy!"

Bennett just chuckles, still holding Autumn on his hip, and the two of them wave bye to Norah and Breezy.

I fight to meet Breezy's eyes the entire time, but she clutches her purse and takes great interest in the ground. So much so, I wouldn't be surprised if she knew the count of every blade of grass.

I step away from the contentious bachelor group without delay, following closely behind the two women as they make haste toward Norah's car. My posture is as sheepish as my flock, however, since the last thing I want to be is antagonistic. She's already upset, and I don't want to make it worse. "Breeze," I implore. "Can I talk to you?"

She shakes her head, and Norah steps in front of her, blocking me like a professional football defensive end. Her small stature suddenly seems like a six-four, three-hundred-pound hologram of Myles Garrett. "Now isn't a good time. Later. Try again later."

"I just want to make sure she's okay."

"She's fine," Norah answers for her again.

"I'd love to hear that from her," I say as kindly as I can. Not only is none of this Norah's fault, but there are two very angry wolves temporarily pretending this is *Show Tunes on Tour* for the sake of the adorable toddler in Bennett's arms. One wrong move, and I'm liable to be worm food. "Breeze, please," I beg.

"I'm good, Tad," she says, but her smile is fucking brittle. "Promise. Upset. A little off, but nothing you need to worry about right now, okay?"

"We'll talk later?" I ask, needing the confirmation for some godforsaken reason. Her avoidance should be the excuse I need to shut down and bug off. Her business *shouldn't* be *my* business. That's part of keeping it casual—leaving the care and emotions at the moment of intimacy, no more, no less.

And yet, if the burn in my chest is any indication right now, when it comes to Breezy Bishop, all my usual careful boundaries left and slammed the door behind themselves a long fucking time ago.

"Yes." She nods. "We'll talk later. I promise."

I take a deep breath as Norah ushers Breezy forward again, settling her into the passenger side of her car and then rounding the hood to climb inside. Her eyes guard everything, and I watch avidly as she cranks the engine and swoops a broad turn around in the gravel drive. I don't take my eyes off the taillights until they're completely out of the driveway.

When I eventually do turn back to Bennett and Logan and the burn barrel, danger is waiting for me in the form of two sets of very ominously keen eyes.

"Ted, I'll be honest. I want an explanation," Logan announces as Bennett fights a wiggling Autumn. "About why you hit me—"

"And why, oh why you have so much interest in Beatrice Bishop in the first place," Bennett cuts him off. "Tell me right now. Are you *sleeping with* my sister? Because trust me, I wasn't exactly believing the whole 'Breezy's helping out on your farm' bulls—crud. And now that I see the way you're looking at her, I'm starting to think she was spending more time in your bed than your god—gosh-darn farm."

"What?" Logan snaps. "You thinking Farmer Ted is plowing Breezy's field?"

Bennett rolls his eyes, but I don't shy away from the answer. The truth is that, yes, Breezy and I have been sleeping together. But we're not teenagers, and her brothers have absolutely no reason for some self-righteous psychobabble about her virtue. I mean, from what Breezy's told me, for most of her life, it's been she who's taken care of their asses. Not the other way around.

"Yes." It's a simple word, but the tone is emblazoned by a chest full of air. "Not that it's any fuuu—mbling business of yours."

"Holy hel—lo." Bennett's jaw drops.

"Hello! Hello!" Autumn chimes in, waving her little toddler hand in the air. "Hello, baby!"

If I weren't being currently stared down by the bull that is

Bennett Bishop, I would probably acknowledge how cute it is and say hello back to her.

"Are you fu—dging kidding me?" Bennett questions through a tight jaw. "Breezy fell for your happy, yapping shi—crap and your sheepy fingers?"

"Bahh, bahhh!" Autumn shouts proudly. "Sheep go bahhh!"

And I have to admit, it makes me smile. She's a sweet kid with a happy disposition and demanding energy. She marches boldly through life, and Norah and Bennett do a great job of enjoying every moment of chasing her, but regardless of how sweet her pigtails are or how big her smile is, Bennett and Norah have still been left with a hell of an empty bucket that will never fill. There's a void when you lose a kid that can't be—

"Well." Bennett grabs my attention, having set Autumn down near her swing set that's safely away from the burn pit and moved closer to me. He's maintaining a soft posture—for the sake of his marriage and his behavior in front of his toddler, no doubt—but from what I can tell, he's been waiting on an answer from me for a while as my mind wandered. "What are your intentions?"

I blink. "My intentions?"

"Yeah, ass—butthole. With my sister. What are your intentions? Do you intend to date her? Marry her?"

A jolt of panic shoots straight through me. My stomach knots. My fingers tingle. Not because I don't know how I feel about Breezy—but because I do.

And that's the damn problem.

I know what happens when you let someone in too far. I know what happens when your entire world becomes them and what it costs you when you believe they'll always be there.

I told myself Breezy was a distraction. Temporary. Casual. But somewhere between the lines of her laugh and her smile and the way she makes fucking everything better, that lie's gotten harder to hold on to. *More like,* impossible *to hold on to.*

"Jeez, Ted. Are you having a stroke or something?" Logan sneers. "Why won't you answer my brother's question?"

"I..." My throat feels tight. "I don't have intentions." I clear it, forcing calm into my tone. "I care about her, and she cares about me, and beyond that, I'd say it's our own, very adult, consenting, private business, wouldn't you?"

"No," Bennett says with an edgy shake of his head. "I wouldn't say that at all."

I shrug. "We're gonna have to agree to disagree, then."

Bennett postures more aggressively now, and I brace myself to earn my own bag of peas.

"Bahh, bahh, bahh!" Autumn exclaims from her perch on the slide of her swing set.

I look up to find my flock making a beeline for all of us and promptly remember the whole reason I ended up at Bennett's in the first place. Crosby, the bastard, is the ringleader heading the charge of fluffy terrorists toward us, and I guess I should be thankful that they managed to stay in the vicinity of the farm while I've been wrapped up over here for what feels like hours now.

All at once, my sheep choose Logan as their victim, surrounding him and circling him like gentle vultures.

Bennett and I back up, him scooping Autumn up and out of the way as she continues to make sheep noises, and Logan folds his arms up and to his chest as they get tighter and tighter around him.

"Yo, guys, you wanna do something about these sheep?"

"Not really," I say, and Bennett actually laughs.

"What are they doing, Ted? Why are they circling me?"

I cup my hands around my mouth and yell. "Don't worry! This is just their pre-attack ritual."

"Pre-attack?" he questions nervously. "And what the hell does that mean?"

"It means when they get done with you, Bennett and I won't have anything but each other to worry about."

Bennett laughs, and it feels like a small breakthrough in the ball of tension we've both been wielding toward each other for years. I never cared that we didn't particularly get along, but now that things with Breezy are the way they are, I don't know...a civil relationship seems more important.

"You shut the hell up, Ted, and get these sheep away from me."

I put a finger to my lips and whistle, and Crosby, Nash, Mackie, and Boris all peel off from the pack and head in my direction first.

"Bahhh! Sheep! Bahh!" Autumn cries excitedly, reaching down in an effort to pet them when they get close. I pull some feed from my pocket and toss it at the ground, and they all freeze up, heads down to get their fill.

"She can pet them," I say to Bennett.

"Pet them?" Logan protests. "You just told me they were about to attack!"

I shrug. "Guess I lied."

"Screw all this bullshit." Exploding out of the circle of remaining sheep, Logan growls and storms over to his fancy Mercedes coupe, climbing inside and slamming the door. I expect him to start it up and pull away, but he reclines the seat instead, crossing his arms over his chest.

"Great. Guess he's not leaving, then," Bennett grumbles before sighing heavily.

"Well, don't cry too hard. At least one of us is. And as a bonus, I'll take the sheep with me."

Bennett smirks and Autumn giggles, and for now, I take that as a sign of making strides.

Gone for now, but I'll be back—just as soon as Breezy is too.

34

Breezy

Is this rock bottom?

I mean, that can be the only explanation for why I'm sitting in Norah's SUV, clutching a plastic gas station bag like it contains nuclear codes instead of a pregnancy test.

"Everyone in that Stop and Go was looking at me," I blurt, words tumbling out before I can stop them. "I know you said people in Molene wouldn't recognize us, but I swear they did. My buying a pregnancy test is going to end up spreading all the way to Eileen's lap and plastered across the front page of the damn *Chronicle*."

Norah laughs, and I scowl. She glances my way briefly, the corners of her mouth still twitching as she steers the car down Josie's long gravel driveway.

"I'm sorry," she says, still smiling. "I'm not laughing at you, really. It's just…the people in the Stop and Go were looking at you because you knocked down an entire tower of soup cans. Also, Eileen wouldn't dare get her gossip from another town. That's not her style. Plus, she hates Brandy Lockwood."

"Who in the hell is Brandy Lockwood?"

"She runs the *Molene Gazette*. Basically, Eileen Martin 2.0."

Once we're in front of Clay and Josie's house, Norah shifts into park and cuts the ignition. Her seat belt clicks free with a sharp snap that ricochets through my skull, and I instantly want to scream.

I can't explain it—this anger that keeps boiling up or the ache that sits heavy behind my ribs. It's like my emotions have staged a coup and I'm just the hostage.

"Well, then," Norah ventures cautiously. "Shall we go inside?"

I nod instead of answering; gestures are all I'm capable of right now with these yo-yoing freaking emotions of mine.

"Right. Going inside, then." She opens her door and climbs out gracefully, moving toward the house like someone untouched by chaos. Basically, the complete opposite of me—with my half-baked plans, nonexistent direction, and a potential life-altering surprise shaped like a tiny human with Tad Hanson's eyes.

Norah lifts her dainty fingers to the door to knock while I drag my legs through metaphorical mud, and the stark contrast between the two of us has my anger renewing tenfold.

I seethe to myself, wrapping my fingers around the handles of the bag that contains the stupid test until they dig into the skin and turn it purple. It's on the tip of my tongue to literally scream Josie's house down like she's one of the pigs and I'm a big bad, possibly pregnant wolf, but she opens the door before I get the chance, and the battle cry dies in my throat.

At the sight of her, I turn weepy.

Her hair is disheveled, her sweater oversized, and her eyes are sunken into the void of two deep, dark circles. Maybe it's that she's the embodiment of everything I'm feeling and then some—a freaking mess and a half and opposite of normal in every way—but one more swing of emotions and I'm going to launch myself right into outer space.

"You look like shit, sis. Are you okay?" Norah doesn't beat around the bush to save feelings.

Josie flips Norah the middle finger but opens the door wider, stepping out of the way so we can step in. "Oh, I'm great. Come inside quick, maybe you'll catch it."

Norah twists at the waist, her eyes widening slightly. "Maybe you're not pregs, Breeze. Maybe it's just a stomach bug." She laughs, waggling her eyebrows with her back toward Josie. "Seems to be going around."

"I'm not puking," Josie contests easily. "I'm just tired. And you're not puking, but you're an asshole."

I snort, and Josie turns her attention to me. "So, you think you might be knocked up, huh?"

I sigh and glare at Norah.

She shrugs in apology, licking at her top lip. "Look, I'm sorry, but I had to let her into the circle of trust. She wasn't going to allow us in the house otherwise."

I groan. I didn't even notice her on the phone, but I suppose she had a few minutes while I was rolling around on the floor of the Stop and Go with the soup cans to make covert moves. "I don't *think* I'm pregnant, but seeing as I've been violently ill and emotionally unstable all morning, I suppose I should make sure."

"You know you have to have sex to get pregnant, right?" Josie teases. "I think there was only one immaculate conception."

I roll my eyes, and she squeals. It's very un-Josie-like, which makes it even more annoying. "Come on. Your sister has already been squealing all the way to Molene and back. Not you too," I say through gritted teeth.

"Breeze!" Josie snaps. "You have to give me a little squealing—a squeak, at least. I mean, this is *news.* Who have you been sleeping with? Last time we talked, you were considering celibacy and a vibrator as your five-year plan."

"I'm not ready to talk about this yet. Maybe after the test, but not before."

"Fine, fine. Then go take the fucker," Josie insists. "Bathroom is the second door on the left."

Plastic bag in hand, I walk the march of shame down Josie's long hallway, glancing at pictures from her and Clay's wedding on the walls and smiling at the pictures of both Summer and Autumn that flank them.

I want to linger—to stay here where it feels safe and good and familiar—but I don't. It's not who I am, not who I've ever been. I face things head on. I make plans and lists, and I get stuff done. If a test is the next step, a test is what I'll take.

Stepping into the bathroom, I close the door behind me and lock it, even though I know Josie and Norah would never betray my privacy by coming inside without permission. It's just a subtle comfort—a reminder of NYC in some weird way, I guess, since locking doors there was like a reflex.

I study my face in the mirror, expecting the poltergeist, but for a woman who's spent the morning retching, I look remarkably at ease. Softer than normal—like I've finally gotten enough oxygen after years of deprivation.

The bag crinkles as I dig inside, discarding it in Josie's small trash can and tearing open the cardboard box to pull out the test.

My hands shake as I try to rip the seam of the blue foil package, failing two times before getting it. I take a deep breath as I read through the instructions carefully, summarizing in my head as I go—*uncap, pee a continuous stream on the absorption pad for at least five seconds, recap, and then lie test flat for three or more minutes.*

It seems simple, but the sheer audacity of needing to take this test for the first time in my life because I might be knocked up by a freaking sheep farmer from one of the smallest freaking towns ever is...overbearing, to say the least.

I lick my lips and set the foil on the countertop next to the sink basin, holding the test with a viselike grip while I pull my pants down and sit on the toilet seat. Josie has a picture of a flowerpot hanging on the wall directly across from me, and I find myself counting the petals along with the seconds as I place the test between my legs.

One, two, three, four, five. Six—just in case.

My hands are trembling—not from clumsiness, but from the quiet, creeping realization that everything could change because of one tiny pink line.

I recap the test and then lay it on the counter beside the foil packaging while I finish my business, flush, and wash my hands.

Once done, my palm drifts to my stomach before I can stop it. The gesture feels foreign, like I'm touching someone else's body.

Motherhood was never something I pictured for myself. Never something I wanted, or maybe just never something I let myself want. I've spent so many years trying to *control* everything, and being a mother has always felt like the opposite of control. It's pure surrender.

Still, the thought of it now—of the possibility—hits me somewhere deep and shaky. Because, if this test is positive, it means something inside me decided I was ready before I ever said I was.

And maybe that's the scariest part.

I exhale slowly and try to steady myself by bracing my hands on the bathroom sink.

I shouldn't be here.

If my father hadn't died, if he'd done right by the years I gave him and Bishop Galleries, I'd still be in New York. I'd still be busy, sharp, untouchable. *And you'd still be pretending that chasing artists and investors and building an empire meant you weren't lonely and subconsciously craving a life that felt like living.*

I sigh. Bottom line, if my father hadn't died, I wouldn't be in Red Bridge. I wouldn't be in Tad Hanson's orbit. And I wouldn't be standing in Josie's bathroom with a pregnancy test on the counter.

And yet, here I am.

Whatever this thing is between Tad and me, I've been telling myself it's light and uncomplicated. I mean, casual is what we said from the start.

But maybe it never was...

God, what will he say if this test is positive?

What will *I* say? What will I *think and feel*?

Checking my watch quickly, I note the time that's passed and blow out another audible breath. There's about a minute left—a minute to wait on one of the scariest answers I've ever dared to ask for.

My phone buzzes in my purse, and I dig it out to look at it.

Tad: *You okay? I'm worried about you.*

Yeah. *I'm worried about me too.*

• • •

My steps are wooden and choppy as I head back down the hall toward Josie's kitchen, her and Norah's voices echoing softly toward me.

They bicker and laugh like only siblings can, and I take comfort in the warmth of familiarity. Bennett and I have always been loving enemies—the type of family that fights one minute and defends to the death the next—and Josie and Norah are much the same way.

Both of their heads come up as I round the corner, and my words catch in my chest.

"Well?" Norah asks gently, glancing back to Josie before settling on me once and for all.

It's all I can do to say the words. "I'm pregnant."

"Oh, Breezy," Norah whispers, joy and compassion and shock all wrapped up in the prettiest of sisterly bows. She's so good for Bennett, but she's good for me too. She's good for all of us. Her softness, her understanding—they're impossible to recreate. And goodness, I sure need them now more than ever.

Josie jumps up and pulls out a chair for me, and I plop into it unceremoniously, sinking my face into my hands. "What the fuck am I going to do?"

Norah's voice is gentle. "What do you mean, honey?"

"I meannn...I'm *pregnant.* I'm basically living at your house because New York doesn't feel like home anymore. I'm careerless. I'm without drive or direction or a plan or...anything. I don't recognize myself most days, let alone what I'm supposed to be as a *mother.* I don't—"

"Breezy, come on," Josie cuts in before I can completely spiral. "Sure, this is unexpected, but you've been kicking ass and taking names for as long as I've known you. You can handle anything—you've handled anything that's ever been thrown at you. If you want a plan, you'll come up with a plan. And if you want help, we'll help you."

"I don't know what I want," I admit. "I feel like, lately, I don't know anything."

"Maybe you needed this slow-down," Norah suggests, a tender hand rubbing at my shoulder. "Maybe...not having a plan or a direction or a job or drive...maybe that's what you needed. You know?"

I scoff. "Yeah. And it got me pregnant with a freaking sheep farmer's baby."

"What?" Josie shrieks. "Farmer Tad? Hot-to-trot freaking Farmer-ass Tad is the father?"

I laugh, but it doesn't feel all that humorous. I shrug. I sigh. "He's... Well, he's been great. And we were just...having some fun," I skirt around the truth of how much time I've been spending with Tad and how intense at times it's been between us.

Truthfully, fun has always been a part of it, but there's been something more intense there. Something that's far more intimate than two people just hooking up for funsies. *Something that's been making you feel things. Deep, deep things.*

Josie and Norah watch me closely, and I'm sure it has everything to do with the nosedive my mood is taking. Or the fact that tears are threatening to flood my eyes again.

I sniffle, swallow hard, and keep the emotion at bay. "I fear that the news of a baby is going to go over about like a bag of rocks."

How am I supposed to tell Tad that I'm pregnant? A baby isn't exactly within the realm of casual we had originally agreed to.

"Are you sure about that, Breeze?" Josie asks. "I mean, I know he's never been much for serious, but we call the man hot for a reason. And he's very nice. I can't imagine him being...I don't know, scummy? Like, it'll be a shock. Just like it is to you. But finding out you're having a baby is always a shock, isn't it?" Her voice lulls me into a weirdly peaceful space. It's so...ethereal. Happy. Hopeful. "Even if it's the thing you've always wanted most in the entire world."

Norah nods. "Of course. Another human? Made by you? It's one of those 'too big to be true' things, but you're way more prepared than you ever think you are because you *have to* be. And when you have to be, you just figure things out."

Yeah.

When you have to figure things out, you do. It's always but always been true for me, even when I've hated it. I am a woman who survives. A woman who thrives, whether the world helps her or not.

I have no choice but to handle this like I've always handled everything else.

Head on. Take charge.

I sure hope Tad sees it the same way.

35

Tad

Norah's car pulls into the driveway at just after five p.m. and rocks to a stop in front of their garage. I watch like a fucking stalker around the side of the sheer white curtain in my kitchen window, holding my breath as Breezy climbs from the passenger side, slams the door, and rounds the trunk to a waiting Norah, whose extended arm settles on Breezy's shoulder and ushers her inside.

I texted her earlier, a little after she and Norah left the Bishops' house in a rush, but I never received anything back.

It goes without saying that hasn't made me feel better about whatever is going on with her, but I'd be an asshole to hold it against her. She was more than gracious and patient and kind when I went twenty-four hours no contact not so long ago.

I don't know what is going through Breezy's mind right now. Is it the surprise appearance of her brother Logan that's sent her into a mental tailspin? Is she sick with some kind of bad virus? Is it a combination of all those things?

I wish I fucking knew. I wish she'd let me in because I can't shake the feeling that I want to be there for her in whatever capacity I can. Certainly not my usual MO, but I guess that's what happens when you care about someone.

And I really care about Breezy.

You more than care about her.

I lean a little closer to the window—trying to grow supersonic hearing or something as the two exchange words on the front steps before heading inside—and end up bumping my forehead into the glass like an idiot.

"What are you doing?" Randy asks from behind me, startling the curtain free from my hand and back into place as I spin to face him.

"Nothing." I smile nervously. "When'd you get inside?"

No one reads me like my brother—no one. We've been through every imaginable high and low together, and he's the only one who knows everything about me. Still, after the hell I've put him through, admitting that I've become inconveniently obsessed with Breezy Bishop and even went to the length of hiring her on as a fake farmhand to create an excuse to have her around all the time feels like a betrayal.

"Five minutes ago." Randy's hands settle on his hips. "I finished fixing the gate lock Crosby got through like *I* said I would. And then I moved over to the hole in the fence on the south side, but when you never showed up with more ribbon like *you* said you would, I just MacGyvered what was there for now. Sheep'll probably be out again in ten minutes, but can't shit out hot wire, now can I?"

"Sorry." I cringe, feeling a little bad for completely forgetting about him out there in the pasture. "It's getting around dinnertime anyway. We can finish tomorrow."

Randy shakes his head. "Fine. But I'm going to the diner for dinner, and if those fuckers get loose before I get back, I expect you to leave me out of it."

"No problem."

With a sigh as farewell, Randy pushes past me out the door and down the steps to his truck, firing it up and turning around to head for town while I peer out the window again. I watch for his taillights to disappear at the stop sign at the end of Maple and then head out the same door he just left through.

Instead of going to my truck, though, I cross the lawn on quick strides, cut through the gate, and make my way up Bennett and Norah's driveway until I'm standing at their front door.

I knock twice with gentle knuckles, hoping not to scare anyone or wake a sleeping Autumn for the second time today, and I wait, arms at my sides and mouth filled with uninvited saliva.

The inner door opens first, revealing a knowing-smile-sporting Norah through the storm door. She pushes it open too and then steps out onto the stoop beside me.

"Hey, Tad."

"Hey, Nor. Can I see Breezy? Is she home?" I ask, pretending I wasn't spying my ass off enough to know the answer to that question already.

"She's here, yes, but she's resting. I really think she needs the sleep, and with how exhausted she was, I doubt she'll be up before tomorrow morning."

"Is she…is she okay, though?"

Norah smiles gently. "Yes. She's fine. Why don't you go home for tonight—"

"Norah," Logan says from behind me, startling both of us before I can dive into more questions about Breezy's well-being. I don't know how he managed to pull in, park, and close his car door without us noticing, but he did, and his timing is really starting to make the two of us seem like a package deal—which is *not* to my advantage.

"Logan, what are you doing here?"

"What am I doing here? The same thing I've been doing here. Trying to set things right with my brother and sister. Please, let me inside so I can try."

Norah shakes her head. "It's not a good idea. Breezy needs

to rest, and Bennett doesn't want you here. I have to respect that. You need to leave until he's ready to talk to you."

"And where am I supposed to go exactly?"

"I hear the Red Bridge Inn is really nice. Or hell, maybe Tad here will put you up."

I scoff. "Not likely."

Norah sucks her lips into her mouth to block a laugh. "Sounds like the Inn is the place to be."

I laugh, and she turns her energy on me, pointing in my face. "You're laughing, but I'm pretty sure I told you to leave too."

I sigh. "Right. I'll try again tomorrow."

Shoving past Logan, I make my way back over the property line to my driveway and consider my options. The house—where I'll be tempted to stand at the damn window all night trying to get a peek—or my truck, which quite frankly, could take me any number of distracting places even if only for a little while.

The choice is obvious.

I climb inside and fire it up, flicking the switch to turn on my headlights only after I've pointed myself away from Norah and Bennett's house.

I don't think much about a plan, and when my truck seemingly pulls itself into the parking lot of The Country Club under ten minutes later, I chalk it up to muscle memory and nothing more.

The number of nights I've spent drinking my sorrows away at this bar could earn me a badge if that were the sort of thing Clay got off on giving out—sidenote, it's not. But over the past two months, that's clearly changed. Nights I used to spend at the bar have been spent at my house with Breezy instead. Well, besides a week ago, when I let myself drown in my fucking misery.

And right now, sitting with my belly to the bar tonight feels odd. Wrong, even.

Sheriff Peeler gives me a nod from the other end, and I jerk my chin back, focusing on the soda I just ordered to avoid all the other eyes.

Clay shuffles in and out from the back room, dragging in

cases of beer for the inevitable weekend rush that's a constant when you're the only watering hole in a twenty-five-mile radius, and Marty works the bar, filling orders and giving shit where appropriate.

Marty's wife, Sheila, is ponied up on one of the stools to my right, her low-cut top and tight jeans screaming "young mother out on the town for the night" in a way that makes me reflective.

The endless nights of feedings and light speed growth from infancy to toddlerdom.

The bittersweet feeling of a night to yourself—finally—only to spend it scrolling through pictures of your little one the whole time.

I shake my head and blow out a breath, considering a real drink.

Before I can think further on it, I wave at Marty to get his attention, and he holds up a finger while he stops on his way from the other end of the bar to flirt with his wife while they make the most of his working during their only chance for a date.

"Hey, Tad," Hillary Howard, Red Bridge's fast-talking real estate mogul, says from my left side, pushing into the bar behind me and throwing her own exasperated arm up at our bartending Casanova. "Ready to put your place on the market yet? I can get you a twenty percent return. I also have a nice little Tudor that would be perfect for you right off Spruce Lane. It was Sandy McHugh's old place before she left to live with her daughter and grandkids in Molene."

My chuckle is brittle at best, tired from the sheer amount of time I've been treading water while shark Hillary circles me. I swear she's been on my ass since the day after I moved in.

Why does she want me to sell the farm? It doesn't take a genius to figure out it has everything to do with my incompetence as a sheep farmer and the green beacon of dollar signs from the commission her bank account is seeking.

But I'm neither concerned with Hillary's bank account nor being good at sheep farming. "No, Hil. Still no interest in selling."

"Fine." She huffs. "But if you change your mind, now's a good time to do it. Supply is really low with places with land like yours, and demand is high with all these city folk looking for a change of pace. I heard even Bennett's sister moved out of the city, so it's only a matter of time before we're flooded."

I don't bother setting her straight on Breezy's temporary status. Frankly, it's none of Hustle Hillary's business, and it's something I'd prefer not to think about. "Okay. But I'm not selling."

"Suit yourself," she says then, huffing before shoving away from the bar and muttering, "Dammit, Marty, stop freaking flirting with the woman. She's going home with you, regardless."

She marches down to Sheila rather than waiting, blabbing at Marty as soon as she comes to a stop. Impatient, always.

But she was at least helpful in a way—dealing with her has shown me that I'm not in the mood to deal with people. I don't need to switch to liquor; I need to finish my soda and get the hell out of here pronto, before the real Saturday night crowd floods in.

Throwing my glass back for a hearty gulp and then wiping at the condensation that's damn near drenched my lap, I glance up just as Hollywood fuckface, Logan Bishop himself, sits down at the bar next to me.

"Jeez," I scoff. "Sometimes this town really is too small for its own good."

"Relax, Ted. I'm just here to have enough to drink that the Inn looks a little nicer. I won't bother you."

Annoyed by his never-ending misuse of my name and his arrogance over the way he's treated Breezy, I turn toward him, my heels hooked on the rungs of my stool and my knees cocked and open. "What is your deal anyway? You just want to torture your brother and sister until they break, or what? Neither one seems to want you here very much, and from what I've heard, I don't blame them."

He frowns, irritation leaching into his features. "Sounds like you haven't heard the whole story, then."

"I've heard their version, and I've got a feeling it's closer to the truth than yours."

Logan scoffs. "Yeah, I imagine you would think that. But the tits of it is, Ted, pretty much every story has three versions—yours, mine, and the third, the actual damn truth."

This guy. I fucking swear. Honestly, the only thing holding me back from punching him again is the fact that remnants of my first two punches are already showing up in the form of blue and purple bruises around his eyes.

"Okay, then," I challenge. "Enlighten me. What's your version so I can average the two of 'em out."

"I...well, I'm not perfect by any stretch of the imagination," Logan answers, though I sense a hint of hesitation in his voice. "I've done a lot of fucked-up shit, and I own that. But I did most of it with pure intentions, and for the last five years, I haven't made any choices I would change."

My eyebrows lift to my hairline. "That's a pretty big declaration. Five years, and you wouldn't change *anything*?" There's heat in my words, stoked by indignation. I know for a fact that he's done some shit here recently. It's how I ended up punching him in the fucking face twice in the first place.

Hell, maybe I shouldn't have kept his bruising war wounds from stopping a third time.

"Circumstances? Yes." He offers a cocky kind of shrug. One that makes it clear he really thinks the world of himself. "Fallout? Absolutely. My relationship with my siblings? Of course. That's why I'm fucking here. But my choices? They've been sound."

I roll my eyes, turning my belly back to the bar. "Maybe I don't need to hear your version."

"What?" he questions, putting both elbows on the bar. "What's your deal, Ted?"

"My deal is that you sound like a damn liar, and what a waste of fucking time listening to one of those is."

"I'm a lot of things, Farmer." Logan lets out an exasperated sigh. "But I'm *not* a liar."

"Then how do you explain the state of things now?" I ask, turning toward him to see the expression on the prick's face.

"What you did to Breezy? Stealing the galleries right out from under her?" I shake my head. "Sounds like a really fucked-up choice to me."

"I didn't steal them..." He growls, frustrated. "See, that's what I mean. There's another version to this, and the version I know is that my dad *left* me the galleries. I didn't lobby for that shit—I'm an actor. What the hell do I want with a bunch of art galleries?" He throws his hands up in the air. "But he was fucking determined to leave them to me in the will. No matter what I said or did, no matter how adamant I was that the galleries belonged to Breezy, he wouldn't change his patriarchal fucking mind. And I thought I had more time before the bastard up and died, but clearly, that wasn't in the cards."

He sighs and runs a hand through his hair, but he keeps going.

"The will was set, and I *don't* have the power to change it. I tried to get Breezy to stay on and run them. But she didn't want to hear it. Which, I understand, of course. It's a real kick in the nuts what my dad did. After all she's done for years and years." He shakes his head. "But I'm not a monster. I'm working with a lawyer to figure out what the hell I'm allowed to even do. If I give her the galleries—the stake my dad gave me in the will—she'll owe fucking millions and millions in taxes. I don't even know if she'd be able to swing it. I don't know if she'd be able to pay and keep them afloat. Not without filing for fucking bankruptcy at first, that is. And that's even if she stopped being stubborn and took the twenty mill my father gifted her in his will." He lets out a long exhale. "I'm trying to figure the shit out. But it's not easy. And the galleries are failing because Breezy is the backbone. I know that. She knows that. My fucking dad knew that. I just wish she'd come back to New York and run the galleries until we can figure out what can be done. Do what she's been doing and just up her salary to compensate in the meantime, you know?"

My head is bombarded with all the shit he just said, and all I can do is shake my head. "This isn't how Breezy tells it."

"Yeah. I know." He snorts, but there's no amusement. Only

frustration. "Because no one will let me stick around long enough to explain it. At least not without getting punched in the fucking face a couple of times."

I wince slightly, stretching my sore hand. "Sorry about that."

He blows out a breath. "Whatever. It's not like I haven't deserved it at one point or another."

"What about Bennett?" I find myself asking, even though I don't really know why. "Why's he hate you so much?"

"I... Well, I slept with his girlfriend once." His head bounces back and forth. "A few times."

I let out a low whistle. "Damn. That's fucked."

"Yeah, I know. It was a real asshole thing to do."

I eye him knowingly. "I'd say it makes you a little more than an asshole, brother."

"I get it. But I did it to break them up, and I can't complain about the results in that aspect. She was a snake. She would have latched on to him until she ruined his life, and he didn't need that shit at the time. He was in a real bad place, mostly because our father was an overbearing, controlling dick." He takes a swig of his drink. "Now, Norah, she's the kind of amazing woman he actually deserves."

The way he talks about Bennett...is not what I expected. I honestly thought he'd ramble on about what an asshole his brother is.

But confessing to the shady shit he's done, and even going so far as saying Bennett deserves an amazing wife like Norah? A plot twist, that's for damn sure.

"So, from what you're telling me here, you're maybe not as much of an asshole as I originally thought. And you quite possibly need to work on your delivery," I add through a shocked laugh. "Maybe you should consider some flowers or chocolates or some shit when you're breaking hard news. Maybe you should drop the egotistical-prick act and offer a buffer of kindness so you have some time to explain your side of things. You can't bulldoze people with hard news, you know?"

"Yeah." He chuckles. "I'll take that into consideration."

I don't know why I'm even offering advice to this guy, but there's just something in the way he's admitting his bullshit out loud that has me warming up to him a little. I'm not thawed out and melted down completely, but I'm not as icy as I was.

"Even a coffee delivery tomorrow morning—when you undoubtedly plan to show up to your brother's house again, begging to be let in—wouldn't be a bad idea," I suggest. "I've not seen anyone in Red Bridge waste a good cup of CAFFEINE coffee before. So you'd have to at least set it down to get hit." I shrug. "But hey, you do you."

"Yeah," Logan says, considering me a little more closely. "That's not a bad idea, actually. Thanks."

I lift my shoulders and take the last pull from my soda, rubbing at the beading water on the glass.

"And what about you?" Logan asks. "What's your deal? Why's Bennett so quick to give you shit? He seemed real fucking pissed over the idea of you and Breezy being a thing."

I lick my teeth, considering how much I'm willing to say. "I guess most people in town don't take the sheep farmer too seriously."

"Yeah. But it's more than that. I don't know... Seems like maybe you don't take yourself very seriously either."

"What's the point?" I contend. "Why shouldn't I just take shit one day at a time? Why should any of it have to be serious?"

Logan squints. "Because sometimes shit is serious. Sometimes life is fucking serious. People die."

I purse my lips. "Yeah, I'm aware."

I am *more* than aware that people die. So fucking aware I definitely should've switched to liquor.

Done with the conversation, I shove off my stool, dig in my pocket, and toss a ten-dollar bill on the bar for Marty. He nods at me, and I turn to leave without saying goodbye.

Logan doesn't push it, letting me walk away without calling after me, and I'm glad because I sure would've hated to aggravate my sore hand again.

Cold air punches me in the throat and burns its way into my chest as I crunch across the gravel parking lot of The Country Club and climb into the single cab of my truck. I can see my breath in front of me—ragged and scattered and messy—and it's all I can do not to get caught up in old wounds.

The first person I feel like calling or texting or going to is Breezy. But it's no surprise. I'm still worried about her. And after having a long-ass, unplanned conversation with her brother, I can't stop myself from sending her a quick text.

Me: *Just wanted you to know I'm thinking about you. Hope you're okay. Hope you're getting the rest you need. And hope you know I'm here. I'm always here.*

I stare down at the phone for a long moment. A part of me hoping to see bouncing text bubbles indicating she's answering me. A part of me hoping she'll help drown out the ghosts that are threatening to suffocate me.

But when nothing comes, I set my phone into the cupholder and crank the engine of my truck.

With a shake of my head, I grab the gearshift and pull it down into drive and aim toward home.

The farm and the sheep will be waiting.

And heading toward them is a hell of a lot better than getting sucked back into the past.

36

Breezy

Sunday, March 21st

Yesterday, after getting home from Josie's house, I crawled straight into bed and didn't move again until the sun forced its way through the curtains.

I just needed a moment to wrap my mind around the life-altering, I'm-going-be-a-mama news. I also needed more moments to cry and throw up and stare at the ceiling for what felt like hours, whispering the same words in my head until they finally stuck.

I'm pregnant. With Tad's baby.

Tad texted me yesterday—twice—but I never responded. Lord knows, it had been a long day of puking, tears, exhaustion, life-changing news, and that didn't even include the pay-per-view worthy fight that broke out between Bennett and Logan and Tad.

I still don't know the whys and hows of Tad ending up in the fray of my brothers' bullshit, but I can only assume the shouting carried all the way over to his farm.

So, yeah. When I woke up this morning and saw Tad's texts still sitting there unanswered by me, I knew what I needed to do.

I don't know exactly *how* I'm going to say the words—*I'm pregnant with your baby* doesn't exactly roll off the tongue—but showing up with his favorite coffee from CAFFEINE feels like a decent start.

Josie's coffee shop is busy as hell, but that's probably because it's Sunday morning. Besides The Diner, this is the go-to spot for the after-church crowd, and no one is ever in a rush to leave.

I put in my order with Josie at the register, and by the look in her knowing eyes, she understands what the order stands for. But she doesn't say anything. Doesn't question or hound me about it. She just nods, types it in, and slides my change across the counter like we're playing poker and she's protecting my hand from the world. Too many ears in the room to say anything else.

Camille makes my two coffees, and I take them over to sit down at an empty bistro table to wait for the rest of my order. It's only a few minutes later when Josie delivers my muffin with a wink and a smile before retreating to the counter, Clay chasing behind her while she swats his hands away from her ass.

"Get away from me, wild man!"

"Don't tempt me, Josie. I'm all prepared to show you wild," Clay taunts.

She giggles, and I tuck my returning smile behind a sip of coffee when she looks back over at me. Josie is the type who wants to be happy—and wants you to be happy for her—but she sure as hell doesn't want to hear about it.

She's a lot like me in that way; she's tough, hardened from trauma and loss and family betrayal. Closed off with a gate and a latch and a lock and a chain to protect herself from what might happen if she lets anyone inside.

But damn, openness looks good on her. Happiness, joy, contentment with Clay—it all looks good on her. I'm ninety-nine percent happy for her and one percent jealous. It's a future for which I'm not sure I'm destined—a future I never really considered wanting—and yet, Josie makes it look almost good. Tolerable, at worst. And truth be told, if my life in New York had been great, I wouldn't have ended up here.

I take a bite of my muffin to settle my stomach and take another sip of my coffee as I pretend to flip through a free *Red Bridge Tourist* magazine I grabbed from the counter to keep myself looking busy. Tad's to-go cup sits waiting next to mine, a stopper to prevent spills in the hole in the lid, and his name scrawled in Josie's handwriting on the side to keep me from mixing them up.

I stare at his untouched coffee for a long time.

Telling him he's going to be a dad feels like standing on a cliff and waiting to see if the ground gives way. But I need to do it. I *want* to do it. The sooner I put it out there in the open, the sooner I can start to deal with it myself.

Josie's coffee is merely a tool for consolation and coming in peace.

Okay, Breezy, time to face the music.

Just as I'm gathering my things, the bell over the door dings, and Logan walks in, his hair combed and a nice shirt belying the casual man I know him to be. He's a jeans and T-shirts guy—so much so, he's worn them on the red carpet before—and seeing him all put together is an unexpected surprise.

An unwelcome surprise, but a surprise, nonetheless. The last person I plan on dealing with today is Logan. I've got too much on my plate as it is—you know, in breaking the bun-in-the-oven news to Farm Daddy.

My brother sidles up to the counter without noticing me, nervously fidgeting as he looks over the menu. I listen a little—I can't help myself—as he clears his throat before asking Josie a question.

"Hey, uh...you wouldn't happen to know Ben and Norah's regular order, would you?"

Josie quirks a skeptical brow. "And why would you want to know that?"

"I...I thought it might be a nice, friendly gesture. A...you know, peace offering of sorts if I showed up at their house with some coffee."

I know for a fact that Logan knows that Josie is Norah's sister, but I don't think the two of them have ever had an actual face-to-face conversation. Josie definitely knows about yesterday's unexpected visit and subsequent tussle, but at his explanation, her icy exterior melts just a little before she glances at me, which makes Logan notice me for the first time too.

"Oh hey, Breeze," he greets affectionately. "How're you feeling today?"

I smile. His eyes are both rimmed with mauvy-purple bruising that yellows slightly right at the edge. "Much better today. Thanks. How's your face?"

He shrugs. "Eh. I'm sure I've deserved worse over the years. I'll tell you what, though. That farmer can punch."

I snort, and it forms a harmony with the sound of the bell over the door ringing with a new customer's entrance.

Norah is instantly recognizable, a pink and purple and orange scarf wrapped generously around her neck and a sweet pair of pink heart sunglasses on her nose. Bennett is right behind her with a pigtail-sporting Autumn in his arms, and she bounces on his hip with unconcealed excitement to get down as soon as she sees Josie behind the counter.

"JoJo!" my cute niece squeals in excitement as she toddles toward her other aunt.

Logan turns his body away from me toward them, and as soon as Autumn spots him, she stops to point her little index finger at him. "Bam Bam!"

I kind of want to laugh over how damn much her little toddler brain can remember, but when Ben makes eye contact with Logan, we're back in the middle of a battlefield. Metaphorical bombs in the form of gritted teeth and sharp exhales explode in the room, and I heave the beleaguered sigh of a woman who's been dealing with this for literal decades.

And now, I'm pregnant—and let me tell you, the hormones aren't doing anything for the patience portion of my disposition.

"What the hell are you doing here?" Bennett demands immediately, no subtle entry to the aggression at all, and Norah doesn't hesitate to grab Autumn and pull her into her arms.

No doubt, she's still on edge from the last time Logan and Bennett were in the same room together. Hell, I am too. Every nerve in my body is clenched tight, and I'm still sitting at the bistro table instead of making my exit.

Logan holds up both hands innocently, and for the first time in a long time, I feel bad for our youngest brother. He's done plenty of shit to deserve his spot in the doghouse over the years, but at this point, all the anger is getting a little clichéd.

"I just came in to get coffee. For myself and for…you guys, actually. Josie's already whipping up your favorite drinks for me. I was… Well, I was hoping if I showed up with coffee, you'd at least take it from me before you started throwing fists."

"I'd never hit someone in here." Norah, Josie, and Clay all scoff, and Bennett rolls his eyes, amending his statement by adding, "*Again*."

"Listen here!" Josie yells, not even waiting for a response from Logan or anyone else. "You're either drinking coffee or getting out. Nothing else is going on in here, you hear me? No cursing, no arguing, and definitely no hitting."

Clay laughs. "Talk about a family reunion."

When the bell over the door rings again, I half expect my dead father to have come back from the grave and arrived in Red Bridge—but instead, it's the one man I've been thinking about all damn morning and night.

Tad. The unwitting father of my baking bun. The sheep farmer with the sperm power of a thoroughbred. And the man whose coffee is sitting right in front of me.

But before I can act or react or do something in the name of grabbing his attention, a frazzled-looking Eileen Martin comes storming in behind him. A stack of newspapers practically weighs down her arms, and when the door falls closed behind her, it knocks her forward with a hit to her ass.

Unfazed, she starts yelling. "Hot off the presses! Hot off the presses! Get the latest issue of the *Red Bridge Chronicle* right here!"

When people ignore her, she turns into a tornado, purposefully grabbing the attention of everyone in the coffee shop by shoving papers in their hands and faces and laps. Sue Nagel, Betty Bagley, Hal Newton, Derrick and Fran, Sheriff Pete—they're all here and being forced to read the damn newspaper, and those are just the faces I can see.

As Norah cracks open the paper, I get a look at the front page—and my name emblazoned in big, bold letters along with Josie's is the first thing I see. Norah moves it quickly before I can get a read on the whole headline, but mayhem explodes quickly enough that I wouldn't bet any money on it saying something good.

"What the *fuck*, Eileen?" Josie yells, all bans on cursing, arguing, and quite possibly fistfighting going right out the window.

I jump up and grab the paper right out of Eileen's stack, flipping to the front and swaying slightly when my stomach flips completely over inside me.

Swans are in the air in Red Bridge: Josie Harris and Breezy Bishop BOTH pregnant!

Logan grabs both of my biceps to steady me as I sway even farther, settling me into the chair across from the one I vacated with worried eyes. "Breeze? Breeze!" I can see his mouth moving, but the sound is nothing but white noise.

I glance from him to Norah, and then Bennett, and then Clay and Josie, who are hugging in front of the counter like being connected is their only lifeline.

And then I swing to the door—to a wide-eyed, completely frozen Tad right in front of it.

His hands shake slightly, his fingers clenched on each side of the newspaper as he stares right at me. I know immediately he'd just as much like to know the truth—if what the paper says is real—as he'd like to time-travel to somewhere in the past and never come back.

He's in real, raw shock. To be finding out like this—I can't even imagine.

I lick my lips and steady my chin, holding it up. And then, I nod. Twice. Once for confirmation, and then again to prove his eyes aren't deceiving him.

After that, I leave the ball in his court, and for as much as I'm hoping he'll rush toward me and pull me into his arms, I can't—I won't—judge him for any other response.

He can run. He can yell. He can faint.

It doesn't matter. I've promised myself grace—for him and for me—and that means giving him the time to process however he sees fit.

The door bursts open behind him, a young, fashionable woman throwing her hands in the air and shouting. "Surprise! I'm heeerrreee!"

It's only then I recognize her as Norah's best friend from New York, Lillian, a weirdness flowing over her as she reads the room. "Okay, whoa. What the hell did I just walk into?"

My eyes jump back to Tad automatically.

White washes over his face, sickness and a sudden problem with digestion, I'm guessing, turning him ill. I wish it didn't make my heart flip in my chest, but it does. I don't blame him, but I do feel bad for myself.

Last night, I finally let myself come to terms with the fact that my life of independence in New York and the boss-bitch persona I played so well was one comprised of loneliness. It was battles fought on my own and tears cried in the shower. It was strong will and the ability to handle anything that came my way—traits born because I had to.

I've always been the caretaker, but so often, when you take on that role, no one takes care of you.

And God, no matter how hard it is to admit this, I desperately want someone to take care of me.

I want someone to comfort me in times of trial and champion my wins. Someone to wade through the mud with me, no matter the depth.

I know this thing with Tad started out as casual, but when I wasn't looking, hope edged in. Longing and dreaming and daring to think, maybe, I wouldn't always have to do it alone.

His reaction is valid. Hell, I'm shocked by the way Eileen just plastered the news everywhere, and I'm already in the know.

And yet…it still stings.

"I can't believe you fucking did this!" Josie shouts at the top of her lungs. "You had no right, Eileen! You had no fucking right!"

"Fu-ck!" Autumn yells in unison, but this time, Norah doesn't even correct her. Sometimes the f-word is all that's appropriate in a tense moment like this.

"This was my news to tell!" Josie hollers, and Clay wraps his arm around her shoulders.

Josie's pregnant too? If I weren't so wrapped up in my own pregnancy and Tad's subsequent outright shocked reaction that's currently taking place across this coffee shop, I'd probably be wondering why she didn't tell me. Or how she managed to get pregnant in the first place. For the longest time, I was one of the only people who knew about the tragic accident that turned her world on its head.

"It's okay, Josie," Clay reassures, squeezing Josie tightly to his side.

Eileen stands there, a mix of delight and outright fear residing in the crow's-feet of her eyes. I think there's a part of her that's flying high on cloud nine for breaking the bombshells of news that are quite literally true for once in her sleazy journalistic life. But there's also another part that's scared shitless as the rage-filled eyes of Josie Harris stare through her soul.

"No. It's not okay!" Josie shakes her head, tears streaming down her cheeks. "I'm pregnant and emotional, and the only thing that will make me feel better is if I get to kill Eileen!"

"Whoa, whoa, whoa," Sheriff Peeler bellows, heading into the fray to stop a homicide. "Let's everyone calm down."

All I can do is look back at Tad. His eyes are as wide as Josie's big coffee mugs, flitting between me and the newspaper clenched tightly in his hands. He gulps once, and then three more times after that.

A cacophony of screams breaks the sound barrier as Josie gets more riled up, and Clay and Bennett join in, shouting at Eileen for her gross invasion of privacy, all the while Sheriff Peeler does his best to make sure their altercation doesn't end in bloodshed.

Norah tries to shelter the newly arrived Lillian from the sharp word bullets being tossed in the air with a quick hello hug, and Autumn clings to her shirt while simultaneously repeating the word *fuck* every time someone shouts it.

But it's all basically background noise as I keep my eyes locked on Tad.

His feet are the first things to move, the rest of his body seemingly in limbo or purgatory—or hell, I suppose—skittering and scampering until they get traction out the door. It falls closed behind him as I watch on in horror as he jogs to his truck and jumps in, peeling out of the spot at the curb and taking off down Main Street at double the speed limit.

When I turn back to reality, my heart in my throat and chaos still living and breathing inside Josie's coffee shop, Logan's gaze finds mine. There's a softness in his face that's been missing for fifteen years or more, and I know with horrifying reality its root cause is pity. *For me.*

I can practically smell tomorrow's headline now.

Poor Beatrice Bishop: Upon pregnancy announcement in paper, Farm Daddy flees town for good.

Boy, that silly nickname didn't age well, did it?

37

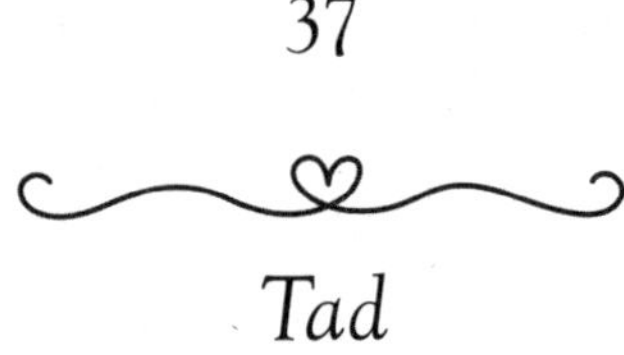

Tad

Breezy's *pregnant.*

Breezy's. Pregnant.

Breezy's pregnant.

Knuckles white and mottled, I grip the wheel and try to focus on the road as I tear out of town past the water tower toward Molene. Thoughts move faster than my wheels, and repeated chills run up and down my spine.

Sweat dots my forehead and drips from my lip as I try to find a way to calm down, but the onslaught of memories is too much, too fast, all at once.

The first day of spring break plans.

The eggs on the stove.

The smell of coffee in the pot as I left for my forty-eight-hour shift.

Veering recklessly off the road and into the heavy, snow-caked dirt on the side of it, I slam on the brakes and skid to a stop, my breathing labored.

Salty tears tinge my previously dry throat.

"I wasn't supposed to do this again," I murmur.

My words are soft and pleading at first until they grow some legs and start sprinting off my tongue. *"Why? Why? Fucking why?"* I shout into the cab, the question an affront to God himself and the plan he saw fit for me. The cruelty. The disparity. The ironic end to a sheep-filled pathetic effort at doing something other than ending it all.

"Why? Why would you do this to me? Don't you see I'm barely surviving? Don't you see?"

Tears fall unchecked now as I plunge forehead-first into the steering wheel, setting off the horn and startling myself back upright. My chest shakes, and tears breach the corners of my eyes. I pull up my shirt and wipe them away, hammering the sick moisture in my throat back down with sheer will.

A dangerous numbness washes over me as I move the shifter back into gear and pull back out onto the road without even looking for traffic. I hang a U-turn, swinging back in the direction I came from, but instead of going back to CAFFEINE, I drive straight home. The lump in my throat is big enough to close it off completely, but for now at least, it's stopped up the tears.

Randy is in the front, repairing a stretch of fence and lining it with the new electric ribbon from the co-op I was supposed to bring back out to him yesterday when I was spying on Breezy, his head rotating up at the sound of me pulling in.

I shift into park and turn the key, but I don't climb out. The truth is, I don't think I can.

I don't know how long I sit there—time disappears into a vacuum of nothing and everything all at once—but the knock on my window from Randy's folded knuckles eventually ends the spell.

I shake my head, the energy to open the window or door as vacant as my sanity. He rounds the hood then, opening the passenger door, climbing inside, and tossing his heavy, yellowish leather work gloves up onto the dash and stretching his arm out across the bench seat.

When I don't move, he squeezes my shoulder. "Rough day?"

"Bennett's sister," I say, the words sounding like they're coming from somewhere—anywhere—other than me. "Breezy. You know her. We've...well, we've been sleeping together."

"Yeah, brother. I know," he answers without hesitation. "The whole farmhand thing wasn't a very good cover, considering farmhands usually do actual work and they don't sleep in your bed or wake up in the house in the morning wearing your fucking clothes."

Yeah. I guess Breezy and I have been spending way too much time together for that bullshit cover story to seem true to my brother. The man might not live in the farmhouse anymore, but he's here every day.

"Eileen announced her pregnancy in the paper this morning. Breezy's pregnancy," I clarify, realizing how it sounds. "Not Eileen's."

He's thoughtful. Silent. Painfully fucking calm.

"It wasn't supposed to be like this," I say, a desperation breaking through the numbness. "It was never supposed to happen for me again. I keep it casual. I don't get serious. I don't...I can't."

"You can." It's guileless. Kind. Patient. It's everything I'm incapable of right now.

"I *can't*." I shake my head against the desperate urge to run away to a whole new place and never look back. "I was never supposed to be in this place again."

"What place?" he asks, his voice soft.

I swallow thick saliva down like a golf ball to clear the path to honesty. "At risk of losing everything."

Randy lets out a deep, sympathetic sigh. "Oh, brother."

"I just don't...I don't think I can do it." I say it like I'm asking permission. I say it like Randy, somehow, can absolve me of a nagging, building sense of guilt because he *knows*. He knows where I came from, what I've been through. He knows how broken I am—how unfit a cracked foundation is to hold up a new house.

"What's the other option?" he asks instead, the gentleness in his voice doing nothing to quell my nausea. "I know there's risk. I know it feels scary and impossible, and I know it wasn't supposed to happen. But it *did*. And as much as you're having a hard time with the risk of losing everything, the fact that you have it to lose?" He shakes his head. "Tad, that's a gift."

My head falls forward, and I bring my hands up to meet it. He reaches out to squeeze my shoulder once again.

"Take a little time to get yourself together. You've more than earned that. But then you move forward. Don't let the past hold you back from this. You've done your time. You've been a shell long enough. You deserve happiness, Tad. You really fucking do."

Emotion clogs my throat, but I swallow it away. My mind still reels at what went down in Josie's coffee shop this morning. The shock of seeing the news of Breezy's pregnancy in the fucking newspaper. How sad and worried her eyes looked when they met mine. The hesitant way she nodded her head to confirm the truth.

And my insane reaction to all of it.

"I ran out of the coffee shop without saying a word to her," I say, but my voice rasps with guilt and shame. "She looked scared, and...and I couldn't do anything but leave."

"Brother, you found out your girl was pregnant in a fucking newspaper in a busy coffee shop," Randy says through a soft laugh. "That would make any man want to run. Even men who haven't been through the shit you've been through."

"I don't know, Ran. I feel awful for fleeing the scene like that. I didn't go over to her, didn't say a word. I just left like a fucking coward."

"Relax, man. You'll fix it." He pats my shoulder. "I know you don't think about this much, but once upon a time, my brother was so confident in himself, he didn't think there was anything he couldn't fix."

Both of us know he's right. But both of us know why I haven't been that guy lately too.

And with no one and nothing but myself to worry about, I

didn't need to be.

That's changing now. Breezy—and the baby we made together—need me to be more. I have to choose to be the best version of myself, for them.

Breezy deserves that.

Our baby deserves that.

And fuck, maybe I deserve that too?

In one smooth motion, he snatches his gloves from the dashboard and pops the door open to climb back out of the truck. Before he can close the door, I stop him.

"Randy, wait."

He turns back, slightly disgruntled. "What?"

"Thank you."

"For what exactly?" he asks, quirking a cocky eyebrow in my direction. "For my years of patience with these stupid fucking sheep? For my sage wisdom? Or maybe it's everything combined?"

I laugh. I can't help it. "For everything combined," I tell him. "You are, obviously, the better brother. I wouldn't have survived without you."

He nods, his jaw rolling. "Oh, I know."

No more.

It's time to start living my life like I'm alive again. It's time to stop focusing on where I should've been ten years ago and start being where I need to be right now.

38

Breezy

Monday, March 22nd

I didn't think the hardest part of being pregnant would be sitting still.

But here I am, perched in a green pleather chair that squeaks every time I breathe too deeply and gripping a clipboard like it's the only thing keeping me grounded. The OB-GYN office smells faintly of antiseptic and lavender lotion, and soft jazz hums through the speakers like it's trying a little *too* hard to be calming.

But it's incredibly hard to be calm when you're newly pregnant and your baby daddy has been MIA since finding out the news.

I haven't seen or spoken to Tad since Eileen dropped the baby bombshell in the middle of Josie's coffee shop, and while it's got me tied up in knots not knowing what he's thinking or feeling or wanting, I've resigned myself to giving him some space.

It's only been twenty-four hours since he found out. Hell, I've only known a day longer than him, and my brain feels like a hamster on a caffeine bender.

So, for now, I'm doing my best to stay hopeful and take this one heartbeat at a time. Sure, Tad could decide he wants nothing to do with me or this baby. But unless he Ubered out of Red Bridge overnight, the fact that his truck was still in his driveway before I left for this appointment tells me he hasn't bolted for the Canadian border.

Silver linings? I'll take whatever I can get at this point.

Women dot the space all around the reception room, some with bellies already swollen with babies and some without. All of us waiting. All of us quiet. And for a moment, it reminds me of New York. The anonymity. The pretending. The guessing who everyone is without ever really knowing.

I used to love that kind of mystery.

Now, even though I'm in a room full of people, it feels solitary to be sitting here by myself.

I click the pen attached to the clipboard and start filling out the medical history forms the lady at the front desk gave me. I understand why they need all the information, but it has to be one of the top five worst chores of adulthood.

Name, address, date of birth.

Easy enough. I write my answers down.

But when I reach **Employer**, the pen stills.

For the first time in my adult life, I don't have one.

I stare at the empty line. Once upon a time, I would've written *Bishop Galleries* in big, confident letters. But that woman is gone.

Now, I'm just...me. A woman who fell into a small town, fell into a man's bed for two months straight, and wound up pregnant with his baby.

I have no career and no official home. I'm a wanderer. Nomadic. A finder of new experiences and a fly-by-the-seat-of-my-pantser.

A week ago, I never would have dreamed my pants would be

flying me to an expanding uterus and an appointment with an OB to confirm what three home tests say are true, but I guess life moves fast when you're a woman without a plan and an eye for the hot sheep farmer next door.

I sigh. *Oh Breezy, how your life has changed.*

The door by the front desk opens with a squeak, and a nurse calls out, "Jasmine Wilks?"

A glowing woman with a baby-ready belly stands and smiles, her husband rising right beside her. They both look nervous but happy. They look like a team.

I bite the inside of my cheek.

Maybe it's better if I don't think too hard about who's missing from my side of the waiting room. *Probably better if I just focus on myself right now.*

I didn't think I'd be doing this by myself—I didn't think I'd be doing this at all, I guess. But when I called the OB-GYN office Norah recommended, I was more than happy to take a same-day appointment.

You can never be too sure that you're pregnant, right?

Plus, I can only assume there's information I need to know about growing another human being. When Norah was pregnant with Autumn, I remember being shocked she couldn't eat cold cut subs or sit in hot tubs, and I don't know the first thing about blood work or glucose tests. Needless to say, my years of working in the world of art won't come in handy here.

Norah offered to come with me to this appointment, as did Bennett. Josie offered too, when she called this morning to see how I was doing and gave me some insight into her pregnancy. *You know, the one Eileen decided to blast all over Red Bridge via the newspaper, right along with mine.* We didn't have a lot of time to chat because she was in the middle of a Monday morning rush at CAFFEINE, but I know she's equal parts ecstatic and terrified. And seeing as she's spent nearly the last decade thinking pregnancy wasn't a possibility for her, I'd say it makes sense why she's been so tight-lipped about it too.

Even Logan offered to be my sidekick to this appointment when he texted me to see if I wanted to meet somewhere in Red Bridge for lunch. *Yes, he's still here. Insert heavy sigh.* I knew that chat would involve the galleries and our father's will and all the things I simply do not have the energy to be thinking about right now, and this appointment was my get-out-of-jail-free-card excuse.

But mostly, I thought having anyone else tag along would make me feel lonelier.

Maybe I should have considered it harder.

On a faint sigh, I focus back on the paperwork. I scrawl ***Unemployed*** across the line, finish my insurance section, sign a stack of consent forms I barely read, and return the clipboard to the front desk.

I'm halfway back to my chair when the door opens again, revealing the person who didn't offer to come but I wanted here the most.

Tad.

My heart stutters hard enough to make me dizzy. He scans the room—all quick, searching movements—until his eyes find mine. Relief flashes across his face like sunlight breaking through clouds.

"Breezy!" he says, voice rough, urgent. "Did you see the doctor yet?"

"No," I say quietly and shake my head. Tears threaten to prick my eyes, and my throat is so tight I'm having a hard time forming words. "Just...uh..." I clear my throat. "Waiting my turn."

"Good." He exhales like he's been holding his breath for hours. "I was afraid I'd missed it."

"Missed it?"

"The appointment." He lowers his voice and pulls me gently toward him, guiding me to a couple of chairs on the far side of the room with a hand at the small of my back. "I went to Bennett's house this morning to talk to you, but Norah said you were on your way here. After she gave me the address, I just got in my truck and drove as fast as I could." He lets out another deep exhale of air. "God, Breezy. I'm so sorry for the way I reacted at CAFFEINE. I... Well, it came as a shock, you know?"

I nod.

"But I'm sure it came as a shock to you too, and I should have stuck around to talk about it. I should've stayed by your side because you shouldn't have to face any of this alone."

"It's okay, Tad." My hands shake, and he reaches out to pancake them with his. Everything inside me settles. "I get it. Really. I'm just glad you're here now."

"Are you nervous?" he asks, his voice so earnest I could cry. It's the care I've longed for, the support I didn't even know how much I needed.

"Yes. I don't see how I couldn't be. I've... Well, I've never been pregnant before, and I sure as heck wasn't expecting this."

He nods before looking down at the floor and swallowing thickly. "The nerves will pass soon, and then the excitement will set in," he comforts. "That first sound of the heartbeat. The first picture of a tiny human inside... We'll never be the same."

I want to ask him where he gets his wisdom—how he's smart enough to recognize the little things in the midst of a scariness neither of us has ever known. It's a whole other level of the human experience to be responsible for a person other than yourself.

"Beatrice Bishop?" the same dark-haired nurse as before calls from the door by the front desk. It's a little awkward, walking toward her, knowing Tad is walking behind me while other women in the room watch just as I did with Jasmine before.

But it's good awkward. It's new. It's joyful. It's fulfilling.

Tad's right. I have a very, very strong feeling I'm about to be irrevocably changed.

Once we're through the door, the nurse leading the way, I glance back at him. For once, I don't bother hiding how nervous I am. I've commanded many rooms in the last two decades, negotiated million-dollar art deals, and stood toe-to-toe with men who thought I didn't belong in their world of obscene wealth.

But this feels like stepping into the unknown.

I'm entering into a new endeavor that has a hell of a lot less room for failure and much higher stakes.

Tad reads it all easily, hurrying his step to put his hand on my back and whisper in my ear, "It's all going to be okay."

I nod. I know he can't know that's true, and I can't either—but somehow, the comfort of him saying it anyway is enough to settle my stomach.

"Step on the scale for me," the nurse directs, gesturing in front of her and waiting as I scramble to hand Tad my purse and sweater and coat and scarf.

He takes it all with a gentle laugh. "Definitely don't get on there with all this shit. It's at least twenty pounds."

The nurse smiles, and I step up on the scale. I expect her to read my weight aloud—like the unbothered nurses in New York always do—but she doesn't, sending me a wink as she writes it on her clipboard instead. "All right, we'll just need a urine sample. Restroom's right behind you, and the cups are on the counter. Label it, cap it, and bring it back out with you. You'll be in room number four, and your..." She looks directly at Tad, and I don't have a clue what to call him.

When *Farm Daddy* is the only title that pops into my head, I just about swallow my tongue and start choking on my own saliva.

"Boyfriend," Tad eventually supplies with a smile that looks completely at ease with the label.

"Your boyfriend can wait in there for you."

"Great," I say through a burning throat, my mind running like a racehorse with extensive training and a need for glory.

Within the span of a few months, I've gone from perpetual single gal in the city with balls of steel to a pregnant, small-town girl who nearly weeps over the simple designation of the title boyfriend by the boy himself. If I showed the Breezy of last year this version of me, she wouldn't even recognize herself.

Slightly embarrassed but on a schedule, I lock myself in the bathroom and do the impossible—point an unruly hose with no aim capacity into a plastic cup beneath me and get it all in without peeing on my hand.

Once I've washed my hands and labeled everything, I head to room four, where Tad's already waiting. He's sitting with his ankle crossed over his knee and his arm stretched along the back of the chair beside him. My things are neatly folded and piled on the empty cushion.

He's just kind of staring off into the distance. He looks relatively calm—calmer than I feel—but pensive, and I try not to call too much attention to it as I enter the space.

"Hey," he says, jolting slightly when I walk in. I set the cup on the counter as inconspicuously as possible and awkwardly climb onto the exam table. The paper crinkles obnoxiously beneath me, and we both laugh.

A knock comes almost immediately, and the nurse reappears, rolling in a small computer cart. She dips a test strip into my sample, then turns to me.

"Okay, while that test is processing, let's talk about your symptoms and a little bit about your medical history."

I nod, trying to look composed even as Tad sits a few feet away. We've gotten close, sure, but this level of intimacy feels like diving off a cliff.

Pretty sure the cat is too far out of the bag to stuff it back in, Breeze.

Yeah. It's safe to say that, whether we like it or not, we're going to be knowing a whole lot about each other for the next nineteen years at minimum. And even after that, pretending we won't be involved is a joke—children are for life, accidental or not.

"When was the start of your last menstrual period, Breezy?"

"Um...I guess like six or seven weeks ago," I answer as honestly as I can. "I was on birth control but...yeah. I guess it wasn't controlling much."

"Funnily enough, I have a five-year-old wild child named

Tilly for that very reason." The nurse smiles at me. "And your periods...they're pretty regular?"

I smile, laughing a little through my nerves. "Normally, yes."

"And any other symptoms. Nausea, breast tenderness, fatigue?"

"Yes. All of the above, actually. Plus, puking and crying a lot."

The nurse nods knowingly. "And have you had any spotting or bleeding?"

"No, none."

"Okay, great. And as far as family medical history...anything genetically significant we should know about?"

I glance at Tad, my heart suddenly thundering. "Well...I had a niece with Osteogenesis Imperfecta Type III. But my brother also has another daughter without the mutation."

She types in her computer, nodding gently. "Okay. Well, the doctor will be in shortly to see you, and then we'll go from there."

"Thanks," I say.

She smiles, leaving the computer behind and exiting through the door she came in before pulling it closed behind her. I hear sounds—like she's messing with the little plastic flag above my door and then silence.

I feel like maybe I should fill it with something, but I'm surprised when Tad does the talking for me.

"I know this is going to sound a little...scary...but I think you should move in with me."

"What?" I gasp. "We don't even have the doctor-confirmed results yet!"

He smirks. "Okay, then, after we do. If it says what we're both fairly sure it's gonna say, I think you should move in with me." He winks. "I mean, I guess I am Farm Daddy after all."

I laugh, but I also groan, because holy hell, my head is spinning. "Okay, if you were trying to distract me from the nerves of the appointment, I think it's working, but you can cut it out now."

His voice is soft and calm as he stands up from the chair and takes my hand in his. "I'm serious, Breeze," he says, and his eyes lock with mine. "I know it's quick, but the baby growing inside you right now really likes to keep its foot on the gas. There are going to be appointments and cravings and sickness and swollen ankles and hard days and good days and everything in between, and for as shocked as I was at first, I'm ready for it now. I want to be around. I want to be a part of it. I don't want to miss something or leave you to fend for yourself. I want to handle it together, with you, every step of the way." He smiles at me through eyes that are hesitant yet sure at the same time. "Please, I'm practically begging at this point, but that's okay. Don't go back to New York. Do not pass go. Do not collect two hundred dollars. Stay in Red Bridge. Move in with me."

"Well, jeez." I scoff, throwing my hands up and sending his flying incidentally. "How am I supposed to say no to a speech like that?"

He smiles and reaches up to brush a piece of hair behind my ear. "You're not."

"And I wasn't planning on going back to New York," I admit the truth. "In a very strange way, Red Bridge has started to feel like home."

"Well, how about you take that a step further and really make it home...with me?"

"Okay..." I don't say the word yes out loud, but I'm definitely nodding as a strong knock on the door grabs both of our attention. It opens, and a blond woman in a white medical coat with bright green eyes and a symmetrically perfect smile walks in. She takes two pumps of soap from the dispenser next to the sink, washes her hands, glances over at the test the nurse left processing on the counter, and greets me all in one fell swoop.

"Hi, Beatrice. I'm Dr. Rickman. I don't believe we've met before, but I can promise I'm, like, seventy-five percent fun and only twenty-five percent scary."

Tad's amused gaze is steady on me, but mine is like an active game of pinball, bouncing from one thing in the room to another at freakishly fast speeds.

"Twenty-five percent scary?" I ask.

She laughs. "Well, yeah. You're going to have a baby. And no matter how you slice it, there are moments when that's terrifying."

"I'm pregnant?" Tears hit my eyes, and joy hits my heart in one fantastic burst.

She nods. "Congratulations."

Oh boy. *A baby, moving in with Tad, completely rearranging life as I've known it for thirty-nine years?*

Yeah. I'd say things are about to be at least twenty-five percent scary from here on out.

39

Tad

Friday, March 26th

We're officially diving headfirst into day two of living together.

Crazy, considering that eight days ago, the idea of moving in together—or having a baby—wasn't on my radar. Or Breezy's, for that matter.

Five days ago, I found out she was pregnant via a damn newspaper article in the middle of a crowded CAFFEINE.

Four days ago, we sat in an exam room, holding our breath while Dr. Rickman turned the ultrasound screen toward us and let us hear the tiny, miraculous *thump thump thump* of our baby's heartbeat.

And now, here we are. *Together.* In my farmhouse.

The sun is shining in the morning sky, and the last remnants of snow are melting off the grass. Breezy reads the paper at the kitchen table, but the cup of coffee I made her a good thirty minutes ago is still full and most likely cold by now.

The silence between us hums a little differently these days. It's not uncomfortable, just...charged.

But that feeling could very well be a *me* problem. *Probably because you're putting too much pressure on yourself to not fuck things up.*

"You hate my coffee that much?" I attempt to tease, but my words come out a little shaky.

Her eyes peek over the paper, and her face is soft as she laughs. "I don't hate your coffee. I'm just trying to switch to decaf after Dr. Rickman gave me the rundown on all the no-gos during pregnancy."

"Oh." I scratch the back of my neck, relieved and mildly stupid. "That makes more sense than my theory that you were silently judging my barista skills."

She laughs again, and the sound loosens something in my chest. "I've had your pancakes, Tad Hanson. Your barista skills are fine."

"Well, that's a relief. Still, I can run down to Earl's and grab some decaf if you want."

"No, really. It's okay."

I shake my head. "It's no trouble. Take me fifteen minutes."

Before Breezy can respond, a presence at the front door pulls our attention.

"Knock, knock," a feminine voice calls from the door, and I wave Norah in when I see her through the window with Autumn on her hip.

"Hey, guys!" Breezy greets, her excitement taking her up and out of her chair and over to Norah immediately to steal Autumn.

"Bee!" Sweet toddler giggles ricochet throughout the kitchen as Breezy bends her backward, tickling her stomach and swinging her from side to side.

"Bee!" Autumn squeals. "Ahhh! Tickle!"

Norah grins. "Good, seems you're feeling better on the

sickness front today."

"Definitely feeling a lot better this morning," Breezy says after pressing a kiss to Autumn's little forehead. "And now, I'm even better after seeing this little munchkin." She tickles her niece's belly again, and Autumn squeals out in delight.

"Well, selfishly, I was really hoping that was the case because I need the two of you to come over to the house for dinner tonight," Norah announces, and her face morphs from grin to apologetic grimace. "Between Logan and Bennett doing their dance to slice each other's throats and Lillian trying and failing to play mediator, I'm losing my mind. I know you're settling into baby-on-the-way-so-we're-living-together vibes, but I am *begging* you. I need buffers."

"Dang, that's quite the request," Breezy comments on a snort. "And honestly, I'm shocked that Logan is still hanging around in Red Bridge."

"Oh, trust me, I am too." Norah sighs. "Which is why I would really, *really* love it if you helped me out here," Norah begs, even putting her hands together in front of her like she's praying. "Just think of how many f-bombs you could prevent from flying out of Autumn's mouth. And also, my sanity. Think about how you'll be saving that too."

"Just curious...why are you having this dinner exactly?" Breezy asks, quirking a curious eyebrow in Norah's direction. "I mean, it kind of sounds like a recipe for disaster..."

"I don't know, Breeze." Norah blows out a breath of exasperated air. "Probably because Logan keeps showing up at my door like a kicked puppy, and I'm too hopeful for my own good. Also, I think you and Josie deserve a little celebration for all the big news."

"And who all is going to be there?" Breezy asks, and Norah throws both hands in the air.

"Welp. Besides Logan and Josie and Clay and Lillian and Bennett and me, pretty much anyone and everyone I can find in this damn town that Bennett can tolerate."

"So, we won't be the only buffers, then?" Breezy asks on a

laugh. Norah shrugs.

"No, but you'll be the *most important* buffers," Norah answers with a big, please-do-it smile. "And you won't even have to talk to Logan if you don't want to, Breeze. I've already prepped him on that."

"I see." Breezy unexpectedly turns to me for approval, her eyebrows rising and a small smirk curving the corner of her mouth in question. "What do you think, Tad? Shall we provide our buffering services tonight?"

My chest tightens infinitesimally, and a slow tingle takes root in my fingertips. This level of trust and intimacy—it's both the best feeling in the world and the scariest and most familiar in ways I promised myself I would never know again in this lifetime.

"Yeah, okay," I say, my voice cracking so slightly I'm hoping no one notices. "I don't know how we can refuse when the invitation comes with that much desperation."

"Oh yay!" Norah grasps her chest dramatically with both hands. "Thank God. I promise I'll try to keep the vibes upbeat and less WWE if *at all* possible."

Breezy rolls her eyes before sticking out her tongue at Autumn, earning a few big belly laughs in response.

And Norah's smile is one of relief as she focuses her gaze toward me. "But hey, Tad, you proved you can throw a punch if you need to, so if it comes to that, I guess it comes to that. Just, please, avoid the china cabinet on the left of the dining room. It has some of my grandma Rose's favorite dishes in it."

"China cabinet on the left is sacred," I repeat with a laugh. "Got it."

"Perfect!" Norah chirps. "I'll see you guys at six, then." Approaching Breezy playfully, she steals Autumn back and tosses a wave over her shoulder on her way through the door.

"Buh-bye! Buh-bye, Bee!" Autumn waves too as Breezy blows kisses with sloppy wet sounds at her.

But the door pops back open just after it's slammed, and Norah sticks her head in. "Oh yeah. Invite your brother too, Tad."

The door bangs again, and Breezy laughs as Norah and

Autumn disappear across the lawn. "Oh man," she says. "Randy's gonna looove this invitation."

"I think I'll just pick him up without telling him where I'm taking him. I really want to see the shock when we drop him in the middle of this crowd."

"How long has he been over at Grandma Rose's old place?" Breezy asks as she heads over to the kitchen sink to fill up a glass of water.

"Almost a year now. Though, he'd been trying to buy it from Josie for years," I update with a shrug. "He's good over there. Happy, even. Hell, the only reason he stayed here as long as he did is because he thought I needed him to."

Breezy turns to look at me, her nose scrunched up in confusion. "Why would he think that you needed him?"

My stomach pitches as I chuckle, brushing it off. "You know how older siblings can be," I say, adding a wink of teasing since she's the oldest in her brood. A heavy bubble of guilt makes a mockery of my steadiness as I search the counter for my keys, desperate for a decaf-procurement-themed escape.

I care about Breezy—deeply. And yet...I cannot bring myself to mire through the anguish of sharing my life story with her. I cannot allow myself the pain of going back to that place—of reliving and explaining that day. And fuck, I really don't want to take her on that pain-filled journey with me. It's too dark.

And trust me, I know weakness isn't a component of a good man, though vulnerability is. Unfortunately, this version of Tad Hanson cannot be the latter without the first, and the first, at its complex cause, is unsurvivable.

The cold, sharp metal of my keys digs into the palm of my hand and soothes the simmering agony inside. I lift my gaze to Breezy's consciously, focusing on keeping the brittle edges of my smile at bay. "I'm going to run and get that decaf, come back, and make you an entirely new, even tastier cup of coffee. Then we're going to get outside and enjoy the sunshine while we have it before the sogginess of late spring in Vermont sets in."

"Do we have to do sheep things in the sunshine or..." She pauses and offers a little grin in my direction. "I already checked on Tom and Betsy and Mabel this morning. They were happy and cozy in the barn. And even Crosby seemed like he was behaving for once in his rebellious life."

"No." I laugh. It's forced, but after a decade of practice, I'm a pro at faking. "No sheep required. In fact, you can pick the activity, and I promise to participate with bells on. Now, do you need anything else at Earl's while I'm there? Any cravings flaring up?"

"Oh!" Her eyes go wide with glee. "Hot Cheetos. And some celery. You know, to balance the Cheetos."

I chuckle. "Can do. Anything else pops into your mind, you can call me or text me, okay?"

Her eyes seem to shimmer as she replies, "Maybe this whole housing and growing a human thing won't be so bad. I've never seen this level of servitude in my life."

Rounding the table, I brush a hand across her shoulder, then dip down for a kiss. It's easy and familiar—like we've been doing this for years—but there's something new in it too.

We pull back at the same time, both smiling and laughing.

Yeah, we're comfortable. That's not the problem.

The problem is I want it to stay this good, and nothing in my life ever has.

40

Breezy

The scent of grilled steak and cold Vermont air mingle as I trail after Norah through the yard, the heels of my boots sinking into damp grass. She's carrying a massive bowl of salad like it's the Hope Diamond, and I pull up beside her, lowering my voice even though there's no one else within ten feet.

"Quick question," I say, tugging lightly on her sleeve. "Why exactly are we having dinner out on the lawn with heaters, in forty-degree weather, while you've got a twelve-person dining table inside?"

Norah cranes her neck toward me like I'm the one being unreasonable. "Oh. Yeah. Well. *Technically*, Bennett still says Logan isn't allowed in the house. So, *technically*, this isn't *in* the house."

A shocked laugh leaves my lungs. *"Norah."*

"What?" She just shrugs. "Plus, there's no need to worry about Grandma's china, so I'd say, overall, it's a win."

"Norah."

She's already sidestepping me, moving toward the long table set up under the string lights. "I've gotta get this salad down and grab the sides. Make yourself comfortable. There are drinks by the firepit."

Behind me, Tad brushes a hand along my back as he passes, his fingers warm through my sweater. The touch is easy and natural and reminds me of how good the past two days of living together have been. I'm honestly starting to feel like we could give this real couple thing a run.

He's been fun and flirty and attentive, and I've done my best not to put up my usual force fields. Of course, we haven't dived into the deepest, darkest pools of intimacy and secrets, but it seems like somewhere we'll get eventually.

It honestly feels like we're only growing closer with each day.

I catch his grin as he moves toward the drink station, pretending not to eavesdrop, and I shake my head before following Norah again.

"Listen, Norah," I say, keeping my voice low as we stop by the table she's busy filling with food. "I know you want to heal the relationship with my brothers, but as the woman who's been in the middle of their crisis management for going on two decades, I have to tell you, it's not easily solved. Maybe we're better off just letting them hold their own space rather than forcing them together."

"Maybe," Norah agrees, flitting toward the table while I follow her. "But we're going to try this first. And who knows? Maybe it'll fix Bennett and Logan's relationship and yours and Logan's too. Stranger things have happened, you know," she singsongs.

I sigh. Goodness, she's feeling way too hopeful.

"Logan wants to be here," she adds, setting the salad beside a bouquet of withering roses, little ice crystals forming in the water of their vase, and spinning to face me before lowering her voice. "He wants a relationship with you and with Bennett. And I know he's wronged both of you, but I can tell by the look in his eyes that he's not here to be an enemy anymore."

"I hear you, I do. No one wants my brothers to find a way back to a relationship more than I do, but some burned bridges cannot be rebuilt." I swallow, the turmoil of my own conflict with Logan over Bishop Galleries edging in. Hell, even the massive bridge my father burned is mere ashes now with absolutely no chance at closure. I mean, he's dead. I can't talk or sort anything out with him. I literally just have to live with the deceit and find a way to make my own peace with it.

Norah starts to open her mouth, most likely to refute, but I keep going. "I've only gotten a little taste of the bitterness Bennett has been feeling toward Logan for years, but I still have to actively work not to smack our youngest brother upside the head." I reach up and squeeze her bicep. "Just…don't get your hopes set too high on a miracle, okay?"

"I promise. I'll manage my expectations." She nods and steps away from me, calling back toward the house, "Lillian, can you bring the dressing, please?"

Shaking my head, I drop the clearly futile subject and move on to interest in Norah's Manhattanite best friend. "How is Lil enjoying Red Bridge this visit? Thinking about moving here too? If she does, we could be making a dent in the NYC census within a couple of years."

Norah scoffs. "Yeah, I don't know about that. Earlier today, in the middle of Main Street, during the Spring Fling Cider Festival, she used the word 'desolate' as a descriptor."

I laugh, of course, envisioning myself saying the exact same thing on every other visit I've ever made to my brother's sleepy Vermont town. It's funny how a big life change can shift your perspective entirely. Red Bridge's population isn't vast, but the warmth of its hug is unparalleled. There aren't even a fraction of the people here who are in New York—but they care *so* much more.

I'd wager if it weren't for Eileen Martin's questionable journalism practices and out-of-towners, there wouldn't be anything but sunshine and rainbows all the time. And, you know, the occasional poker tournaments because nothing says "for the kids" like a little competitive gambling.

"What's so funny, Breezy?" Lillian, the new topic herself, asks, skipping down the stairs with an armful of every variety of salad dressing known to man. Norah passes her with a brush of elbows, headed back toward the house for more food.

"You are, Lil," I say directly, taking a load off on one of the folding chairs set up at the outdoor dining table that we're apparently going to freeze our asses off at and eat dinner at the same time.

"Well, of course I am." She winks. "I'm also incredibly smart and beautiful too, if any men happen to be sniffing around, by the way."

Norah cackles, returning with a Crock-Pot full of something steamy, thanks to Bennett's handoff at the door. He doesn't look thrilled, but I'll be honest, sometimes that's just my brother's face.

"Oh, Lil, Lil, Lil," Norah tsks. "Didn't you say you were taking a break from the bruter sex for a little while? Since that thing with the billionaire's son and the other thing with the musclehead from Jersey and then the final, *final* thing with the mystery guy you refuse to give any details about whatsoever?"

Boy oh boy, does that description of the dating scene in New York sound familiar.

I see myself in Lillian a little and, I suppose, have had a soft spot for her since the moment I heard what she did for our Norah. Helping her run out on a wedding destined for disaster, giving her the tools to get out for good, and facing harassment from Norah's mom and ex-fiancé, all without complaint, are the markers of a great woman and an even better friend.

Frankly, without Lillian's intervention and support on Norah's behalf, my brother Bennett might still be self-destructing in the wake of Summer's passing, and as much as I'd have wanted to, I don't think I'd have been able to save him on my own.

"You doing okay?" Tad asks, settling into the chair beside mine. He sets a glass of lemonade on the table in front of me, and I smile over at him.

"Yes. A little chilly, but I'm sure I'll be hot-flashing soon anyway."

He reaches out to rub my sweater-covered arms. "Want me to

go get your heavier coat?"

"Hell no." I snort. "It's covered in glitter from the pageant parade earlier. The girls were tossing it with both hands! I don't know if I'll ever get it all out."

He laughs. "To be fair, I tried to warn you. The Spring Fling Cider Festival never lets you out of its clutches without physical consequences."

I stick my tongue out at him. "I was picturing quaint. Cheery. Small-town. Not the teeny-tiny pageant queens with buckets full of sparkly dust!"

"Here," he offers then, contorting slightly to wiggle his arms out of the sleeves of his heavy blue flannel shirt-jacket. "Take mine." He winks. "I did a better job of dodging."

Accepting it willingly now that my hands are beginning to feel like knives, I settle into the smell of Tad and turn fully toward the table as everyone starts to sit down.

Norah and Bennett take the seats directly across from us, Autumn in a snowsuit and high chair in between them, and Josie and Clay, coming out of the house and each carrying a side dish, take the ones at the far end.

Randy walks to the table with a glass of lemonade in his hand, looking pretty neutral about the whole freeze-your-ass-off-and-eat extravaganza. He was adamant he'd drive himself to this shindig and just arrived at the same time as Logan. He settles into the seat beside his brother Tad, directly across from Lillian, and Logan gets sequestered to the lone chair at the end.

Gang's all here, I guess.

I can't deny I imagined a lot more buffers—possibly Sheriff Peeler and Deputy Rice—but I'm certainly not going to ask any questions.

"Well," Norah chirps, breaking the awkward silence first. "Thank you so much for coming, everyone. It's so nice to get everybody together, especially with such amazing news for two of our most-loved people, Breezy and Josie, and the new opportunities to love and be loved they're bringing to the family."

My throat tightens, but to be choked in this way feels astonishingly good. It's family. It's support. It's the exact opposite of how Bennett and Logan and I grew up, and for the first time since Norah suggested this stupid dinner, I can see the reason.

"Thanks, Nor," I say, smiling and crying a little all at once. For a woman who just found out she's nearing month two of pregnancy, I refuse to think about how many more things are going to make me weepy over the next eight months. Of course, my brain decides *now* is the perfect time to think about our baby's first ultrasound in Dr. Rickman's office and the little heartbeat I saw and heard. More tears start to fill my lids, and I do my best to swallow back the ball of emotion that's turning into a boulder inside my throat.

Good grief, Breeze. Cool it on the tears.

A hiccupping breath escapes my lungs and Tad's hand finds my knee under the table and rubs.

Josie's attention seems split between Norah and hushed whispers with Clay, but when he gives her a gentle elbow to the side, she pipes up too. "Yeah. Thanks, Norah. It's so freaking cold I might get hypothermia and the whole miracle pregnancy thing will be for nothing, but at least you got us all together."

I suck my lips into my mouth, and Clay guffaws, waving his fork-filled hand. "Don't mind her, guys. It's the hormones."

Tad and I exchange wide eyes before a hush falls over the group, the clinking and clanking of forks and spoons and dishes the only sounds among us. Logan is on some of his best—quietest—behavior I've ever seen, and Clay and Josie are still exchanging many, many heated whispers. After what he said, though, I'm kind of surprised he's still alive.

"So," Randy says, completely clueless to the family dynamics holding the rest of the tongues at the table hostage. "How's everyone enjoying their visits to Red Bridge?"

Lillian is the first to open her mouth—unsurprisingly, I suppose, since she's the only true visitor and the most removed from all the other drama. "I'm having a great time! I mean, there's nothing to do that I've noticed, and everything is literally closed by eight p.m., even on the weekends, but I don't know, maybe someone with the lay of the land could help me find something...*interesting* to do." She tilts her head toward Randy with a soft smile that borders on flirty mischief.

And Randy looks behind him like it's possible Lillian is talking to someone else, but eventually, he looks back across the table at her, pointing to himself and asking, "You want *me* to show you around Red Bridge?"

"Depends," she says, her tone teasing and her eyelashes fluttering. "Do you know anything fun to do around here?"

Randy laughs. "Fun's a relative term in Red Bridge. We've got the diner, the hardware store, one bar, and a church."

"Sounds thrilling." Lillian giggles and leans forward a little. I don't miss the way her breasts push up against the table and create undeniable cleavage. Randy doesn't miss it either. "Maybe you could take me on the grand tour and show me *all* the sights. I promise to act impressed."

He scratches his jaw, uncertain but clearly flattered. "You're serious? You want a tour of Red Bridge?"

"Yeah," Lillian says with a cheeky little smile. "You're hot and handsome and seem really nice. Not *at all* like the guys in New York." Her eyes flick to the end of the table and then back to Randy. "I don't see why not. I'm not seeing anyone, and I think we could have *a lot* of fun together."

Randy struggles to clear his throat at the obvious flirtation, Norah rolls her eyes, and Logan, evidently, sees this as the perfect moment to lay years of repressed regret and resentment out on the table. He shoves his chair back so hard, I startle.

"You know what, Ben? I'm done!" Logan shouts. "Done begging you to hear me out, begging you to give me a chance to apologize, begging you to fucking *grow up* and get over yourself."

"Ohh boy," Tad mutters beside me, and bless him, it makes me laugh. I know things are about to get ugly between my brothers—again—but I swear if I don't let myself find the humor in these things, I'd be crying all the time.

"Good!" Bennett fires back. "Maybe you'll actually leave then, and I can stop pretending to enjoy eating in the freaking Arctic Circle!"

"Guys," I hedge, panicking when tears spring to Norah's eyes, the defeat of failing at mending their relationship again taking its toll.

"I'm telling you!" Josie shouts at Clay, standing from her chair and pointing dramatically, detracting from the ongoing sibling rivalry with spectacular flair and shocking us all. "I see something in the bush over there! See! There's a glare!" Her chair falls as she shoves away from the table and charges away, her scream escalating. "Eileen Martin! I see you in that bush, and you'd better get out here and face me right now before I find Ben's shotgun and start shooting!"

"Oh, sweet Jesus," Norah mutters, worried for her sister and the paycheck her bravado might not be able to cash when she catches the person she supposedly sees in the shrubs. "Ben, can you do something, please?"

Clay is already moving after her, but mere seconds later, Eileen Martin actually appears and starts walking as fast as her geriatric legs will take her. Tad, Randy, Bennett, and Logan all get up and jog in sneaky Eileen's direction behind Josie, even chasing down the nosy old busybody when she takes off at a run. Thankfully, the men are faster than Josie and she's several feet behind them when Tad wrestles Eileen—gently—away from the passenger door of a waiting car on Maple while Randy helps a young woman out of the driver's side at the same time.

Norah, Lillian, Autumn, and I all watch from the front lawn while Josie catches up to them all and starts shouting threats toward Eileen.

I don't know who the young woman at the wheel of the getaway car is, but she looks scared out of her mind as the men march the two of them back up to the house and sit them down in our recently vacated chairs at the outdoor table. Eileen looks half thrilled, but I imagine that has more to do with Tad, the object of weekly articles for as long as I've been reading the Red Bridge paper, holding her tightly by both arms along the way.

I understand her crush, obviously. I, myself, am currently impregnated by him.

"All right, Eileen," Josie says, pointing an index finger directly in her face. "It's time to put up or shut up! How in the actual hell did you know I was pregnant?"

"And me!" I interject.

"Yes, and Breezy," Josie continues, "before we announced it! It's a violation of privacy! An invasion! And just plain fucking wrong!"

"Fu-ck!" Autumn yells, making Norah sigh. All of us have been horrible influences on our sweet toddler girl lately, but not even Norah dares to interrupt her sister to chastise her for language right now.

Tears are in Josie's eyes, and she's genuinely upset. With everything she's been through—with her history with pregnancy and loss—this isn't the cute little spoiler story Eileen seems to think it is.

Not to mention, this is so far from the first time Eileen's written an inappropriate article about a member of our family, it's not even funny. From following Bennett and Norah's every move while they were dealing with Norah's ex, to invasive pieces into Josie and Clay's history and heartache, to weekly fluff articles on Tad, and declarations of a threesome for me, Eileen's been pushing this group toward a hostile response for a long time.

"I want to know how you knew, and I want to know right now!" Josie demands. Clay holds her arms gently at her sides, but I have a sneaking suspicion that if he weren't, Josie would have one of Norah's butter knives to Eileen's slender throat.

"I'll never reveal my sources!" the crazy woman declares, somewhat unwisely.

"That's it. Someone'd better call Pete and tell him this murder I'm about to commit is one hundred percent premeditated!" Josie screams, her body thrashing in Clay's hold so much, Tad steps closer to back him up.

"We went through your trash!" the accomplice admits, the pressure too much to bear as the volume of the entire group escalates. "I'm so sorry, and I didn't think it was a good idea, but Aunt Eileen insisted!"

"*Aunt* Eileen?" Josie questions.

"Dammit, Millie!" Eileen screeches.

"I'm sorry," Millie cries. "But I'm not cut out for this kind of journalism!"

"Yeah," Josie says sarcastically. "Theft, breaking and entering, spying in the bushes—it's not for everyone!"

"Oh, piss off, Josie," Eileen grumbles. "I'm just doing my job."

"Doing your job? Doing your job! You know, Eileen. You, of all people, with your nosy-ass tactics and years of hit pieces, *you know* what Clay and I have been through. What a big deal it is to be *pregnant*. And yet, you found it appropriate to spoil it for us in this way? How do I know this weekend's paper isn't going to publish my due date? For Pete's sake, Eileen, I'm not even out of my first trimester yet!"

"Neither am I," I add, a newfound panic at the idea that a pregnancy I never even knew I wanted isn't guaranteed. Tad rounds the table toward me, his voice kind but commanding as he takes control in a way I've never experienced before.

"All right, guys. I think that's enough for tonight," he announces. "Eileen, take this as a warning that if you pull this shit again, the response won't be nearly as friendly. You know I love and respect your hustle for reporting the news in a town that doesn't make much—but this is too far."

Eileen nods, a sadness I don't expect creeping in at the castigation from a man she admires. "I, well…I'm not sorry."

"Eileen!" Tad snaps, and she holds up her hands defensively.

"But! I can see where you're coming from, and out of deference to you, Tad, I promise to take a break from reporting on the Ellis, Bishop, Hanson family circle for a little while. I've got a few other leads that are getting hot anyway."

"Great," Tad says, sarcasm tainting the positive right out of the word. Reaching for my hand, he pulls it to his chest and clutches it there subconsciously as he says the rest of our goodbyes before Josie can fly off the handle again. Clay's holding her back ten feet away, but the best analogy I can give is like a jockey holding back a racehorse in the starting gate. Tonight may be over for us, but I won't be surprised if Josie and Eileen go a few more rounds before it's truly done. "Norah, thanks for the invite and for the little bit of food we managed before all hell broke loose, but it's time for us to call it quits. I want to get Breezy home."

As Tad turns to lead us back across the lawn while the rest of the group is left to take care of their own shit on their own time with their own minds, a relief washes over me. I've never had someone willing and capable of handling things for me. Never.

Beyond that, I've never not been responsible for handling other people too.

But with Tad at my side, I don't have to be in charge.

It feels so good, I don't know if I can ever go back.

41

Tad

Breezy lies back in bed, her hands on her stomach as she caresses the tops and sides and bottom with a thick, creamy lotion she keeps on the nightstand. Her mouth is upturned, despite the chaos of the dinner turned vigilante justice we spent the evening at next door, and I find myself watching her.

Soft hands move across her stomach, a slight crease between her brows forming as she shifts from one side of her hips to the other, just above the top edge of her sexy black lace panties. Her skin is supple and tight, but I know in the next few months it'll stretch to untested capacities at an unprecedented rate. And yet, I know for a fact that she'll still be sexy—truthfully, she'll be even more so. The top of the lotion jar sticks as she tries to screw it on, binding on mismatched threads.

"Here, let me," I offer. Our hands brush lightly, and I complete the task with ease. The sound of her breathing amplifies.

"I should be grateful, I know I should, but deep down in some hormonal place, all I feel is annoyed." My smile grows as she continues, though I do my best to hide it to save myself from hidden weapons. "What is it about growing a human that has to mess with coordination and brain capacity? Like, hello, can't we contain the symptoms to the uterus? Ugh."

"I know it's got to be frustrating...having your body hijacked and all. But this is the role of the man in times like these anyway. To be the doer, the getter, the fixer. You might be operating at sixty percent, but I'll cover the forty you're missing as best I can."

"How?" she asks as I adjust my shoulders and the pillow behind them.

"How what? How will I help?"

"No." She shakes her head and those blue eyes of hers peer into mine. "How do you manage to say things like that out of the blue?"

"Say things like..."

"Perfect things, Tad. The things I need to hear most. Things that put me at ease."

Every edge, every wound, every heartache softens. "Breeze."

"You've managed to make me feel comfortable in a skin I never knew I'd wear within a matter of a couple of days, and I... well, I can't thank you enough. This could be so much rougher of a transition—going from fling to cohabitation. But you've managed... you've managed to turn it into something of a help, rather than a hindrance." She shakes her head, sighing. "I guess what I'm trying to say is, it feels nice to be a team."

A bolt of discomfort rips into my chest as old words, old wounds, old heartache return with a vengeance. *We're a team, Tad.* My wife Abigail made a habit out of saying it, and hearing it now is a stabbing reminder of my failures.

As Breezy lies back, I count my breaths to steady them, setting my old world aside again and searching out the light. The hope, the clarity, the direction—they're all aimed at the future. At a life to be built with Breezy, and the baby—our baby—she's growing inside her.

I find purpose in centering myself on them—on focusing on

what will be instead of what was.

I know it's still too early to feel the baby kick or anything, but I remember…

"Would it be okay if I…well, if I talked to the baby?" I ask, and Breezy's gaze jumps to mine. "I know it can be a little weird at first, and I'd like to put my hand on your belly too, so I just thought I'd check if—"

"Of course you can."

I smile, scooting closer and leaning toward her stomach before settling a shaking hand on the side. Her body jumps a little, but her breathing is even and comfortable as I rub gently.

"Hi, there, little one. I'm…well, I'm your dad. We haven't met formally yet, but we will soon, and I just wanted to introduce myself and tell you a little bit about me." I shift even closer, lowering my voice. "I'll love you through it all, even when it seems like I won't. I'll always be a listening ear and someone you can turn to. And I'll always, always do my best to protect you and your mom."

Saliva thickens, actively working to plug my throat, but tonight's events are a tunnel to life-sustaining air.

"Especially from nosy newspaper ladies who like to hide in the bushes."

Breezy's laugh is melodic. "Oh my God, I still can't believe tonight was anything but a fever dream. The tundra dinner, Josie grabbing Eileen by the collar, Lillian flirting with *Randy*." She snorts. "I thought your brother was going to choke on his tongue."

"He's not as celibate as he seems," I defend, escalating Breezy's enjoyment exponentially.

"Oh, don't worry. Lillian's lore for rendering men speechless precedes her everywhere she goes. Last year, when Norah and I did a girls' weekend at a spa in New York with her, I heard some stories that, if told right now, would give all three of us nightmares."

"Hear that, sweetheart?" I say, talking directly to Breezy's stomach again, my hand rubbing gently. "Your mom is already protecting you too."

I glance up just in time to catch Breezy's breath as it leaves in a silent gasp. Her hand cups my face, the warmth of her palm radiating gratifyingly into my cheek.

"Thank you. Thank you for making what could have been awkward and scary and uncertain feel secure."

"We're a team," I find myself saying aloud before stretching tall, leaning forward, and putting my lips to hers. Unshed, salty tears flavor the back of my throat, the words a bleeding, fatal wound.

But the knowledge that comes with them—the experience in how amazing life *can* be—and Breezy's earnest need for my partnership might be the only things that can save me.

And even if they can't, I make the promise to myself and to her and to the ghosts of my life past and to the universe that I'll do nothing less than die trying.

The kiss deepens, and just like that, everything else is gone. At least, for a little while, it's just the two of us.

42

Breezy

Wednesday, April 7th

"Ah, come in, come in!" I welcome Norah and Autumn, waving to Tad as he pulls out of the driveway in his truck to the tune of tire-crunched gravel, headed to meet Randy on an errand to Molene. Norah's hair is windblown and Autumn's tiny cherub cheeks rosy with the nip of fresh morning air. I waggle my fingers until the handoff of my sweet niece is done, swinging her in a circle that makes her giggle.

"Beeeeee!" she squeals as I press big kisses to her cute cheeks.

"You seem to be feeling good," Norah remarks, unwinding her scarf from around her neck and discarding both it and her coat on the back of the nearest kitchen chair.

"I am." I smile, tickling Autumn's belly before unzipping her coat and putting it on top of Norah's. "I think the sickness is passing, and energy-wise, I feel like I just got a burst. I'm going to tackle as much as I can today while it lasts. What have you two been up to this morning?"

"We were at the park downtown," Norah supplies, turning to the cabinet behind herself to grab a mug and fill it with the freshly brewed coffee in the pot before dropping a bomb of information. "With Uncle Logan."

"Oh, Norah."

"Well!" She huffs out a sigh and dramatically holds out both of her hands. "It's been two weeks since the disaster dinner, and he's *still* in town. You and Bennett are both ignoring him—which I'm not criticizing—but I mean, come *on*. How can I not feel a little bad for the guy?"

"I'm not ignoring him," I correct. "I'm just protecting myself."

She snorts. "By ignoring him."

My sigh is much heavier than the air it's composed of. "I want to get over it. I do. But every time I see him, I see our father, and I get angry." I look down at Autumn's innocent face, the sparkle of her eyes remarkably reminiscent of the one Logan always had as a kid. So much purity, a well of good intention and kind thoughts every human starts with before life and hardship pump it out of them. "But I guess you're right. Maybe we can try another dinner. At a restaurant, perhaps." I rub my nose gently against Autumn's. "Also, a temperature-controlled environment where you don't have to make my cute niece eat dinner in a snowsuit would be preferred."

Norah laughs, but that's quickly followed up by a hum that's full of satisfaction, and impressively, it's all the gloating she does before changing the subject. "You know what's weird?"

"What?"

"I'm getting so comfortable standing in *Farmer Tad's* kitchen that I'm pouring my own coffee."

I chuff. "Yeah. Tell me about it, sister. I'm getting comfortable enough in Farmer Tad's house that I'm considering it my own. Gonna go through some stuff and clean it out when you all leave and everything."

"Well, technically, it *is* your home. I mean, you live here now." She winks. "And holy moly, I never would have predicted you two as a pairing," she admits. "But Breeze, the man looks really freaking good on you."

"I know." I laugh, setting Autumn down on the floor as she squirms. "Trust me, I know. It's wild. The art snob and the sheep farmer, procreating and settling into a happily ever after."

"Maybe there's, like, a sheepish niche in the art world you don't know about yet. Or at the very least, rustic, rural pieces."

I snort. "Yeah, I don't know… I might just be done."

"Really? I mean, I support you in whatever direction you want to go, you know that. But stepping away for good? That's a big deal."

"I know it is. I won't decide yet, while I'm hormonal and emotional and jaded and everything. I'll wait until I have a clear head." I shrug. "But I think it speaks volumes that I've yet to respond to that shark of a headhunter you sent my way. Over the past few months, he's sent me more offers than I can count and I just…don't want anything to do with any of it. And that was before I found out I was baking Tad's baby bun in my oven."

"It certainly says something." She nods. "And being here with Tad? It's good?"

I smile. I can't help it. "It's amazing, Nor. He's patient and helpful and funny and…" I sigh. "I'm having a really hard time remembering what I liked so much about living alone."

"And the sex? That's good too?"

I cackle. "Norah!"

"Sexxxx," Autumn repeats, and Norah's eyes widen.

"Whoops." She drops her voice to a whisper. "But it's good?"

"Norah, *please*," I chastise before smirking. "But I *am* pregnant after all, so I suppose you can be the judge."

She hums, snuggling into her coffee mug. "Oh yeah. *Hot* Farmer Tad."

I snort. "You're asking for trouble with your husband today. First Logan and now the lust?"

"I'm not saying for meeee. I'm just happy for you. I have my own hot things, but I'm betting you don't want to hear about those because they have everything to do with your brother and how good he is at…" She waggles her brows, and I pretend to cover my ears.

"Lalalala."

Her laugh rings throughout the kitchen and spreads to Autumn, who's made a playground out of the Tupperware cabinet in the corner. She bangs a lid against the wooden floor, and an overwhelming peace falls over me at the sight of her.

Maybe, just maybe, slow life in Red Bridge is exactly what I needed.

"All right," Norah declares, rinsing her coffee mug in the sink and giving it a quick cleaning before setting it in the strainer. "We'll get out of your hair for now. But call me later, you know, when you're ready to mend the fence with Logan."

"You're relentless."

Norah smiles, coming toward me quickly and pulling me into a hug so fierce, I almost tear up. "I love you. You're my family, and selfishly, I want all the eggs of my family in the same basket before Easter."

"I'll try. But not today. After Tad gets back from Molene, I think we're going to go on a date."

She pulls back and claps in between us. "Okay, then. Let's go, Autumn. Aunt Breezy has some nesting to do before she can get done in the much better, much dirtier way, and as is obvious by the mess you've made of this cabinet, organization is not this age's strong suit."

I roll my eyes and kiss Autumn on the cheek, and Norah scoops her and their belongings up, waving at me before they shove through the door. Without their distraction, it's officially time to clean.

• • •

I've seen avalanches with more structure than the closet in Tad's guestroom on the first floor.

Straddling the stack of clothes I just knocked off the bar, I wobble like a newborn deer and grab the top box from the leaning tower of chaos before it topples. "My gosh, this is like Monica's secret closet on *Friends*," I mutter, shimmying back and trying not to fall or break something. "Who knew Tad was such a packrat when he's so neat everywhere else."

My phone chimes from the nightstand, and I detour through the mess, climb over a stray boot, and grab it.

A text message from Tad is the only notification on the screen, drawing my cheeks up and out as I click to read it.

Tad: *Coming back into Red Bridge now. Dropping off Randy, and then I'll head toward home. Want me to pick up lunch on the way back? I can get nachos if they're still calling to you, or something else if that craving joined the witness protection program.*

I laugh under my breath. The nacho craving has, in fact, fled the country and assumed a new identity somewhere in Fryville.

Me: *Nachos are out, Farm Daddy. Cheeseburger and fries are in. The greasier, the better.*

Tad: *Understood lol. I'll call the diner and put in a to-go order. See you soon, Farm Mommy.*

Me: *Oh my God. Don't even try to go there. That nickname doesn't hit the same for me.*

Tad: *But you're a mommy on my farm…feels kind of apt.*

Me: *How about you just focus on my food?*

Tad: *Farm Daddy's on it.*

Reinvigorated by the promise of food, I turn back to the heap of clothes like a woman on a mission. It's me versus this closet, and right now, the closet's winning.

I start scooping hangers by the handful, stacking shirts like I'm competing in some sad domestic Olympics. After a few trips from the closet to the bed, I've unearthed a mix of flannels and coats and old sports teams' T-shirts. I silently wonder about a younger, obviously trimmer Tad who used to wear all these and why he didn't get rid of them when he outgrew them.

Funnily enough, they look like they might fit me pretty well, and with a belly I know will be growing by the day, I'm going to be in desperate need of some temporary wardrobe additions.

Red Bridge isn't exactly a shopping paradise like New York.

I tug one of the flannel shirts on, pulling it up and over my shoulders and cinching the front. It's about two sizes too big, but for right now, loose is perfect.

I set it to the side and try on another and another and another until I have a stack of fifteen shirts to add to my options for the next couple of months. And I fold and organize the other pile to ask Tad about donating when he gets back home from Molene.

Perfect, I think, until I reach the back corner and drag out a box heavy enough to make me regret my life choices. *Tad's muscle is definitely needed for this one*, I think as I swap it out for a lighter one.

But when I fold back the flap, I pull out a nondescript photo album and open it to the first page to find a picture of Tad.

He's handsome as ever, smiling and standing in front of a firehouse in a navy pair of pants and a T-shirt, and he's holding his hand up to the camera as though the photographer is a member of the paparazzi.

I study the photo a little closer.

His body is still fit and his arms still tanned like now, but his smile is different somehow—bigger and brighter. It's weird to see, considering Tad comes across as one of the happiest-go-lucky guys on the planet, but in this photo, his eyes are different.

I lean in slightly, intent on examining the lettering of the embroidery on the chest pocket of his tee, but I startle hard when a question comes from out of nowhere.

"What are you doing?"

The voice is harsh and close and jump-scares me so much I drop the album right back into the box as I turn abruptly.

When I see it's Tad, my shoulders relax a little bit.

The to-go bag from the diner still hangs from the fingers of his right hand, his coat in place and his keys in his left hand as though he sought me out as soon as he arrived. I don't know how I managed to miss hearing him come in.

"Oh, shoo, you scared me," I tell him, rising to my feet. "I got bored earlier, and I don't know if it's nesting or just anxiety, but I got the urge to start figuring out a potential space for the baby, and when I got in here, the closet surprised me with how packed it was. I figured I'd start there."

"This is *my* stuff."

"I know," I say carefully, trying not to read too much into his clipped tone. "I was going to ask you about all of it before I did anything, but I thought if I went ahead and presorted everything, it'd save you some time and heartache. No one likes cleaning out closets—"

"I'm not getting rid of any of it. In fact, you can just go." He holds up the bag of food. "Go to the kitchen and eat. I'll put it away."

His shoulders are tense, and his voice grated. I hate the thought that I've upset him by going through this stuff, but for the life of me, I can't understand why it would be such a big deal.

"Tad, what's going on? I'm sorry I didn't ask you before going through things, but with the way we've been, I just assumed—"

"Are you wearing one of the shirts?" he asks harshly, noticing my attire on a full-body jolt that shakes the house, my world, and what little foundation we've built in this new, complicated relationship. His entire being is as frozen as the road was the night we crossed paths on my way into town, and his eyes have never felt so cold.

"Uh..." I look down carefully and then back up at him. I suddenly feel incredibly embarrassed and unsure, but I don't even know why. "I...uh...thought I might be able to use some of this to carry me through the rest of the spring thaw while I'm getting bigger, so I don't have to buy new stuff..."

"No. Take it off." His voice breaks, then steadies. "I'll buy you new stuff, okay? Just…please, take it off."

It's all so confusing because this isn't the first time I've put on one of Tad's shirts…

I slip out of it slowly, confusion thick in my throat. He snatches it from me, staring at the fabric like it's made of glass.

"Tad, seriously. I'm really sorry if I unintentionally did something here, but if you don't tell me what's going on, I can't know what I need to avoid in the future. What is this stuff?"

He shakes his head. I don't know if he's trying to clear his thoughts or reset or ignore me completely, but in the end, it doesn't matter. He doesn't answer me, regardless.

And déjà vu from his dark day hits me like a freight train.

"This is never going to work if you can't let me all the way in," I whisper.

"I can't do this." The reply is tortured enough that I know better than to curse him out, but a sick twist grabs hold of my stomach and doesn't let go. "None of this is any of your fucking business, okay? Just leave it. Leave all of it." Charged air and burgeoning tears distort my vision. He's never ever talked to me this way.

He's never ever looked as distraught as he does right now.

"Tad?"

He backs out of the guest bedroom with his hands up, fabric still gripped in his fingers and his eyes on the wooden floors, and when I move to go after him, he just moves faster.

The sound of the kitchen door slamming closed and the engine of his truck firing up are the last things I hear, my heart in my throat and my hand on my chest as I will the universe to keep him safe on what I know will be a dangerous, distracted drive.

I want desperately to go back to the box and the photo album. To dig through until I get the answers he's not willing to give me himself.

But I don't.

I know, no matter how badly I want to know, he'd never forgive me for the intrusion of privacy in this moment. *Hell, I'd never forgive myself.* Whatever these clothes are—whatever life he lived before—there's so much more to them than meets the eye.

I set the bag of food on the kitchen table untouched, the hunger long gone, and then head to the living room to stoke the fire in the woodstove.

I'm tear-stained and chilled to my bones.

But the more wood I add, the more obvious it becomes the cold I'm feeling has nothing to do with lack of heat. The fire rages, burning so much it could stand to lose a little energy. I mess with the vents Tad showed me, but when I can't get them to move, I settle for leaving the front door cracked a little.

I pad softly down the hall, shutting the door to the guest bedroom with a quiet click, all while trying my best not to sob.

He'll be back eventually, right?

Right?

Yes. He *will* be back, and when he is, I want to be in the right headspace to meet him where he needs. I can't be like this—heart pounding, gut churning, right on the verge of breaking down completely. Somehow, I have to find a way to calm down.

I walk back down the hall to the master, close the door, and head to the bathroom to run myself a bath. I light a candle, pour in some gentle suds, and strip down, climbing into the soothingly warm water.

I close my eyes and blow out a deep breath, cradling my stomach with gentle hands and willing my mind to stop racing.

I don't know much, but I know, without a shadow of a doubt, what happened with Tad is the result of a man grappling with things that changed him forever.

A man who's been through it all.

A man who's barely hanging on.

It's only after I've settled in that a thought jolts me upright. *My phone—I left it in the guestroom.* If Tad reaches out, I need to see it.

I climb out carefully, wrap a towel around myself, and tug a T-shirt over my still damp skin before stepping back into the hall.

But the world tilts hard to the side.

"Whoa," I whisper, catching the wall as the edges of my vision pulse gray and wooziness slaps me in the face.

I stumble to the wall just inside the bedroom, sliding down until I'm sitting on the floor.

Fuck, I should have eaten.

Head spinning and heart racing, I lie all the way down and blink up at the ceiling as the overwhelming notion that I'm about to pass out overtakes me.

Yep. This is happening.

The last thing I see before the world fades is the ceiling swaying above me like it's underwater.

Then everything goes black.

43

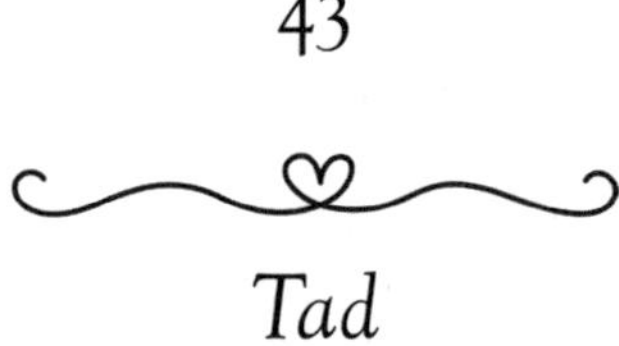

Tad

Abigail's shirt rests in my lap, the smell of her mingling with the scent of Breezy as it clings to the fabric. I fiddle with the glass of water in front of me, watching as condensation beads up and runs down on the wood surface of Clay's bar, puddling in a ring.

Clay and Marty rush around behind the bar, serving customers, but I don't pay much mind to anyone other than the people in my thoughts.

Breezy. Abigail. Lucy.

Two lost forever, and the other probably well and gone and on her way to somewhere, anywhere but here with me.

Fuck.

I can still hear their laughter, still see their smiles—still feel the guilt of letting them down like it's fucking yesterday. And now, I'm failing again. Breezy and the baby. Myself. Randy. Everyone who's ever fought for me—I'm disrespecting every fucking one. All because I can't find a way to cope out loud.

Can't find a way to get the stupid words out of my throat. Can't find a way to—

I shake my head. *Fuck, I need a drink.*

Whistling down the bar to get Clay's attention, I set Abby's shirt on the stool to my left and sink my head into my hands. A million memories of all the fights we had, from big to small, run through my head like a fucking torture chamber. All the stupid reasons, all the stubborn moments I kept my head in my ass instead of apologizing, all the chances to say I'm sorry I didn't take nearly fucking fast enough...

"Hey, kid," a deep voice says, startling me from the right. I'm expecting it to be Clay, but instead, it's the sheriff, sliding onto the stool next to me uninvited. "Little early in the day to be looking so much like shit, isn't it?"

"Little early in the day to be at the bar while you're on duty, isn't it?" I toss back, but it only makes him laugh.

"Just came in for a glass of water, that's all."

"Yeah." I snort. "Sure."

I know Sheriff Pete's dirty little secret—that he sneaks in here from time to time for a drink or two just to get through the day. Nobody else thinks much of it, I guess, but I know why he does it, unfortunately. I know just as well as him—sometimes it's the only thing that'll numb the pain. His wife passed away not too long ago, and he's never been the same since. Sure, he plays at flirting with Eileen from time to time, but he's never moved on to anyone else for real.

"What's got you so churned up?" the sheriff asks, and I shake my head.

"Don't want to talk about it."

"Yeah, I can see that. I ain't blind. Still. Maybe you should talk about it anyway."

"Listen, old man, if I was gonna talk about it, I wouldn't talk about it with you. I'd talk about it with—"

Blunt realization hits me between the eyes like the sharp end of a pry bar. If I were going to talk about it with anyone, it'd be the very woman I've been boxing out. Breezy isn't just a houseguest or a fling or a casual fucking lay like I thought she'd be—she's my future.

She's the spark I've been missing, the reason I'm willing to live again.

I fucking love her.

And holding back now isn't protecting me or her—it's destroying us in a bout of self-sabotage that could be studied by the world's foremost psychologists and still not be understood.

"Pete, I gotta go."

"Yeah." He grins at me like he can actually see inside my fucking head. "That's what I thought. Glad I could be of service getting your head outta your ass."

I still have a chance to make this right. To tell her my story and beg her to forgive me for holding her at arm's length for so long.

A chance to have her and our baby and grow old together. A chance at happiness I never thought I'd have again.

I dig in my pocket for some cash, tossing a few bills on the bar and waving at Clay and Marty with a two-finger flick. They both jerk their chins in reply, and I grab the flannel from the stool next to me and head out the front door, my eyes adjusting to the soft light of the fading sun with a jolt. I look up to the sky, stopping there and taking a deep breath.

As I let the air out, I feel cleansed by clarity. What I want, what I need to do to have it—it all seems so simple now.

Sheriff Pete bumps into my back as he comes running out the door behind me, apologizing blindly until he sees it's me, and then freezes dead in his tracks, his eyes troubled.

"What's up, Pete?" I ask as he rubs the top of his head frantically. Sirens in the distance catch my attention before he can answer, growing closer by the second until the fire trucks are in sight and flying by in a hurry.

I turn back to Pete, his upset making sense—too much sense—in one, soul-crushing moment.

Sheriff Peeler is contrite, doing his best to be comforting, but

I'm already a mile deep on a spiral no other human on this earth could possibly imagine. "I'm sorry, Tad. It's your place. Nor and Ben just called it in, but said your truck had come and gone, so you wouldn't be home."

"Fuck!"

"Tad!" Pete yells as I take off for my truck at a run.

"Breezy's inside!" I yell back without stopping, jumping in and starting it so fast, I swear my tires are spitting gravel before my ass even hits the seat.

Time slows down into a chasm, and my nightmares take shape in the light of day.

I can't fucking do this again.

I won't survive it.

44

Tad

Ten Years Ago
March 14th

The first sight as I wind around the bend and come over the hill is a punch to the gut in every sense it can be, a glowing mix of orange and thick black and ash curling into the otherwise blue sky.

My memories, my things, my home, picked for its perfect, quaint setting and idyllic white fence—up in flames. My legs move first, jumping from the truck at a run before it's even stopped, my thoughts a mask of emptiness to let my brain protect itself just a little longer. My knee jolts on the loose, snow-melted, sloppy ground, but I don't slow.

I'm already equipped with my air tank and respirator, having strapped in during the ride, and I breathe carefully to conserve my limited supply of oxygen.

But the glow of the fire as it rolls through the broken glass of blown-out windows is all I can see—all I can feel—as I cross the distance, and before I know it, I'm gulping over the sound of my own frenzy.

I hit the front door with a shoulder, snapping the wood frame with ease and barreling into the house in what feels like a fraction of a moment.

My foyer is dismally dark, the normal laughter of jokes and banter created with love replaced by a smoke so thick I can't even see my hand six inches in front of my face. My lungs feel heavy but not with soot—with the real, raw reality that my limitations as a human are on the precipice of being challenged. I overpower the feeling with urgency. I can and will do *whatever* I have to do, no matter the cost.

There is no other option I'm willing to consider. In this moment, I can do anything. Because I have to.

Fear coats my movements, forcing me to rely on my training and muscle memory fully. I can hear my own breath in my ears, feel the thud of my heart in my chest, and see the film reel of a life in this house as it's eaten by the lick of unbearably hot flames.

Palming the wall, I walk along it blindly with nothing to guide me but the experience of walking it a thousand times before and the determination to see if she's all right—to see if *they're* all right. To get them to safety as quickly as possible.

"Where are you?" I yell, my voice muffled unbearably. "Are you in here?"

Ash and water mix with still-hot embers as they rain down on me, the crew outside fighting to knock down the flames enough to keep the structure standing. Beams above me burn near clean through, and the walls feel hollow to the touch. I use my elbows and fists to knock through barriers, but it gets harder and harder with every step I take forward blindly.

This should be a hall—open and free from debris—to the back of the house, but it's nothing more than an obstacle course now, burned and beaten by a fire that's been unattended for just a little too long.

When I left for my shift at the firehouse this morning, all was well. Now, my whole world is on the verge of hell.

Words don't seem clear or crisp right now, so I revert to anguish, screaming loudly instead. I listen intently, the sound of my breathing and the harsh crack of failing wood fading into the background.

It's subtle, but there's a cry back—one of desperation and pain that chills me to the bone in spite of the temperatures over five hundred degrees all around me.

The call wasn't wrong. They're *inside.*

Some part of me believed they weren't; some part of me ignored the description of the dispatcher when she said *people may be trapped.*

Fuck.

I move more quickly, ignoring the creak and crackle of succumbing wood and pushing myself to my knees to go farther when structural collapse denies me at my full height. I have to get to them. I *have* to.

Randy's muffled yell rings out behind me, but I ignore it, pushing forward anyway.

I can save them, and I will.

Tad Hanson can do anything when he has to. There's no other option.

"Abigail!" I yell, choking on the lack of air my rapidly shallowing breaths are bringing to my respirator. Panic doesn't help—ever. And yet, I can't seem to turn off the personal connection that it's not just anyone in here. I can't seem to compartmentalize that it's my wife and my daughter and that they need me to be the one who can save them. "Lucy!"

"Tad," my brother Randy says, his voice muffled by his own air mask and gear. "Let me by!"

I don't listen, pushing forward instead and contorting my body to fit through a tight space formed by two fallen beams. The alarm on my air tank already rings its warning of approaching depletion, but I ignore it.

Even upon arrival, I could see the house was lost. The flames licked twice as high as the roof, and both walls on the sides had started to give in, and now, as each moment passes, it claims more of the beloved structure my late father-in-law built with his own hands.

But my wife and daughter are inside. I won't leave without them.

I can't.

I'll keep going until I can't anymore—even if it kills me.

45

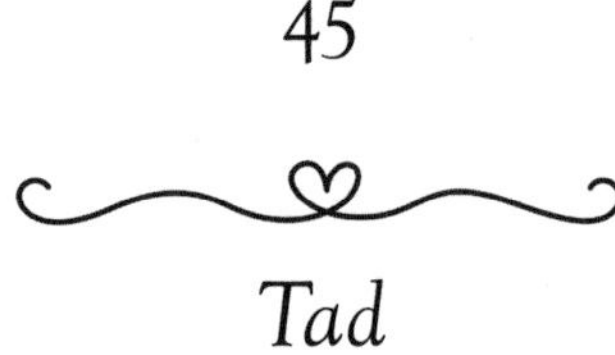

Tad

"Dammit!" I scream, slamming my phone down onto the floor of the truck as I fishtail around the corner of Maple, not even pausing for the stop sign before making my turn.

Breezy's still not answering her phone, and Bennett isn't picking up either. Randy's the only one who answered, and I hung up on him as soon as I got the message across—*my place is on fucking fire, and Breezy is probably inside.*

Sheriff Pete slides around the corner behind me, his lights and sirens going as I floor it until the speedometer hits sixty-five. Trees pass in a blur, and the distance between me and the tail end of the fire truck in front of me closes at a dangerously fast clip.

I cut off the turn, just missing the culvert and ditch as I pull into my driveway alongside the fire truck and come to a stop a millisecond too late, the front end of my truck blowing a hole in Randy's newly repaired fence.

I don't bother shifting to park or turning off the ignition before jumping out and taking off at a run for the house.

Fire rolls unchecked from the seam of the roof, and smoke billows wildly from the windows at the right side of the house.

"Tad!" Norah yells as I hit the porch at a run, ripping the storm door open with brute force and hitting the interior one with a flying shoulder.

"Breezy's inside!" I yell back. I don't look in their direction after that, but by the sound of Norah's scream as she calls Bennett's name, I'd say he isn't far behind me.

I don't care. My *only* focus is getting to Breezy and getting her out of this house alive.

The heat is instant and suffocating and there's smoke everywhere.

Fuck!

I drop to my hands and knees to limit my smoke inhalation enough to keep from passing out and crawl through the kitchen and down the hall toward the living room. It's fully engulfed, a hollow shell of what it used to be and by the looks of things, the likely source of the fire. I keep moving, my throat burning and my eyes in tears from the fumes. There's a harsh bang, the sound of something giving way in the living room and falling across the hall behind me, and I hear Bennett curse loudly before more muffled screams take up just outside.

My ears ring, my heart racing and my head pounding from the lack of air for even just a couple of minutes starting to get to me. Sweat pours down my face and off my body as I fight to put one hand in front of the other in a bear crawl.

Twenty feet feel like a hundred yards as the heat and fumes and closing flames beat against me, but when I finally make it to the back of the house, a small glimmer of hope renews me with a burst of energy.

The door to the master bedroom is closed, and the flames in the attic have yet to break through the ceiling above.

Climbing to my feet temporarily, I put a shoulder to the door and shove, breaking it from the jamb and splintering the wood on the bolt side. Smoke curls wildly at the ceiling, but for the first time since entering the house, it's not thick enough to cut off my sight yet, and I move quickly around the bed to the other side of the room.

Oh, thank God.

Finally, a breakthrough. Relief and anxiety and urgency fight for supremacy as I see her.

Breezy—horizontal across the floor, just outside the bathroom door, in a T-shirt and wet skin.

"Breezy, baby," I whisper as I pull her into my arms. My voice is choked, and my eyes scan her face and body wildly. "*Fuck.*"

My pulse is a hammer. I press my ear close to her mouth and feel the breaths push from her lips.

Her body's warm. Chest rising. Lips still pink. *Breathing.* Thank God, she's breathing. But her eyes stay closed, lashes still.

She's not conscious, but she's here and she's breathing and she's alive, and I made it to her.

My throat is nearly closed, the raw burn of smoke and tears mixing in a potent form of poison, and yet, I take my first full breath since I sprinted out of The Country Club.

"Okay, okay. You're okay. I've got you. You're okay." I don't know if I'm telling her or myself. My throat's on fire, lungs clawing for air, but all I can focus on is getting her out of here. *She needs a hospital. Now.*

I scoop her up and into my arms, gathering her carefully and pulling her T-shirt up over her mouth and nose to help with the smoke as much as I can.

"Hold on, Breezy. Hold on for me."

Moving quickly, I take the shortest route to clean air, exiting the bedroom and pushing past the spray of cascading water as it falls on us from the ceiling as the firefighters outside soak the attic where the fire has spread across the entire roofline.

Out the sun-room and the back door and onto the deck, I move quickly around the house as fast as I can without hurting or dropping her.

Sheriff Pete is the first to spot me, pointing and whistling to a couple of guys off to his left. I don't stop or slow down, but they match my speed, running toward me. Halfway through the front yard, we meet.

"She's alive, she's breathing, but she's not conscious!" I shout at them even though we're mere feet apart. "We need to get her to the fucking ambulance! To a fucking hospital! Now!"

Nate Woodall and Barry Flyshman, two of the volunteer firefighters for Red Bridge and guys I've avoided getting to know for all the years I've lived here, take Breezy from my arms and carry her to the stretcher waiting behind the lone town ambulance. I try to follow, but I trip over my feet as my legs give out, a cough of smoke and debris rattling out of my chest and landing on my hand.

Mud and water soak through my jeans and onto my knees in the grass in front of what used to be my house. Smoke still rolls, though lessened significantly by the work of the firefighters behind me, and the heat of smoldering flames licks at my back and fights the chill that invades my bones.

Bennett and Logan rush toward Breezy while Norah stays back with Autumn, and I struggle to my feet, willing myself to carry forward. Randy stops me with a hand at my shoulder—I think, at first, to halt me—but ultimately helps me over to my truck and lifts me inside. He runs to the driver's side and pulls out in a cloud of gravel behind the ambulance, and I fight the urge to rub at my stinging eyes with my dirty, shaking hands.

"It's going to be okay," Randy assures me confidently, eyes on the road and one tight fist clenched around the wheel. "You got her out...you got them out."

I nod. I know. I did. And the feeling is poisonously bittersweet.

To think I made it this time when I couldn't for Abigail and Lucy. To think, even now, I still don't know if Breezy and the baby are okay.

I pray to a God I abandoned long ago, and I do it without shame. I beg for mercy. I beg for compassion.

I beg for Beatrice Bishop and the baby in her belly.

I beg.

Please, God. Please let them be okay. Please don't let this end in devastation a second time.

Please don't make me regret where I should've been a second time.

Please, I beg. *If you have to take someone, take me instead.*

46

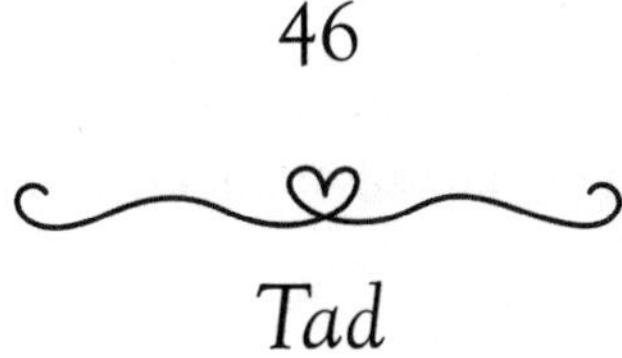

Tad

Ten Years Ago
March 14th

Debris falls all around me as my oxygen alarm rings out into the quickly dwindling space. Thick black smoke cloaks my face and robs me of my sense of direction, and a heat unlike I've ever felt licks at me from every bearing.

Water sprays on me in waves, droplets splattering across my mask through the cloud of smoke and rendering me even more useless. A sooty paste coats the clear surface, smearing badly when I try to rub at it with my glove. I swallow, choking on an airlessness as the tank strapped to my back depletes, but I won't be deterred. I rip off the mask and toss it aside, sinking to the floor to find any bit of clean air I can.

Hands pull at my legs as I try to crawl forward, and my lungs get heavier and heavier by the millisecond. I hold my breath, but after a minute or two of very slow progress forward, the edges of my consciousness start to fade. My brain feels thick, my decision-making officially gone. I collapse to the floor, using every vestige of control I have left to submit myself to God himself.

I'm not going to make it. Abigail, Lucy, me—none of us are going to make it out alive.

I hug the floor, memories of Abigail and Lucy and me at the kitchen table over the weekend filtering into my sluggish mind. I see Abby's smile and hear Lucy's laugh and feel the warmth of their hugs as they pile into my lap and rain kisses all over my face.

My skin tingles, and my heart slows.

And then, in one peaceful moment, it's all over.

• • •

"Tad!"

A voice slams through the ringing in my ears as a strip of white light cuts across my eyes. I flinch, coughing hard enough to split my ribs open, air tearing down my throat like glass while someone tugs and stabs at my arm, dragging me back into full, panicked consciousness.

"Abby!" I yell, shoving at the person at my arm and struggling to sit up.

"Easy, Tad. Easy."

My head turns toward the voice, and through the blur, I see Randy. His helmet is off, his face is soot-streaked, and his eyes are bloodshot and wet. His turnout gear is half unbuckled, the reflective tape warped and blackened.

"Take a deep breath, Tad." His eyes meet mine, blocking the light in severe shadow. His hand puts weight on my shoulder, pinning me down.

"Abby—" My voice breaks. I grab desperately at his arms. "Where's Abby? Where's Lucy?"

My cry is broken. My questions, statements.

I know where they are. I *know*.

And he doesn't answer. His mouth opens, closes, but he can't look me in the eye because he fucking knows too.

"It's okay, brother," he whispers, his voice clogged with emotion. "It's going to be okay."

The ambulance rocks beneath us, siren wailing into the air. Oxygen hisses from the mask hovering near my face, and the sharp scent of antiseptic cuts through the smoke still clinging to my skin. A paramedic leans over me, latex gloves squeaking against my arm as they reach for the IV, but I shove them away.

"Where are they, Randy?" I demand, louder now and a sob strangling my lungs. "Where *are they?*"

I want him to say it. I want him to tell me what I already know to be true. But fuck, I want him to tell a different fucking version. I want him to tell me a fucking miracle occurred. I want him to tell me that Abby and Lucy made it out.

But he doesn't. Because he can't. *Because he fucking can't.*

Because everything that was important to me—everything I loved and cared about, my entire fucking world—is gone.

"No. No. No." I shake my head, a violent yell breaking free from a hell within me I wouldn't wish on my worst enemy. "Nooo!"

"It's okay," Randy says again, his words a hollow, deceitful weep of his own. "It's gonna be okay."

It's not going to be okay. It's never going to be okay. We both know it.

Because Abigail and Lucy are gone. But because of my brother, I'm still here.

I should be with them. The three of us should be together.

"Nooo!" I cry again, fighting their holds with the intent of jumping out of this fucking ambulance and running straight back into the fire and letting it take me. Randy pins me again, and I just catch his nod to the paramedic at my side before it all goes black again.

A temporary peace from a permanent kind of pain—one I'll never recover from.

47

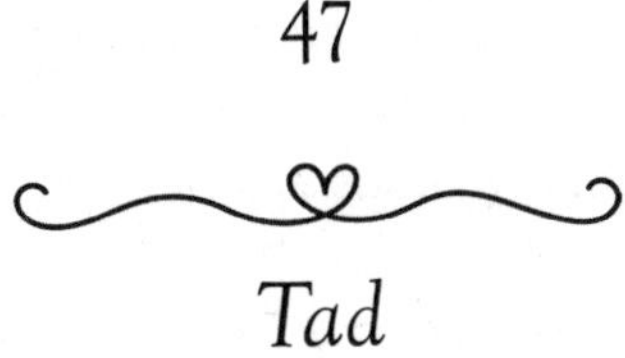

Tad

Doctors and nurses move around me in a flurry, holding me back with a hand on my chest when I try to follow them toward the restricted area I saw them take Breezy into when we arrived.

They had her out of the ambulance before Randy could bring the truck to a stop, moving to the back too fast for me to catch up. Memories of being too late—of being the only one to survive—cascade like waves over my shoulders and sink me to my knees. I can't do it again.

I can't lose them. I *can't*.

Tears fall unchecked as I put my face in my hands and roar into the empty hallway. My chest implodes with the force of my yell, and I don't let up until every last vestige of air has been wrung from my lungs. A gentle hand falls on my shoulder and squeezes, and when I look up, it's straight into the sage, sad eyes of Sheriff Pete Peeler. He must have driven like a bat out of hell from the house, just like Randy did.

"Come on, son. Let's find a place to sit down."

I shake my head violently, unwilling to leave this spot until I'm forced. "I'm not leaving, Pete."

"I don't want you to leave, boy. I want you to sit. Shit, I think you got smoke clogging your ears."

He guides me with a hand under my arm, effectively helping me up and over to the wall, where I slide down to the floor with my back against it immediately. He climbs down to the floor beside me, lumbering as his knees crack.

Randy comes to a skidding stop in front of us, having found a spot to abandon the truck and made it inside finally, and when I meet his gaze, it's nearly as tortured as mine. I don't often have the fortitude to consider anyone's pain but my own, but Randy's been serving the penance of his demons just as long as I've been living with my own.

He knows I've never forgiven him for saving me, eternally punished for doing the right thing. It's not right of me, but it's not wrong either. It's just...purgatory.

His back slides down as he sinks to his ass against the wall across the hall, mirroring my posture entirely, legs flat out in front of himself, body limp. "Fuck."

He's in rough shape, but I'm arguably rougher, choking on saliva, soot, and a pure adrenaline crash as I try to keep it together.

"Take deep breaths," Pete commands easily, his hand finding my shoulder and gripping tightly. "Both of ya. Take some deep fucking breaths."

"Breeze!" Bennett yells, moving down the hall at a run with Norah and Logan hot on his heels, his eyes wild and searching as he yanks open doors and looks inside up and down the wing to our right.

I try to talk—to call his name out in acknowledgment—but all I manage is a strangled cough before Pete takes over.

"Over here, Ben," he says calmly, climbing to his feet next to me again.

"Where is she? Is she okay?" Bennett asks frantically, his

demeanor aggressive in every sense of the word as he charges toward us at a jog.

Pete puts a hand to his chest, but his feet keep churning, essentially leaving him treading tile. "We don't know anything yet, Ben. We haven't seen her."

"Haven't seen her?" Logan yells from behind Norah, stepping forward with his chest out like he can force his way through our assumed stupidity with sheer ego. "Why the hell not?"

"They won't let us back there, son," Pete says, trying to hold on to what little reason is available in the tight air of a very tense hall.

"Bullshit, they won't. I'm going," Logan insists, slamming into a set of doors that won't budge—the very same dead end that stopped me. Emotions are high, but evidently, security in hospitals is higher. "Fuck!"

"All of ya," Pete insists then, his patience waning from wading through too many buckets of bullshit. "Sit your asses down, right now. Come on. Take a load off."

Bennett and Norah hug each other tightly, and Logan slams down next to Randy. Without saying a word or lifting his gaze at all, Randy reaches out to put a hand on Logan's shoulder, just like Pete did for me earlier. It's an olive branch of humanity I don't know that I'm capable of right now.

"Tad," Norah whispers, surprising me entirely by being directly in front of my face. She's squatted down, her ass at her heels, and when my eyes find their focus, I see a sheen of tears in her eyes and a messy smear of mascara beneath them.

"Where's Autumn?" I ask, my voice hoarse.

"She's outside with Clay, Josie, Sheila, and Marty. They all left the bar as soon as they heard."

I nod. It's all I can do.

"Tad, honey, we should get you seen by a doctor too," Norah says, gently touching my arm. "You were in there a long time. Took in a lot of smoke, you know?"

I shake my head. I'm not leaving this spot until I hear about

Breezy and the baby.

"Tad," Bennett says then, shocking the shit out of me by using my real name. "Get checked out. I promise you, I'll come find you as soon as—"

The door to the restricted area swings open with a thud, interrupting Bennett and bringing me to my feet so quickly I sway. Pete puts a hand under my armpit on one side, and Bennett grabs on to the other as the doctor asks, "Tad Hanson?"

"That's me," I rasp desperately. Shards of glass against a chalkboard would sound better than I do right now.

"Beatrice is asking for you."

She's asking for you. That means she's speaking. That means she's thinking.

That means she's *okay.*

The weight of the world leaves my shoulders, and my balance suffers the consequences.

I collapse. Voices shout. Everything goes hazy.

And just like that...I'm officially ousted as the one making decisions for myself as my consciousness takes a road trip.

I guess, maybe, the time has come for me to get checked out.

48

Tad

The sting of antiseptic hits first, sharp and sterile in the back of my throat. Then come the sounds—oxygen hissing, monitors beeping close and far away—and the ache that sits heavy in every inch of my body.

Bright light greets me through my blinks, the simple act of breathing burning like never before. I try to clear my throat, but it's useless.

"He…hello?" It's gravelly and hurts like a son of a bitch, so I close my eyes on a groan.

For a moment, there's only the noise of machines and the weight of pain pressing me down.

Then soft, familiar, and *home* fills my ears.

"Tad?" Breezy's sweet, strong, healthy voice urges me to open my eyes again.

"Breeze?" I push myself up the hard mattress, craning my neck until I see her. She's in a hospital bed parked directly beside mine, and she's crying. Silent tears of relief and fear and a hundred other emotions stream down her face and make her lips quiver.

Shuffling quickly, I spin to the side and climb from my bed. The IV line tugs hard at my arm, monitors erupt in panicked beeps, and pain tears through my chest with every movement, but I don't stop as I move toward her bed on quick feet, carelessly dragging cords and an IV pole with me.

"Tad, stop. You're gonna hurt yourself!" Breezy declares in a panic, but not a thing in this world would stop me right now from pulling the woman I love into my arms and convincing myself she's safe.

I pull her up and off the bed, into my arms in a tight hug that I know has to hurt. I try to loosen my hold, but the relief is too strong, the emotion too overwhelming. For her part, she's selflessly silent, squeezing me tightly back.

As gently as I can, I lay her back to rest on her pillow, taking her waist in my hands and putting my face to her hospital-gown-covered belly. I want to look her in the eyes, but I can't yet. It's too much.

Breezy rubs her hand firmly across my back, her lips falling to the skin at the back of my neck and staying there. "Shh," she comforts. "It's okay. I'm okay. The baby's okay."

Back bowed and head low, a sob bucks me as the weight of my life comes raining down on me. My losses, my gains—the sweet confirmation that Breezy and the baby are both, by some miracle, okay.

"We're all okay," she whispers, and it simultaneously breaks me and breathes life into my soul.

I swallow hard against the tears lodged in my throat, nodding against her belly and fighting the shake in my hands before reaching out and grabbing hers and squeezing until her knuckles turn white.

My own ID bracelet, strapped on me sometime while I was unconscious, boasts a reminder that I got to Breezy's room by way of my own hospital bed. Thankfully, our family and friends saw to it that we are together. I don't know if they truly cared, or if they just knew I'd tear this place to fucking shreds if they didn't, but either way, waking up to Breezy's safe, warm, tear-streaked face will forever be ingrained as one of the most satisfying, clarifying, beautiful moments of my life.

I don't just care about her—I love her. And it's about damn time I started acting like it by letting her in.

"Breeze. I'm sorry I haven't been able to…" I shake my head and meet her eyes. "I'm sorry I haven't shared my life with you. That I haven't let you in."

"It's okay. I know we're still in the phase of earning trust, and—"

"No, baby." I cut her off, not to be rude, but to steel my nerves. I have to get it all out—I have to release it before it makes me explode. "No. It's not you. It's not us. I… Breeze. I've done this before."

"Done what before?"

My throat is thick, and my heart feels like it'll explode at any minute as I face my demons head on.

"Loving someone. Building a life." I pause, letting out a shaky breath. "The fire."

It takes everything inside me to say it aloud, but I force it out with sheer will. "Breeze. I had a wife, Abigail, and a daughter… Lucy." I close my eyes as two tears fall along the ridge of my cheek, opening them again after licking the salty liquid from my lips.

"I was a firefighter with Station One of the Elgin Fire Department just outside of Chicago, and one day, a few hours into my shift, I got a call to a house, fully involved with two people trapped inside." I swallow. Sickness lingers just in the back of my throat, fighting for supremacy with my next words. "My house, Breezy. My people inside."

She covers her mouth, instant emotion shining in her sweet eyes.

Tears fall unchecked down my cheeks. I choke trying to clear my throat, but I don't stop. I can't now. With news like this, the only way to get through it all is to free-fall.

"I was too late that day. The electrical short that caused the fire spread through the entire attic first, before Abigail and Lucy even knew it was burning. It was early, just after sunrise, so they were in bed, and by the time the alarms went off, collapse was already starting. I couldn't get in, and they couldn't get out. The only reason I'm alive is because Randy pulled me out after I'd gone unconscious. He was a firefighter with Elgin, too. Same station as me. Same shift that day when we got…the call." My whole body quakes with grief and sadness and shame—for failing and, especially, for the unfortunate truth of my next admission. "For a long time, I really wished Randy hadn't saved me."

"Tad." My name in her voice is soft. Broken. Tortured. It's all the things I've been feeling on my own for the last ten years in living color—all the weight I've been carrying in undeniable sound—and somehow, the pit I thought had been permanently carved in my stomach is suddenly gone because I've shared the burden with her. My spine is straighter; my heart is stronger. I can breathe.

It's raw, inflamed—just like my throat is from inhaling so much smoke—but for the first time since it happened, it feels like there's a chance it could heal.

"Today, Breezy. Today is the first time since it happened, I've seen the blessing in him pulling me out. Being with you. Making this baby—this beautiful miracle together—it's the happy ending I never thought I'd have. Never thought I deserved." My whole body shakes. "I think they sent you to me, Abigail and Lucy. I think they helped save you today."

Tears stream down Breezy's cheeks, and her hand covers mine as I cradle her face in my palm. The earnest burn in my chest pulls my next words from somewhere deep inside.

"I love you, Breezy. With my entire being, including the parts I thought died with them. You make me want to be more. Better. You make me want to *live* again."

49

Breezy

Fingers in Tad's brown hair and thumb at his pink, tear-drenched lips, I fall into the comfort of his warm eyes and let his words wash over me.

His unbearable grief, his willingly shared love—his declaration that I, somehow, have given him the will to live out loud again.

I don't feel worthy of the crowning, but I know with every shred of my being I'll spend the rest of my life trying to live up to it.

Because for as much as Tad thinks I've saved him, he's saved me.

I was whirring through life with little to no regard for any of the parts of it that truly mean something. Love, purpose, joy—I gave them all up for success.

"I don't know that I'll ever find the words to express how much it means to me that I'm able to give you your life back." I cup his cheek in the palm of my hand, and he leans into it. "The words to express my gratitude for you sharing this giant piece of yourself with me—for trusting me with it. The words to tell you just how much I hope Abigail and Lucy and Summer have somehow found company with one another in heaven until the rest of us get there."

My voice shakes as tears steal its steadiness, but I keep going.

"But Tad, I will spend all of my days trying to find them. I will spend all of my days telling you I love you, thanking Abigail and Lucy for sending you to me, and finding the absolute joy in the privilege of being with you. Because you saved my life too, and baby, I don't just mean today."

His lips find my knuckles and then my arm and my cheek and my lips, and then we're kissing, deep and slow and so soul-exposing, I'd feel it in another universe.

"I love you," I whisper, breathless and desperate to say it again as soon as he pulls back enough to let me.

"I love you too."

Pulling gently at his biceps, I direct him up and into the bed with me until we're hip-to-hip and head-to-head. He intertwines our fingers, rubbing at the backs of my knuckles with the other hand.

"So, from fireman to...sheep farmer?"

He chuckles, a soft sadness metering the tone. "I needed something as far away from my old life as I could think of."

"And Randy?"

"Left his whole damn life and career in Chicago..." He pauses, shaking his head, and his hair rubs against the side of my cheek. "To follow me to Red Bridge and face the consequences of his actions...saving my life when I didn't want it saved." Glancing around, he surveys the room. "Speaking of...where is everyone? Don't get me wrong. I needed this time with you, but I can't believe our families willingly gave it."

"Yeah," I say, "They...didn't."

He sits up, turning to face me. "What do you mean?"

"I mean, they were all here. Randy, Ben, Norah, Logan,

Josie, Clay, Pete, Sheila...hell, half the town was here, so much so the doctors were getting touchy. But then...Eileen showed up."

"You're kidding. After everything she—"

"Wait. There's more." I grimace. "Tad, Eileen had a heart attack."

"What?"

I nod. "She showed up here, and everyone assumed, naturally, that she'd heard about the fire and was coming to capitalize on our suffering and anxieties. Josie got into her immediately—I didn't hear everything since it happened out by the main entrance, but I know it wasn't good. But Eileen's niece came running in not long after, and...baby, Eileen got so upset when she heard about you and the house, she started having chest pains. She came here to get checked out. I haven't heard an update in a little while, but they said she had a heart attack."

"Shit. That's horrible."

"I know. Bennett promised he'd come back as soon as they knew something definitive."

He studies me, worry creasing his face. "And what about you? What are the doctors saying? When I found you, you were unconscious."

"I passed out," I admit softly. "After we fought and you left, I took a bath to calm down, but I hadn't eaten the burger you brought me." I cringe at my own stupidity. "Hadn't really eaten much all day, honestly, and when I hopped out of the bath to get my phone from the guestroom, I never made it there. The doctors said the heat of the bath, mixed with not eating and the diversion of blood flow to the baby, is enough to explain why I passed out on the way there." I shake my head. "I...I didn't even know the house was on fire until I got here and they told me," I admit. "Tad, I'm so sorry. I think...I think I left the woodstove open and that's probably what started it, and—"

"Breeze, it's okay," he comforts, and his voice is all warmth and ache and makes a ball of emotion clog my throat. "It's okay."

A few tears fall down my cheeks. "But the clothes. The

photos. They're Abigail's and Lucy's, right?"

He nods, quiet but certain.

And I start to cry. "I'm so sorry."

"It doesn't matter." He pulls me back into his arms and hugs me against his chest. "All that matters to me is that you, and the baby, are okay."

"I am. And our baby is." I sniffle, trying to steady myself. "The doctor did an ultrasound to check. Heartbeat was strong and everything," I update, and a new wave of tears threatens to spring to my eyes just thinking about the relief I felt when hearing our little baby's heartbeat on the monitor.

"Thank God." His shoulders drop with relief, and he presses a kiss to my forehead before rubbing a gentle hand over my belly. "Thank God. You're both okay."

"They have me on a little oxygen to be safe and something called a bronchodilator," I add. "Randy said the doctor told him they're doing the same for you, as well as an antibiotic and corticosteroids because your inflammation is so bad. They're keeping us both overnight, but if our oxygen levels are okay tomorrow, we can go home. Or...well, somewhere."

"Ha. Yeah. I'm sure Randy will let us crash with him for a little while."

"You're sure Randy will do what?" Tad's brother asks, walking in our room at just the right time with Norah, Bennett, Autumn, and Logan all trailing behind him.

"Let us stay with you until we have a house again," Tad repeats, doubling down.

"Of course."

"You can stay with us too!"

"Good, our house is full."

The first is from Randy, the second from Norah, and the third, of course, from Bennett.

Logan chuckles, pushing through the crowd until he makes it to the bed, leaning down to pull me into his arms. "Don't worry, Breeze. I'm not welcome either." It's a long, slow hug, filled with weeks of regret and a simple conclusion that family, even at the tense times, is what matters the most. I pat him on the back and then the cheek, working my lip with my teeth when a sheen exposes the waiting tears in his normally cocky eyes.

As he pulls back, I touch his cheek, whispering. "We'll talk, okay?"

Bennett steps forward for a hug too, followed by Norah and Autumn, and then finally Randy. Tad waves them all off, and I can't help but roll my eyes with a laugh.

"Too manly for hugs, huh?"

"No," Tad disagrees easily. "Too naked. I'll hug you all tomorrow, when I'm not in this gown."

It's a much-needed moment of levity, but the nagging unknown of Eileen's condition brings it to a swift end.

"How's Eileen, Ben?" I ask. Bennett and Norah share a look before he replies.

"She's doing okay. Shaken up. Wrung out. Doc said it was a minor heart attack. Josie's actually still with her and says she's going to stay for a while to keep her niece company. Eileen says... well, she says she's retiring, but I don't think any of us will believe that until we see it."

"Retiring? Who the hell's gonna run the paper, then?" Tad interjects.

"Her niece, I guess," Randy answers with a shrug. "That's supposedly why she's here in the first place. Eileen said she would have been done a while ago, but she liked having lunch with you every week."

Tad's response makes my heart squeeze. "We can still have lunch every week. Tell her that, okay?"

I get unexpectedly teary, and Tad pulls me into a hug that buries my face in his chest. From behind me, I can hear Bennett taking charge.

"Okay, guys, let's get out of their hair for now. Breeze, Tad, if you need anything, you call. We'll check back on you tomorrow."

Pulling it together quickly, I turn and waggle my hands to get hugs from Autumn and Norah and Bennett and Logan and even Randy again. Tad waves them off once more, which results in a trail of laughter as they leave the room.

His look is sly as he cups my face in his hand. "For clarification, babe...the naked thing? Not an issue when it comes to you."

Oh yeah. I'm in love. I'm in love in a big, big way.

50

Breezy

Wednesday, April 14th

The lid of my to-go cup clicks under my fingernail as I sit in the little park at the center of town, the smell of espresso and fresh-cut grass tangling in the air. Across the table, a second cup sits waiting for a meeting that's long overdue.

My phone buzzes beside it.

Tad: *Love you. Don't forget to eat something with that coffee.*

Me: *Bossy.*

Tad: *Damn straight. Farm Daddy takes your and our baby's health very seriously.*

The corners of my mouth curve up before I even realize it.

It's officially been a week since the fire, six days since our release from the hospital, and every moment has been a whirlwind. I'm still finding my footing, but it feels good—this life fits.

Of course, Tad's been hesitant to let me out of his sight, but I haven't minded at all. Even now, I miss him.

Logan's silver rental car pulls into a spot in the parking lot and shuts off, and I take a final deep breath to prepare myself to say all the things I want to say. The hard things, the good things, the things that can't help but feel like a little bit of both—I've loved Logan since the moment he was born and every moment in between, even when I hated him. With family, it's not always logic that wins; sometimes it's love.

His smile is warm and gentle as he arrives, leaning forward to place a kiss on my cheek before taking the seat across from me. "Thanks for the coffee."

"You're welcome. Thanks for...everything you've done in the last week."

Logan shrugs, minimizing his efforts in a way that's unbecoming of a supposedly snobby, cocky Hollywood big shot and much more telling of who he really is.

"No, Logan. It's a big deal. Randy said you had a crew there working the next day on our house, and I don't know how you pulled it off, but I appreciate it. I went by there this morning, and they've already got a new basement dug, the foundation poured, and the walls studded out." I shake my head. "At this rate, we could be back in there in a month, and with the baby on the way, I... Well, it means a lot."

"I know it might not seem like it sometimes, but I'd do anything for you, sis. You practically raised us. You..." He swallows, looking down for a long moment before meeting my eyes again. "You're the reason I'm anything at all."

"Logan."

"Breezy, you are. That's why I've been hanging out here, waiting. I knew I couldn't leave until I made it right. And believe me, I tried to fix the gallery mess. My lawyer and accountant looked for every loophole they could find to transfer them back to you, but apparently, the tax implications are a nightmare. You'd have lost all your net worth on fucking taxes just trying to take full ownership of them." He exhales a deep breath. "And the last thing

I wanted to do was make shit worse for you."

I shake my head, completely at a loss for words. "I didn't realize you were doing all that."

"They were yours, Breeze. I never wanted to stand in the way of that." He reaches out to gently hold my hand. "And I…I set up trusts, for you and for Bennett. I don't know if that's what you would've done, but when you said you didn't want the money, I did my best to figure out the best thing to do."

"Trusts? What are you talking about?"

"Breeze, just because you and Bennett didn't want Dad's money doesn't mean it disappears. He left it for you. Unless you designate it to some other purpose, it has to go to you. So, I put it in trusts for you both. Bennett's money is in Autumn's name. Yours is currently in your name, but we can change that if you want, after you have the baby, or whatever you want."

"I…I don't know what to say."

Logan shrugs. "It's done. If you want to make a change, all you have to do is say, and I'll call the lawyer."

"Well, thanks. I appreciate your handling it, and I appreciate it—"

"Breezy, you don't have to do this. You can still be mad at me about the galleries. I'll understand, really. I'd love for you to run them still, but I understand if you don't want to." His shoulders bounce. "I'm okay with it if you need to hate me, so long as you still let me love you."

"Oh, baby brother," I whisper raggedly. "I don't hate you. I couldn't. Ever. And honestly, Dad leaving the galleries to you is the best thing that's ever happened to me."

"What? You don't mean that."

"Three months ago, I wouldn't have. But, Logan, right now, I do. I needed this. I needed the change, the push, the end of a trail of excuses. I'm finally chasing *my* happiness. No one else's. And I was never going to do that in New York, when I felt like the responsibility of the family was on my shoulders."

"So, what now? What are you going to do?"

I laugh. "Slow down. Choose me. Live happily ever after, I guess."

"Fuck yeah. Life here looks damn good on you, I'll tell you that."

"Thank you." I smile at him and search his face closely. "And what about you? What are you going to do?"

He sighs. "Well, I don't think I can hang around here much longer. I thought Bennett would thaw eventually, but I don't think I'm getting anywhere, and I don't know, maybe I'm better off just leaving him alone. I'm headed back to New York next week." He shrugs. "Time to start handling things there. I need to get the galleries steady—find the right people, make sure what you built doesn't fall apart just because the wrong Bishop's name is on the paperwork." He smiles at me, but it's a little sad around the edges. "But just know, anytime you need me, you call me, and I'll be here."

I nod. I understand. I understand it all too well because it used to be me, dancing on the periphery of really living my life. "I love you, Logan. And I'll work on Bennett. We'll find a way to be a family again, okay? I promise."

His smile is sad but handsome as ever as he leans over the table to hug me, whispering in my ear, "Walk me to my car, okay? The crew found something in the fire before they started demo, and I felt like it was something you guys might want."

I do as he asks and wait patiently as he grabs it from the back seat. When he hands it to me, my breath catches in my chest. *The photo album from the guest room box, full of Abigail and Lucy and the Tad who loved them.* This is the best news I've gotten all day.

"Logan Bishop, you are full of surprises."

When the moment is right, I'll be able to give them to Tad. And then, our family will really be whole.

51

Tad

Monday, June 28th

Paper crinkles with Breezy's heavy breaths as the ultrasound tech moves the goopy wand across her adorably blossoming bump, trying to get the best view. Our baby bounces and kicks and rolls, and Breezy's laugh as she watches it all happening in real time is the best sound in the world.

"We've got a wiggle monster on our hands, folks, but I think… yep, I have, finally secured the money shot." The tech smiles, moving the wand around again and clicking the ball in the center while the machine bings several times. "Do we want to know what we're having? Or are we waiting for a surprise?"

I look to Breezy, who simultaneously looks to me, and we both smile.

"It's up to you," I tell her, and her smile grows.

"But I was going to say it's up to *you*," she counters, and the sonographer laughs.

Breezy turns back to the screen, trying to get a peek, and with that small gesture, I know her answer without her having to say it.

"Let's hear it."

"Ah, yay!" the sonographer cheers quietly. "I love this part." Reaching down below to the printer of the machine and handing us both the photo, she smiles. "Congratulations, Mom and Dad. It's a...boy."

"Oh gosh," Breezy laughs with joy-filled tears shining in her pretty blue eyes. "Between the Bishop and Hanson testosterone track record, I think I'm going to have my hands full."

She's never sounded happier to be put out, and I feel the exact same way.

Leaning forward to touch our lips, the sting of my nose warns of happy tears I don't dare try to hold back. "A boy. A perfect, beautiful, amazing baby boy, made by the two of us."

Breezy nods, our foreheads rubbing together. "I love you."

"I love you too, baby. More than anyone in this world will ever comprehend."

She touches her lips to mine again, and the tech shoves back in her chair while another round of pictures prints from the machine. "Congratulations again, guys. You're one of the sweetest couples I've seen in here in the last...well, five minutes or so."

Both of us laugh, and I reach across Breezy to shake the young blonde's hand while Breezy takes the string of black-and-white photos. The sonographer returns the gesture with a strong hand and then focuses on Breezy.

"Take your time getting up, okay?" she instructs. "It's normal to be a little light-headed after being on your back for so long, and you can use this rag to clean the goo off your belly before you put your clothes back in place. When you come out, just check out at the front desk like normal. The report will be in your portal by tomorrow, but baby looks very happy in there, okay?"

"Thank you so much," Breezy replies, her heart so obviously in her throat by the sound of her voice, I can't help but squeeze her hand in mine. When the door closes behind the tech, she turns to me. She's never looked more beautiful, and this is a woman who's never looked anything but for her entire life, I'm sure of it. "What did I do..." She shakes her head. "What did I do to deserve this beautiful life?"

My grin isn't just ear to ear—it's clean off my face. "Funny. I was just wondering the same thing."

• • •

Hand to Breezy's back, I usher her around the checkout desk into the main waiting area, point her toward the door and home. I've got big plans to show my girl just how thankful I am for this life in our new bed, in our newly finished house, on my old land, as soon as we get home, but the sight of Clay's smiling face is a completely unexpected addition to the process.

"Hey, man," I greet with a handshake and a grin, Breezy's excited laugh providing a sweet soundtrack in the background. "Fancy meeting you here."

"Where's Josie?" Breezy asks. "I'm assuming you didn't figure out how to have an appointment at the OB-GYN without her."

Clay laughs. "Had to visit the little girls' room before the drive home. She says her bladder is nothing but a trampoline these days."

"Same," Breezy agrees. "If I hadn't gone just before the scan, I'd be joining her."

"Is it your twenty-week too?" Clay asks excitedly.

"Yes! I still can't believe we're due around the same time." Breezy's face is warm. "After everything you guys have been through to get here." I nod as she finishes. "Clay, I'm so, so happy for the two of you."

"Thank you. Really."

The door opens then, Josie stepping out and bumping right into us with surprise. "Oh my gosh."

Breezy and I both nod, laughing, and Clay rearranges us to

pull Josie into his side. "Yep. Here at the same time. Isn't it wild?"

Then the door opens again, bumping us in the back enough that I start to move us to the exit with our goodbyes. "Good seeing you guys. Congratulations—"

"Oh, Mrs. Harris, I'm glad you're still here!" someone calls behind us. "You have pictures of baby B, but Shalisa forgot to print pictures of baby A. She gave them to me and asked to see if you were still here. I'm so glad I caught you."

Frozen in place, Breezy and I have no choice but to be shameless in our eavesdropping as the biggest Red Bridge news of the year drops right in front of us.

Josie and Clay—after loss and trauma and hardship that would cow most people—are having twins.

Life is a miracle.

I know because I'm living it for the second time, on a second chance, with a second love that feels like the first.

If it weren't for Clay Harris standing in front of me, getting the biggest news ever, I'd be a shoo-in for the luckiest man alive.

"Holy moly!" Breezy squeals in excitement. "Josie Harris!"

"Well, I guess the cat's out of the bag, huh?" Josie says, laughing and smiling at the same time.

I shrug. "Good news, though. With Eileen retired, the chances of you reading about it in the paper tomorrow are much, much lower."

Josie cackles. "Thank God."

52

Breezy

I take one final look at myself in the bathroom mirror and rub a hand over my rounded belly.

Goodness, I can't believe we're having a boy.

I also can't believe Josie and Clay are having *twins.*

And I thought me having Farm Daddy's baby was a big surprise. Once Red Bridge finds out Josie Harris is carrying two little bambinos in her belly, she might have to avoid downtown for the rest of her pregnancy.

I close the bathroom door and flick off the overhead light, and the bedroom glows with the low amber of the bedside lamp. Tad stretches out on the bed, his black boxer briefs the only thing concealing a small section of skin. His feet and chest are bare, his eyes dancing, and his hands are tucked behind his head against the headboard as he watches me cross the room.

"What's got you so giddy?" I ask as I walk toward him, my long satin nightgown trailing lightly behind me as I pad toward the bed.

Now that we're in the new house, all of my stuff from New York is finally here. I even sold my Chelsea apartment last week. Thanks to the crew Logan hired, we've been moved in for three weeks, and for the first time in forever, everything feels settled. I haven't tripped over a box in days.

"You. Me. Our *boy*," he says, voice low and content. Then his grin turns wicked. "And you looking so fucking sexy I'm already hard."

My giggle is obnoxious—and I love it so much it hurts. I'm not the serious, overworked woman I used to be, and with every moment I spend in my new life, with my new love, it shows.

"What doesn't make you hard these days?"

Tad laughs. "Other women. Your absence. Cold soup."

I snort.

"Hey, can I help it if I landed the sexiest woman on the planet who's only getting sexier by the day as she grows my baby?" He launches forward from his spot on the bed, pulling me close with splayed hands at my hips and his mouth dangerously close to mine. "You're it, baby. You're the turn-on." His lips dive forward, capturing mine in the sweetest, hottest kiss of the last five minutes.

It'd have a more impressive record if it weren't for the fact that my guy always knows what he's doing.

"Tad," I whisper, climbing onto the bed on my knees as he pulls me gently back.

"Yes, baby."

"Tad, I should get some sleep." I don't mean it, of course, but man, he's fun to tease.

"After," he says easily, spinning me around until I'm lying on my back with my head on the pillows. Slowly, painstakingly, he lifts my satin gown until I'm exposed from the breasts down, my growing baby belly protruding obviously now that I'm getting further along. "For now, though, you just relax. I'll do all the work."

"You'll do all the work? Can I get that in writing?"

He laughs before leaning down to kiss my belly, then my chest, and finally, my lips. When he pulls back, his eyes are as serious as

I've ever seen them.

"Just tell me where to sign, Breeze. I'll do anything you want, and I'll do it forever. For the rest of our lives."

"Tad."

"I love you," he says, pressing a soft kiss to my lips again. "And I know, without a shadow of doubt, I'm exactly where I'm meant to be."

Epilogue

Breezy

A year later
Saturday, June 17th

Our newly fenced backyard is a sea of whispered laughter and terrible hiding spots. Friends, family, and half the town are crammed behind trees, picnic tables, and lawn chairs—everyone buzzing with excitement as we wait for Tad to get home.

"Shh, shh!" I say loudly, grinning as I try to hush the crowd. I swear, the more I shush, the louder they seem to get.

Pete, of course, is elbow-deep in the chip bowl instead of taking cover. Josie smacks his hand and pulls him down beside her on the blanket where she's hiding with our babies—three squirmy, sun-dappled miracles lined up like the world's cutest parade.

Rose and Danny, Josie and Clay's fraternal twins named for her late grandmother and father, are little carbon copies of their parents. Rose, with her blond hair and bright green eyes, is Josie's tiny twin in a ruffled pink romper and a sun hat that keeps sliding sideways over her face. Beside her, Danny is Clay's mini-me with the same dark hair, same golden eyes, same mischievous grin, wearing a little blue onesie that reads *Ladies' Man* across his chest.

And then there's Hayes McCoy Hanson, Tad's and my whole world. He's a perfect mash-up of the two of us, with my blue eyes, Tad's mouth and hair, and a grin that already gets him out of trouble.

His outfit is the simplest of the bunch—a soft white tee and tiny denim overalls—but on him, it looks like perfection.

It's hard to believe the babies are already seven months old now, but they're growing like weeds, and I know, very soon, we won't be able to contain them this easily.

Across the yard, Clay and Bennett take their places at the sign I made them hang between two of our trees, ready to unfurl it at the perfect moment, facilitated by my having texted Tad ahead of time to tell him Hayes and I were playing in the backyard.

Even Tad's dad and Uncle Cal have traveled to Red Bridge for the occasion and are chatting with Randy from camp chairs on the far side of Josie and the babies.

As expected, the gate unlatches with a click, and when it opens, we all jump in excitement. "Surprise!"

Tad takes a step back, his smile catching joy like a thief who just got away with the world's biggest heist. I clap, which is copied quickly by Sheila and Marty and Autumn, who's playing with the water table in between them in a strawberry-adorned swimsuit and little bitty heart sunglasses, and the sign in between Clay and Bennett in the back of the yard rolls open with a snap.

"Congratulations!" I say, rushing forward to wrap my arms around Tad's neck as he reacts to reading the same word on the banner.

"Oh jeez," he cries, wrapping his arms around me tightly and burying his face in my neck so deeply it tickles. "What in the hell is this, Breeze?"

I palm both sides of his head and pull him back, pressing my lips to his and rubbing at the sweet purple bags under his eyes. He's been working so hard for us, for his new job, for Red Bridge—I swear he never even saw this coming.

"We're celebrating you. Congratulations, Mr. Red Bridge EMA Director. We are all so, so proud of you."

"I love you," he whispers raggedly, the tenuous emotion of taking his life's—his real life—purpose back by the horns a landslide it's nearly impossible to hold back. We still have the sheep, but neither one of us is pretending they're anything but pets these days.

"Oh, Farm Daddy...I love you too."

He snorts, smacking me on the ass before turning to a loitering Randy to shake his hand. The two of them have been through so much together, and somehow, are finally coming out the other side. Randy, like Tad, is moving back to his true purpose and has officially taken the position of Red Bridge Fire Chief.

Six months ago, just after our beautiful baby boy Hayes was born, the town voted to fund and form an official, paid city fire department instead of the volunteer setup they were operating on before. Nate Woodall and Barry Flyshman, two of the volunteers who helped save my life the day of the fire, took the other two full-time positions after finishing their certifications last month.

I, for one, feel safe and sound in the hands of everyone who's poured their blood, sweat, and tears into making this new department a reality, and I can wait to see my man shine in the welcoming arms of his true calling.

And he's not the only one feeling fulfilled these days.

A few months after I came out of the fog of postpartum life, I started an art history program at the library, and it's become one of the brightest parts of my week. Watching the kids of Red Bridge discover color and creativity—watching them light up the same way art once lit up my world—has brought my life full circle in the best possible way.

Lately, I've even been thinking about using some of the trust money to open a small gallery downtown. It would be a nonprofit space where the children of Red Bridge would be the featured artists.

Tad loves the idea, and honestly, I do too. I've realized I'm just as much a part of Red Bridge as it is of me, and giving back to this community that gave me everything feels exactly right.

And now, standing here surrounded by everyone I love, it feels like all of it—every hard, messy, beautiful part—led to this.

I move away, uncovering food on the picnic table and waving an arm at everyone to come eat while Tad does his due diligence of shaking hands and making nice with everyone in attendance—which, in addition to his brother, dad, and uncle, is pretty much *everyone* from town. Betty, Fran, Harold, Earl, Pete, Melba, Camille, Todd, Felix, Lee, Eileen, Millie, and sooo many more—we're surrounded by a support system of people and small businesses that would do anything to help us and anyone else in this town if they needed.

It's part of what I love about living here—and it's part of what I'm still getting used to. Everyone knows everyone, along with all their business.

It only took one trip to Earl's for hemorrhoid cream after I had the baby to teach me how quick Red Bridge plays the game of telephone. I thought they'd set up a billboard about me at one point, I got so many questions.

"Great party, Breeze," Pete says, scooping a handful of chips from the bowl and directly into his mouth. One or two don't make it, taking up residence on his belly instead. I chuckle. "Thanks, Pete. More chips in the house if those run out."

"Excellent."

I check on Josie and the babies quickly before heading back for the house, intent on getting the rest of the food out, when Tad pulls me up short, a big hug and a huge kiss taking us into seriously dangerous public display of affection territory. If Eileen hadn't retired, this would be in the paper before the last guest left tonight.

"Wow," I say with a smile, my breathing heavy as his lips let go of mine. "What was that for?"

"I love you, Breezy."

I laugh softly, biting my lip and rolling my eyes. "I know you do, Tad."

"Yeah...but I bet you don't know this."

"Don't know—" As Tad backs away and settles onto one knee in the grass, my words evaporate into a mist. "Oh my God," I whisper instead. "Tad Hanson, this party was supposed to be about you!"

A collective gasp ripples through the yard—then cheers, whistles, and a few sniffles from the peanut gallery that is all of our family and friends.

His smile should be illegal, it's so fast and loose, and everything I've ever dreamed of appears right before me in a flash.

"It is. Everything about me is about you, and I suppose, that's the whole damn point. I don't want to have a single day without knowing you're mine forever. Beatrice Bishop, please, I'm begging...be mine forever. Will you marry me?"

Snot and tears mix in an ugly display of the happiest moment of my life, save the birth of our son, and even at that, this is a pretty sure tie.

"Yes. Yes. Of course, yes!" I nod, and Tad jumps up, pulling me into his arms and into a kiss that makes the last one seem demure.

This moment, right here. This is the best it's ever been.

• • •

Tad

I linger on the outside edge of the party, a beer in hand and a smile on my face as my fiancée flits from person to person, showing off her ring. It's an oval diamond in yellow gold, with a smaller teardrop diamond set at the side of the main stone. I designed it myself three months ago, at a jeweler in Burlington, while finishing my EMA certifications. It's a nod to Breezy's unique beauty and the idea that she is the keeper of my tears—the safe spot for my vulnerability.

I've never felt more at home with every part of myself than I do as Breezy's partner, and I cannot wait to make her my wife.

My dad and uncle follow her around to everyone she talks to, butting in with excitement every chance they get. I know they're thrilled to see me moving forward with my life—and I get it. But I'm glad they're suctioned to Breezy's ass instead of mine. They've been here to visit once a month since the baby was born, and I can't imagine they'll slow down anytime soon.

Ten years is a long time to wait for your son to come back to life. I understand that now in a way I never did before. It's amazing how your own wounds can blind you to the pain of others.

I'm trying to be better—Breezy makes me want to be better.

Randy makes small talk with Eileen's niece Millie, and I say a little prayer that he'll take that somewhere so I don't have to deal with his grumpy ass every time I don't approve some shit he asks for at the fire department. We've moved on from the sheep, but he's got a decade of a complaining habit I'm going to be fighting against.

"Happiness looks good on you, kid," Pete says from behind me, surprising me with his presence by appearing from behind the congratulations banner Breezy had special made. He's drinking a bourbon, like he usually is these days, and a loose smile matches perfectly with the glaze in his eyes.

"Thanks, Pete."

"Never happier in my life than the years I spent with my Helen." I nod as he continues, putting a hand on my shoulder. "I know you won't take it for granted, though. Ain't many of us who really understand, but I know you do."

"I do. And I won't. Take it for granted, I mean."

"I know, kid. I know." My eyes find Breezy in the crowd and focus in on her smile as she does some ridiculous chicken squawk at Autumn, who belly-laughs in Bennett's arms so hard, he has to bend at the hip to keep hold of her. Breezy glides through the motions as she hugs Norah, putting her purse on her shoulder for her since her arms are full of several trays of food, and I find myself thanking God for both the good and bad put together.

"Hey," I say, turning to Pete to ask him—really ask him—how he's doing, but to my surprise, he's already gone. I guess my admiration let time get away from me.

Shoving away from the tree I've been using as a prop instead, I make my way to my soon-to-be wife as she picks Hayes up out of his high chair and spins him around, coming up behind her and bending my head into her neck before she even sees me coming.

She gasps and then melts, her body finding comfort in the warmth of mine. "Hello, my love," I say into her delicate skin, shifting to kiss it when goose bumps appear.

Eileen appears in front of us, stealing Hayes right out of Breezy's arms and swirling away so quickly it makes the two of us laugh. Since retiring, she's been an unexpected staple in our life and a pseudo-grandmother figure to Hayes in ways I can't exactly comprehend. She's happy and helpful—still nosy, though not quite as much. But all in all, I think claiming an unofficial spot in our family has breathed new life into her.

Breezy, hands free now, spins in my arms and wraps hers around my shoulders, pushing up on her toes to put her lips to mine. "Hi, fiancé. I haven't seen you in a while."

I laugh. "I know. Maybe we can sneak away for a little bit and see a whole lot more of each other." I waggle my eyebrows, but we're rudely interrupted by the sound of Breezy's phone going off with a text message, and seeing as we've just been with pretty much everyone we know and they're all on their way home on the roads at the same time, she pulls it out to check it.

Her gasp is soft but noticeable. "It's Logan."

I know she hasn't heard much from him in the last couple of months, since the last time he visited the baby and got the same old hostility from Bennett, but every time he does reach out, she gets excited. She misses him, and as weird as the first time we met makes this sound, so do I.

"Oh no." She flips the phone to show me, and I read the message to myself.

Logan: *Sorry to do this, Breeze. I know you've got a lot going on there with your own life. But I've got a problem. I need your help. What do you think? You up for a trip?*

I don't like the sound of it, but he's family. And family, I know for so many reasons, is everything. "Does this mean we need to go to NYC?"

Breezy sighs. "I think so. But I'm getting back here as quickly as possible."

"Yeah?" I ask. "Don't miss the big city?"

She shakes her head. "I'm not giving up this life for anything."

"Me either, baby. Me either."

Exclusive Bonus Content

Bonus Scene

Breezy

My grip tight, I hold the album to my chest with both arms and perch on the edge of the couch, staring at the door.

Tad's on his way home from the grocery store on an errand I instigated in the hopes of getting him out of the house and setting the mood—with flameless candles—to deliver the gift I've been holding on to since Logan gave it to me three days ago. I would have given it to Tad sooner, but since Logan left town, Tad's been overwhelmed with the jobsite at the house, trying to keep things moving.

We're staying in a place Sheriff Pete owns on the far side of town, something passed down from his late wife's parents. It's a cute space and plenty comfortable for us, but I know we're both eager to be back on Tad's property next to Norah and Bennett and Autumn. With how hard everyone is working, we will be soon.

I glance at my watch before staring at the door again, my breath catching as Tad's truck's lights cascade against the window at the side of the house and shut off along with his engine. There's a brief beat and then the slam of his door, his boots moving swiftly across crunchy gravel.

The air leaves my lungs as soon as the door opens and his smiling face finds mine, and I can't wait even a second longer. "I have to show you something!"

My statement is jarring and a little harsh, if I'm honest, but the regulation of my emotions I'm normally so at home with has left the building in a big way.

Tad, for his part, is getting to be a little too good at handling the swings in my hormones and answers with a level of patience that would impress a monk. "Okay. Is it a good thing or a bad thing or a medium thing, and should I be sitting down when you show it to me?"

"It's a good thing," I say quickly, but upon further consideration, add some context. "But you should also sit down." I point to the spot on the couch my zeal made me abandon, and after tossing his keys and the bags of groceries on the kitchen table, he walks right toward me, presses his lips to mine, and then sits there.

It's only then, with me facing him and the cross of my arms at eye level, that he notices what I'm holding.

"Is that..." He swallows, and I nod, licking my lips before I sink to my knees in front of him.

"Yes. It is." My voice drops to a whisper as he rubs a single, slow hand down the front of his face. "Logan gave it to me before he left town. He...well, the demo crew found it in the debris."

"Have you looked inside it?" he asks softly, and immediately, I shake my head.

"No. I thought... Well, I thought we could together. If you're okay with that. If not, I just...I wanted you to have them, Tad. They should be with us, you know?"

He takes my mouth in a kiss that brightens all my senses. It's a thank-you and a cry and terror all in one. When he pulls back and touches his forehead to mine, a single tear cascades from his cheek, splash-landing on mine. "Thank you."

Pulling the album from my chest and shuffling back, I set it in his lap and take the spot next to him on the couch.

And together, we bring Abigail and Lucy home.

Abigail in the hospital with Lucy in her arms.

Tad in front of the firehouse, a tiny baby at his chest.

Lucy, in front of their house in Illinois on the first day of school with pigtails in her hair.

The three of them, together, laughing at the camera with cookie dough on their faces and a messy kitchen in the background.

Every single picture is an instant in time, every moment a memory.

And together, we'll cherish them always.

ACKNOWLEDGMENTS

To all of the most important people in our lives. You know who you are. We couldn't do this without you. We love you.

To our husbands, Craig and Peter. We're both endlessly grateful for your overwhelming love and support. You're exactly the kind of men we write romance books about...go figure. LOL.

To all of our reader friends, THANK YOU FOR READING. You have our gratitude every single day for making it possible to have this dreamy career we love.

To our Entangled Amara Team, thank you for helping us make our dreams come true. Jessica, thank you for believing in us. This series channels something in us we'll be forever grateful for.

To Summer, thank you for changing us forever and bringing us this perfect, flawed, loveable Vermont town.

And to Tad and Breezy, thanks for reminding us that the best plans are often the ones we don't expect and the best things in life often the things we don't even know we need.

XOXO,

Max & Monroe